ABOUT THE AUTHOR

Lexie Winston has been an astronaut, rock star, princess and time traveller. In her dreams. But none of the dreams have lived up to what becoming an author has been like. She gets to live in a world of pure imagination, and her heroines get to do the things she's always wished she could.

When not writing books, Lexie is a mother of two gorgeous teenagers and the wife to a patient and understanding man. They live in Western Australia and are lorded over by a black toy poodle. She loves camping, reading and if her iPad was stolen, her world would explode. (It has the kindle app on it.)

And check out my website at lexiewinston.com

And you can find all my links at
https://linktr.ee/LexieWinston

ALSO BY LEXIE WINSTON

The Collectors Division

(Paranormal Reverse Harem Series)

Guardian

Guardian's Blood

Guardian Ascending

Collector's Division Omnibus

Neighpalm Industries Collective

(Enemies to Lovers Reverse Harem)

Abandoned Girl

Broken Girl

Tormented Girl

Wanted Girl

Cherished Girl

Loved Girl

Superficial Girl - Jacinta's Story Part 1

Superficial Girl - Jacinta's Story Part 2

Neighpalm Industries Collective 1-3

Neighpalm Industries Collective 4-6

Seductive Sins Collection

(Reverse Harem Series)

Glorious Gluttony

Gangs, Guns, and Glory

Galaxy Circus

(Sci-Fi Reverse Harem Series)

Apprentice

Stagehand

Whisperer

Mama - Galaxy Circus Novella

Performer

A Night Most Wicked - Galaxy Circus Novella

Broken Promises

(Dark Poly Romance Series)

Secrets Kept

Lies Untold

M.I.T.H.O.S

(Contemporary RH)

Spies Like Me

Coming 2022

WHISPERER

LEXIE WINSTON

NEIGHPALM PUBLISHING

First published by Neighpalm Publishing in 2022

Whisperer: Galaxy Circus Series

Mobi format: 978-0-6453753-8-1
Print: 978-0-6453753-9-8

Cover design by Raven Ink Covers
Content Edited by SCW Editing
Line Editing by Elemental Editing

✹ Created with Vellum

Whisperer is the third Galaxy Circus novel, a fast-burn RH series that contains some adult situations which may be triggering, such as dub-con.

Galaxy Circus will also contain MM and male appendages of a somewhat interesting nature.

CHAPTER ONE

Lila

"Mine!" At those growled words, a number of things happen simultaneously. John gasps and collapses with a hand pressed tightly to his chest, and Xavier and Cas jump up, putting themselves between me and the feral Vilaxian, stopping him from grabbing me with his outstretched clawed hands. Saxon's short black hair is standing up, and his magenta eyes are glowing with an inner light. His fangs are extended and dripping venom, and his body vibrates as a growl rips out of his mouth.

"John!" Eric shouts, panic lacing his tone as he moves to his brother's side, drops to his knees, and scans John. "Link! Will, go see if Link's okay. We need him."

A sense of dread and growing panic infuses my

body, freezing me into inaction. Do I go to my grandpa's side or stay where I am so I don't incite the already feral Vilaxian? My head bounces back and forth between the two options, and I can practically feel the smoke leaking out of my ears as I try to make a decision.

William's pinched eyebrows and blown pupils hardly mask what he's feeling. He looks torn as his head whips from the door to his brother who's lying on the ground and the growling sanguinista.

"It's okay, William, we've got this," Xavier assures him as Cas changes into half form. William nods his thanks and edges past Saxon, who hasn't stopped growling and trying to reach me, snapping at Cas and Xavier every time they block his path.

Before William can leave the room, Link's there with a cut on his temple oozing silver blood, and I watch in fascination as the nanotechnology within his body speedily repairs the damage. The skin stitches itself back together, and then the remaining blood absorbs back into his skin. He makes his way quickly toward my fallen grandpa as if the gash wasn't even there.

Even through all of this chaos, I can't help but appreciate how fucking cool that was.

Caspian and Xavier are doing a good job of blocking Saxon, putting their bodies between him and me, but that won't last forever, and I'm torn between wanting to be with my grandpa and trying to help the sexy blood drinker who looks to be out of his fucking mind, his growls sprinkled with shouts of "Mine!" and "Blood rose." My gaze moves away from Saxon and back to John. His eyes are closed, but he doesn't seem to be convulsing or foaming at the mouth or showing any other signs of what's wrong, so I return my attention to Saxon. Maybe if I calm him down, that might make the situation easier.

"Hey there, ah, Saxon. Why don't you just take a deep breath, and we can talk about this some more?" I hear the words that come out of my mouth and roll my eyes. *Yeah, right, Lila, like the feral blood drinker is going to calm down after taking a deep breath.*

"He seems to be showing signs of a panic attack. There doesn't seem to be any other cause, but I'd like to take him to the hospital wing so I can check him over thoroughly," Link says, running a diagnostic hand over my grandpa who is still out like a light.

Xavier waves a hand, and a hover stretcher appears next to him. Link nods his gratitude as William and Eric gently lift John onto it. Eric holds John's hand, while William brushes his hair back from his face.

"What about Saxon?" Cas asks, his agitation crystal clear in his voice as he stabs a finger at the feral Vilaxian while they play keep away from Lila.

"I can't re-sedate him. If I do, it may kill him. I know it's not ideal, but we should allow them to bond. Lila said she was okay with it, and I think we should respect her choice," Link reasons, looking at Cas and Xavier then me, and I nod my assent.

"Yeah, I did, but I was hoping for something a little calmer and rational. I don't relish having my throat torn out." I reach up instinctively to protect it, and a slight tremor runs through my body at the thought.

"Everything I have read says that a Vilaxian instinctively knows when to stop drinking when bonding with his blood rose. It's a survival mechanism, otherwise they could kill the only person whose blood will nourish them thoroughly." Thank fuck for Link's knowledge, or else I'd be going into this blindly, not knowing if I'd survive or not.

"You better be right about this," Xavier growls at him as Link programs the stretcher to follow him, and he strides out followed by the two remaining brothers. Fuck, I'm so torn. I've only just found my family, and I want to be where they are, making sure John's okay, but I also have a duty to myself and my new mate. He is not going to be rational until we get this done.

"Good luck," he calls over his shoulder. "And Lila? Make sure you drink plenty of fluids when you're done so you don't end up dehydrated."

"Dehydrated?" The word squeaks out of my mouth. "I'm pretty sure that's the *least* of my worries."

I move around the room now that we have more

space and less people, and Saxon's glowing magenta eyes follow my every move. "Now what?" I ask.

Xavier and Cas exchange a glance before they both shrug. "I could teleport you to your room, and we could let him find you," Xavier suggests, and Saxon's growl gets deeper and louder. "Or not." I'm not sure if he was serious about that or not, but I kind of have the urge to smack him upside the head for it. There is no need to antagonize the already crazed Saxon.

"What about—" Before Cas can finish what he's saying, a beeping sound interrupts us. It's loud and insistent, and Xavier throws his hand into the air before pushing a button on one of the consoles. A face appears on the holoscreen—a face that is very similar to the one now scowling at it. Saxon tries to make a run for me while Xavier is distracted, and a small scream escapes my mouth, but Cas is there, his half shifted body growing before he snatches the enraged Vilaxian with his tentacles. They ripple and pulse as they try to contain Saxon who continues to struggle.

"What is it, Xane? I'm in the middle of some-thing," Xavier snaps tersely as he joins Caspian in restraining Saxon. They wrestle him into submis-sion. He keeps growling, but he's still for a moment, his eyes still fixed on me.

"I'll make it quick, since you seem to be busy," the voice replies, and my warlock snorts, unamused.

"You think?"

"Two humans just arrived on the doorstep of the Pleasure Inn. They managed to get through the gate, and the female has a hint of warlock manipulation in her. *Your* signature to be specific."

Fuck. He could only mean Susie and Mark.

Xavier stiffens and looks at me, and I feel my stomach drop with dread. Well, even more dread, because, you know, an enraged Vilaxian who wants to drink my blood to seal us together for all eternity is only a few feet away. Okay, maybe not dread, maybe anticipation if I'm really being honest. I swear I must have hit my head at some stage, because I'm thinking with my vagina and not rationally at all.

"Are they okay?" Xavier asks, his concern for my friends completely endearing. I sigh. He's so wonderful.

"They seem to have had a car accident, and the female is injured, but not badly. I instructed Crimson to seal the wound," the voice on the screen shares, and it's too much for me. I need to know if my bestie is okay.

"Who are you and what have you done with my best friend?" I demand, and the infuriating being shrugs nonchalantly.

"Nothing... yet!"

I can feel my hands tighten into fists as the desire to bitch slap this arrogant prick into the next galaxy plays on my mind.

"Fuck!" Xavier shouts, and I'm suddenly frozen

along with everything and everyone else in the room.

This can't be happening right now. How dare he silence me? I swear when I get my hands on that warlock, he's going to wish he never met me. It's my bestie who is in trouble, not some random walking on the street. I watch in silence as I try desperately to break through the spell.

Xavier is breathing heavily from wrestling with Saxon, and he shoves a hand through his disheveled hair.

"Well, cousin, you look to be having fun." The being smirks with a smile that makes me want to smack him. "Who's the chick? Have you fucked her? She looks like she could be feisty in bed," he asks, and I turn my ire from my warlock to the now walking dead man I can no longer see.

The guy has a set of brass fucking balls, that's for sure, especially since he's mocking my relationship with Xavier. He better run if we ever come face-to-face, because he's racking up a list of offenses right now, and my protective instincts are on high alert. Our encounter will end badly for him.

"Do not talk about my intimate like she is a piece of meat," Xavier bellows, and I feel the room shudder from the power in his words. I'm slightly mollified by his statement, and if I could smirk, I would. I bet warlock dude is crapping his pants at the moment.

"Your intimate is a human? How the fuck did that happen? She won't be able to sustain you, Xavier. You must be wrong." The voice is incredulous, and I start having murderous thoughts again. I wonder if I can program the transporter to deposit Htaed in his bedroom and have him crap in his sheets... or better yet, eat him.

If I have my say, I'd vote for option two. Problem solved.

I listen to the rest of the conversation as they discuss Mark and Susie, practically foaming at the mouth to be involved. Finally, Xavier does the right thing and unfreezes me, and I immediately scowl at him.

"Let me make sure I understand what just happened, Xavier. Did you cut me off mid-rant? When I was trying to ask what had happened to them?" I demand, crossing my arms while tapping my foot on the floor, waiting for his response. Xavier, to his credit, winces and starts to murmur lame excuses.

"Dude, did you give her your balls?" the asshat on screen jokes, and I whirl, turning my wrath on him. Seeing him flinch is magical, and Xavier steps up next to me, wrapping an arm around my shoulders, trying to give me comfort, but it's a little too late, I'm fired up.

"Lila, honey, this is my cousin, Xane. He resides at the 'bed-and-breakfast' Susie was telling you about, the Pleasure Inn." He does bed-and-breakfast in finger quotes, and I narrow my eyes on him.

"Not a B and B?" I ask, and he shakes his head, looking a bit sheepish.

"No, it's an alien brothel. A lot of the aliens that use Earth as a holiday destination are not compatible with humans. Aura, the brothel's master, keeps a stable of alien sex workers and bots to cater to any need or kink."

Mind fucking blown. An alien brothel. Now I would like to be a fly on the wall in that place. Purely for research purposes of course. I mean, I'm not that kinky…

I look between the two warlocks and instantly know the perfect way to wind the asshat up. "And your cousin is one of these workers?" I ask, making direct eye contact with Xane. I know his reaction will be priceless.

The asshat bares his teeth at me, and I feel a jolt of smug satisfaction. Hurts, doesn't it, to have assumptions being made about you without knowing all of the facts? "Certainly not," Xane sneers at me, not liking that the tables have turned.

Xavier sighs, pinching the bridge of his nose because he has to deal with two unruly toddlers. "Xane is one of the master's… partners, for lack of a better word."

"How shocking, a warlock prince and master," I sneer, not ready to let bygones be bygones just yet, and Xavier shakes his head.

"It's not like that. Unlike Earth, where a master or madam is considered taboo, the title is a revered and coveted spot in the galaxy. Aura, the master, is a very powerful person. Sex pays, and it pays well. Look at what everyone has told you about Link and Pleasure Bot Industries."

"Oh, how is the gorgeous doctor? Hmm, now that is a tasty morsel." I see red at the suggestive words coming out of the warlock's mouth, and I can't control the change. I don't even want to. My beast pushes to the surface and forces a half shift, my tentacles flying. I'm growling and baring my teeth, trying to get at the figure on the holoscreen.

Xavier scowls at his cousin before pulling me into his arms and cooing sweet, reassuring words that have a mollifying effect on my beast. She settles down, and I allow Xavier to rain little kisses over my face between the whispered words of assurance.

"Holy shit, what is she?" Xane asks, pointing at a tentacle. "That's… That's not a Skarrian thing."

Xavier huffs in annoyance while rolling his eyes. "You know Skarrians are polyamorous. One of her mates is a kraken shifter, and she's also courting the doc, so maybe keep your goddamn opinions to yourself."

"My apologies, Lila, that was rude of me." Xane bows slightly, seeming genuine in his apology, and I can finally shift back to normal. My bottom half is naked, having shredded my clothes in my spontaneous shift, so Xavier waves a hand to clothe me again.

After Xane grovels a little bit more, asking for my forgiveness, we finally have a discussion about my two friends. After a few interesting tidbits of information are imparted, I'm almost certain there's another conversation going on I can't hear. Damn telepathic warlocks! Some facial expressions don't match up with the verbal discussion, and their replies are often delayed, but I don't care for now, so I make a decision.

"As long as their consent isn't taken away, I guess there's no harm in inviting them to join in. They can always say no." I'm a little hesitant to trust this complete stranger, but I know Xavier would tell me if I couldn't. He doesn't seem concerned in the least, and when he spoke about the master, he seemed like he had a lot of respect for them.

"Yes, and we'd muddle their minds again so they wouldn't remember. I can't do what Xavier did and remove the memory, but I can manipulate it so all they will remember is staying overnight until a tow truck arrived," Xane assures me, but to be honest, I *want* them to remember. It would also be good if the master took an interest in them and invited them to stay longer. That way, they would be protected from anything or anyone who may try to pump them for information about the circus.

"I'm saying you can try. I really would like them

to be protected," I finally agree, and both warlocks look surprised, but Xane's shock quickly turns to anticipation.

A growling sound behind us penetrates my consciousness, and I turn around, startling when I realize Saxon has started to break free from the stasis Xavier had him and Cas in.

"Fuck, I knew it wouldn't hold him long in his state. Got to go, talk soon." Xavier cuts off the call and looks at me. Thoughts of Mark and Susie drift away as I swallow the lump in my throat that returned as soon as my focus shifted back to the present.

"Make a decision, Lila, and make it quick," Xavier orders, snapping me out of my daze. The fear of the unknown is what's affecting my decision making. It's like playing Russian roulette with my life.

"Shit, fuck, I don't know. Like, I *want* to bond with him, but how?" I can hear the slight tremble in my voice as my usual confidence waivers and my pulse begins to thump loudly in my ears. I try to sync up what my soul is saying with what my mind is thinking, but it's pointless. I just don't understand why they can't be on the same fucking page.

"Link said it would be his natural instinct to protect you. I think Cas and I are going to have to let him go and let it happen, Lila. If we try to inter-fere any more than we have, he could get more dangerous." Xavier is wearing a look I haven't seen on his face before—helplessness. I know he wants to fix things, but he can't.

My heart is racing a million miles an hour, but I understand what Xavier's saying. If he and Cas stay in the same room, it might trigger his protective instinct, and then Saxon may end up attacking them, and they are struggling to hold him now. I don't want either of them to get hurt in the crossfire just because I'm nervous.

"Okay. Can you two find out about Grandpa J for me?" He quickly agrees, and I nod, gesturing for him to unfreeze Cas. "It's okay, Cas. Let him go."

"Fine, but if he looks like he's going to go too far, I won't hesitate to shift into my beast and eat him," Cas growls to the both of us. I can only hope Saxon actually hears it, because I don't think Cas is messing around. He really will eat him to protect me.

I brace myself for what happens next, but nothing could prepare me for what does. Cas releases him from his tentacles, and Saxon strikes, his fangs bared and lips peel back with feral intensity. He leaps for me, but instead of snatching and tearing into my vein, he gathers me gently into his arms, a growling sound still rolling from his lips. He nuzzles my neck, and I brace for the pain, but all he does is inhale deeply.

"Mine," he growls again before picking me up bridal style and flashing out of the room. I feel nauseous just like the first time he moved me too fast and groan. Saxon must hear me, because he slows to a normal walking speed. The immediate relief I feel at his consideration eases a bit of my anxiety. We get to the elevators, and he presses a button. Before long, we are in front of a door on the sleeping quarters floor. He puts his hand against the panel, and it slides open, and then he steps in. The room is shrouded in darkness, my eyes refusing to adjust, and I can't make out much except for a few lumpy shapes. I don't know if they are people or furniture.

Talk about an ominous start to our bonding. Nothing woos a woman quite like not being able to see her environment.

"Saxon, you're back," a hopeful voice calls through the darkness, and then we are surrounded by people—up close and personal and Vilaxian, if the fang-filled smiles have anything to say.

"Brother, are you well?" A Vilaxian I don't know steps in front of all the others, holding up a hand to stop Saxon from going anywhere. "Put the human down. You know nothing good can come of this."

"Mine," Saxon growls, and there is a feminine gasp. A wave of possessiveness washes over me at hearing those words. I like being claimed by him, and I'm ready to throw that "mine" stamp on his ass too.

"So it's true. You have found your blood rose?" The man in front of us is still frowning. "The queen said as much. It is unusual that she is not Vilaxian, but it is not the first time this has happened. That's why she asked me to bring the goblet! Happy bonding, brother." The man loses his frown, and his smile is blinding as he slaps Saxon on the back before clearing a path. "Get out of the way. You know not to come between a Vilaxian and their blood rose."

"No, it can't be true." One of the pretty females crosses her arms and stubbornly refuses to move out of Saxon's way. From the corner of my eye, I see Hale, but he's not interfering. He just has a small, amused smile on his face. I continue to play possum in Saxon's arms, not wanting to stir him or any of his clan members up.

"Why? Just because it isn't *you*?" Another woman, the one I'd seen dancing with Magenta at the club the other night, steps up with a stubborn set to her jaw. Suddenly, we're surrounded by super tall, super buff vampires who all intend to give their opinions, whether positive or negative, on me, the *human*, being Saxon's blood rose.

Assholes.

They argue noisily, and I feel Saxon grow more and more tense, his body vibrating with annoyance. He roars and takes off into the air, flying over the arguing group.

I'm not ashamed to admit I screamed when he took off like Superman. I had fully expected for us to hit a ceiling, but we just kept moving through the air, avoiding any objects in our way. I can see that we're in a horizontal shaft of some sort, with low lights illuminating sporadic gaps in the wall. He lands on one of these gaps. Leaning over, he pushes his hand against a panel, and a door slides back, revealing another dark space.

Note to self, Vilaxians love the dark.

He floats us into this space before setting us down on solid ground again. He then stalks through the pitch-black room, causing me to get a little disoriented since I can't see anything. I pat him gently on the chest, trying to get his attention.

"Where are we?" I ask quietly, hoping not to agitate the already super agitated vampire even more.

I get no response, but my neck is still intact, and I'm not dead, so I'm calling that a win. Suddenly, I'm flying through the air, on my own this time. A small screech leaves my mouth, but as gravity kicks in and I land on a soft bed, the noise cuts off. Heaving a sigh of relief, I try to make out my surroundings again, but it's still too dark for me to see much. Soon enough, however, Saxon follows me up onto the bed.

The curious part of me can't wait to see where this goes.

CHAPTER TWO

Lila

I hadn't noticed before when we were with my grandpas, and I'm not sure how I didn't notice it when Saxon carried me to his bedroom, but the gorgeous Vilaxian is naked apart from a tight pair of briefs. As he prowls across the bed like the lethal predator he is, I can just make out the ripple of all those delicious muscles as he moves, and although his eyes are glowing and I can see his fangs because his lip is curled back in a snarl, he's more controlled than I thought he would be.

I thought I'd be a goner, he'd be lost in a feeding frenzy, and there would be Lila splashed all around the room, but apart from the growls and uber possessiveness, which, let's face it, is hot as fuck and my panties are dripping wet because of it, he's been an extraordinarily patient predator stalking his prey, and now he has me right where he wants me.

As nervous as I am, I am so here for this. Being his sole focus is exciting and intoxicating.

Sign me the fuck up, and let's get this bonding started.

"Ah, yeah, so hi?" I can't stand the stifling, tension-filled silence any longer. At the sound of my voice, Saxon shakes his head slightly, and when his gaze meets mine again, he's lost some of the feral intensity. I'm surprised and slightly disappointed. The feralness was scary but mildly intoxicating too.

"Little girl, do you know what you are to me?" he asks, his words a mouthful of growly deliciousness. I could orgasm just from hearing his voice, and it's totally cliché to say, but still, it's totally true.

"Yup, your blood rose." I say it simply, yet it's anything but simple.

He sits back on his heels, his fists clenched at his sides like he's holding himself back, which I have no doubt is what he's doing. His jaw is clenched, and he cocks his head slightly to the side. "And do you know what that means?"

"Sure, you're wifing me up." I tilt my head to the side as I think about my situation. "Well, actually, it's more like I'm husbanding you up, although I already have one with two more potentials. Anyway, it means I'm yours and you are mine." The last word comes out in a growl. My kraken makes herself known, and I can feel how thrilled she is. She wants to test her strength against this predator, and I feel her try to force the change. I grit my teeth and hold onto my human form with every bit of stubbornness I possess.

Stop fighting me. You'll get your turn, but let's not scare him before we've even locked him down, I caution her, and I almost feel her roll her eyes before she disappears again. So. Damn. Dramatic.

He low-key growls and pounces forward. I react instinctively and throw a hand out, smacking him on the end of the nose. "Bad vampy." He startles backward, his eyes wide as he cups his nose in utter disbelief.

"You hit me?" He blinks a few times, trying to make sure that what he experienced matches the words he just spoke. "Nobody has landed a hit on me in fifty years."

"Well, you scared me." I arch an eyebrow at him while crossing my arms. "You can't go around scaring a woman into being your blood rose. You need to be gentle."

"No ravishing," he mutters quietly. "That stupid merman was right."

"Oh, hold up, wait a minute. No one said anything about *no ravishing*, you just need to ask first." I think about it a little, realizing my statement was partially correct, and then shrug. "Well, actually, consent isn't even really needed. I like the idea of you taking what you want, but I'm also human, and you ripping my throat out is not going to go well for me. This" —I wave a hand between the two of us— "would be over very quickly, and it wouldn't end well for either of us." A shudder rolls through my body at the thought of blood splattering across the room all because he was impatient.

His frown clears as he contemplates what I just said, then he nods his head decisively like it all makes perfect sense. Thank fuck he understands. "Yes, you are right, of course. I need to change you first before we can finish the bonding."

I hear the sound of tires squealing as my brain comes to a complete halt. "Change me?" I squeak out as he gets off the bed and disappears into the darkness of the room. "Hey, can we maybe get a little light? You've got me at a little bit of a disadvantage because I can't see a thing."

He's suddenly in front of me again, and I can't stop the little yelp that leaves my mouth. He lifts my hand and places a kiss on the back of it. "My apologies, my beautiful blood rose. I must admit I'm a little nervous," he says, not meeting my eyes, but I see him swallow roughly. "It's affecting my reasoning, but I will endeavor to do better." He releases my hand and disappears in a flash again.

I blink my eyes, the flashing starting to make me feel vaguely ill. Shortly after, though, the room's lighting increases slightly, and my eyes adjust to the change. It's still fairly dark, but I can make out more of my surroundings.

Before I can get a good look at the room, Saxon returns once more, and in his hand is an ornate silver goblet with some interesting markings on the outside. Although his facial expression is blank, I can see one of his eyes twitch involuntarily.

Is Saxon nervous?

"In order for you to be my blood rose, I need to make you Vilaxian. It's not an easy process, and it's not a common one. The only time it is ever performed is for a non-Vilaxian blood rose, and this has only happened a handful of times over the centuries." He pauses for a moment, like he knows it's a lot to take in, letting me digest how rare our bond truly is. My racing heart slowly returns to a steady beat before he continues. "This goblet is spelled and was sent to me by the queen. It is kept guarded in the royal vault, and only brought out in situations such as this. The Vilaxian with the non-Vilaxian blood rose can appeal to the monarch to use it, and that's exactly what I did. Her being my aunt made things easier, and she readily approved it."

He looks down at the goblet thoughtfully before holding it out for me to take, our eyes locking. My hand shakes as I reach for it, so I take a big calming breath. Holy crap, Saxon is turning me into a vampire, or some sort of vampire, a blood rose who will survive the bonding and be able to provide for my mate. I hadn't even considered what might happen. Sure, when I bonded with Cas I got the ability to shift, but fuck, I haven't really thought about any of this, or maybe I chose not to.

Either way, this is nerve-racking, the fear of the unknown weighing heavily on my mind and warring with my heart and soul. Deep down in my bones, the overwhelming sense of the rightness of being his blood rose calms me down again, so I breathe in and out twice before reaching for it again. This time, my hand is steady. I'm ready to bond.

"The liquid inside will change the structure of your bone marrow so that it will produce more blood, so I can drink from you without killing you. It may also give you some Vilaxian characteristics, but that does vary by blood rose. It may be uncomfortable for a few moments as the spell rewrites your DNA." Again, I breathe in and out, only seconds away from losing my shit as he reveals more of what I can expect. "Do you want to ask any questions?"

I quickly shake my head and bring the goblet up to my mouth, but he puts a hand on mine, stopping me before I can drink. When I look up at him, his eyes are soft, and he wears a gentle smile.

"Are you certain, Lila? You don't have to do this. I'm sure we can come up with another solution," he says softly, but we know the truth. Without me, he will wither away and die, and I can't have that on my conscience. Yes, again, I'm marrying someone I know next to nothing about, but look at how good that turned out with Caspian. And, I mean, this guy is sexy as fuck. Even if we have nothing else in common, I'm almost certain sex with him is going to be off the fucking charts. If that sucks, I can slit my wrist and fill a cup of blood for him every day. I mean, there are worse things I could have to do.

"I want to do this, Saxon," I tell him and gently peel his hand back, and before he can say anything else, I throw back the goblet like a frat boy at happy hour. I gulp down the liquid, but it's not until I'm almost done that I recognize it's hot and thick and tastes like copper. My brain stalls out as it puts two and two together.

Blood.

Oh my god, I'm drinking Saxon's *blood*. My nonexistent gag reflex decides to make itself known, and I struggle to swallow the last mouthful, but I do, forcefully, and I clamp my lips together in the hope that I do not bring all of that back up. I can't imagine what it tastes like going the opposite way. Groaning, I keep my lips tightly shut as the goblet falls out of my hand and instinctively roll onto the bed in a fetal position. Placing my hands over my stomach, I pray to every deity I can think of to not let me vomit blood everywhere. I can't even imagine how insulting it would be to Saxon, so I need to put my big girl panties on and digest his blood like a champ.

I feel Saxon climb up onto the bed behind me

and run a hand over my now feverish forehead. "Hold on, Lila, it won't be long. I promise." Just as he finishes saying this, I feel my body start to seize up. My muscles lock into place, and the blood beneath my skin begins to heat. Soon, it feels like I'm boiling from the inside, but I can't even open my mouth to scream because I'm frozen in place. My eyes roll back in my head as the searing agony feels like it's rearranging my insides. All my bones beneath seem to throb, and my skin stretches so tight across my body it feels like it could split at any second. An inferno rushes through my internal organs, and when it hits my heart, I finally blackout.

A thudding sound in my ears is the first thing I notice when I return to consciousness. No, it's a double thud, kind of like two hearts beating followed by a rushing sound, like water running through a drain. I cock my head to the side, trying to work out what I'm hearing. My mouth is dry and my gums ache, so I try to swallow. It feels like knives are stabbing me in the throat, and I groan and roll onto my back, but I move so fast, I roll too far and land on the floor with a heavy thud. Pain shoots through my tailbone.

A quiet chuckle has my eyes shooting open before I scream and clamp my eyes shut once more, slapping my hand over them as I try to block out the obnoxiously bright light.

"Well, it seems my blood may have changed you

a little more than I thought it would." Saxon's voice is growly and deep and oh so sexy.

"What's going on?" I ask and squeak as I clamp my hands over my ears. What the fuck? Did I just scream that? I feel Saxon help me to my feet and move me back to the bed, my eyes still slammed shut.

"Just a moment," he tells me, and he disappears but returns in a flash, a small breeze washing over me. "Okay, try to open your eyes now." I reluctantly peel them open, and when I'm not instantly blinded, I look around and sigh in relief before removing my hands from my ears. I go to say something, and he presses a finger to my lips. "Just whisper until you adjust to your new senses." I nod, and he removes his finger

"Oh thank god. I'm not sure what you did, but fucking hell, that was bright." I go to sit back down on the bed, but my body smashes into a wall instead. A blinding pain shoots through my skull as I slide down the wall into a puddle of Lila at the bottom. "What the fuck is happening to me?"

I may have screeched that at a nearly inaudible level, but I'm having a small freak-out here. I put a hand against my throbbing head, hoping to ease the pain.

"You seem to have gotten the Vilaxian increased senses and speed. I've dimmed the lights back down to what they were when we first came in." Huh, it seems like broad daylight in here. How am I going to cope with being out in the rest of the ship? I'm not sure about the strength, because the walls are reinforced. "I would be careful for the next few days until you get used to the changes in your body."

He speaks those words so fucking casually, like it's no big deal, but before I open my mouth again, his advice shuts me up.

Changes in my body? I think about what else I know about Vilaxians. They drink blood, are fast and strong, and…. "Oh my god, do you think I can fly?" I exclaim, not even hiding my excitement. I have absolutely no chill, but this is *flying*. Like a superhero. My brief episode when I drank the water was enough to hook me.

Once again, Saxon helps me to my feet and guides me back to bed, not removing his hand like he's afraid I'll disappear if he releases me. He may be right, because my body is practically vibrating with energy. He helps me down onto the bed —again.

"I don't know, but a little later, we can go out into the arena and test your abilities." Gone is the feral vampire, and in his place is the calm and rational man who was going to teach me to shoot. I can't believe the change in him. Is this just from him giving me his blood?

"Why are you so calm all of a sudden?" I ask suspiciously, narrowing my eyes at him. "Before you were like a rabid beast. I thought for sure you were going to rip my throat out."

"Blood rose bonding does tend to make a vampire crazy, but I managed to get myself under control once I heard your sweet voice and your assurance that you wanted to do this. Having you drink my blood managed to lock the rest of the feral beast down… for now. I'm sure it will return the minute I smell your own sweet nectar." My blood quickly rushes to my cheeks as they turn red at the thought of *him* smelling *me*, but I realize he's actually referring to my blood as his eyes lock onto the side of my neck.

"So how do we bond?" I'm low-key vibrating with nerves and excitement over all these changes I hadn't even dreamed of.

"We need to do a blood exchange. Although mine has changed the structure of your DNA, allowing for you to be compatible with me, it was spelled through the goblet, so we need to do this part simultaneously to activate the bond."

It's a struggle, but I manage to keep my face blank. I don't want him to see how the thought of drinking his blood again revolts me. It really was gross, and it took everything inside me not to vomit it back up. "Ah, okay, but how? I don't have fangs like you." I look around for a knife, but he leans back against the headboard and gestures for me to come to him.

I move extra slowly as I crawl up the bed and into his arms and successfully avoid hurting us both. I breathe a sigh of relief as I settle between his legs, my back to his front. He wraps both his arms around me, cradling me. "I will bite into my wrist, and while you drink from it, I will drink from your neck. Is this okay?" he asks, holding me like I'm precious glass and he's afraid to hurt me—both physically and emotionally.

"Will it hurt?" I can hear the hitch in my tone, and I feel him shake his head behind me.

"There may be a brief pinch, but then it should be all pleasure after that." His voice has dropped an octave, and I feel him harden against my lower back.

Well okay then.

"Okay," I agree, and he leans down. His breath brushes across my ear, causing a shiver to run down the entire length of my body, and goosebumps appear on my skin.

"Thank you, Lila. You do not understand the gift you have given me, but I promise I will do everything in my power to protect and cherish you for as long as we're both alive. I am forever your servant." Without waiting for me to respond to the beautiful words he just floored me with, he brings his wrist up to his mouth and bites down, the pop of his skin echoing in my ears.

He brings it around in front of me, and the smell suddenly hits me. Holy. Fucking. Shitballs! He smells like toasted marshmallows and chocolate. I feel a click in my mouth and a searing bite of pain that quickly diminishes. When I use my tongue to investigate, I cut it on one of the fangs that have unexpectedly erupted from my gums. My mouth waters, and I feel my rational brain take a sidestep for something similar to my beast—something primal and possessive—and with my own tiny growl, I grab his arm, bringing it to mouth. I run my tongue over the blood welling there, and my eyes roll back in my head as the flavor hits me. The heavy groan that leaves my mouth portrays my need. I seem to lose all rational thought, and it's like I'm watching what is happening through a TV screen.

Feral Lila growls when the flow of blood slows and uses her own fangs to rip his skin open to get at the luscious liquid inside. As the blood flows more freely, his healing restricted by my venom, I guzzle the flavorsome red liquid, lost in the taste and sensation, but behind me, I feel Saxon's body stiffen and the length against my back harden even further as he moans a long keening sound.

CHAPTER THREE

Saxon

"Fuck." I can't help the guttural groan that leaves my mouth. Having Lila's fangs in my skin feels like nothing I've ever experienced before. Even with her rough and uneducated fumbling, it still sends an exquisite burst of pleasure rushing through my body.

She instinctively swipes her tongue across the mess she made of my wrist, healing it almost instantly before she spins in my lap. She straddles me, grinding down against my cock, and my fangs throb with need. Her beautiful green eyes have taken on an ethereal glow, and they narrow. Before I can do anything, she strikes again, sinking her sharp fangs into my chest before withdrawing and suckling on the wound. It's too much for me, and I lose my shit. My rational side slips backwards, releasing the tightly coiled monster inside—the one who I had to force back down so as not to scare Lila completely. He's out now, though, and he's not going to go back until he's drunk his fill. Her blood sings to me, beckoning me. Roaring, I lurch forward and strike the fat, pulsing vein in her neck. She stiffens beneath me, but my pleasure venom releases, and soon enough, she's grinding even harder against me, her suckling turning desperate as she feeds from me.

Fuck. This is everything!

The rush of pure adrenaline that flashes through my system as the flavor of her reaches my taste buds is nothing short of mind-blowing. She tastes like lava fruit, a delicacy found on Vilax that, if compared to human food, tastes like apple pie. I gorge myself on her, drinking and thrusting up to meet her core, but it's not enough. I need to feel her tight pussy wrapped around my cock while her delicious, life-giving blood flows down my throat. I close up her neck and coax her away from my chest, my monster and I working together to get us what we need. She whimpers and claws at me, not ready for the blood drinking to end. Her strength is already enough to rival my own, not that she realizes it.

In a flash, I flip us over, tearing her clothes from her body in a movement too fast for the human eye to track. Lila matches me for strength and movement and has my briefs shredded and tossed to the ground only moments after I finish undressing her.

We roll around, my monster crowing at her struggle. He revels in the fact that his mate is strong and capable and can hold her own against us. With her teeth bared, and her pretty green eyes glowing with her own internal monster, she's frenzied in her attempt to dominate me. It's breathtaking. *She's* breathtaking. Lila momentarily overpowers me as I admire my mate, my blood rose.

To finish the bond, I need to be buried deep inside her with our blood mingling on our bodies and then say the magic word, so I pin her down and start to bleed her. First, I bite into her neck, then her chest. Moving to her arms, I bite holes in her elbow creases and wrists, then slither my body down to her pussy. The scent of her desire almost overwhelms me, and I'm dying to swipe my tongue through her dripping folds, but I want to ensure I bond her to me properly. I bite holes in both creases of her legs and then in her thighs. I sit back and admire my handiwork. Lila is lost to the pleasure my venom is giving her, writhing and moaning as her blood drips out, coating her body. Using my hands and tongue, I paint her whole body in the crimson liquid before biting her again, this time holding back on the venom and allowing the pain to bring her around slightly.

"Lila," I murmur, coaxing her to look at me. "I need you to bite me in the same spots I bit you," I tell her, and before I can say anything else, I'm flat on my back and she's on top of me, following the path I took on her. I try to keep my head up, gritting my teeth as her own venom slides into my system once more. I need to say the words to bond us, but the minute she slides her fangs into the thick vein on my dick, I'm done for. Pushing her back, I fly us across the room until she smashes into a wall, my dick at the entrance to her core.

She rubs her slippery body against mine, mixing our lifeblood together, and I say the words, "As we share our blood, I pledge my life, my heart, and my soul to you. I will be your protector, shelter, and the one you can rely on forever," and thrust myself deep, both with my fangs and cock.

Lila screams out as I pound into her with a speed she has never experienced before. Her orgasm explodes into life, and she comes hard, her pussy rippling around my dick. My eyes widen as I feel suckers latch onto my cock as she lodges her fangs in my neck. I stop pretending that I can last longer, and I fucking explode. My cum drenches her womb with my seed. Growling, I continue to drink as I think about my seed making her stomach round with our child. Our bodies slide together in a smooth, erotic glide as I bring us back to the bed and position us so she's on top of me. I continue to thrust lazily as we both drink our fill, our bodies providing the blood necessary to complete the bond. Our souls lock together, binding us as one forever.

After that initial bonding, I lose track of time.

Lila and I fuck and suck for what could be hours, our bodies constantly connected in some way, whether it be tongue, lips, fangs, or fingers. We give each other hours and hours of orgasmic bliss, finally stopping when I hear Lila's heartbeat, which had synced with mine, slow and start to beat irregularly. I have to coax her to release her suction on her latest bite, and I drag us off the now sticky, blood soaked sheets and guide us toward the bathroom.

Turning on the shower, I sense Lila's body weaken as she starts to feel the effects of what we just did. Although her body is now changed to be able to sustain mine, a blood rose bonding is no small feat, and I'm certain she is almost at her limit. I sit her down on the seat in the shower when it reaches the right temperature, and then I flash back to get my communicator from next to my bed, returning before she can even slump to the side.

I press a button while I support my gorgeous mate, worry erasing everything else that I have been feeling. I was so lost in all the sensations, I didn't pay attention like I should have.

"Is Lila okay?" Link's voice asks before I can even say anything when he answers my call.

"Mostly, but our joining took a lot out of her." I cringe from the admission. "I would appreciate it if you could come and check her over," I say to the doctor and her potential mate. Although it is not the Vilaxian way to share mates, somehow in my sedated state, I knew that I was going to have to share mine and had come to terms with it before I was even released from sedation. I must question how the release happened, because I think I surprised everyone—including myself. They were not expecting me to appear like I did. Granted, I was fairly feral, but I do not think it was planned based on the expressions on their faces and one of Lila's grandpas passing out.

"I will be right there," he assures me calmly with no hint of worry, the ultimate professional, and hangs up before I can even reply.

I send my brother a message, telling him to let the doctor in and show him to my room in our quarters when he arrives.

"Lila, my beautiful rose, let's get you cleaned up so your doctor doesn't have his own heart attack," I encourage her, listening to her heart. Although it's slower than normal and there is the occasional skipping of a beat, it seems to be okay for the moment. Using a cloth, I wash Lila's blood-covered body, a red ribbon of water swirling as it slowly disappears down the drain. If anyone else saw it, they would think both of us were gravely injured, but all our wounds are now sealed.

Lila is listless in my arms, and I start to worry more than I was. I could try to feed her more of my blood, but I don't think it's going to work. Her poor body underwent a huge shock and change today, and the mating didn't help any. I'm sure Link will know what to do. Maybe food and rest will be all she needs. I hope.

I message my brother again and ask for him or one of the others to change the sheets on my bed. Normally I wouldn't want anyone in here, and I certainly wouldn't want to remove the sheets yet, but Lila needs to rest, and I'm not ready to let her return to her own room yet. In fact, I'm feeling a little unsteady. Yes, we mated, but what will happen next? We all have our own rooms in the circus pod. Will she ask me to move into her quarters on the big ship? Do I want to leave my clan? I think about what all that means, and although there is some inner doubt and concern, it's more about whether she will want me in her space and absolutely nothing about leaving my clan. I had already planned to ask for a dissolution, so that is not a problem for me. I will need to talk to them about it, but that can wait until I'm certain of Lila's decision. They are not stupid, they know things are going to change.

All the while I've been thinking about our future, I've been gently washing my gorgeous mate. I need to wash myself, but I'm reluctant to let her go. I'm worried she may fall off the chair.

A knock on my door has me putting Lila behind me and growling at whoever disturbs us. It's not really rational considering I invited people to help me, but it's an instinctive response I can't control nonetheless.

"Saxon, it's Link," a voice calls through the door before it slides open slightly. "I'm here to check on Lila just like you asked." I can hear murmuring behind him, but I can't make out the words because of the shower and the growl still vibrating through my chest. I guess it's one of my clan members doing what I asked, as well as making sure I don't attack him. I take a few deep breaths, knowing they are not here to harm her.

"Come in," I call back, unable to stop the snarl in my voice. "But just you, Link." There is no way I want anyone viewing my mate while she is in such a vulnerable state.

He slides in and quickly shuts the door behind him. He's carrying a bag, which he sets on the floor, and then he studies us through the glass shower screen. His eyes widen when he sees me, but then he quickly schools his features. Fuck. Do we look that bad?

"How about you pass her to me and you can wash yourself?" he suggests gently, slowly holding out his hands so as to not antagonize my feral side. I look down at my own frame and realize that although the blood was washed from Lila, I still have it on parts of my body. I'm sure he's wondering if Lila was as bloody as I am. "And I can look her over and see what she needs to fully recuperate."

Nodding, I gesture for him to come forward, and he does, sliding the shower door open and holding out his hands. Pressing a kiss to her cheek, I cautiously slide my naked wet mate into the arms of another. I take stock of how I'm feeling, because I expected a reaction. It's easier than I thought it would be, and when I catch a glimpse of her shoulder, I realize that's why. Link is one of the marks on her skin, I know this, and for some reason, my monster is okay with it. He has accepted he will be one of a few and that she made the change for him and didn't just let him die, which means everything to the both of us. Who are we to deny her nature when she's done nothing but accepted and adapted to ours?

Link wraps a towel around her limp and shaky body before scooping her up. "Your brother cleaned your bed and changed the sheets, so I'll dry her off and put her in your bed while I check her over. Is this okay?" Link is still being very slow and deliberate about how he's interacting with me, like he's afraid to move too fast or use the wrong words and upset me. I guess it's understandable, considering what state I was in when he last saw me.

"Yes, that's fine, I won't be long," I tell him, reaching for the soap, and his eyebrows jump in surprise at my rational response. Fuck. Me too.

"Well, ah, good then." A hint of disbelief laces his tone, and he appears to be at a loss for a moment before shaking his head and retreating into my bedroom as I hurry through cleaning myself up. God, she's only been out of my arms for barely a moment and the need to be near her almost over-whelms me. I also want to be there when Link checks her over. I want to be able to watch him and listen to his heart for signs of untruths. Although I'm sure the doc could hide it, I'm hoping out of respect for me and the fact that I'm her mate, he won't. If I have to threaten him just a little, well, that won't be a hard ask either.

Once I'm done, I turn the shower off and dry myself, wrapping the towel around my waist before joining him and Lila back in my bedroom.

He's dressed her in one of my shirts, and she's lying on my bed, her eyes closed and chest rising slowly as he examines her. I'm not sure if she's asleep or actually passed out, and I pace back and forth while he runs a hand scan, muttering to himself as he goes. It's so quiet that even with my advanced hearing, I can't make it out. It kind of makes me want to shake him or smash my fist into a wall, but I clench them instead and try for patience.

"Wow, I'm not sure what happened, but Lila's whole physiology has changed. Her muscle and bone densities are bigger, and so is her heart. It looks like it grew to compensate for all the extra blood her body will make to feed you. Her stomach is also adjusting to digesting your blood. I think her body has kind of shut down while it does all that." A thoughtful yet fascinated look passes over his features. The doctor side of him is clearly loving this new knowledge. "Other than that, it seems to be just exhaustion. She needs to rest, eat some real food, and maybe lay off the blood drinking for a few hours so she can recover." He fists his hand and steps away from her before turning to face me. "We will have to monitor your blood intake and her vitals over the next few days. Vilaxians have two hearts to compensate for the extra blood production, but she doesn't have that, and even though it seems to have grown, I'm not sure if it will be enough to keep her healthy. The Vilaxian queen sent me a few studies on non-Vilaxian blood roses. Sometimes the Vilaxian mate would have to supplement their blood intake by taking from others. That will be something you will have to discuss with Lila. I'm not sure she will be happy if you use a Vilaxian donor, so we may have to organize blood deliveries." He stops and thinks about it. "Or she may be okay with you drinking from one of her other mates. It's something you will have to talk about, but for now, she just needs rest."

I heave out a breath of relief I hadn't realized I'd been holding. I was just going through the motions in an attempt to not think about the possibility that I may have hurt my mate during our bonding.

"Why don't you climb into bed and rest with her? It's five in the morning, and neither of you are needed right now." He pats the bed next to Lila, encouraging me to get in beside her.

I frown slightly. I've never been a cuddler, but I

guess I can give it a go for my mate. Then I remember something that happened back in the Adams brothers' office, now that my mind is clear of the bonding frenzy. Fuck. "Is John okay?

Link sighs heavily, his brows pinching together, and shakes his head. "Yes and no. For now, he is in no immediate danger, but he has been poisoned. It is very slow acting and nothing I've ever seen before. I've settled him into an induced coma to slow down the poison's track through his body, but it is beyond my capabilities to fix. I don't know what it is, so I have no clue what the antidote is. Xavier also had no luck pitting his magic against whatever it is. He is going to need to see a Celestian. They are the only ones who may be able to help him now. Eric and William have decided to cancel the rest of the Earth shows."

How will Lila react to this news? Guilt starts to eat away at me since I kept her away from her family for so long. Will she be mad at me?

Link pauses before clearing his throat. "Take today to rest up and connect with your new mate. Tomorrow, we'll receive the detainee the Earth authorities are holding—William says Lila needs to know that process—and then we'll leave Earth. We have a number of stops we need to make on our return to Skarr. It's going to be a busy few weeks, and Lila is going to see things she never imagined. She's going to need all the support she can get, especially with no powers."

I feel a smile cross my lips, and my monster preens within me. Link raises a questioning eyebrow. Smiling is not my thing, so I can't help but be proud of how I helped my blood rose. "She may not have any powers, but she is no longer vulnerable. She has the strength, speed, and senses of a Vilaxian now. Not full strength, but better than she was. I will work with her on her self-defense. I promise, she is no longer as vulnerable as she used to be."

I watch Link sag minutely, his own breath of relief audible to my ears. "Well, that is some good news. Thank you, Saxon. Thank you for protecting our girl." He pats me awkwardly on the shoulder, and I decide to give the poor cyborg a break. I reach out and grip his forearm, shaking it in the Vilaxian way.

"I am honored to be her mate, and I look forward to getting to know you better," I tell him formally, and a small smile lifts his lips.

"Alright then. I'll leave you to it. When you wake, will you let us know? Eric and William want to be the ones to tell her about John."

I swallow roughly but quickly agree, and he takes his leave. I pull back the covers and slide in behind my girl. She's curled up on her side, and her breathing is even. When I tune into her heart, it is beating in a steady rhythm again and synced with one of mine. I feel a deep sense of contentment when I hear it, and I reach around her waist before snuggling into her back. I breathe in her delicious scent and sigh in bliss before closing my eyes. Vilaxians don't need a lot of sleep, but I can certainly see the appeal of snuggling with one's mate. I may just rest my eyes for a little while as I wait for my mate to wake so I can feed her real food. I can't wait to discover all her likes and dislikes.

CHAPTER FOUR

Link

I hurry out of the room, leaving the two of them to rest, relieved that Lila survived becoming Saxon's blood rose. I go back to the medical room where John is being monitored. I don't have anyone else in the hospital wing at the moment, so I haven't erected a barrier around his bed to keep anyone out. Eric and William are still there, keeping an eye on their brother. The expressions of anguish and helplessness on their faces makes them seem closer to their actual age for the first time. The wrinkles on their foreheads and at the corners of their eyes are rarely visible, but with their pinched eyebrows and frowns, those signs of age are more prominent than ever from the distress they are feeling.

I desperately want to cure John, but even I have my limitations, as hard as that is to admit. I put those negative thoughts aside and focus on the present.

They look up as I come into the room. "How is Lila?" Eric asks, not giving me a chance to catch my breath, wringing his hands with worry.

"She's fine. She and Saxon are now bonded, and she made the transition to part Vilaxian beautifully. Her body has adjusted to produce extra blood for Saxon," I tell both men hesitantly, and William narrows his eyes.

"What *aren't* you telling us?" he asks suspiciously, picking up on my nonverbal cues.

I sigh and take a seat on the lounge next to William. Eric is across from us in a single seat with John in a bed behind him. I have the bed set to scan his vitals every ten minutes and to sound an alarm if anything changes within that time.

"Nothing you need to worry about. Lila's exhibiting more Vilaxian traits than I thought she would. Saxon confirmed she has developed their senses, speed, and strength as well as a taste for blood. Her muscle and bone mass has increased to compensate for the extra blood her body is now producing, and her heart has enlarged in size to cope with pumping that extra blood through her system. In short, Lila has taken on almost all Vilaxian traits. We will need to test her to see if she can fly."

I hope ripping off the Band-Aid quickly was the right decision to make. They asked, and I answered as factually and as scientifically as I could. There's still a lot to learn about Lila's new traits, but I can't treat her like a science experiment.

Eric and William exchange hopeful glances. "So does this mean that Lila is as fast and as strong as them?" Eric asks, a tinge of optimism in his voice.

"Yes, that's correct," I confirm for the two men who smile gleefully, Eric slapping William on his back happily.

"Well, finally some good news. We certainly needed some of that!" William exclaims, leaning back into the sofa, and I see some of the tension drain from his body. The two of them must have been concerned about how her bonding with Saxon was going to go. "That's fantastic. We won't have to worry about her so much now that she has those going for her. Now, we just need her to bond with Xavier and have her memories and magic returned to her."

The grandpas are ecstatic, and I'm happy for them. They have been so worried about John, furious that he's been poisoned. We tossed around some ideas on how or where it happened, but we are clueless. I did find a small puncture mark on his hip, and I assume that's how the poison was administered, but we're still at a loss as to who it was or when it occurred. Thankfully we don't have to worry about it being in the food or water supply. The type of poison is something I'm not familiar with, and my database is huge. Although I don't want to put a damper on their good mood, I need to express my concerns.

"I can't help but be worried about Lila. I haven't done enough research into Skarrian matings, so correct me if I'm wrong, but usually mates take on some of each other's powers, right?"

"Yes, that's right," Eric confirms, then he waits to see where I am going with my question.

"So far Lila has mated a shifter and a Vilaxian, and a warlock is her next possible mate."

"Or a cyborg." Eric winks at me. I'm not an eye roller, but I'd love to roll them now.

"Is it common for a Skarrian to have mates from lots of different races?"

The two exchange a glance, and William shrugs. "To be honest, eighty percent of Skarrians only end up with Skarrian mates. It's really only the ones who travel the galaxy that end up with mates from outside races. It's not uncommon for Skarrians to experiment with tourists, but a holiday visa to Skarr is only five days long. Not many people want to seal a bond with someone that quickly, and there are many tourists to play with, so why settle? When Skarrians hit adulthood, they usually have a good idea of whom they want to form family units with."

"That's not saying it doesn't happen, but it is unusual," Eric adds.

"And what about these Skarrians? Have there been any studies completed on how they cope with having such a broad range of powers?" I ask carefully, but I think William and Eric finally get where I'm going without me directly saying it.

"You're worried about whether Lila's body can sustain so many changes." William rubs his chin thoughtfully.

"Yes, not to mention she's pregnant. I don't think it occurred to either her or Saxon to be careful. They may not have been rational enough. Saxon certainly would have had tunnel vision."

"Are the babies okay?" A quiet voice at the door has me spinning around. Standing there are Xavier and Cas, and Cas's normally bright complexion is washed out with worry.

"Yes, my friend. It was the first thing I checked. The eggs are happy in stasis. Lila's kraken sent me smug feelings of satisfaction. The fuck me vibes are well-sated for the moment," I reassure him, feeling guilty it wasn't the first thing I did. He is her first mate, after all, and he must have been sick with concern this entire time.

He slumps against the doorframe and exhales loudly. "Thank fuck."

"Come in, you need to be here for this." William gestures to both men, but neither of them takes a seat. Xavier leans against the wall, adopting an air of nonchalance, but I can see how tightly coiled his muscles are, ready for anything, and Cas paces back and forth.

"Sorry, my kraken is not so reassured, and pacing keeps him contained for now. I'm going to go for a swim shortly, but I want to hear why you're worried."

"Just the fact that with the four of us alone, Lila is going to end up with a large range of new abilities, not to mention her own Skarrian ones once they are unlocked. That's not even adding in that idiot merman who is the final mark on her shoulder," I blurt in frustration. I hate not knowing all the answers.

William's and Eric's eyes widen at this news. "And does Lila return his interest? She was always muttering about the can of tuna fish." Eric chuckles, but William doesn't look as amused. I think he's finally getting what I'm saying.

"Her mark is on his shoulder, he showed me," Caspian confirms. "But that could also be the kraken fuck me vibes interfering with real interest."

William shakes his head. "No, that's not how it works. There needs to be genuine interest from both sides in order for the mark to appear."

"Well, anyway, I think we need to hold off on any more bonding until I can do some more research. Maybe the Celestians will have some information that my databases don't." My frustration levels are almost through the roof. With all the data I have at my fingertips, there is nothing that reassures any of my concerns.

Xavier scowls, but before he can argue against my recommendation, I hold my hand up. "I'm not saying it's permanent, but she's gone through two huge changes in the space of a couple of weeks on top of getting pregnant. Let her body adjust before we throw anything else at her. I know we planned to go straight to Westalin after we left Earth, but in light of the situation..." My gaze slides to John before returning to the group. "I think Celestia should be our first stop. We can have them cure John and ask them about Lila. They have magical ways to heal, which I just don't possess."

"Fine, but do not ask me to wait to have my parents return her memories. She needs those to feel the intimate bond we have." Xavier stubbornly crosses his arms, the most powerful being in the world looking like a toddler who had been told no.

"No, Xavier, I promise I don't want to stop anything, just slow it down," I assure him. I'm not sure if my words placate him, but he must know it's the right decision.

William stands up and claps his hands once before brushing them down his pants. "Good. I'm glad we've got a plan, but if you don't mind, I need to go cancel the rest of our tour and do some major sucking up to our Earth promoters. Eric, when Lila finally surfaces, I'm going to need you to teleport with her to Area 51 to pick up our detainee for deportation. We are expected to pick him up in a little over twenty-four hours."

"I expect she will sleep for a good portion of that," I tell them, and Eric nods, relief all over his face.

"Okay. I will go and advise the performers and crew of the situation then if you are going to handle the Earthlings. Please let us know if there are any changes," he requests, and I quickly agree.

"Of course. If Xavier and Cas can get Lila some food and a change of clothes when she wakes, I'll stay here and monitor John." I could sense they needed to do something to help Lila and be able to see her.

"Actually, there is one thing we haven't discussed." Xavier pushes off the wall he was leaning on and comes over to look down at John, brushing his hair off his face before turning to look at us.

"Oh?" William arches an eyebrow curiously.

"Who let Saxon out of sedation?" He points at one of the other beds at the end of the room. It's turned on its side, as well as the surrounding equipment, including the sedation fluid I had flowing into his system. I haven't had a chance to clean up the mess yet, too busy scouring my data-bases for anything remotely resembling the poison inside John. I also thought maybe Xavier could do some warlock mojo and pick up a clue as to who it was.

"That is a *very* good question, and one I don't have an answer to quite yet. I haven't had a chance to examine any of the security footage," William admits, his agitation evident as he continues running his hands up and down his pants.

"We also need to ascertain how Viggy got on the Vegas strip," Eric reminds us.

Shit. With everything else that happened, I had forgotten about Viggy's tour down the Vegas strip, which could have been disastrous. That would have been hard to explain if he actually stomped on or ate someone.

"Allow me the pleasure of finding *and* punishing the people involved." Xavier's dark voice sends a shiver down my spine. The threat and promise are as clear as day. "I have no doubt their motives were less than pure, and I can drag that information out of their minds. It will help me pass the time."

"I'll assist him." Caspian's eyes glow, and I can see his beast peeking out, his voice becoming more guttural. Heaven help whoever it was, because these two don't look inclined to be forgiving. Normally I'd try to dampen their casual killer instincts, but today I'm just going to turn a blind eye.

"Thank you, that would be most helpful." Eric can't even hide his grin of glee at the thought of them finding the culprits and enacting their punishment.

The four of them leave, and my machines run another scan of John's body. Lighting up a panel on the wall, I watch the progress of the toxin in his bloodstream. It's almost parasitic in nature in that it spreads through the blood but attaches itself to various organs and feeds. I have never seen anything quite like it before, and my concern is that it is not a natural poison but something that has been synthesized in a lab. It almost attacks like it has intelligence. It feeds from something long enough to cause pain, but then it allows that part of the body to rest and recover while it moves on to another part. That's why John grabbed his chest. The poison was attacking his heart for the moment, but it has moved onto his lungs now, leaving his heart to recover once more.

There's just something about this that seems familiar, but I can't put a name to it. I'm hoping the head healer at Celestia can help me, and if not, I may appeal to one of the queens. I know one of them has immense healing powers, but after the loss of their child, she fell into a great despair. I just hope she isn't too far gone, because healing powers may be John's only hope.

I lose track of time while I sit there monitoring John. I have my tablet open with a reference book that has every toxic substance known to the galaxy and whether there is a possible cure or not. That's not to say there aren't more undocumented ones, and I'm coming to the conclusion that's exactly what this is. Just when I think I find something similar, there's always something that doesn't match up.

I'm reluctant to leave, but I receive a message from Xavier asking me to meet him at the security office. After setting the monitors to send updates and alerts to my watch, I make my way to the security room. That's where all the camera feeds are monitored and recorded. He wouldn't have asked me to leave John's side if it wasn't something vital to discovering what happened to Saxon.

When I get there, I find Cas and Xavier in deep conversation with Terrans, the Skarrian head of security. I take a seat and wait for them to finish their conversation.

"So what have you found?" I ask with anticipation as Terrans pulls up some video footage on a few of the screens.

Xavier scoffs, slamming a fist down on the table. "I swear that my harem members' brains must have been damaged at some stage in their pathetic existence. For them to think that they could hide any of this from me is laughable, though I do have to admit that I think two of them have leveled up from feeding from me. I didn't think either of them had the power to muddle the minds that have been messed with already."

He waves a hand at the screen, and we watch as three females leave a room. "Those three should not be down here. They have been banished to their quarters on the big ship. I'm afraid I have been slightly distracted with Lila. I never thought they would disobey my direct orders, so I never spelled them to their rooms." His tone is regretful, even though his jaw is still clenched tightly with barely contained anger. He isn't shrouded with mist, and Terrans keeps side-eyeing him. It is unusual for Xavier to appear without it in front of the crew, and I don't think Terrans knows what to make of it.

They make their way through the circus pod until they get to the loading dock that houses the dinosaur cage for when they are transported for the show. There, they meet up with Phillip and Fiona and another figure that makes me gasp in surprise.

"That's Josa! He was supposed to return to Cybertronia on the transport that brought Silac and Tirrian." I watch as the six of them huddle together, smart enough to speak quietly and hide their mouths so we can't actually hear or read their conversation.

"Can we make that louder?" Caspian asks Terrans, pointing at the whispered conversation.

Terrans shakes his head. "No, I've tried to, and it just distorts. It's almost as if there is a spell in play."

"There might be." Xavier shrugs. "Again, not something I thought either Nambra or Lexus could do, and Elyan is powerless, so she's definitely not capable."

"What about Phillip or Fiona? Do either of them have those kinds of powers?" Cas muses. We know the siblings are sneaky in their own way, but I hadn't even considered the possibility that they could be the culprits trying to sabotage the circus.

"Who knows? I don't actually know much about them except that they are the Adams brothers' wife's sister's grandchildren. They are supposed to have animal powers, which is why they are working with the dinos, but they certainly didn't display or use them the other day when Htaed went crazy in the ring," I point out, and Xavier snorts in disgust again.

"Clearly," he deadpans.

We watch as the group finishes their huddled conversation. Phillip and Fiona leave the camera view, and Terrans presses a few buttons. We follow their progress to the teleporting room and watch as they teleport back to the big ship.

"You'll need to access the camera files on the big ship to find out where they went next. Once you arrive, speak to my brother Ferron. He will be able to do what I just did," Terrans explains to Xavier. "I can't access the footage from here just in case anyone human actually finds their way into this room. Security protocol."

"I'll be going there next. I want to have all my farlucks in a row to present my findings to William and Eric."

Terrans returns to the loading dock, and we follow the warlock girls and Josa's path through the circus pod. Finally, the direction they are headed in is obvious as they make it to the medical wing. I freeze and watch in horror as Nambra and Lexus hold hands and manage to override my security wards.

"Remind me to fix that for you so it will never happen again," Xavier says through gritted teeth as he leans forward. I know he's not mad at me but at the situation. Even if that may be the case, a sense of guilt washes over me because the security I have is weak. I've never really needed it in the past. There has never been a situation like this since I've been with the circus.

The camera shot switches again, showing the security footage inside the room. Nambra and Lexus stand back against the wall, exchanging frightened glances as Elyan and Josa step up to the sedated Vilaxian. With my wards now broken, Josa pushes a few buttons on the medical screen, over-riding my commands and taking control of the programs.

"I'm just going to reduce his sedation. I would stand back, though, because when he comes out, he could be feral," Josa warns Elyan, their voices not hidden this time. Maybe the Adams twins were responsible for the sound distortion when they were huddled together after all.

She huffs and rolls her eyes but moves backward. "As long as he kills that bitch during their bonding, I don't fucking care."

"How did any of them know about Saxon and

Lila? It was supposed to be kept quiet. The Adams brothers asked the Vilaxians to keep it to themselves for now," Cas muses as we watch Josa reduce the sedation and Saxon's eyes snap open. It doesn't take long for him to recover, and he roars his fury, ripping himself from the restraints keeping him on the bed before tearing the fluid lines from his veins.

"Well, they didn't," Terrans states matter-of-factly. "Radella and Estrella have been denying it to anyone who will listen. It's all anyone has talked about for days in the dining room. None of you have been there though. They are even placing bets on how long she survives the bonding."

The three of us exchange a glance, and I can see the two of them are as annoyed as I am. Xavier shrouds himself in shadows, and Terrans shudders, flinching back in fear. I think he'd temporarily forgotten whom he was talking to. Xavier waves a hand in his direction, and his eyes glaze over slightly. I'm sure Xavier is making him forget what he looks like. When they clear again, he shrinks back when he realizes who is in the room with him.

"I think it's time I reminded everyone who I am, what I'm capable of, and that Lila falls under my protection. We will worry about the twins later. For now, I have three warlocks to punish. Care to join me?" He directs the question at the kraken and me.

Cas quickly agrees with zero hesitation, but I shake my head. I'm more of a pacifist. Yes, they deserve to be punished, but I don't need to be involved. I know whatever Xavier and Cas have planned will be more than enough. "No, I'll return to John. I wouldn't want anyone interfering with him. Now that I know Josa is still on the ship, I need to change codes. I hadn't before because I thought he was gone. I thought the medical unit was *safe*."

I can't help but swallow roughly, and guilt settles heavily in my stomach.

"Let us know when Lila and Saxon surface, and we will have a meal together and get to know our new husband-in-law." Cas sounds excited about the prospect, and his eyes flash back and forth from his beast. "I know it has only been about twelve hours, but I miss her dreadfully." He rubs a spot on his chest and grimaces like he's in pain.

Xavier sends out his mist to surround Caspian. "That's your new bond. It will be like that for a while. Come on, I'll let your beast toss the girls around a bit. That should distract him and keep him happy for a while." Although I can't see them now, they both chuckle evilly, and I shake my head. Who would have thought the all-powerful warlock would be capable of comforting someone? Wonders will never cease.

"Have fun, boys. I'll see you later," I tell them before leaving the room and returning to my patient, anxious to make sure he is protected.

CHAPTER FIVE

Xavier

We teleport back to the mothership. I'm hoping once Lila and I seal our bond that my teleporting reach may extend, but for now, I still can't personally teleport such a large distance. I did a location spell and discovered my wayward harem members had returned to their quarters. I'm not sure how they thought they could hide the shitshow they created. I'm wondering if I damaged Elyan's brain when I removed all her power—though she wasn't all that intelligent to start with. I know she had to have been the ringleader. Neither Lexus nor Nambra have the guts to do something like this on their own.

From the teleporting room, I teleport us to my rooms, landing us on my side of the quarters in front of the adjoining doorway. I allow my mist to peel back from Caspian. "Do you want to change into half form for this?" I ask him, sensing how close to the surface his beast is.

"It's all I can do to hold my beast back, half form might make it easier to manage him," he agrees and quickly strips, allowing the shift to take over his body. I don't take my eyes away as he gets naked in front of me. Shifters usually don't care, and I think he and I have moved onto a relationship where modesty is probably a thing of the past. If we share a mate, the likelihood that we will end up fucking that mate at the same time is high… very high in Lila's case. I won't deny it though, Caspian is a very sexy man, even sexier in half form. His tentacles intrigue me. I've never had a lover with tentacles before, and I would very much like to take them for a test ride.

He grunts, and although he can't see me admiring him, I'm almost certain he can feel the lust in the air because I don't do anything to curb my feelings. Lila has changed me. Much like my harem, I had grown good at hiding everything I was feeling, but now I don't care who knows. I think about this realization for a moment. Oh, that's why Nambra and Lexus may have more power than I thought they had. I haven't been keeping a lid on anything, and they have been feeding from it without permission. It's yet another blow to my trust, not to mention taboo in the warlock world. You never feed on someone without their permission, especially if they are your harem master or mistress.

I reel in every single feeling I have and lock them down tight. I see Caspian sigh with relief and chuckle. "We can revisit all of that at a later time, okay?" he suggests. I can't help but notice his voice became a little deeper as he spoke.

"Yes, sorry. Lila has made me weak," I grumble out in apology, and he shakes his head.

"No, my friend, Lila doesn't make you weak at all. In fact, she strengthens all of us. You'll see once your intimate bond has been fixed."

I allow my mist to fade and push the button for the door to slide back, giving me entrance to the harem side of my quarters. It's mostly quiet, but I can hear the murmur of something farther in the room. I feel Caspian follow behind me, but he lets me take the lead, although I know he's dying to inflict a little damage to the idiots who clearly have a death wish—a wish I am happy to make come true.

In the living area, I find Ara and Jastia, my remaining two loyal warlocks, watching a space opera on the couch. Both of their eyes are glued to the screen as something dramatic happens to the characters. Farther down the couch, Zanorn, my metamorph, is in his preferred form with a tablet in hand. His long white hair is pulled back into a messy bun at the back of his head. He has on a black tank top and black wide-legged pants that I favor for comfort when in my quarters. His dark skin glints where the light hits it, and there's a small smirk on his lush lips. I would guess he's reading something erotic. He is an avid reader, and he thoroughly enjoys smut. He looks up when I get closer, wearing a soft smile.

"Hello, Xavier," he calls out, the relief in his voice strong. I had been avoiding the rooms altogether out of respect for Lila. I will have to dismiss them all from my harem eventually, but they are doing no harm staying here for now. Zanorn picks up on my mood and frowns. "What is wrong?" He puts down the tablet and stands up, gaining the attention of the two warlock girls.

"Where are Lexus, Nambra, and Elyan?" I question, not explaining why I'm asking, but my firm tone lets them know I'm impatient and not fucking around. He frowns and waves a hand in the direction of their rooms.

"Where you left them, I'm assuming." He exchanges a glance with the girls who look equally confused.

"They haven't left their rooms since you banished them there," Ara says, her voice quiet.

"Hmm, well, I actually have proof that they have left their rooms. Go get them please. Sinath and Topirey might as well witness this too." My voice is flat. I'm not sure how this harem got so out of control. Obviously my inattention has caused them to forget their places.

Caspian undulates out of the shadows and stops just behind me, and all three of them startle. None of them had been paying attention to anything else but me. Although these three are not my targets, I'm pleased I caught them off guard, and I'm hoping the others will be downright terrified.

Jastia turns and hurries to do as I bid, while Ara and Zanorn sit down again. "What did they do this time?" he asks flatly.

"I'll wait until Jastia returns, if you don't mind. I don't want to waste my energy by repeating myself."

It's not long before she does. Sinath and Topirey look confused, or as confused as the two of them can look with their unusual features, but Elyan, Lexus, and Nambra look terrified, and so they fucking should. I get a burst of energy from the terror in the air, and I suck it down quickly. The three girls pale even further as a wicked grin slides across my lips.

They all go to take seats, but I wave my hand, forcing the three culprits to remain standing so they know I am here solely for them. "Do you three know why you are here?" They stupidly shake their heads, trying to look as innocent as possible. With their hands clasped in front of them and avoiding eye contact, I can sense they are going for the submissive route.

Caspian huffs in disgust behind me. Their eyes quickly flick to him, and I'm not sure what they see, but all three of them blanch. Elyan steps behind the other two before they focus their attention back on me.

"Seriously? That's how you're going to play this? Stupidity?" I can't say I'm surprised, but to have the fucking audacity to lie straight to my face shows they have a serious lack of self-preservation. Good.

"What did you do? Why couldn't you have just obeyed him? Why do you have to go around stirring up trouble?" Ara spits out. The usually mild-mannered warlock practically vibrates with anger. "Wasn't Mithus's betrayal enough? Elyan, you've already been stripped of your powers. You couldn't even keep your head down and behave in the hope he'd return them?"

Ara's words prove to be too much for Elyan to hold her tongue, and she lashes out. "He shouldn't have taken them in the first place." Now I just have to wait for them to confess, they won't be able to help themselves. "I was just protecting our master from the vile Earth bitch. Why does he need her when he has *us*? She can't sustain him like we can." Elyan's hands clench at her sides, and her lip is turned up in a snarl.

"Exactly. She's even that awful Vilaxian's blood rose. We knew if they sealed their bond there would be no way Xavier would stay interested."

And there it is.

Nambra just admitted to the crime.

I throw my head back and start to laugh, and

Caspian chimes in behind me. Lexus scowls at him. "I don't know why you're laughing, your mate's a slutty *whore*." She brazenly takes a step forward like she's going after Caspian. Yes, she clearly lacks self-preservation. He doesn't let her get far, as one of his tentacles shoots out and snatches her up, hoisting her into the air. She screams and starts to cast a spell, but I render it null. She struggles and gasps as his tentacle tightens around her, cutting off her air supply and her ability to talk.

"Wow, Lexus. That's a bit rich coming from *you*." Zanorn has stayed quiet up until now, knowing to stay well out of the firing line, but I guess her utterly ridiculous comment was enough to set off the most placid person in the room.

"My mate is magnificent. You would never be in her orbit, let alone in the same solar system as her. Think about how powerful she will be once she bonds with all of her mates. I wouldn't want to be the person who pisses her off," Caspian cautions with a smirk. I can hear how much he admires and respects Lila in his voice. The threat, however, rings loud and clear, but the two other girls scoff, foolish not to heed his warning, and roll their eyes, even as Lexus starts to turn pale from lack of oxygen.

"Please, a kraken shifter is no match for a warlock, and she won't survive bonding to the Vilaxian. He will drain her until she's a husk, just like Mithus was, and she won't survive it." Elyan is so flippantly confident she is right.

"So why hasn't this one gotten free yet if you warlocks are so special?" Cas shakes Lexus, and her eyeballs bulge, and the veins start to pop inside them. Her face and lips turn a light shade of blue, a sure sign she's being suffocated. Cas pauses for a moment before he releases her, and the jealous warlock drops to the floor like a piece of lead. The dramatic thump makes me grin in amusement.

I haven't stopped my chuckling, and I can see the innocent ones of my harem watching me with caution.

"Not only did she survive, but her body chemistry has become part Vilaxian with their strength and speed, oh, and their taste for blood," Cas crows, the pride in his voice obvious.

This shuts the girls up, and then all hell breaks loose. They turn on one another without hesitation. It's obvious their so-called alliance was a joke. "You said she would die," Nambra accuses Elyan. She crosses her arms and glares at the former warlock.

"And you said that you two were powerful enough to hide us from the cameras. That was a dirty fucking lie. You're still the pathetic worms you always were," Elyan sneers, and it proves to be too much for Nambra, who waves a hand, sending Elyan flying back, her body smashing into the wall behind them. Elyan groans and slides down onto the floor, shaking her head. Seeing the girls turn on each other is no surprise, but it doesn't lessen my anger one little bit, I'm just waiting to mete out my own vengeance.

"I might be weak, but you are nothing. Nothing. You are worthless to anyone and everyone. Practically human. Maybe you should be left behind on Earth when we leave, because nobody is going to want a powerless warlock. The only thing you'll be good for is some outer ring brothel, and you might not even survive that," Nambra sneers, and Lexus nods, having recovered slightly from Caspian's treatment of her, but she doesn't move from her spot on the floor. They have all momentarily forgotten about us while the three of them have their own argument.

I clear my throat, and their attention turns to me once more. They blanch at the look of fury on my face. I guess they really had gotten distracted. Elyan stays on the floor, which is probably the smartest move she's made so far.

"So you have nothing else to say for yourself?" I ask. "You don't want to plead your case any further or change your story?"

They both get a stubborn set to their chins. "She made us do it." Nambra points at Elyan, throwing her completely under the Vilaxian starship. Elyan immediately tenses, her body freezing in place, and before she can open her mouth, Nambra shuts her up. "She said that *she* would be nothing but trouble. That she's already caused her to lose her powers and it was only a matter of time before she whispered in your ear and we would be losing ours too."

I cannot believe the audacity and sheer stupidity of these women. "What the fuck was I thinking when I contracted them to my harem?" I mutter under my breath, but Cas hears me.

"You probably weren't thinking with your brain." He snorts quietly, and he's not wrong. All three women are luscious and lusty, and it was no hardship to feed from them in the past. I'd like to think I've matured though, not to mention knowing Lila is my intimate changes everything.

"Did you not consider that there is a reason I stripped Elyan of her powers and told you all to leave her alone?" I step closer to the three of them, and they flinch. Seeing that makes me smile internally. They have finally remembered who I am.

"Pfft, no. It's no secret you have a wandering eye, and even I can see that Lila, despite being a powerless slut, is sexy." Elyan finally staggers to her feet, rubbing her shoulder where it hit the wall. Lexus is still down, and I think Cas may have damaged some ribs.

"Lila is my intimate," I announce to the room, and the immediate silence that follows speaks louder than words. I don't think anyone even breathes for a short moment, and then chaos erupts. Nambra whirls on Elyan.

"You stupid bitch. We never should have listened to you!" she screams.

"Your intimate? How can that useless slug be your intimate?" Elyan is shaking with fear now, but she still hasn't learned to keep her words to herself. I doubt she ever will.

"Silence! Lila is not as powerless as she seems. My parents locked her powers down years ago. You know what the penalty for attacking a royal's intimate is, don't you?" The girls fall silent, and I see Ara shudder out of the corner of my eye. "But I am feeling generous. If you tell me where I can find that cyborg nurse responsible for freeing Saxon, I will wave the death sentence and only remove your powers like Elyan. All three of you will be stripped of your positions and family names and banished from Westalin."

As much as I'd rather kill them all, I have to look at the bigger picture. I focus my attention on the three women, waiting to see who will share the nurse's whereabouts. One, two, three seconds go by before one of them develops the nerves to speak up again.

Nambra is quick to offer up the information. "He is hiding in the lightning cats' living quarters. One of the caves is unoccupied, and he has managed to mute his scent with his nanotech, so they have no idea he is there. Not to mention their own infighting has them distracted." I nod my head at her, surprised at how much information she has to give. I guess they have been working together longer than I assumed, which in itself is also worrying.

"Thank you." I hold out my hands and start to absorb Nambra's and Lexus's powers. Nambra joins Lexus on the ground, tears flowing over their cheeks as they plead with me to spare them, but I have not one drop of sympathy or guilt. My body shudders at the influx of power, small that it is, and I breathe deeply while I adjust. When I'm done, they are both curled up in fetal positions on the ground, quietly sobbing. "Get them out of my sight," I tell the others, and Sinath and Topirey hurry over and remove the girls, returning them to their rooms.

There is no point in locking them in. They are powerless now, and I don't think they will be able to convince the others to do their bidding. They also don't have self-healing, so I hope they are not stupid enough to have sex with the two males again. They will die.

I turn my attention to Elyan. "I can't believe that stripping you of your powers wasn't enough to get you to keep your head down," I start, sounding deceptively calm. I like the thought of luring her into a false sense of security.

She shrugs casually like this conversation isn't going to be one of her last. "I knew my daddy would make you give them back when we got to Westalin." And there it is, the source behind her unwavering confidence.

Ara and Jastia giggle hysterically, and Zanorn scoffs. I shake my head at her delusions.

"Oh, and how would he make me?" I ask, wanting to hear her reasoning.

"Because he's more powerful than you. Our family has always been more powerful than yours. You don't deserve to be the ruling family of West-alin, and it's only a matter of time before we over-throw you." She practically vomits this word bile. "My daddy says yours is going to meet his maker very shortly, and then I will make you bow down at *my* feet. You will be *my* plaything, and I will use you whenever and wherever I feel like it." During this tirade, she's been moving closer and closer to me as I see the now obvious manic light in her eyes. I'm not sure if stripping her of her powers caused this mental break, or if it happened previously and I just didn't notice.

"Well, I look forward to seeing your father battle mine for supremacy, but unfortunately for you, you won't." I sigh, bored with the conversation and unconcerned about any of the rubbish she just spouted. I wave a hand and watch as her body slowly starts to crumble, peeling off and floating onto the breeze like the first gentle flakes of snow at the start of winter.

"Damn it, man, you promised to involve me."

I startle slightly, turning my head away from the crumbling warlock in front of me. She finally realized what is happening and is desperately trying to hold herself together, but it is like trying to hold water with a bucket that has a hole.

"Fuck, I'm sorry. I kind of forgot. My temper got the better of me."

Cas rolls his eyes and puts his hands on his hips. "Fine, but I get the cyborg," he retorts, and I wave my hand in agreement.

"Of course my friend, he is all yours."

"You are fucking psychotic. You will regret this, Xavier!" Elyan screams, her mouth still intact. "Don't do this, please!" she begs, and I ignore her and turn to the remaining three.

"I am sorry you had to see that. I am terminating our contracts as of today. You will be paid out fully, of course, and I will provide you with excellent references so that you can find another harem to join, if you wish."

The three of them aren't really paying any attention. They are too busy gaping at the horrific spectacle that is Elyan. It's actually wasted on them, so I project a video of what is happening to the whole ship. I want everyone to know what happens when you cross a warlock, and worse when you threaten their intimate. Hopefully this will make them think twice about going after Lila again.

"How long will this take?" Cas asks, waving at the disintegrating girl, and I shrug.

"No idea." I watch in awe as she continues to fall apart. I've never used this punishment before, but it's quite entertaining and certainly dramatic

"Well, come on, let's go find that cyborg. My kraken wants to rend some limbs." He's clearly on edge as he cracks his knuckles menacingly, and his eyes flash back and forth from purple to black.

"Fine, I'll deal with them later. Hopefully someone will clean the mess up." Nobody moves at my words. I think everyone else is too scared they'll catch my attention.

I turn, thankful that I no longer have to deal with harem drama, and make a note to tell my dad about Elyan and her father's plans. Hopefully Dad won't kill him before I can return and watch.

CHAPTER SIX

Caspian

I'm kind of a little stunned at what Xavier did to his harem girl, but also kind of not. I would have killed her too, except I would have most likely just shifted and eaten her. The fact that he basically made her disintegrate slowly is kind of disturbing. She was watching as little bits of her body floated away. I don't think it hurt, and there was no blood or gore so cleanup should only require a broom and a dustpan, but still, it was a pretty hardcore way to die. I should probably be scared of his power, but I'm not. I only feel grateful that he's another line of defense for Lila.

I don't think anyone is going to forget about that anytime soon, especially since he broadcasted it to the whole ship.

Xavier made inquiries as to where the cats were

—either up here or down in the pod—and discovered they are actually on the main ship. As we make our way to the lightning cats' quarters, every screen we pass shows exactly what happened to Elyan. People are gathered around, whispering and pointing at it, all wearing horrified expressions. Xavier has assumed his mysterious persona once more and is cloaked in mist, but they all blanch or shrink away when they see us walk past. Hopefully it goes a long way in keeping Lila safe, though bonding with Saxon has obviously helped her, as well as her ability to shift into a kraken.

I rub a hand across my chest at the pang in my heart when I think about my mate. Although I am happy for her and Saxon, it's been too long since I've seen her, and it's time she was returned to me. I need to reassure myself and my beast that she is fine, despite being told that she is. Seeing her in person will go a long way in calming us both down.

Going after those responsible for her being placed in a vulnerable position is the only thing keeping my beast from bursting through my skin and rampaging back to the circus pod to find her. We are definitely ready for our turn with her. We don't even want sex, we just want to feel her in our arms again and listen to her belly to reassure ourselves our eggs are safe.

I asked Link, and he assured me that they were fine after he scanned her. He said that although her body has changed, nothing within her womb did.

The only thing he wasn't sure of was if our little darlings would now also have a taste for blood. He told me he didn't say anything to Saxon, and Lila was asleep. Also, our beast forms like blood anyway, so it really isn't a big deal to me, and we will deal with it if they happen to enjoy blood.

The trek from the warlock's quarters to the lightning cats' accommodations takes about ten minutes. We could have used the sideslip elevators, but Xavier wanted to be seen just to drive home the seriousness of the situation. People's reactions to seeing him were hilarious. Most of them found new places to be very quickly, but I think the message has been driven home—Lila is under his protection, and death will be the only outcome if you mess with her.

There is no room for negotiation, just an automatic death sentence.

We get to the door, and he pauses and turns to me. "It's going to be freezing in there. May I give you some magical protection?" he asks, looking me up and down. I visibly shudder at the thought of being cold. My kraken is most definitely a tropical water kind of creature. In my full form, I can regulate my temperature if I have to, but in half form, I will turn into a Caspian popsicle in there, and that is not my version of fun.

"Yes please," I reply, and his mist peels back, revealing his waving hand. I feel a warm barrier cover my entire form. I look down, thinking maybe he'd put a sweater over my top half, but no, I'm still naked, and I can see a shimmer of magic coating my torso and tentacles. I raise an eyebrow at him, and he shrugs.

"It would be a shame to cover all that." He gestures to my form before the mist recovers the hand and he turns his attention back to the door. I'm pretty sure he didn't need to peel the mist back to protect my skin. Instead, he did it to reassure me.

That's the thing about Xavier. As I get to know him better, I can see how thoughtful he is when he cares about someone. Not everyone would understand that side of him.

I hear him clear his throat, and the air starts to prickle with the intensity of his magic. "Stay close in case one of the lightning cats goes on the defensive. I should be able to deflect their lightning if need be. Let's go and get us a cyborg."

He overrides the locking mechanism, and the door slides back, causing a blast of air and tendrils of fog to roll out of the door. Hopefully he has protected the underside of my tentacles as well, otherwise this is going to be painful. I grit my teeth and move forward when he does, heaving out a sigh of relief when the extreme cold doesn't touch me. We stand in the entrance to the quarters, and I think we both blink in surprise. Although I knew it was going to be freezing, I had no idea their quarters would look like this. In front of us is a simulated frozen tundra that looks exactly like the landscape on Iceen. There are a couple of large rocks and an open space covered in ice with dips and crevices, and behind that is a rock face with a number of different openings.

I knew the main ship was set up to accommodate each species' specific needs, like the mer tank, but I didn't realize they had caves in here until Nambra mentioned Josa's whereabouts.

I can see five different entries along the bottom, and then farther up are another two. I guess they need to climb the rocks to get up there, and based on what I've seen during the circus, they are quite agile, so it wouldn't be a difficult task for them.

A growling sound has me focusing on the middle cave. The light in here is quite dim, and I watch as Xavier produces a ball of light before launching it into the air, illuminating the area a little more. I can make out the shadow of a cat, but still no color to give me a clue which one it is. The shadow keeps growing in size as it makes its way closer to the entrance and us, the growling accompanied by a sizzling sound.

Lightning.

"That sounds like one pissed off cat," I mutter to my warlock friend whom I feel increase the energy of his own power. It's like a clash of the titans. Soon, the area is rippling with the residue of both creatures' powers, and I feel my hair start to float as static electricity clings to it. Finally, I can make out the color of the cat, and I feel my stomach sink. I was hoping it would be Maxsim, the alpha of the clan, but unfortunately, I can tell by its pale blue fur and the black mane that it's Natalia, the vicious she beast. I should have guessed it would be her from the immediate hostility, but lightning cats can be territorial, so it might have been one of the others. She steps out into the clearing, her body buzzing with tension as electricity swirls around her. She roars out a warning before piercing her tail into the air and launching a bolt of lightning at us. The blast of power hits an invisible barrier in front of us, which doesn't even tremble at the contact, and bounces off, landing harmlessly against the rocks where it dissipates with a few sparks.

"Enough!" Xavier bellows, the sound reverberating off the rocks, but she doesn't listen and launches another bolt at us, roaring her displeasure again. Before it can hit the invisible barrier, a figure leaps from the caves above and intercepts the lightning, his large body absorbing the electricity as he lands lightly on his feet between us and the enraged she-cat. Maxsim's ombre blue body is twice the size of Natalia's, and his roar is ear splitting, shaking the ground beneath us. He quickly puts her in her place, causing her to flinch back and bow down in front of him. The alpha is finally here.

Xavier and I watch as Maxsim's body shimmers, and then he changes form. It's a fast process, but it looks uncomfortable. Unlike a shifter's change, which is aided by magic, their bones seem to rearrange themselves until he stands upright in humanoid form, his muscular fur-covered ass on display with his tail lashing back and forth in agitation.

"Holy shit," I mutter as I take in the lightning cat in front of us. I don't know what I was expecting. Of course he isn't covered by his normal loincloth or circus uniform.

"Close your mouth, squidlet. You're drooling," Xavier mutters, laughing quietly. I bet he's looking just as much as I am, but his perving is hidden behind that damn mist.

"Fuck off," I growl at him, and he chuckles again, a little louder this time.

"Change," Maxsim bellows at the female cat, the alpha command rattling even me. My beast champs at the bit to test his mettle against this worthy opponent, but his thoughts confuse me for a moment until I listen closer.

Cat good mate for Lila. Strong, virile, and sexy. Fucking hell. Poor Lila, my kraken is basically acting as her pimp.

Calm down, asshole. She has enough on her plate. Let her settle into the mates and powers she has already, and Xavier is next, you know that, and don't forget Link.

He purrs in response at the reminder of the sexy doctor and warlock, and then he settles back down. Fuck my life, that was close. Next thing I know, he'll be taking them for a test run for her, and that is not really acceptable without Lila's approval.

Natalia's change is much slower than Maxsim's and looks much more painful, with it taking longer for her bones to reform into the desired form. A forced change isn't easy on any kind of shifter. When she finishes, she looks up at him with a scowl and snarls. She struggles to her feet, and I avert my eyes. I don't need to be looking at a naked woman who is not my wife. Xavier must understand my dilemma, because I feel his power flex, and then she's covered with their traditional loincloth garb. Unfortunately, so is Maxsim, and we hadn't gotten a look at the front yet. My kraken grumbles deep inside.

"What were you thinking, attacking like that?" he demands angrily, stepping toward her aggressively, and she rolls her eyes. Natalia is a beta and below Maxsim in the pecking order, so she is being incredibly disrespectful. I guess her mother being the matriarch has made her cocky. I have a feeling she will end up regretting her attitude.

"They barged into our den *uninvited*. I was well within my right to do so," she sneers before baring her teeth at us and hissing. Down, kitty.

"This is not Iceen. Those are not the rules we live by here," he scolds her before turning to look at us, raising an eyebrow and crossing his arms. "Natalia isn't really wrong though. You did come in uninvited, which in Iceen would get you attacked. What is it you want?"

The lightning cats tend to stick to themselves.

They don't come out and join the rest of the crew to socialize between shows, so I don't really know anything about this streak except for the information they shared with Link, and that's not really anything personal about each individual. It's a shame they remain aloof from everyone else, but I guess if they have their own internal issues, they wouldn't have time to cultivate friendships.

By now, the rest of the cats have joined us. Three huddle around the entrance of one cave, staying well out of the way. I guess they don't want to draw an irate Natalia's attention. Above us on the ledge of the other cave, the pure white cat, Echo, lounges, his head resting on his paws as he watches everything silently.

"I have it on good authority that there is a cyborg hiding in your caves," Xavier explains, still in his mist form. "He is wanted for treason. He assisted in trying to kill the Adams brothers' granddaughter, Lila, and I would like your permission to search for him."

This has Maxsim's eyebrows jumping in surprise, but Natalia just scoffs behind him.

"Unlikely, warlock. We would know if he were here. We could smell a stranger in our area, so he would not be able to hide himself." She sounds so confident and smug, it'll be nice when Xavier proves her wrong.

"Well then, either you know and you are in on his treason," Xavier suggests, which is something that had already been rolling around in my mind, and it has Natalia paling, "or he has managed to get past you. Either way, I still require permission to search for him." Xavier's mist rolls back from his body, and he shows himself to the lightning cats. It is the same glamour he assumed for his harem, and not the one that I know is his real form. He puffs up his chest and his body crackles with power. I see the fur on the tips of their ears stand on end. "Actually, I don't even require permission, I can search, but I thought I would try the polite way first."

Natalia's fur bristles, her claws lengthen on her fingers, and her tail crackles with electricity once more as she starts to growl. "You will not," she says through a mouthful of teeth, but Maxsim holds up a hand, silencing her.

"Quiet," he demands before bowing his head in consent at Xavier. Natalia cowers under the alpha command, but the look she gives him would strip skin from a body.

"I will show you through the caves. I apologize for my streak member's rudeness. I will inform her mother, the queen, that she will need a few more lessons in diplomacy when we return to Iceen." He turns to the three cats huddled in front of the left cave. "I'm assuming there is no cyborg hiding in your caves?" All three of them shake their heads in unison, and I have to smother my chuckle. They look like cute kitties at the moment, but Natalia proved how deadly they can be. "Very well, they are not in my and Echo's either, which leaves us with five to search."

Natalia screeches. "You're not suggesting I am hiding the cyborg, are you?" she demands, putting her hands on her hips and standing defiantly in front of her cave. "I will not let you search my private quarters."

Because *that's* not suspicious at all. The chuckle I was holding finally releases in the form of a choking cough. I wouldn't put it past her to be conspiring with Josa. She doesn't like Lila either, and getting rid of her would solve a problem for her.

Maxsim starts to argue with her, but Xavier quickly steps in, putting his hand gently on the big alpha's shoulder. "That's okay, we don't actually need to see inside her den." He waves a hand and produces another flickering ball of light similar to the one that is floating above us, lightening up the area. It splits into five other balls, and my mouth drops open as they shoot off in the directions of the five different caves. The one heading for Natalia's shoots cheekily between her legs, causing her to jump and scream. Xavier chuckles with amusement.

"They will tell me which one he is in, and then it is only a matter of dragging him out," he explains to Maxsim.

We all wait in silence, anticipation prickling the air around us, and I see Xavier shudder. I step up next to my friend, putting my hand on his shoulder. "Are you okay?" I ask as one of my tentacles sneaks out and wraps gently around his leg in comfort, uncontrolled by me.

"Yes, of course. I can just feel his terror, and it is quite heady." He sways slightly, almost like he's getting drunk off the emotion. Ah, so he's absorbing the cyborg's utter despair. "I can't wait to take a crack at his mind before you dispose of him. I've never rifled through a cyborg's brain before, and I'm looking forward to the experience."

Xavier sounds absolutely giddy.

I drop my hand back down to my side, but my tentacle caresses him reassuringly before it drops as well. *Stupid horny beast. You're almost as bad as the damn merman.*

This is why Xavier is terrifying. He can talk about rummaging around in someone's mind quite casually, but to everyone else, it's horrifying. I'm just glad I'm not on the receiving end of that torture.

He stiffens and turns to face the cave on the far right. "That one." He points at it, and the three cats that are still in cat form race toward it and disappear into the darkness, their footsteps silent over the icy terrain.

I go to follow them, adrenaline rushing through my veins, but Maxsim puts a hand against my chest, stopping me in my tracks. I glance down at it before looking back up at the alpha cat and arching my eyebrow. "Let them bring him out. There's nowhere for him to go, the cave is a dead end. Now that they know he's there, he won't be able to hide from them like he has been."

I remove the cat's hand from my chest but does as he asks, grinding my teeth with impatience.

This psychotic cyborg is *mine*.

CHAPTER SEVEN

Maxsim

I can feel the tension running through both the warlock and the kraken. The cyborg has really stepped over the line. On Iceen, trying to kill off your competition is common practice for females, but I know this is not the case elsewhere. I cannot believe he was hiding here in our quarters underneath our noses and I had no idea.

I eye Natalia suspiciously out of the corner of my eye. There is no way he should have been able to get in here without some kind of assistance, and I would not put it past her to be the one who helped purely out of spite, because that's just who she is. Once the others leave, I will demand answers from her. I can't wait to leave Earth and make our way back to Iceen. I am done with this vile bitch. I will be making it known that neither my family clan nor Echo's will support her family as our leading matriarch. It is time for a change in leadership.

The sound of a scuffle reaches my ears, and I can tell by the way the other two stiffen that they can hear it too. Before long, Trace, Sim, and Fuse drag out a man wrapped head to toe in thick furs. The only feature I can make out is a tuft of metallic green hair sticking out from underneath a hat that is lodged firmly on his head. He's struggling and yelling obscenities at them, but the three of them have a good grip on the cyborg with their teeth.

They deposit him unceremoniously face down at our feet, hissing at Josa before backing away and returning to the entrance of their cave. The three cats decided to share a den, since they are better protected from Natalia's wrath and manipulation as a group, and I fully supported their choice.

Xavier rolls the man over with a heavy foot. The encroacher tries to clamber back to his feet, but the kraken shoots out a couple of tentacles and pins him to the ground. Another one shoots out and peels the cap and scarf off the man, exposing the telltale shimmery skin of a cyborg.

"Josa," Caspian sneers, and his unveiled hatred of the cyborg is palpable in the air as his tentacles flex a little tighter in response. "Look at you, hiding like a mitavin like you have something to be afraid of."

The warlock doesn't say anything, just stares down at the defiant creature with his arms crossed.

"I'm not scared. You can't do anything to me."

"Why?" Caspian asks, genuinely interested, and Josa looks confused, his brows pinching together as he tries to follow the kraken's train of thought.

"Why what?"

"Why don't you think we can do anything to you?" Caspian clarifies.

"I've done nothing to deserve punishment," he snivels, and Caspian starts to chuckle.

Looking over at Natalia, I watch her face. She has a sneer on her face, her claws are extended, and her fur is bristled, but I can smell the fear wafting off of her. She knows her involvement in all of this will not go unpunished. In fact, she may have just accidentally secured a way for me to keep Echo permanently safe. I turn back to look down at the cyborg. His own fear is also visible. His skin trembles slightly, and I can see a drop of sweat roll down his temple. I can't believe he's been here under our noses the whole time.

"You and I and all of the kitties know that's not true."

I growl under my breath at the kraken calling us kitties, and he just smirks at me before he continues to bait the cyborg.

"You were supposed to have left the circus on the transport that dropped our new performers off nights ago. Imagine our surprise when we saw you on the security footage."

The cyborg blanches at this and mutters, "The Skarrian twins said we wouldn't appear on the footage."

I see Caspian and Xavier exchange glances. "Well, that's one thing solved. We will need to deal with that at another time," Caspian comments to the still silent warlock. He turns back to the cyborg without waiting for a reply. "They lied. They distorted your voices—it didn't even do that once you separated—but the camera still picked up your images. We know you released Saxon from his sedated state, and boy, did you fuck up." The kraken takes a dramatic pause, letting each of his words sink into the cyborg's mind, and each word that's spoken causes fear to transform his features. "What you didn't know is that Lila is Xavier's intimate."

My gaze shifts over to the warlock, trying to gauge his reaction to Caspian being so forthcoming about his relationship with Lila, but all I see is *mist*. Nothing is visible to differentiate any features of his body.

A strangled cough has me looking back at Josa.

The cyborg's shimmery skin tone loses his glimmer and turns almost muddy, like it's tarnished, and he starts shaking his head. "No, oh no. Nobody said anything about that. Those fucking warlock girls set me up. Fucking bitches."

"Well, actually, they didn't know either, but you

were still hoping that Saxon would kill Lila—Lila Adams, the Adams brothers' granddaughter, and my mate—so it doesn't matter if you didn't know about the warlock, you knew about *me*." Caspian has lost all pretense of humor and is now vibrating with fury. His eyes flash to his beast's before returning to normal. "So before I kill you, Xavier is just going to root around in your brain and see what other shitty things you've done without anyone knowing."

"No, please no, please don't." He starts to scream and holds his hands against his head like they can protect his mind from the warlock. The cyborg actually seems more scared of Xavier than the threat of death from the kraken, and I find that very interesting. What else does this cyborg not want anyone knowing?

I hear Echo whimper slightly above us and step forward. His distress is sour to me and makes me very unhappy, and there's nothing I won't do to keep my mate happy.

"While I appreciate that you are protecting your mate, I must also protect mine, and Echo is a sensitive soul. Would it be possible for you to remove this yalani dung from our den and continue your interrogation elsewhere?"

"Of course. I apologize for the intrusion, Maxsim, and please give your mate my apologies for upsetting him." The warlock waves a hand, and the cyborg is instantly secured with light ropes.

Caspian peels back his tentacles, and the cyborg lifts into the air. The warlock waves his hand again, and he starts moving toward the door, followed by Caspian and the wrapped up cyborg. Caspian turns and waves at me.

"Thank you for helping us find this useless creature, and again, we apologize for trespassing in your space." He stops suddenly, and I can see him fighting internally with his beast. He finally grits his teeth and shouts, "Fine!" then he sighs and runs a frustrated hand through his blue hair before continuing. "We would love it if you and your mate could join me and mine for dinner one night. It is a shame we haven't gotten to know you better, and we would like to rectify the situation."

He doesn't seem a hundred percent sure, but he is being polite. The last thing I should do is outwardly reject his offer. "I will talk to my mate and let you know. Thank you for the invite."

He smiles and nods, seemingly okay with my noncommittal response, and hurries after the warlock and their prisoner who have already left our den.

The door hasn't even slid closed before Natalia is screaming and launching bolts of lightning at me, but they are easy to absorb. Her power is no match for mine. "How could you do that? I am the *matriarch*. I am in charge of this streak, and you will not get in my way. Wait until I tell my mother what has occurred. You will be lucky if she lets you live."

I stand with my arms crossed, waiting for her to physically attack me. If she raises a hand to me, I won't take it. I chuckle at the thought of her running to her mother. A strong female lightning cat wouldn't need someone else to put me in my place, she would be able to do it herself, but I haven't found many who could best me. My own mother, sure, but I've never given her any reason to. My chuckles seem to make her even madder.

Trace, Sim, and Fuse retreat into their cave, smart enough to get out of the line of fire. Although they are alphas, Natalia's viciousness knows no end, and they have learned it's easier to avoid than engage. They plan on keeping their heads down and staying out of her way until she finally leaves the ship. Nothing good comes from drawing her attention. It's taken all of my cunning to stop her from attacking Echo. The alpha command works temporarily, but it soon wears off. I'm not sure how she manages to circumvent it, but as soon as she does, she's attacking him again. He basically confines himself to our den with the forcefield on so she can't enter—a prisoner in his own home. The physical attacks were exhausting, and being on high alert twenty-four seven is no way to live. I couldn't believe she had the audacity to do it during a performance. I'm just surprised the Adams brothers haven't demanded to see us about it yet. I thought for sure we would all be kicked off the show. The Adams brothers don't tolerate any infighting or bad behavior from their employees.

Natalia continues to rant as I walk away. "Don't you turn your back on me, Maxsim. I will have your respect," she demands, so I whirl on her.

"You didn't seem too surprised to see that cyborg. In fact, you seemed downright suspicious when you said no one could search your quarters. If I go in there, am I going to smell someone else's scent?" Natalia shuts her mouth the instant I bring up searching her cave again. She knows I know she is hiding something, but I won't let her off the hook. "Let me make this clear. There is no way he could have hidden in here without someone helping him, and I think that someone is *you*."

She sneers at the accusation. "Bullshit. You are too busy with that abomination omega to even know what is going on in this den. I could have a parade of men through here, and you wouldn't notice or care."

"No, you're right. I really wouldn't. You could fuck the whole ship, and it would make me happy because it would mean you're leaving all of us alone." I can't hide the venom in my tone as I knock her down a few pegs. She flinches, my words obviously hitting a nerve.

Up until now, I've played peacekeeper, not encouraging her but also not telling her it isn't going to happen. I thought our actions were clear enough, but I underestimated how stubborn and delusional she is. No more. This female has been pandered and catered to for far too long, and she needs a reality check—one I will be more than happy to deliver.

"I will never mate with you. Even if you had considered Echo as a possible mate as well, I never would have considered it. He is mine, and all you have done is try to kill him. You're lucky I haven't killed you out of respect for your mother," I bellow, my anger finally getting the better of me, and lightning crackles around my body. "I suggest you do yourself a favor and stay in your den, away from everyone else, because I promise you this, Natalia—I will no longer hold back. If it comes out that you had a part in trying to kill the Adams brothers' granddaughter, I will see you disgraced and shunned. You will never find a streak, and you will be an outcast. Keep your head down, and maybe, just maybe, you will find someone who will make you happy one day." I turn my back to her, knowing that even if she strikes at me with her lightning, I can withstand her attack, since I am stronger than she is.

I leap carefully from rock to rock until I reach the entrance of our den where Echo is waiting for me in cat form. He stands as I approach and swipes an affectionate and reassuring tongue over my hand. The hundreds of little spikes are flattened so he doesn't tear the skin from my bones, but it's still a rough texture and it tickles slightly. I run my hand through his snow-white fur, wiping the slobber off the back of it and chuckling before gripping his mane and tugging him with me. He follows, walking next to me as we traverse the rocky corridor into our den. All of the dens on our level are shaped the same as dens back on Iceen, both the caves and family dwellings. The long, narrow entrances make it harder for enemies to attack before it opens into a large, communal structure with a curtained off bedroom area and a separate bathroom. The Adams family was adamant when bringing different species to the circus that they would be comfortable when they were not performing.

Echo and I have lots of furs and soft furnishings strewn around the area with a small kitchen off to the side. Most of the time we don't use it and only use the replicator, since neither of us are cooks. We mostly prefer to catch our food in animal form when we are home, but that's just not possible here.

I release him, and he pads over and jumps down into the sunken hole he has made into his nest, curling up and purring with contentedness. He's happy now that we are away from the hell beast and safe in our own space. I lean against the cave wall, thinking about what happened. I can't believe that cyborg managed to hide in here without any of us knowing. Natalia had to be involved. There is no way he would have survived in the cold temperatures without assistance. Sure, he was bundled up in furs, but they wouldn't have been enough. I'm tempted to shift and go sniff around in the den he was found in. If I pick up her scent, there's no way she can deny her involvement, and it's one more black mark against her.

I push off the wall and head back the way we came, but Echo growls from the bed and calls to me with a high-pitched whine that makes me turn back. I don't like to hear my omega in distress. I return to his nest and climb into it with him. He rolls onto his back and exposes his tummy for me to rub, and I chuckle.

"What's wrong, my omega? I just want to examine the den. I should be able to sniff out whether or not Natalia has been in there. I want to know if she is responsible for the cyborg being in our living space. I'm not sure what it is about the human girl that makes all the aliens on this ship so fucking crazy, but I won't be complacent if someone is trying to hurt her." He bats at my hand with his paws before shifting back into his humanoid form so we can converse. He curls up in my lap with his head resting on my thigh, his lithe body stretched out for me to admire. I know Echo is approaching his heat. I was hoping that Natalia would be gone by the time it came around, since it is too dangerous for him to go through it with her here. I will be lost to my desires and unable to protect us to my full ability, so it would be the perfect opportunity for her to attack. I continue to rub my hand through his hair, and he purrs with happiness.

"I like the little Earth girl," he whispers quietly, his voice soft and melodic, and my hand stills.

"Really? I didn't know you'd spoken to her."

He shakes his head. "I haven't, but my cat likes her. He wants to roll around in her scent. She smelled delicious the other night during our performance. That's why I tried to stop Natalia when she attacked the glass in front of her."

I feel my eyebrows jump in surprise, and I have to smother the huge wave of jealousy that washes over me. My claws want to come out so I can scratch her face off, but that wouldn't be fair to my omega. Omegas often have more than one mate, but I wasn't expecting him to be attracted to a non-lightning cat. "She smells good to you?"

He nods slowly, not meeting my eyes. "Yes, she smells as good as you do. I want to steal one of her shirts and bring it into my nest so I can breathe her in and combine her scent with yours." He turns his head as if he's ashamed to admit it to me, and I can see him tighten with tension, like he's afraid I'm going to fly off the handle and be angry about how he's feeling. I take a deep breath and will my jealousy down.

"Well, that's interesting. What would you like to do about it?" I ask him, and he rolls away, burying his face in his nest.

"I don't know!" he wails, and I scoot down and tuck his back into my front, nuzzling my face into his neck and nipping it while I purr reassuringly.

"We don't have to worry about it right this moment. I'm pretty sure she is going to start working with our act soon, so maybe you can see how you really feel about her when that happens," I suggest awkwardly, not wanting to upset my omega but not really sure how I feel about it myself.

He shrugs, but I feel his body relax. Phew, I said the right thing. It's a tricky line to walk, and sometimes I'm not as sensitive to his moods as I should be.

"Okay, I just need to go check out that den. I want to know if Natalia was involved. Are you going to stay here, or would you like to come with me?" I ask my mate, and he stands up, stretching. There's nothing covering his body except for his fur, and that doesn't run down his chest and groin region. His cock is lying against his thigh, and I feel a twinge in my own when I see what color it is. Normally, it's the same hue as his skin, but as he gets closer to his heat, it starts to change to red. At the moment, it's a pretty pale pink color, which means we've still got a while.

A clearing throat has me looking up into the laughing eyes of my mate. "I thought you had something you wanted to do, and it wasn't *me*." He pouts playfully, his eyes twinkling with amusement.

I growl and tug him into my body and bite his neck over my claiming mark. "Keep it up, brat, and I'll have you impaled on my knot quicker than you can blink."

He squirms, and I feel his dick start to harden. "Yes please." His words are breathy, and I see his eyes glaze over.

Well, maybe exploring the other den can wait until I've taken care of my mate's needs. I pull him in tight and take his mouth with mine. Both of us have our fangs retracted, since it's not easy to kiss with a mouthful of them without doing damage to the one you're kissing.

He sags into me, allowing me to take the lead, but I pull away and tip his head back so he has to look at me.

"Present for me, omega," I demand, and he whimpers and does as bid, with his ass up in the air and head down, leaning on his forearms. I see him shiver with anticipation.

I get down on my knees and caress his ass cheeks. His tail wraps around my waist, caressing me, as I lean down and press a kiss to my omega's back. "Don't you look so pretty for me." I reach around and stroke his long length, using the fluid leaking from the end to assist me.

He whimpers again and shudders. "Please, Alpha, I need you."

Suddenly, the blaring sound signaling a ship-wide announcement reverberates through our den. Echo groans with frustration as I pause my actions.

"Attention all. There is an all-crew meeting with compulsory attendance to be in the dining hall of the mothership in ten minutes. Do not be late."

The announcement cuts off, and I rest my forehead against his back. Taking a deep breath, I lift my head, look down at my mate displayed before me, and growl in frustration.

"We can miss it," he rasps, panting heavily, and I slap him on the ass before standing up.

"Sorry, brat. We will need to continue this later. I want to check out that den so when I see the Adams brothers, I can speak to them about getting rid of Natalia. I won't stand for her behavior any longer."

He collapses onto his stomach dramatically and rolls over, pouting. "Fine."

"Well, are you coming? Maybe the Adams girl will be there." That gets him moving quickly. He hurries to our bedroom area, and when he returns, he's wearing a loincloth similar to mine. We have circus uniforms, but we are off duty, and we only wear them when we are working.

He stops in front of a mirror and combs his mane, and I smother a smile at his preening. I only hope the Adams girl doesn't outright reject him. Echo is sensitive, and that could send his mood plummeting. He throws the brush on a table and hurries out of the room, completely forgetting about me. He's lucky I'm not insecure, or I might take his actions as rejection, but my mark on his neck and his on mine assures me that nothing and no one will ever come between us.

I hurry after him. In his excitement, he's forgotten that Natalia will attack him if she sees him on his own, and I will not let any harm come to anyone who is mine.

CHAPTER EIGHT

Echo

My heart races as I hurry toward the exit of our den. I can't wait to catch a glimpse of the little Earth girl again. I have no idea what draws me to her, but her scent is intoxicating, like sunshine and warmth, which we don't ever get on Iceen. I just want to rub my body all over her so I can carry it on my skin no matter where I go.

"Echo, wait!" Maxsim's bark has me screeching to a halt just before the exit of our den and shivering with desire at the same time. I love my big, growly kitty, and he would never use his alpha bark on me detrimentally.

When he catches up, I get a whiff of his fear, and I suddenly feel guilty. I realize what I've done, and I'm lucky that I didn't get farther away from him than I did. He wraps an arm around me, and I sink into his warmth, relieved to have him next to me now that I'm thinking more clearly. How did thoughts of the Earth girl distract me so badly that I forgot about my safety?

That vicious beta bitch has been trying to kill me for months now. Ever since she walked in on us knotted and she realized I'm an omega *and* she doesn't stand a chance with Maxsim, she's been hell-bent on trying to kill me. Her single-minded focus is scary and borderline obsessive, and only Maxsim's strength, as well as the other three acting as a buffer, has kept her in check. If we can find more damning evidence to get rid of her, well, I'm all for it.

We leave our den, and the temperature program of our quarters has turned frigid. There's a raging storm, and the snow is practically sideways. I take a deep breath and sigh with pleasure. I just want to turn around, head back to our den, and snuggle down with my mate in my nest and finish what we started, but I know it's important that we don't.

Putting my head down to protect my face from the weather, I follow behind Maxsim as he leads the way. We go down a path that lets out at the far right of the quarters, next to the entrance of the cave we need. Maxsim lifts his nose into the air, checking the area for danger, aka Natalia, but when he smells nothing, he continues with his task. His hand is warm in mine, not as warm as we would be if we were shifted, and I keep close, grateful for the heat his body is giving off. I do love this kind of weather, but I prefer my animal form to this one as it's much warmer like that.

We head down the corridor of the unused cave, finding no sign of anyone having dwelled in here, but smells don't seem to linger on the frozen, ice-covered rock walls. Soon enough, we're in the living area, where again, there is no lingering, recognizable scent. There is one that is new, but I'm assuming that's the cyborg's. I didn't get close enough to him to get a good sense of how he smells, but it reeks of electronics and desperation, which is not pleasant at all.

Maxsim huffs his annoyance at the intruder's scent. It's faint, but it does linger on a couple of surfaces. He did a good job of containing it, and I would like to know how he was able to. Not much can outsmart a lightning cat in its own environment, and we are skilled trackers and hunters.

While he continues to ponder the scent, I drop his hand and move toward the bedding area. Since it's tucked behind a thick curtain, I would expect to be able to pick up a stronger trace of the cyborg there, but when I pull back the drapes, the scent that hits my nostrils makes my eyes water.

"Holy shit." I wave a hand in front of my nose, trying to dissipate the overpowering odor. It seems like Natalia may have been doing a little more than just assisting the cyborg.

I feel Maxsim crowd in behind me and hear

him draw in a breath, and I growl slightly at the thought of him smelling that disgusting beta's sexual scent. She must have been fucking the cyborg. There is no other way for it to smell like it does in here. Maxsim strides up to the bedding pallet and yanks back the sheets. The fluids on the sheets are still damp, and I grimace with disgust. It hasn't been that long since they copulated. She must have been in here with him last night, but it's strange that neither of them smelled like it when we confronted them. One of them must have gotten their hands on a scent blocker. My guess is Natalia, because the cyborg would have no reason to.

How did none of us notice? Trace, Sim, and Fuse stay far away from her, so I guess it's understandable that they didn't, and the same goes for us. To be honest, unless we're preparing for our show, none of us want anything to do with her.

"Well, I would say that is the smoking gun." I try not to sound too disgusted, but Maxsim's growl rattles out of his chest. "Good riddance to bad news. I hope it's enough to have her thrown into the brig until we get to Iceen."

"The warlock and the kraken will want to know. I'm almost certain the cyborg will not survive his interrogation. As much as I would like to hand Natalia over to them as well, we do not need a war with her mother, but I think it's time for a new ruling family, one who cares about every one of our people, not just what benefits them. Natalia is not fit to rule. Although killing is accepted on Iceen, it is not the practice of other races, and killing the Adams brothers' granddaughter is not good for political relations. They have the ability to have us blackballed throughout the galaxy."

My growly kitty drops the covers and steps out of the bedroom area, and I release some of the tightness that had been building in my shoulders. He must hear my sigh of relief, because he loses the growl and the frown and gives me a gentle smile. Although I know he's not growling and angry at me, it still upsets me if he's upset.

"My poor omega, was the stench of that beta bothering you?" He grabs my hand and tucks me under his arm again as we make our way back the way we came, leaving behind the scene of the crime and the proof.

I shudder at the memory and nod my head, snuggling into his side as I enjoy the physical contact. "Yeah, it was horrible."

"Unlike the Earth girl's scent?" I hear the question and hide my smile. My poor alpha is suffering from a touch of jealousy, but he loves me enough to try and shove it back down, and I love him even more for it.

I'm almost certain if it had been another alpha lightning cat, he would have torn them apart already. The fact that he's acting levelheaded makes me wonder if he's not as oblivious to the appeal of Lila himself.

I don't answer his question, deciding to let him stew on it a little bit. I like it when he gets demanding and growly, and maybe he'll *make* me tell him how it feels.

"Come on, we need to hurry. We'll be late for the meeting. It has to be something important. Crew meetings only usually happen at the beginning and end of a tour." I pull his hand to hurry him along, and he does, grumbling quietly to himself.

"There's been nothing but upheaval since we arrived on Earth. Personally, I will be glad to see the back of it. I really don't want to do the rest of the shows. The sooner we can ditch Natalia, the better."

That last bit is said as we step out into the furious snowstorm. Ahead of us, I can see Trace, Sim, and Fuse huddled together, making their way to the door, while Natalia, once again, is nowhere in sight.

"Hurry, let's catch up to them. I feel like we haven't spent any time with them lately." I drag my alpha along, and he chuckles. Apart from our visit to see Link and have their birth control checked, we haven't seen them unless it's prior to a performance, and even then they prefer to stay in cat form.

Once upon a time, the five of us thought we'd find an omega and become a streak together. That was back before I presented as an omega. Once that happened and Maxsim mated me, the other three became close to Minx. She was supposed to be on this trip. The four of them were going to create their own streak, but Natalia put a stop to that when she manipulated her way into the circus. I bet they can't wait to return to Iceen and be reunited with Minx. I wonder what will happen to the act. With all the drama that has been happening lately, it wouldn't surprise me if the Adams brothers decided to pack it in completely and call an early recess to the tour.

We catch up with the other three, and when the door opens, we stumble out into the relative warmth of the rest of the ship. We stomp our feet and brush off the snow that has accumulated on our bodies. Like Maxsim and me, the other three only have loincloths covering their groin regions. Their coats are varying shades of blue. Of us all, Maxsim is the only one with black markings.

I hug all three of them in greeting. Once upon a time, we were all lovers, and while I miss their company, I don't have those kinds of feelings for them anymore. They are more like my favorite older brothers. Thankfully Maxsim knows this, so there is no tension when I do show them affection. Touch is integral for an omega, and I just can't seem to help myself with the people I love.

"Hey there, Echo. Are you okay? I could feel your distress when the warlock and the kraken were here earlier," Trace asks, holding me at arm's length and running his eyes over me to make sure I'm okay. I'm not sure what he's looking for, but it's sweet.

"I'm fine. I was worried Natalia was going to hurt them and Max," I explain, worry still mixed in my tone, and he reaches up and ruffles my mane before dropping his arms again.

"When are you going to learn that Max is indestructible? He's a force of nature. Nothing can damage him, he does the damage. Roar." Trace makes some claws and pretends to be ferocious, and Sim, Fuse, and I dissolve into laughter while Maxsim crosses his arms and frowns at Trace.

"Ha-ha, asshole." He flips him off and grabs my hand, dragging me in the direction we need to go. I can hear the other three following us, their giggles echoing in the hall. I smother my grin, proud as can be of my fierce protector. Once we get to the elevator, we all pile in together. There aren't many other quarters on our level, only Zala the larnuk mistress, who has enough space for her horses as well, but I don't see any sign of her, so either she's already there or still to come. I don't know her very well, but she's quiet and solemn and kind to her animals, so she's okay in my book until she proves me wrong.

When we get to the correct level, we exit the lift. There are a lot more people around. A few wave and say hello, but most are wary when we venture out into the ship. Natalia hasn't always been very welcoming, so it makes people reluctant to approach us. Even though we stick to ourselves, their reaction always sends an uncomfortable pang to my heart. It would be nice to make some friends while we're here, maybe someone to have a drink or meal with between shows, to play a game of Conqueror with, or to invite to hang out.

As we reach the dining room, the crowd grows even bigger, and the sounds and smells of our fellow performers become invasive, but not unpleasant. My fur bristles with excitement at being here all together.

I sigh wistfully and look around at all the interesting creatures involved with the circus. Out of the corner of my eye, I spy the Vilaxians. There are three new ones who came on a day or two ago, and there looks to be some friction between them and two of the regular females. They are arguing in one corner, their body language is stiff, and the harsh expressions they are wearing reflects how unhappy they are. They are speaking too quietly for me to pick up what they are saying though, which is a shame since I do like to keep up with all the circus drama.

The five of us take a seat at a free table, and I continue my perusal of the crew. I pause on the two new shifters who also came on board—another dragon to replace the previous one, but a naga as well. Naga shifters aren't common, and I don't think I've ever seen any others before. There is another snake-like species in the galaxy, but they are not shifters and only have one form. I study the naga closely, his green, orange, and black scales shining in the artificial light. His massive body is curled up underneath him as he carries on a conversation with the dragon, and he has no shirt covering his top half. I can see glinting rings in each nipple, and he has rippling muscles down his abdomen. His body tapers into his tail, but there are two elongated bumps under his scales in his groin area, which is where my eyes lock onto.

Fuck me. Does he have two *cocks?*

A hand grips my mane, turning my head away from the interesting shifter, and I find myself staring into amused silver eyes.

"What are you looking at, my omega?" Maxsim's words are quiet and grumbly, and accompanied with his tight grip on my mane, it sends a shiver down my spine.

I see Maxsim's nose flare as the scent of my arousal drifts to his nostrils. I'm getting closer to my heat, and it's getting harder and harder to control my desire.

"Nothing?" I hedge sheepishly, and his grip tightens. A moan is begging to leave my lips, especially since we were interrupted by the announcement. Maxsim knows what he's doing to me.

"You weren't admiring the pretty snake and his double cocks, were you?" He growls a little more, his jealousy stoking my arousal even higher. I try to shake my head, but it's useless. He knows I'm lying, and his grip is just too tight.

"No," I mutter, and his amusement changes to lust in an instant.

"Oh, you are a brat for lying to me. I will enjoy doling out your punishment in the form of my pleasure." He releases my hair, and I shake out my mane before continuing my perusal of the crowd, being sure to skip over the naga and his two cocks. Truthfully, I'm looking for the little Earth girl. Maybe if I can study her closely, I can figure out what has me so interested, but she's nowhere to be seen. I'm about to ask Maxsim if he can see her when two new people sit down next to me. It's the merman and his sister, both in their human forms. I'm a little surprised that they are sitting at the same table as us. Everyone mostly avoids us, but I guess without Natalia around, we might be able to make more friends. I feel excited at the prospect and smile at both of them.

"Hello, ferocious ice kitty. Have you seen my little coolmy shell? She doesn't seem to be here."

I blink a couple of times, surprised that the merman is talking to me. He is another creature who hasn't been particularly social, if the ship gossip is to be believed. His golden hair shines in the artificial light, and his green skin sparkles vibrantly. He preens when he sees me looking at him. "Ah, I see *you* see how magnificent I look in this light. I was hoping my little starfish would admire the wonderfulness that is me as well. I am thinking maybe the dim lighting of my cave made it so she couldn't appreciate my brilliance." He pushes back his golden hair as my mouth drops open.

Maxsim snorts not so politely on the other side of me, and I can see Trace, Sim, and Fuse are just as stunned as I am, but the arrogant creature doesn't acknowledge our reactions. He just puffs up his chest and continues to look around the room.

"No, it won't be hard to convince her to stroke my fins when she sees me in this light. It will be all she can do to control herself."

He doesn't even sound wistful, he sounds confident.

I try to form words to make a coherent sentence, but I can't, and I don't have to, because a blue hand on the merman's shoulder has him looking up into the eyes of Lila's kraken mate, Caspian.

"You wouldn't be thinking about forcing yourself on my mate, would you, fish?" His growl is almost as impressive as my alpha's, and I feel my toes curl slightly. Damn heat hormones. Max's hand comes down on my knee and stops my leg, which had been bouncing up and down. I grimace, but he just looks amused, thankfully.

"No, I remember consent is required, but how could she say no with all of this wonderfulness?" Nikos waves a hand up and down his body, and I spy Caspian's hand tightening on his shoulder before the merman winces slightly. Clearly, he doesn't like pain.

"Good, see that it continues." Caspian releases him and undulates up to the front where he stands off to the side with the warlock.

I wonder what happened to the cyborg. I guess we will never know, and that might be a good thing, especially after watching what the warlock did to part of his harem.

The crowd settles into silence as William and Eric Adams enter the room. There's no sign of John, and both the brothers wear scowls. This was not an unusual occurrence prior to Lila's arrival, but since she has been here, they have been all smiles. What could have caused them to be so upset? I suppose we are about to learn what's causing their distaste.

CHAPTER NINE

Lila

When I crack my sleepy eyes open, I have no idea what time it is or where I am, only that my body is surrounded by the most wonderful warmth and weight. Looking down, I see a pale, muscular arm wrapped around my waist, and when I lift the blankets, I notice a fair, muscular, naked leg is thrown over my own naked body. Huh, I'm naked. There's no rising heart rate or low-key panic about being in this situation, though, so I instinctively know I'm where I'm meant to be.

I drop the blanket and snuggle back into the body behind me. It's radiating heat like a furnace, and it's a solid strength that gives me comfort.

Okay, Lila, think. What happened? What's the last thing you remember?

I rack my brain. Everything is slightly foggy and

like looking through a frosted mirror, but my memory slowly comes into focus. Mark and Susie, and that gaudy hot pink convertible. We were driving down the strip. Viggy! Okay, good, I remember what happened, and we got him back to the circus with no international—or would it be galaxian—incidents.

Thank fuck for small miracles.

I was in the office speaking to my grandpas, and then… Saxon! So that solves the weight at my back. I must have bonded with the Vilaxian. Hmm, he's a lot warmer and snugglier than I thought he'd be. I shuffle back even farther, like I'm trying to merge with him.

This feels so freaking good. Before Caspian, I was not a snuggly person. I was a 'thank you for the orgasm but I'm out' kind of girl. Snuggling leads to things like *emotions* and possible *second dates*… ew—or that's what I've always thought.

I was wrong.

Snuggling fucking rocks my world.

"If you keep rubbing that tight little ass against my dick, I'm going to think you want me to stick it in you." The rumbly words behind me and the tightening of the arm around my waist has me stopping momentarily. Lost in my rambling thoughts, I hadn't even noticed his cock getting hard. How I didn't notice that pole thickening between my legs, I have no idea. I freeze, but Saxon grabs my waist and rolls me to face him. He's grinning, and I'm momentarily lost in the gorgeousness of this man. Holy shitballs. No wonder he doesn't smile often, he would start a fucking riot. I put my hand against his cheek, running a finger over his bottom lip, and it's a struggle not to give into the urge to lean forward and bite it.

"Oh, Grandma, what big teeth you have," I whisper, and his grin drops and he looks slightly befuddled. His brows pinch together while he searches my eyes.

"Grandma? Lila, are you okay? Fuck, maybe our bonding damaged your brain," he mutters out loud, and I snort, moving my hand down his body and wrapping it around his dick.

"Oh, Grandma, what a big dick you have." I giggle as he fights his instinct to groan with what I'm doing, still concerned about my mental health.

Saxon is an enigma.

"Lila, sweetheart, I need to call Link to come check on you. Do you want to let go of my dick? You have gotten very strong, and I kind of like it where it is."

Poor, confused, sweet vampire. I must reward him for being so caring, but first I should put him out of his misery.

"Relax, big guy, I'm fine. It's a line from a children's fairy tale on Earth. Red Riding Hood says it to the big, bad wolf just before he eats her, which is what I plan on doing to *you*." I press a quick kiss to his mouth before sliding my way down the bed. *Holy shit, I'm fast.* Within a flash, I'm face-to-face with his… I don't think dick describes it well enough, maybe anaconda. I feel my slutty pussy weep with joy. She knows this beast intimately, and like Pavlov's dog, responds accordingly.

I slide my tongue along the length of it. It's so pretty, pale, thick, and long. There's no way I can fit this whole thing in my mouth, but I'm going to give it a fucking good college try.

Saxon's fingers thread into my hair as I spit some saliva onto it to help my hand slide up and down the bits my mouth can't reach. I get it good and lubricated before I slip my lips around the head. Hollowing my cheeks, I give it a small suck, and I feel him thrust a little before his body goes rigid. Oh no, that won't do. I want him to get lost in the sensations, not hold onto his iron control. I reach around his body, grip his bubble butt, and get good handfuls of those delicious globes, pulling him into my body. His cock slides deeper into my mouth, and I breathe through my nose as tears leak out of my eyes, my tongue flicking the underside. It's a full-service blow job. I may not be able to get it all in, but what I can will certainly never forget what it's like to be in my mouth, especially with the suckers lining my throat.

His hands tighten in my hair, bordering on painful, but again, my slutty pussy just leaks more. I like a bite of pain with my pleasure. Bobbing up and down on his cock, I encourage him to thrust as one of my hands leaves his ass, and I cup his round balls. Sliding off his cock, I bend down and take one into my mouth, casually loving it before moving to the other. Saxon's breath is now coming faster, but I want to hear him groan and say my name.

Visions of our bonding come back to me in tiny pieces, like an old, flickering black and white film, except in these memories, there's another color—red. Our bodies are covered in blood, slipping and sliding as we take our pleasure from one another. Holy fuck, it was hot. I remember it all now. My mouth aches, and I feel a click as my fangs extend.

Remembering the taste of Saxon's blood on my tongue, I move completely on instinct and run my tongue along the thick vein on the underside of his cock. The popping sound of my fangs piercing it makes my nipples pebble even harder as Saxon shouts and thrusts as I latch my lips around the two holes and suck. His blood tastes like chocolate and heaven, or what I imagine heaven would taste like. The blood flows fast, and I struggle to swallow it, a little leaking out of the side of my mouth, painting his cock in that beautiful crimson color. Swiping my tongue over the punctures, I heal the holes and sit back to admire my handiwork. His dick is now coated in his blood and is even prettier than before.

"Lila, your venom! I can't stop. *I can't fucking stop*!" Saxon groans, pulling my hair to bring me closer.

I open my mouth, taking in as much of his dick

as I can. It pulses and floods my mouth with a completely different liquid this time. It's saltier than his blood, but no less delicious. Fuck my life. Why can't human men have cum that tastes like dessert?

I drink it all down, the blood painted on his dick mixing with his cum, sating my thirst. Saxon mutters words of praise and thanks some deity I've never heard of for gifting him a blood rose. What a sweet man. Sliding his dick out of my mouth, I grin with pride as I make my way slowly back up his body, giving love to all the bits I missed on the way down. That V that leads to the D gets covered with kisses, as does his eight pack, before I move even farther up to his two perky brown nipples, the only patches of color on his pale body. I spend extra time giving them the love they need, biting into each and taking a little sip of blood, before healing them again. I wouldn't want them to feel left out. That would be rude of me.

Saxon finally reaches the limit of his patience and hauls me the rest of the way up, his mouth taking mine before I can get a word out. Our kiss is not gentle, our fangs tearing into lips and tongues, flooding our mouths with blood, but it only enhances the kiss. Knowing that my blood can sustain this man is nothing short of awe inspiring, and I feel like I could shout it to the world with how smug I feel.

He rips his lips away from mine, and I find myself chasing after them. Saxon chuckles darkly as he rolls me onto my back, his huge body looming over mine as he settles between my parted legs. "You are so beautiful, my blood rose." He runs his lust-filled gaze down the length of my body, his magenta eyes glowing. "And so very, very naughty." The last words are punctuated with a growl, and I shiver, my pussy weeping even more and my nipples hardening to the point of pain. "You will need to be punished." He rubs the tip of his cock against my opening, and I just about sob with joy.

"Yes, please punish me," I beg, turning my head and offering him my neck, the thick vein under the surface begging for him to put his fangs into it. "Please, Saxon, take from me what I offer freely." The words feel right, although I have no idea why. Saxon's lips peel back in a snarl, his fangs dripping with a clear liquid.

At the same time he strikes, his giant cock thrusts deep into my pussy. I scream, unable to stop the sound from leaving my mouth. The intrusion on both ends is painful, but that quickly morphs to pure fucking pleasure as his venom flows through my body, and my cunt adjusts to his huge length.

This, right here, is heaven on earth. It's everything and nothing I ever thought I'd need.

He is without mercy as he pounds his dick into my tight channel while sucking the blood from my body. All I can do is hold on and enjoy the exquisite sensations as they roll through my very being. My nerves tingle as pleasure is roughly dragged to the surface. I fucking love it. I throw my head back and close my eyes, the onslaught almost too much to bear. The more he sucks, the tighter my pussy gets, until I know he's struggling to keep moving.

"Those suckers… they are like nothing I've ever felt before." He pulls away from my neck, wild-eyed as my blood drips from his mouth, and it's too much. Seeing this strong, sexy man undone sends me over the edge, and I orgasm like nothing before. I see stars as waves of pleasure batter my body like a tsunami on the shores of Japan in a never-ending cycle of pleasure as he, too, can't hold on any longer. He comes so hard I can actually feel it, and I orgasm again, or maybe I haven't stopped, but feeling his cum inside of me is amazing.

I definitely have a kink, because I felt the same way with Cas. Do I have a breeding kink? Is that what this is? I hold him to me tightly, my legs wrapping around his hips so he can't escape, and I feel a chuckle deep inside me. Oh, okay, that's my kraken. She's the horny kinky bitch. I feel her thoughts now that I've tuned into them. She's wondering how Vilaxians procreate and telling me I need to find out. I tune her out and just ride the pleasure wave with my newest hubby.

His lips find mine again, but this time they have lost the feral intensity of before. With his beautiful eyes locked on mine, this kiss is sweet and sensuous and loving, and I feel my heart skip a beat as I fall a little in love with this intense man.

I'm not sure how long we lie here making out, his hard dick still lodged deep inside me, but eventually, he pulls away and leans his forehead against mine, sighing.

"Link says I need to feed you real food, and I should let him and your other mate know you are awake. I've been selfish long enough." His eyes open, and they shine with passion. "Thank you, Lila. You have no idea how much this means to me."

I don't, but I'm starting to get an idea. I give him a quick kiss. "I'm looking forward to getting to know you better, and I'm sorry to ruin this bubble we're in, but can you let me up? I've got to pee." I push gently at his body, but with a shout and wide eyes, he goes flying backward so far and so fast he slams into the wall in front of the bed. The wall caves in slightly, and Saxon groans as he slides down into a crumpled heap on the floor.

"Holy fuck." I look down at my hands in astonishment, my eyes widening. "Are you okay?" I hurry off the bed, my and Saxon's combined fluids sliding down my thighs as I race to check on my new mate. I go to grab him, but he holds his hands up, and I flinch back, fearful that *he* might be afraid of *me*. Seeing my reaction to his rejection has him grimacing.

"No, Lila, it's okay, you are just adjusting to your new abilities. It's going to take a few days for them to settle. I'm okay, I promise, just a little surprised, that's all. I have been hit a lot worse, but never by a female." He pushes himself up off the floor and comes over to me.

I hold my hands up to stop him, frightened I'm going to hurt him again, but he just pushes them to the side and gathers me in his arms.

"You just need to concentrate on your movements a little more than normal. Your abilities will probably fluctuate up and down until they settle, but they will settle, and you will adjust and be magnificent," he promises, placing a kiss on my head. He is so tall he towers above me, and being in his arms must be what it's like to be hugged by a grizzly bear minus, you know, the fur and death. "Come on, let's shower and then find your mate and some food. You'll feel better once you see him and your other potentials."

I relax a little more at the thought of seeing Cas, Xavier, and Link, but my nerves start to get the better of me again when I realize how careful I'll need to be with them too. I'm like Lady Thor on steroids, and as much as I like knowing I can protect myself, I don't want to unintentionally hurt anyone. The picture of Saxon sliding down the wall will haunt me for a while. Despair starts to pierce my heart in a throbbing ache the more I think about my strength. What if I do that to my other mates? They don't have the same kind of resilience that he does. What if I hurt one of them?

Fuck my life. I don't want to get sucked into this rabbit hole.

I let him lead me into a bathroom off to the side. I now realize that the light in here and in the other room is very dim, but because of my new eyesight, everything is as clear as day for me. I'm not sure how I'm going to cope with being in normal light. I see why the Vilaxians like the dark now, and I remember reading that their planet only has seven hours of daylight or something like that. Their eyesight must have evolved to adjust for the darkness.

Saxon points me to the toilet cubicle, and I close the door and pee, allowing myself a couple of deep breaths as I get my bearings. I don't have time to freak out right now, but I will set aside some time for it a little while later.

Ten o'clock, lose my shit. I'll add it to my calendar.

I'm sure everyone will understand. Maybe I'll shift and go hide in the pretty grotto at the bottom of the mer pool. If I'm quiet, hopefully that randy can of cat food won't find me and I can freak out in peace. Sure, I knew that I could change when I bonded with Saxon, but I had no idea it would be to this extent. I'm sure once I calm down and get a moment to breathe, I will decide it's cool as fuck.

"Lila, my beautiful blood rose, are you okay?" A knock on the door and Saxon's concerned tone has me taking another couple of deep breaths before wiping and flushing. Putting on a small smile, I step out.

"Yeah, just taking a moment, you know." I don't have to explain. I see his eyes soften and know he understands.

"Hop in the shower, and I'll find you something to wear." He points at the already running water, knowing I need a few more minutes to myself. He presses a kiss to my forehead and disappears in a flash.

Sighing with relief, I climb under the hot spray and take another moment to myself. If the water hides a few tears, well, no one will ever know.

CHAPTER TEN

Lila

When Saxon and I finally surface from his room, it's almost lunchtime. I'm wearing a pair of baggy sweats and a shirt a million times too big for me, but they smell like Saxon, so I'm uber happy to be wearing them. I have nothing on my feet, and I'm not sure what happened to the clothes I had been wearing prior to bonding. Maybe someone sent them out to be cleaned.

I'm champing at the bit to find Caspian, Link, and Xavier. There's an ache in my chest that I know will be fixed once I see them. I'm also desperate to find out if John is okay. Now that the bonding is over, I survived, and we are doing well, my anguish has returned tenfold. I'm ready to leave our self-imposed confinement and reenter the world and reality. The only thing that slows my exit is the fact that I dread having to trek through his quarters, not relishing another run-in with his clan. When we get there, though, the rooms are eerily quiet and empty, which is somewhat of a relief.

"Where is everyone?" I ask, looking around. We walk down a corridor lined with rooms before reaching a communal living area with a small kitchen and replicator. Do Vilaxians eat real food too? I rack my brain, trying to remember if I know the answer, but come up with nothing. So. Much. To. Learn.

Saxon looks as bewildered as I do. "I'm not sure. I would have thought Xenos would be here to celebrate our joining. It's unusual that he isn't, same as Hale and Velorina."

"Xenos?" I ask, remembering the strange Vilaxian I hadn't recognized when we first entered the quarters.

"My brother. I was surprised to see him too. I can only assume that the queen sent him to replace me while I was incapacitated. He brought the blood rose cup, which allowed you to transition to be compatible with me." He's smiling at me now, wearing a look of pride and warmth. I can't believe the blatant difference between who he is now and the cold, stern soldier tasked with working on my self-defense.

"Oh, wow, okay." My heart races in panic. I'm going to meet my husband's family. Shit, I don't think I've ever had to impress a family member before.

Fuck with a capital F.

Saxon chuckles, his eyes crinkling adorably, and I'm blinded by his smile once more. Holy hell, my husband is hot… *Both* of my husbands are hot. God, I love calling them my husbands.

"I can hear your heart rate speed up at the idea of that. Do not worry, my beautiful blood rose, my brother will love you. Right now, let's get you some food. I don't want the good doctor getting pissy at me for not following his strict orders and feeding you properly."

I giggle at the idea of Link growling protectively at Saxon. It's slightly preposterous, but Saxon looks like he's serious. The Vilaxian is nervous about a cyborg's reaction—or more like Saxon is uneasy about how Link will react even though he's not my mate. I like this show of respect.

He sweeps me up into his arms and strides toward the door, and it slides back as we approach it.

"Put me down, you big oaf, I *can* walk." I pound on his arm in an attempt to get him to put me down, but he ignores me and nuzzles my neck.

"Allow me the privilege of carrying you, at least until we get where we're going. I know I will have to share you with your mate and other suitors then, and I want to make the most of what's left of our time alone."

Le sigh, isn't he wonderful? I cease my useless smacking of his glorious biceps and settle back to enjoy the ride. Who am I to argue with that?

Once we leave the room, he flashes us to the dining room in the circus pod. Strangely enough, this is empty too. "Where is everyone?" I ask again, starting to get a little concerned. He steps up to one of the communication panels in the wall and presses a button.

"Call Hale," he commands, and I see an image of Hale appear in the little screen as it buzzes, waiting for him to accept the call.

Finally, live action Hale appears on the screen, scowling at Saxon. "What?" he snaps quietly. I can hear Grandpa William's voice in the background, talking.

"Where is everyone?" Saxon asks, and Hale scowls.

"Did you not hear the ship-wide announcement for a compulsory meeting?" Hale whispers quietly.

"No, we must have been in the shower. Where is it?" Saxon questions urgently.

"In the dining room on the mothership. Dude, you need to get your asses here. Shit has officially hit the fan." Hale side-eyes me before cutting off the communication.

My heart starts to race again. What could have gone wrong now? "How are we going to get up there if everyone has been required to attend? There won't be anyone to transport us."

Saxon presses a kiss to the top of my head. "Don't worry, I know how to operate the transporter." He flashes us again, moving through the ship faster than I can track, but this time, I no longer feel nauseous at the speed. My body has adjusted, and it doesn't feel like I'm being flung around at warp speed.

We stop in the transporter room, and Saxon puts me down gently. He goes over to a cabinet and pulls out a small remote. Next, he grabs my hand, and we both stand on the transport platform. He pushes a button on the remote. I hear the transporter fire up, and within an instant, we are landing on the transport platform on the mothership. This room is empty of crew as well.

Saxon places the remote in his pocket. "We need to return it to the pod when we go back. Want to try running at full speed?"

I quickly shake my head. I am so not ready for that. "No, not yet. I want to try everything out in the arena where there is less chance of me breaking anything, anyone, or hurting myself." I shrug, hoping he didn't notice the hitch in my voice at the thought of doing anything Vilaxian related in public.

"Okay." He swings me back up into his arms and flashes us once more. I can feel the pressure of the air against my face as he runs, my hair flowing behind me. It's almost a freeing feeling.

When we stop at the door to the dining room, I

hear a cacophony of voices. The doors open, and I blink in astonishment. I hadn't been to this dining room yet. I was confined to my room because there was concern for my safety from some of Saxon's clan. I'd like to think I could withstand a little bit more now, but I don't doubt that I will need some instruction in self-defense from my new hubby. I can't deny I'm looking forward to getting hot and sweaty with him, maybe rolling around on some mats and getting pinned to said mats...

"My beautiful blood rose, whatever you are thinking, you need to stop. Your arousal is quite potent, and I'm afraid it will distract a lot of the crew from the meeting." Saxon's voice is low and growly, and I feel my cheeks heat in embarrassment.

Great, everyone's going to know I'm horny. I'm not sure how I can be horny again. It has to be those damn fuck me vibes. Can't my children give me a damn break for once? I just spent the night fucking, so surely my vagina has to be closed for maintenance.

We enter the room, and I cross my fingers, hoping that no one notices, but sure enough, the minute we step in, almost everyone turns to look at us. I move slightly behind Saxon, using him as a buffer between me and the crowd. No one is hiding their otherness today, and it's a bit overwhelming to have all eyes focused on me.

"Ah, Saxon, Lila, so glad you could make it." Eric waves us forward and points to a table at the front of the room. Xavier, Caspian, and Link are all seated there. Next to it is a table of lightning cats—minus the female—Nixie, and… damn it, the horny can of cat food.

Unfortunately, my eyes meet his, and he puffs up like a puffer fish, shaking his golden mane of hair like a horse and winking at me. It's a little bit scary, because it actually looks like he's having an epileptic fit, but Nixie soon catches a glimpse of what he's doing and slaps him across the head. He scowls at her, but it's enough for him to be distracted, and I hurry past him and slide into a seat with my mate and future mates. My butt hasn't even hit the chair before Cas is dragging me into his lap, shoving his nose into my neck, and breathing deeply. His tentacles wrap around me until I am completely encased in them.

I sigh in pure bliss. Instantly, the dull ache in my chest eases, and I melt into him, enjoying being wrapped up in his love. Even my kraken relaxes, and I'm glad she'll chill the fuck out for now.

"God, I missed you," he says, heaving out a deep breath like he'd been holding it the whole time I was gone.

Saxon takes a seat at the table and nods to the others before turning his attention to my grandpas.

"We'll catch you both up on what's happening in a moment. For now, I want to reassure you that the show will continue, but there will be a short hiatus. When we arrive in Celestia, if you would like to make arrangements to return to your home planet until we reconvene, then that will be acceptable. You just need to inform us of your plans before we leave Earth's orbit so we can arrange for transport for those who do want to depart." He pauses for a moment, letting the words sink into every creature's head. My curiosity is piqued by this announcement though. "All right, you are dismissed to discuss this proposal with your teams and contact your families. Once again, we thank you for your time and patience, and I hope you will all rejoin us once we resume." William's words end the meeting, and people get up to leave the room, the noise almost deafening.

I stay put, unable to move if I even wanted to, and William and Eric come to me. Cas releases me just enough for them to both give me a hug and a kiss before joining us at the table. I hear them welcome Saxon to the family with slaps and manly hugs. I can't stop the smile of happiness that spreads across my lips. My little family just keeps growing and growing, and if things go the way I hope, it'll continue. I know I've been on the fence about all this chosen mates, out-of-my-control stuff, but honestly, I'm freaking thrilled. To go from being a foster kid no one particularly wanted to having everyone want me is heady and intoxicating, and I can't get enough.

I look around the table at my other potential mates. Okay, who's next? I know I can't mate with

Xavier until his parents release the spell on me, so I guess it's my delicious doctor.

I shiver with excitement, and I feel Caspian chuckle beneath me, his entire body moving. "Wow, I would have thought those fuck me hormones would have been well sated after your marathon bonding with Saxon, but I can smell how horny you are," Cas comments quietly, and I notice how much attention I'm getting from others around the room.

The lightning cats, the Vilaxians, and both Silac and Tirrian are staring at me with an intensity that borders on scary, but it's Nikos who once again steals the attention.

"Lila, my little starfish, why don't you allow me to ease the ache in your loins? Obviously your mates aren't capable of taking care of you like I can." Saxon and Caspian both growl at his comment. Xavier just snorts in disgust, and Link smothers a chuckle. Some help they are. Assholes.

"How about you don't," Grandpa Will replies dryly. "Now get, all of you, I have to catch Lila up on what she missed." It doesn't happen quickly, but eventually, it's just us—my two hubbies, and two fiancés, Will, Eric, and me.

"How's Grandpa J?" I ask as soon as the room clears. It's nice not to be surrounded by so many creatures, especially with my Vilaxian senses being so sensitive. Taking a deep breath, I listen in shock and worry as they explain what is wrong with John and the actions they have decided to take.

"So we're canceling the tour?" I ask when William finishes.

"Yes, just until we can get John healthy again. We don't know how long it will take, and Link says it needs to happen as soon as we can get there. You and I just need to pick up the detainee from Area 51 that Agent Smith told us about," Eric explains. "We will leave as soon as you get something to eat and can get changed."

Area 51? Holy shit, it *does* fucking exist. After seeing all of the creatures on this ship, it's clear the government is lying about extraterrestrials, and now I get to see the facility up close and personal.

"I would like to check her over once more as well, just to be sure she's okay," Link requests, and both of my grandpas agree.

"Well, while you're doing that, how about Xavier and I help Saxon move into our quarters?" Caspian suggests behind me, and I watch as Saxon blinks, kind of bewildered, before gracing us with that blinding smile again.

Fucking swoon. I feel Cas suck in a breath behind me, and I chuckle. See? I am not the only one affected. Even Xavier, who peeled back his mist once everyone left, looks a little dazzled, but he and Saxon have a history that I'm just dying to hear more about.

"Would you like that?" I ask Saxon, not wanting to assume anything. I can't imagine he's going to be happy leaving his clan, but he grabs my hand, easing my doubt. Caspian reluctantly releases it so Saxon can lift it to his mouth and place a kiss on top.

"Nothing would make me happier. I will inform my clan of my intentions to leave. The Lila Adams clan will now be my family, and I couldn't be happier. We may need to mediate the dissolution though. Radella and Estrella are not going to make it easy, but Xenos can facilitate that." Saxon shrugs like it's no big deal, but my happiness dims a little at the challenge.

"Right, let us know if they cause any problems for you. Now, what did you find out about that damn nurse?" Eric asks.

"I may be able to shed some light on that situation." A voice at the doorway has us all turning to find Maxsim and Echo, the lightning cats, standing there. Had they been lurking at the door, waiting for the opportunity to interject?

"Did you find more information after we left?" Xavier asks, gesturing for them to join us. I watch as the two cats cross the room. They have this graceful, predatory way of moving that is downright hypnotic, and their feline features, fur, and tail make them sexy as fuck.

"Yes, unfortunately I need to report that Natalia was indeed helping him. I believe it was in return for sexual favors."

Cyborg? Natalia? Sexual favors? What the fricky frack am I missing?

Also… gross. Just gross.

"Ah, yes, there's still some information you don't know. Maybe Xavier can get us up to speed," William suggests. I must have said that out loud. The temptation to face-palm myself is real, but I am far too curious to let my slight embarrassment get the best of me.

Xavier proceeds to tell Saxon and me exactly what happened to set our blood rose bonding in motion, and by the time he's finished, I practically have steam coming out of my ears, and I can see Saxon isn't much happier.

Those scheming motherfucking D-bags.

"Where are those bitches? Let me get my hands on them." I struggle to get out of Caspian's embrace, but his tentacles hold me tight. "Saxon, I must rely on you to avenge me," I cry dramatically when I'm unable to free myself, and the room falls silent before everyone bursts into laughter, including my Vilaxian hubby. *Damn traitors.*

"Well, I removed Lexus's and Nambra's powers, and they will be shunned, and Elyan is a pile of ash on the floor of my harems' quarters now. I'm assuming since they were all here at the meeting, no one has had time to clean her up."

"And the cyborg?" I ask, arching an eyebrow at Xavier. I hope he met a similar fate as Elyan.

"Dead," Caspian rumbles behind me, and Saxon pouts before nodding his approval.

"Well, okay then." I settle down, slightly mollified by their response.

"And we will personally return Natalia to Iceen. I think it's time I give our support for a new elected matriarchal family." William nods at Maxsim. "I would like to nominate your mother as the new candidate. It's time for a change. Iceen has been stagnating with that family for years."

Maxsim bows his head. "I will let my mother know you will support her challenge. She, too, is ready for change, and I know that the other top four families will support her as well."

Echo has been quiet all this time, hiding behind Maxsim. I'm having trouble looking anywhere else but at both of them. They are so exotic and sexy. I desperately want to reach out and run my hand through their fur to see if they will purr for me—especially Echo. There's something about him that draws me to him, a vulnerability of sorts. I just want to wrap him up in blankets and smother him with snuggles… and maybe my breasts. Or both. Definitely both.

Eric claps his hands, and I jolt out of my daydream. "Well then. Natalia can join our soon to be detainee in the brig for the return journey. Can I leave it up to you to retrieve her for us since she never attended the meeting?" He looks from the two cats to Saxon and Xavier, and all four of them appear almost feral with excitement as they agree.

"What about the twins' involvement?" Xavier asks my grandpas. "Unfortunately, I can't find any video footage showing that they were responsible for Viggy being on Earth. The transport operator is showing a blank space in his mind, but I have no idea how, or who, would be capable of such a thing." I can hear the disappointment in my warlock's tone, and I feel disappointed along with him. Those two have been nothing but a pain in the ass since I arrived.

"What about compulsion? Some of my clan have those capabilities," Saxon suggests, and Xavier rubs a hand across his chin in thought.

"Maybe. I would have thought I would be able to sense *something* or tell the difference, but maybe not."

"What are we going to do about them? Even though we may not have proof of them releasing Viggy, we still have them on the security footage with the others, right?" Link asks, and William and Eric exchange a glance.

"Nothing for now. We will continue to monitor them, and they will eventually mess up." William stands, brushing off his hands and effectively ending that conversation. I'm slightly annoyed, but I guess they have more pressing problems on their hands. "Right then. We need to retrieve the circus pod, so Caspian, while Link is checking over Lila, can you ask Magenta to help you put out the holo emitters and get the takeoff procedure started? It will be a mostly empty ship, since only the flight deck crew headed back to the circus pod once the meeting was finished."

Eric also stands up, joining William, and it's like a cue for everyone to start moving.

"As soon as Link is done, Lila and I will go to Area 51. It shouldn't take long unless Agent Smith is in one of his moods, but then we should be ready to leave Earth's orbit and set a course for Celestia."

My stomach lurches. This is it, we're finally heading farther into space. It's equally terrifying and exciting at the same time, but first things first—Area 51. I'm so excited I could squeal, but I won't. *Be cool, Lila, be cool.*

"Alright, you know what to do. Let's get moving. Time is of the essence." William clears his throat before dismissing us all and then leaves, followed by the others, including Caspian who manages to untangle himself from me before planting a kiss on my lips that leaves me breathless and panting for more.

"See you soon, mate. Maybe we can go for a swim together once we hit lightspeed." He waves cheerfully, obviously refreshed from having himself wrapped around me.

Saxon kisses me swiftly before promising to see me soon and hurries off with the two cats and Xavier, who, to my disappointment, just waves an absent hand at me. I can't deny that his response, or lack thereof, hurts, but Link soon distracts me.

"Come on, beautiful, let's get you and those babies checked out."

"Oh fuck, the babies." My hand goes to my belly, and I sigh with relief at the small bump that is still there. I'm a total failure as a mother. I hadn't even considered them while gorging myself on all the blood. Link must see my fear, because he quickly wraps an arm around me and pulls me into his side.

"They are fine. They were the first thing I checked, but it doesn't hurt to be thorough. I have machines which have better diagnostics than my hand scan."

I sag against him, my relief almost taking me to my knees. "God, I'm going to suck as a parent. It's because I had no good examples growing up."

"That's partially untrue. For your first few years, you had excellent parents, and when you get those memories back, you will see." Eric pats me on the hand as we make our way around the big ship to Link's office. "Let's get this done for everyone's peace of mind, and then we have a prisoner to wrangle." Eric looks positively gleeful, and I roll my eyes at his enthusiasm. Trust him to consider that fun.

I jump up on the table and lie back, closing my eyes. I'm ready to get this physical over with so I can get on with the fun.

CHAPTER ELEVEN

Lila

Link scans me and confirms everything is okay with the babies and my new body. When he tells me that my heart has enlarged and he needs to monitor it for a few days, I agree to let him inject a monitor under my skin. It will keep track of my vitals for the next day or two just to make sure everything is hunky-dory after my change. Once that's done, he takes me back to the dining hall and orders me a crap load of food, which I proceed to consume.

"Oh my god, I think my babies have been joined by a couple of food siblings." I pat my stomach, feeling full and satisfied and sleepy. "I could easily head back to my rooms, settle down on the couch in front of the picture window, and take a nap."

"Well, I don't have time for that shit, and neither do you." Eric drank coffee while I devoured all my food, but now he's looking at the display screen of his communications watch. "We need to get moving. You need to change and meet me back at the transport platform in half an hour."

I groan, and Link holds out a hand to help me to my feet. "Come on, I'll keep you company until Saxon has a moment to work with you on your new Vilaxian skills. You probably need to be careful around other people." The caution in his voice mirrors my own thoughts, but I allow him to tug me to my feet.

"Yeah, about that. I've already—and this was purely accidental—shoved him into a wall. Believe me when I say I don't want to do that to anyone else. He said the trick is to do everything super slowly, which will actually be normal speed if that makes any sense."

Eric rolls his eyes. "But I need you to hurry up so we're not late."

"Yeah, yeah, slow your roll, Gramps. I'll be there. You just worry about *you* being there on time." I can't help the sass that easily rolls off my tongue.

"Fine, I will go check on my brother then and get changed. I'll see you soon." He hurries away without a backward glance, and Link and I exchange our own.

"He and William are really worried about John.

They just want to head to Celestia, and the delay is killing them minute by minute." My heart aches at the thought of my grandpas in pain, and one of them is barely holding onto life. This whole situation is fucked up.

"Do the Celestians know we're coming?" I ask, and he nods as we make our way through the ship to the elevator and then my rooms. We pass people, and we get a few polite nods and greetings, but everyone seems preoccupied. I guess the announcement changed things for a lot of beings.

"Yes, I sent a message to them before the staff meeting. They are expecting us in three days, which is how long it should take us to get there once the pod has returned to the ship."

We walk hand in hand, and I decide I need to do a mental health check on Link. I can't help but wonder how he feels about me bonding with Saxon. "So, um, I was wondering if you are okay with this," I ask, not really wanting to look at him in case he isn't, and the awkwardness coming from me isn't really something I'm used to.

"With what?" He pauses for a moment, sounding a little confused, and I kind of don't blame him, since I am all over the place.

"With me and Saxon and what just happened, and I guess everything. I guess what I'm asking is, do you still want to be my boyfriend?" How fucking teenager of me to make it sound so blasé when it's not, like it wouldn't break me in two if he decides this is not for him.

He chuckles and squeezes my hand. "Is that what I am?" he asks, and I feel my stomach sink. Shit, maybe that's not what he wants. Maybe I am a bit much for him. Me and all my shit…

"Ah… Um…" I try to pull my hand out of his, completely embarrassed now, but he holds on tight and pushes me up against the corridor wall, blocking me in. I could probably get away with my new strength, but I really don't want to hurt him.

"Lila, look at me," he demands, putting a finger under my chin and lifting it so I have no choice.

I feel my cheeks flush with shame. How high school am I? Shit, this is why I never did the boyfriend thing in the past. I'm so freaking awkward, and I don't do awkward.

"Lila, I like you. *Really* like you. What I feel for you… I've never experienced it before, and I hope you will seal the Skarrian mating bond with me one day. As a cyborg, I don't have a fated mate like Caspian and Saxon, and I can't form any kind of bond with you myself. The only thing I can do is extract some nanobots from my body and inject them into yours. That's what cyborg marriages are. It's symbolic of a couple joining together to do that. But it won't do anything to you, it's purely a romantic gesture." His silver eyes shine with emotions, and I relax, hearing him say the words I needed to hear.

"Well, we have half an hour, and I'm pretty sure we can knock out a mutual orgasm in that time." *Yeah, way to go, Lila. He gets all sweet and romantic, and how do you respond? By suggesting a quickie. High. School. And so emotionally stunted.*

Link doesn't seem to mind, though, and the love in his eyes quickly turns heated as the corner of his lips tips up in a wicked grin.

Yes. Please.

"I could give you five in that time," he tells me and steps back, freeing me from the wall and grabbing my hand. Our journey to my rooms is quick, and by the time the door slides open and allows us entrance, Link and I are already stripping off each other's clothes. Link doesn't have much to do because I'm only wearing sweats and a shirt, so I'm naked as soon as they come off. It takes me a little longer to extract the delicious doctor from his uniform, but soon enough, we land on the couch. His naked body is cooler than my flesh, but it seems to warm from contact with mine, and by the time I'm finished with him, he'll be smoking hot.

Forty-five minutes have gone by since Eric demanded I meet him at the transporter. That's actually fifteen more than I was supposed to take, and I can tell he's pissed when I finally get there.

"Sorry, sorry!" I apologize profusely as I hurry onto the transport platform, waving at Officer Kirk who is operating it today.

"I knew I should have insisted you return to your rooms *without* one of those blasted men," Eric grumbles, and I raise a surprised eyebrow.

"What's crawled up your ass? Usually you're all Team Lila and getting her some men."

He has the grace to look embarrassed, and he sighs. "Sorry. It's this thing with John, and I loathe dealing with Agent Smith. There's something that is untrustworthy and creepy about him. He just rubs me the wrong way. It's almost like he doesn't like aliens. I'm not sure why he has the liaison position if that's the case, and he's being extra mysterious about this new detainee. We have almost no information about him except for his designation, Alien A. I'm not sure what he's done to warrant deportation. Most of the time it's some trumped-up charge or an accidental reveal to a human, something that could be easily overlooked, but he is a hard-ass. We never had as many aliens being deported with his predecessor. Though I must admit this has been the least amount for years. Usually he has a whole heap of them he's decided to ban from Earth."

I wait to see if my grandpa takes a breath after the verbal diarrhea spewing out of his mouth. He seems to have a lot on his mind when it comes to Agent Smith.

"So what do I need to know?" I ask, and he loses the lost in thought look and straightens up.

"Just follow my lead. You're here to observe. It's fairly straightforward. We sign some paperwork, and then they will bring the detainee out and hand him over to us. Whether he returns to the ship in cuffs and gets put in the brig until we can return him to his home planet or he gets assigned a room until they decide where they want to go next depends on the crime. Usually they return to their home planet and answer to their own authorities. Most charges get thrown out because they are pretty bogus. Earth is never understanding." He brushes his hand down his clothing, and for the first time, I realize he's wearing the Galaxy Circus jumpsuit like mine. Normally he's just in jeans and T-shirts, unless he's wearing his ringmaster costume.

"Okay, Obi-Wan Kenobi, I will be your faithful apprentice."

He just cocks an eyebrow and looks unimpressed. Yes, they have Earth classics available to watch on their streaming service, and it's obvious he knows whom I'm referring to.

"Oh, and here." He holds out his hand, and when I look down, I recognize a gun similar to the one Saxon had been trying to teach me to use before he got a whiff of my blood. "That's the one calibrated to your blood so no one else can use it if you happen to have it taken away."

"Oh no, no way. I have no idea how to use that thing." I shake my head, stumbling back like the fucking thing is going to bite me.

"Just aim and shoot, and don't fire it unless you intend to kill. To be honest, you shouldn't need it. It's more of a show of force than anything, though I bet Agent Smith would like to get his hands on this technology. Up until now, we've resisted giving them weapons that kill aliens. They only have the ones that can incapacitate."

I reach out and take the blasted thing, tuck it into a pocket of my pants, and promptly pretend it's not there.

"Send us, Kirk," he commands, and our bodies dissolve into tiny little particles, only to reform on a platform in a galaxy far, far away. Well, actually, we're still in the same galaxy and not all that far away if you think about it reasonably.

I look around the room we arrived in, noting we are surrounded by black-clad military men all holding weapons trained specifically on us. Eric tsks, but it's quiet enough for only me to hear it.

A siren blares, and more military men run around farther into the room, but for now, I don't move a muscle, not wanting to risk that one of the guys currently pointing a big-ass weapon at me has an itchy trigger finger, but Eric is not so patient.

Shaking his head, he lifts his hand, and all the

guns fly out of the men's hands and into the air where they hover high enough to be out of reach.

"What have I told you about threatening us?" my normally happy-go-lucky grandpa growls at someone off to the side.

"And I've told you that we can never be too cautious. What if someone else other than you tele-ported into this facility?" A weaselly, familiar-looking man wearing a black suit and Ray-Bans—how cliché—steps through a gap in the soldiers and stops in front of the platform, his hands on his hips. I want to laugh at the visual, but it would be inap-propriate when things are so tense.

Eric shakes his head again. "And who else would be? We're the only ship that comes into Earth's orbit. That was the agreement set up many years ago, and it is one the whole galaxy abides by. You are unnecessarily jumpy." Eric steps down off the platform now that weapons are no longer pointed at us, and I follow after him. "Agent Smith, this is our granddaughter, Lila. She is our heir and is learning the procedures surrounding the circus. She will be taking over for us once we decide to retire." He turns to me. "Agent Smith has been our Earth contact for the past twenty or so years. He came on just before your parents died."

Agent Smith holds out a hand. "Yes, it was a tragic loss. Imagine my surprise when you popped up over twenty years later. I thought you had perished with your parents." He hasn't taken his glasses off, so I can't actually see his eyes, which bugs me to no end. I hate not being able to get a read on a person, especially when I hear insincerity in his tone, but I take his hand anyway. It's clammy and limp and not what I was expecting at all. I shake it quickly, reminding myself to be gentle, before releasing it and wiping my palm discretely against my pants.

If he had a theme song, it would definitely be "Creep." He officially gives me the creep-a-zoid.com vibes, and now I'm glad Eric gave me the lowdown on this dude.

"Yeah, I got lost in the foster system. I can guarantee I was just as surprised as you when I found out I had family and they are alive. I must have blocked out all those memories." I'm not willing to tell him that I had my memory erased.

"Well, if you come this way, I will get you to sign a few forms, and then we can hand over the prisoners." He gestures for us to follow him.

"Prisoners? As in plural?" Eric stops and taps something on his watch. "According to this manifest, you only have one."

"Ah, yes, well, we performed a raid early this morning. Got a tip from an informant about some illegal alien activity. We revoked a lot of visas, and they will all need to be transported off the rock." Smith hasn't stopped walking, so Eric and I hurry to catch up with him.

"Uh, excuse me, can we get our weapons back

please?" someone calls from behind us, but Eric ignores them.

"What did you raid? Where did you raid? We're not allowed to congregate in large numbers per Earth protocols. The only exception to that is a couple of alien run businesses that have exemptions, and the only one nearby is the Pleasure Inn. I can't imagine Master Gasm breaking the laws."

My stomach lurches, and a wave of nausea rolls through me. Oh my god. Mark and Susie! That's where they stopped overnight. I'm trying everything I can to keep my cool, but I must not be doing a very good job of it, because Eric keeps looking at me out of the corner of his eye.

Agent Smith reaches a door, and as he pushes it open, he pulls off his glasses. I almost flinch away from his pale, watery stare. It's kind of unnerving, but I manage to get control of myself before I do.

"Oh, but he was, and he doesn't get a free pass. He and the rest of the current management have had their visas revoked. We gave the rest of the alien guests and workers a fine and sent them on their way, but there are four who will need to leave immediately. They will also not be allowed to return. We also have two humans who will need to have their minds wiped before they can continue on their way. Funnily enough, when I ran their background checks, I discovered that you know them well, Lila."

Fuck. Susie and Mark have been caught up in

the raid and are now on the government's radar. This is the worst possible thing that could happen, and now I feel responsible for the shitshow they found themselves in.

Eric's jaw is tense, and I can see him grinding his teeth, but he acts natural. "Well, let's get this show on the road then, shall we? Lila and I have limited time."

A wide, smarmy grin stretches across Agent Smith's lips, giving him an almost psychotic look. He knows he's gotten to Eric and seems quite pleased about it. His creep vibes have another vibe to add to the mix—douchebag. I do not like this man one little bit, and I get the impression the feelings are *very* mutual.

"Yes, let's."

CHAPTER TWELVE

Lila

T he room we enter is empty, and it looks like an interrogation room, with just a table in the middle and a few chairs on either side. Covering the table is a whole bunch of paperwork. I feel Eric sigh beside me.

"Agent Smith, how many times do I need to tell you that paperwork is meaningless to us? Everything needs to be digital for our records."

The smarmy, self-important grin doesn't leave Agent Smith's face as he takes a seat, placing his sunglasses on the table before picking up a pen.

"Ah, but you know we need paper for our records." He passes Eric the pen, who glares at it like it's offending him, before he hands it over to me.

I take it, but I call bullshit. I know almost everything is done electronically on Earth now too. He gets off on making things inconvenient, and his assholeness is wearing on my nerves.

"Okay, so you need to sign here, here, and here." Smith points out three separate places to sign on a page, but frowns when I don't instantly comply.

"What is the legal process for aliens? Are they entitled to representation and allowed to defend themselves against the crimes they have supposedly committed?" I ask the agent, taking a seat next to him. Eric hides a smirk and sits on the other side of the table, crossing his arms and waiting for a response. I'm sure he already knows the answer, but I can tell my question has annoyed the agent, and Eric seems childishly pleased about it. His reaction is only encouraging me to ruffle the Earth liaison's feathers even more.

"Well of course not, they are *aliens*. How would we explain this to a lawyer?" Agent Smith sneers, talking to me like I'm a brainless twit, and I shrug.

"I'm almost certain we could provide an alien lawyer if need be." I look at my grandpa, and he nods, remaining silent.

"Absolutely not! They broke the rules. One strike, and you're out," Smith snaps. I see spit fly from his mouth, landing as little wet specks on the papers and the table. Ha! Clearly I hit a nerve, and his temper is getting the better of him.

"I get the feeling that you don't like aliens,

Agent Smith. Are you sure you are the right person for this job? Maybe we need to speak to your supervisors. I'm sure there is something in the American constitution about being given due process." I'm completely bullshitting at this point. I have no idea if there is or not, but I'm feeling defensive. I'm also internally freaking out about Mark and Susie, but I don't want him to see that, so I'm distracting him with smoke and mirrors. Isn't that what the circus is all about?

Smith splutters, unable to form words, before growling and stabbing at the paperwork. "Just sign the papers, Miss Adams, or maybe we can revoke the rights of every alien on Earth if I *speak to my superiors*." His threat finally has my grandpa reacting. He sits up in his chair and leans forward.

"Now, Agent Smith, I'm sure the president would be unhappy to hear that we will no longer be negotiating alien technology for him, if that's the case. I think making this decision is above your paygrade."

Agent Smith scoffs. "Technology? Please, you haven't provided anything interesting since you handed over the plans for virtual reality headsets. Our requests for advanced weapons have gone on deaf ears."

This gets an even bigger reaction out of Eric, as he stands up and slams his hands on the table, the noise echoing through the room. "The one time we did offer you advanced weapons technology, you blew up Japan. No, you have proven incapable or not advanced enough to handle that kind of responsibility." The two of them are involved in a heavy stare down, and I have a feeling this is not the first time this argument has come up.

"Okay, fine. Look, how about you read the charges, and I will sign off on them? Let's get this show moving, because we have places to be." I try to diffuse the tension from the room. It doesn't seem to have much of an effect, but it is the distraction they need. Smith stabs at the first bit of paper.

"Crimson, race Vilaxian, Savannah, race Celestian, Xane, race Warlock" —hearing Xavier's cousin's name has my eyebrows jumping in surprise, since I would have expected him to avoid capture if he's anything like Xavier— "and Aura Gasm, race Morpheian. All four are management at the Pleasure Inn and have been found guilty of harboring humans on the premises, as well as an alien with no authorization to be on the planet. All have been stripped of their residence status and must be detained and punished by relevant authorities. I trust you will see they are punished to the full extent of the law."

Eric goes to argue, but Agent Smith rudely holds up his hand. "I haven't finished. Ricky, race Cybertronian. He is the unauthorized alien. We have interrogated him, but he has no knowledge regarding how he came to be on Earth, or so he says, and Master Gasm is denying knowing as well.

He said Ricky arrived on his doorstep with a spell on him. He thought he was a…" He looks down at his notes and frowns. "Sex robot. What is a sex robot? Are there other kinds of robots? War robots? Why don't we know any of this?" His nostrils flare, and his lips turn white as he snaps these questions.

Eric rolls his eyes while I snort at his ridiculousness. "You are on a need to know basis, Agent Smith. I'm sure if you needed to know about any kind of robot, then your superiors would tell you. Just think of them as a big blow-up doll. They are not really all that scary when you think about it."

"Nope, they are programmed to fuck," I state blandly, and Agent Smith shifts his focus to me and narrows his eyes. "They are hardly the 'take over the world' kind of variety. Plus, robots are the least of your worries if any alien species turned their focus on Earth. How about we forget about the sex bots and focus back on the fact that—Ricky, was it? —seems to have been kidnapped and Master Gasm was set up."

"None of that is my problem, Miss Adams. They broke the laws, so they have to go. Lastly, before I was rudely interrupted, is Mark Simmons, race Celestian." The smug smile that appears on his lips makes me want to slap it off him.

My mouth drops open in shock, and I exchange a glance with Eric before shaking my head. "No, that's not right, Mark's from Earth. He's not an alien."

"Oh, I assure you he is, or that's what they all claim. They also claim the other one, Susie, is Skarrian. I'm sure you can understand how I find that hard to believe, and if they are both here, unregistered, then they need to be deported as well." This fucking prick has a set of brass balls for being as mouthy as he is.

"Well, there is one way to get to the bottom of this. I will have our warlock come down, and he will ascertain the truth." Eric shrugs his shoulder, relaxed in his chair like Agent Smith hadn't just dropped a bombshell on us. I'm not sure how he's holding it together. My body is practically vibrating with agitation, and the fangs in my gums are throbbing with the need to rip this motherfucker's throat out.

Oh dear.

Shit, shit, shit. This is not what I need right now.

Smith stiffens, pales minutely, and mutters something under his breath that I miss even with my uber sensitive hearing. He pushes back the chair, the screeching sound loud in the nearly empty room.

"Fine, I will escort him here."

"Oh, and Smith, don't pull any of that weapon crap on him. He won't be as nice about it as I was," my grandpa warns as he opens the door. Smith nods and leaves, the door banging shut ominously behind him.

Eric lifts his watch to his mouth and presses a button. "Xavier, get your fucking ass down here. We have a problem."

"I'll be there soon," is the tinny reply, and I see my grandpa heave out a sigh of relief. He must be really worried, but he's doing an amazing job of hiding it. I wish I had the ability to keep my worry locked down tight too.

I start to ask a question, but he holds his hand up and tugs on his ear. "Wait until Xavier gets here."

I nod my understanding, and we sit in silence. Everything we had just found out rolls around in my brain.

Mark and Susie are aliens?

Surely that's just a cover they are telling the authorities. I can't deny I'm dying to see them. I want to get to the bottom of everything, and I can't wait to get out of here. The longer we sit, the more the creepy vibe seems to stick to my skin, and it's all I can do not to scratch at my arms to remove the phantom feeling. I wonder if my grandpa feels the same way.

Within ten minutes, the door opens again, and Xavier, shrouded in mist, steps into the room followed by an even more agitated Agent Smith. His skin has the redness of someone who is angry, and his fists are clenched at his sides. "I demand that you go back and return my men to the ground," he yells at Xavier. I can't see my warlock's face, but I can guarantee he's wearing that infuriating smirk, and I struggle to contain my own.

"How many times are your men going to point those insignificant weapons at me before you realize they are useless, Agent Smith? It really is quite insulting that you continue to do it every time I come here." Xavier's tone is all imposing warlock, loud, and defiant, and basically a big fuck you to Agent Smith. He is so getting a blow job when we get back to the ship.

"I did warn you," Eric chimes in, still perfecting an unconcerned pose. "If you could give us a moment so we can get the warlock up to speed on the situation, that would be great. If I had known we were going to be escorting so many prisoners, I would have asked him to accompany me in the first place."

"Fine, but be quick. I have one more prisoner for you to sign off on." He gestures to the papers that we haven't signed at all.

Shit, maybe we need to do that, because then at least Mark and Susie will be our responsibility. Eric must feel the same way, because he casually leans forward with a loud sigh, like it's all too much work for him. "Fine, we will sign these and catch the warlock up on the situation, then he can then ascertain the truth of the alien status of the two we are suspicious about. If they are aliens, we will take them with us, and if not, they will remain your responsibility." Smith's eyes light with excitement. I think he's expecting them to be human, and that worries me. I don't like the idea of leaving my friends behind. They are on this agency's radar now for associating with aliens, and that can't be good. This is why I wanted their memories removed in the first place, so nobody could use it against them.

"Excellent. I will give you exactly ten minutes. I am a busy man, and I don't have time to waste." Smith leaves us again.

I start to talk, but again, Eric stops me.

"Xavier, if you could fix the listening ears, please."

Xavier waves a mist shrouded hand, and a bubble of purple smoke appears and wraps around us, cocooning us from the cameras. Xavier lets his own mist pull back and reaches for me at the same time I push my chair back and leap into his arms.

I release a sigh of relief as his strong arms wrap around me, all the tension I'd been holding drifting away. Xavier is slimmer than both Saxon and Caspian, but being in his arms offers no less comfort. He practically radiates power and reassurance. I feel him draw some of the tension out of my body, feeding on it and easing it for me.

"Thank you," I tell him, my forehead resting against his chest.

"Anything for you, *phoeall.*"

"Right, this is a clusterfuck." Eric gave us our moment, but now his patience is gone. "Somehow, Aura and their family have gotten arrested. It sounds like a setup, and Susie and Mark are involved. Aura is claiming both Susie and Mark are aliens, and if they are, then they become our responsibility."

"So do we want the truth or for me to lie so that we don't leave them in the hands of this creep?" Xavier asks, playing devil's advocate so wonderfully.

"Lie," I say at the same time Eric says, "Truth."

I look at my grandpa in disbelief. "And what, leave them in this asshole's hands? Over my dead body."

"No, of course not, but it might start a witch hunt. If they are, what's to say there aren't others here on Earth? Do you think the agency would be happy that some might have slipped through the cracks? No, they will start hunting, and no extraterrestrials will be safe. I'm sure there are some who are hiding relationships with humans. It's bound to happen."

I think about what he is saying. "I guess you're right. So you think Aura is lying to protect Susie and Mark?"

"Almost certainly. Neither of them remotely registered as anything but human," Eric replies, and I cock an eyebrow.

"And you can tell this?" I ask in disbelief, and he at least has the grace to look sheepish when he shakes his head.

"No, not exactly, but Xavier could have." He

points at the man still wrapped around me, and I feel him huff a chortle of amusement.

"It wasn't really something that crossed my mind to test for. As far as I was concerned, they were one hundred percent human."

Eric waves his hand impatiently. "Yes, well, no matter, let's just get on with this. I have a bad feeling about the situation. If Aura is being deported, then who is running the Pleasure Inn now, and will they be taking care of the workers like Aura did, or will they be exploiting them?" He gnaws on his lip, his worry showing when he's been calm and collected so far.

"Is that our concern?" I ask, stepping out of Xavier's arms and looking between the two men. Both are frowning, and Xavier nods.

"Kind of. We are the only way on and off this rock. If something happens and they need an escape, then they have to wait until we come back around."

"Are there any backup escape plans? Or a kind of alien witness protection or safehouse, so to speak, they can go to?"

Grandpa Eric sighs and looks sad. "Yes, there was. Your parents were the ones who ran it. When they were killed in the car accident and you disappeared, we decided to leave the house abandoned. Over the years, people believed it was just an old, deserted house with no family to come and claim it, but underneath is a large network of safe rooms for aliens needing to hide until we return. They are still able to access the facility through a hidden tunnel that starts in an old mine shaft about a mile away from the house. Anyone who needs us will activate a beacon when they arrive, so we know to do a trip there and extract anyone who needs it."

"Oh." Finding out more things about my parents is kind of bittersweet.

"We haven't had anyone use it in a really long time. I wonder if everyone remembers it's there. Maybe we need to send a reminder bulletin to all aliens on Earth—kind of a heads-up that maybe the agency isn't being as tolerant as they have in the past and to watch their backs."

"What about aliens on other continents?" My curiosity is getting the better of me again.

"There are safehouses on all continents. We have the ability to beam aboard the big ship from any of those locations," Xavier explains as Eric taps the paperwork in front of me.

"Okay, enough with this topic. I still haven't heard the charges for the prisoner we originally came here for, but you can sign these and claim responsibility for the others."

I sign in all the places indicated on every sheet. "Are we now going to return the others to their home planets?"

Eric shakes his head. "It varies from case to case and the charges. What Aura and their family have done doesn't warrant any punishment, so they are free to choose where they'll go. They just won't be able to return to Earth for the time being. If the charges were serious, then there would be a process that we would need to go through. We would advise their home planet, and then they would decide whether they chose to retrieve them or have them charged by the galaxy federation, but it is the home planet's responsibility to retrieve them from us."

The door slams open, and I hear Agent Smith call, "Time's up." I'm surprised I can actually hear him, because I know he can't hear us, otherwise Xavier and Eric wouldn't have talked so bluntly. I also know he hasn't given us the allotted ten minutes, but I'm pretty sure Agent Douche is pissed because he can't hear what we're saying and he's being petty. Xavier's mist seeps out, covering him from sight, and then the purple smoke surrounding us peels back.

"If you would follow me, I will have some guards escort us to the prisoners in case they decide to be difficult."

Xavier laughs out loud. "I am more than enough to handle the prisoners."

The smarmy smile that suddenly creeps across Smith's lips creates a small lump in my throat. He looks awfully pleased with himself, and that can't be good. At all.

"Oh, I wouldn't be too sure of that if I were you. The only thing keeping you all safe from one of the prisoners is this."

He holds up a little black remote, and both Xavier and Eric blanche.

"Those are only supposed to be used on prisoners if they are a known dangerous and deadly species, and as far as I know, there are none on Earth that would require that," Eric snaps, finally revealing how agitated he is to Smith.

"Well, I guess you don't know everything. There wasn't just one unregistered alien on Earth, there were two, and if there are two, how many more are out there?" Agent Douche's words are exactly what Xavier and Eric were worried about.

"What race demands the use of the control collar?" Xavier questions, and although we can't see him, we can hear he means business.

Agent Smith smirks like he just won the fucking lottery. "Aaz'axian."

CHAPTER THIRTEEN

Xavier

I'm so shocked at the words that come out of Agent Smith's mouth that I almost lose hold of my mist for the first time in thirty years. I couldn't have heard him right.

An Aaz'axian on Earth?

And how does he even know what that is?

Their race has basically been extinct for many years now. There are barely any left galaxy wide, so it's incredibly unlikely for one to be here on Earth. They scattered and stayed hidden once their tyrannical leaders had finally been defeated. Over eighty percent of them were forced to fight and die for a cause they did not believe in, and then their women began to perish from a mysterious wastage disease until there were but a handful. They are carefully protected and cherished, but are no longer able to bear children. Some say it was their god punishing the Aaz'axians for their hubris, but why punish the many for the depraved acts and decisions of a few? With the ability to glamour, there hasn't been a sighting in years. They chose to keep their heads down and exist in peace, so no one has seen an Aaz'axian in either of their natural forms in over a hundred years. To be honest, I thought they had become extinct. They were a very long-lived, slow aging race, so I guess it is possible for there to still be some around, but highly unlikely.

"No, that can't be true. That race is extinct." Eric shakes his head in denial. "You must have a Morpheian or another with ability to glamour, and they are tricking you."

"There is no way to hold a glamour when you have thousands of volts coursing through your system. I assure you, he *is* an Aaz'axian." Smith waves the damn remote again, and it's all I can do to stop myself from blasting it out of his hand with my power. That wouldn't go down well, however, so I rein in my anger. Barely.

"Very well. Lead the way, and I can use my powers to ascertain the truth there too," I say mostly to reassure Eric and Lila. My intimate has been following along with the conversation, even if she doesn't quite understand the full significance of it. I'm not even sure if she's heard of the Aaz'ax and their war with the Una's over the orb of power. She is still willfully behind on her alien knowledge.

We need to fix that as soon as we get a moment to breathe. We can't have her making mistakes.

Smith doesn't wait for us, he just takes off in the direction of the holding cells. There are not as many people running around now. Most of them used their brains and made themselves scarce after I proceeded to lift the idiots pointing weapons at me into the air. Although, I did make sure all their weapons wouldn't work first, and it's not like they can use the weapons Eric must have already floated up there. It isn't zero gravity where they can float around—they are held in place by my magic.

He takes us down a level, and although I'm distracted by what he just told us, I make sure to keep an eye on my intimate. Lila is easily distracted, and I don't want her wandering off and getting herself shot by some trigger-happy maniac. Everyone here has itchy trigger fingers when it comes to us, but as we pass a large black door that has a big "No Entry, Authorized Personnel Only" sign, she slows and turns her head to look back at it before stopping, her beautiful face frowning. She walks back toward it, and her breath hitches and she roughly grabs at her chest.

"What's wrong?" I ask her quietly, not wanting to draw Agent Smith's attention. He and Eric are far enough ahead though, and they haven't noticed we've stopped.

"When I walked past this door, I got this deep ache right here." She points to her sternum. "It's almost like I need to go in there. Something's calling to me, Xavier."

I eye the door suspiciously now. Whatever could be calling to Lila? Do they have more aliens stashed behind there? I reach out with my magic, but before I can allow it to seep under the door, Agent Smith finally realizes we're not with them.

"What are you doing?" he demands, his voice echoing down the corridor. "That section is off-limits to everyone but people with Level 1 clearance, which you do *not* have. Hurry up, I don't have all day." He sounds impatient, but when I turn to look at him, he also has a glint of worry in his eye. Interesting. I'm torn between doing as he demands to keep the peace and saying fuck it all to hell and investigating behind the door, but before I can make a decision, Lila does it for me.

"Come on, let's rescue my friends. The weird ache is gone now, so maybe it was just concern for them and not what's behind the door." She reaches through the mist and grabs hold of my hand, tugging me to our destination.

Reluctantly, I let it go. I can always sneak back in and check it out at another time. As much as Agent Smith thinks this base is protected and the only way in and out is via the teleportation platform, I can teleport in without the platform. I don't like the idea that they have an area that is off-limits on this level. It's supposed to be the EAA level, and access should be granted to anyone from the

Galaxy Circus as representatives of the Galactic Federation.

Smith opens the door to the holding area, and we approach the cells. It's clean and sterile and blindingly bright. There are quite a few forcefield fronted cells down here, with special protections to cater to all the different aliens that may be placed in them. A warlock, probably a grandparent of mine, placed the spells on them many years ago when we started coming to Earth.

I can see directly into the first few. There is only one person in each. They must have all been separated when they were brought in. Susie is in one, and Mark is in another. On the opposite side, I see Aura, and next to them is Xane. My idiot cousin looks like he heaves a sigh of relief at the sight of me, and I feel a smug grin lift my lips. I'm never letting him live this down. His eyes drift from me to Lila, who is still holding my hand through my mist, and I see him scan her body, his eyebrows jumping with surprise before he gives me a nod of approval. Idiot. Like I care if he approves or not.

"Well, let's get on with this. Do your thing." Smith waves his hand in the direction of the two humans, and although I would like to strip his skin from his body for speaking to me like that, Lila squeezes my hand before she drops it, easing the impulse.

Right, must not kill the agent. Diplomacy is probably not a strength that I would claim for myself. I'm a little too blunt, which is appreciated throughout the galaxy, but not so much with these Earth Alien Authorities. It's why the Adams brothers tend not to involve me with them.

I step up to the first cell, and Smith brings down the forcefield. Before I can send out my magic to assess Susie, Lila pushes me out of the way, and both girls break into sobs as they throw their arms around each other. Thankfully Lila remembers her new superstrength and doesn't literally kill her friend with kindness. They are both talking a million miles an hour, and I'm having trouble following their words.

"Miss Adams, remove your arms from my prisoner before I shoot you." I turn slowly to look at Agent Smith, thinking he wouldn't be dumb enough to point a weapon at my intimate, but sure enough, the idiot is, and my vision goes red. Growling, I thrust my hands out, choosing the least physically damaging way to incapacitate the asshole. The weapon in his hand disintegrates before he goes flying backward, his body slamming against the forcefield of the cell behind him. There, his body starts to convulse from the shocks, and I see his head flop to the side as he loses consciousness before dropping to the ground.

"Xavier," Eric admonishes, but not too hard, and the grin on his face is the complete opposite of the tone coming out of his mouth.

"He dared to point a weapon at my intimate.

He deserves much worse, but I am aware of the delicacy of the situation, so I allowed him to live. I will make sure he doesn't remember." I wave my hand and turn off all the cameras in the room, as well as erase the footage of the last couple of minutes while we wait for the girls to calm down.

Finally, the two girls pull apart, their faces streaked with tears, and I allow the mist to pull back from my body now that there are no extra eyes. Susie and Mark have seen my human punk glamour but not my real form, and Susie's eyes widen as she takes it all in. Her gaze flicks to Xane and back again before she gasps.

"You two look similar."

I scoff. "Please, he is but a poor imitation of the real thing." Susie frowns, and Lila smacks me as I see my cousin flip me off from the other cell. He must be able to hear me, but when he says something, the words don't penetrate. "Well, that's not a nice way to greet the person who is saving you, Xane. Maybe we'll just leave you here."

Lila smacks me again, and I sigh. "You just wait, you'll be begging me to put him back after five minutes in his company."

Although I'm acting put out, I'm relieved my favorite cousin is okay. He was my best friend growing up, and I would hate for anything to happen to him.

"Okay, Miss Susie, what is this we hear about you being an alien?"

Susie's eyes drift to Eric who asked the question, and she frowns. "Wait. Who are you?" she asks, and Eric chuckles again.

"Ah, yes, you would remember me like this." He activates the glamour he had been wearing when they had first met.

"Holy shit, Grandpa Eric!" Susie exclaims, looking at Lila. "Dude, your grandpa is smoking hot."

Lila's skin tone turns a little green like she might vomit, but Eric preens like a damn peacock as he lets the glamour fade away.

"How about we drop all the forcefields so everyone can be involved in the conversation," Eric suggests and begins deactivating them all.

"Wait." A blond dude with shimmery skin like a cyborg steps out of one of the cells and stops Eric from deactivating the last cell. "Not that one. Leave it for now."

I wander down to the cell and peer into it with Eric, but it's dark, and we can't see beyond the first couple of feet. Shrugging, we return to the others.

It's noisy and confusing as the seven captives hug and reacquaint themselves with each other. Eric, Lila, and I stay out of the way while this happens, letting the group have their moment. Lila watches with a small, genuine smile on her face as both Susie and Mark are embraced and kissed by four of the five aliens. She nudges me, and I lean down so she can whisper in my ear.

"I think Susie and Mark must have given their consent, and from the looks of it, it was *enthusiastic*." She giggles but looks pleased with the situation, and I allow the breath I'd been holding to ease out. All of them look really happy together, and I'm thrilled for my cousin. He deserves all the love he can get. Not everyone finds their intimate, but this much love more than makes up for it.

"Okay, shall we get the introductions out of the way? I want this all to be done by the time the agent regains consciousness again." Eric steps up, obviously impatient to get out of here. "Aura, it's a pleasure to see you." Eric holds out a hand to the Morpheian. They are wearing a male glamour at the moment, which I'm assuming is for the agent's sensibilities. I also know, like me, they don't like to show their true form to just anyone.

Aura beams and pushes Eric's hand out of the way before embracing him, kissing him on both cheeks. "Eric, you sexy man, you are a sight for sore eyes," Aura gushes, and Eric's cheeks tinge pink with embarrassment, which is a completely different reaction from when Susie said something similar. "Thank you for coming to our rescue. I'm afraid we've been set up." They drop their arms and let go of a blushing Eric.

"Yes, we had assumed as much. You can share it all with us when we get back to the ship, but it's Susie and Mark we need to worry about now. What did Agent Smith mean when he informed us that they are both aliens?" The color in his cheeks returns to normal, and his brows pinch together as he tries to figure out the truth.

"Let me introduce you to my family first. I think you know Xane, but this is Crimson and Savannah, and Ricky is our new friend. This is Eric Adams, one of the proprietors of the Galaxy Circus, Xavier Colest, heir to the warlock empire, and..." They trail off when they get to the female still plastered to my side.

"This is Lila, my intimate," I tell them all, beaming with pride, and Aura's eyebrows jump.

"Well, congratulations, my friend, that is amazing news."

"And what he's also forgetting to tell you is that she is our granddaughter and heir to the Galaxy Circus." I didn't think Aura's eyebrows could get any higher, but they manage to outdo themselves.

"Well, Saturn's rings, that is simply wonderful news. I know you've been searching for her for a long time." Aura pulls Lila out of my arms and hauls her into theirs, hugging her tightly. "Welcome, child! We are so excited to finally meet you."

Lila graciously hugs Aura back when Susie gives her a quick nod of reassurance. Everyone else exchanges polite hellos before Eric huffs, his foot tapping with impatience again. I know he must be desperate to leave and make the journey to Celestia.

"Can we get to the story now?" he grumbles,

and Aura rolls their eyes and blows out a raspberry at him.

"Fine, so both Susie and Mark were scanned by a Jelliad who informed us of their extraterrestrial origins. Mark is a Celestian who was kidnapped as a baby and hidden on Earth. Without the Celestian maturing ceremony, he never gained his powers or wings and has been passing as a human."

You could have heard a pin drop in the room as Eric, Lila, and I take in this information. The three of us stare at the man in question, who squirms uncomfortably under our inquisitive gazes. Savannah reaches out and grabs his hand. When they meet, hers glows, sending him reassuring vibes, and he relaxes.

"Holy fuck!" Lila whispers. "Out of all the people in the world, the lost alien ends up with my roommate."

"Well, actually, we think that may be why." Xane, who has been silent up until now, steps forward. "It seems that living with Lila may have activated a dormant Skarrian gene inside of Susie. Most humans have lost all signs of ever being from anywhere else but Earth, but occasionally, a mutated gene will appear. Nothing usually comes of this, but we think living with Lila, who is Skarrian, somehow triggered that gene. Then, when she was visiting with you, she must have come into contact with Skarrian water. She is probably only a couple of bottles away from activating any latent powers."

Now we all swing our attention to Susie. "Did you drink the unlabeled blue bottles of water in my fridge at the hotel?" Lila asks her friend, cocking her head to the side quizzically.

"Yeah, they were freaking delicious. I meant to ask the hotel where they got them from, but I forgot. I assumed the no label thing was a funky marketing ploy." Susie's chocolate brown curls bob as she answers. The sweats she's wearing are practically swallowing her, and she has bare feet, but she doesn't look like she's been treated badly.

"Well, that answers that question. Those were bottles of Skarrian water. I've been basically mainlining them in the hopes they will activate my powers."

The room sinks into silence again as Eric and I digest the information we just heard. Suddenly, Eric claps his hands, breaking the silence and causing Ricky, who I think is a cyborg, to jump. Aura quickly snuggles him into their side in reassurance. "Okay then. Overlooking the fact that you had a Jelliad on the premises—I am not even going to ask —it seems that Susie and Mark are indeed our responsibility." He turns to the two in question, his eyes softening with sympathy. "I'm sorry, but you can't return to your everyday, Earthling lives. You are both on Agent Smith's radar now. You have damaging knowledge, and even if you weren't an alien, I doubt he would let you go. I'm afraid you are going to have to come with us."

Susie sidles up to Mark's other side and grabs hold of the hand Savannah is not holding.

"We are fine with that. Knowing what we know now, we couldn't return to our old lives and be happy. If we have access to a phone and the internet, both of us will resign from our positions with the hospital," Mark says, not upset about it at all, but Xane, Eric, and I exchange a loaded glance.

You tell them. I don't want them to be upset with me, Xane begs me quietly in my head, and it's all I can do to stop myself from smiling at seeing my cousin smitten with these two. To ease his concern, I slightly nod my head in confirmation.

"I'm afraid it would be better if we faked your deaths—a car accident on the way back from Vegas, and due to the older nature of the car, neither of you survived your injuries. We can teleport back to your home and retrieve any belongings you wish to keep."

"But what about money? How are we going to be able to live without access to our money or jobs or anything?" Susie sounds distraught, her voice going an octave higher on each word, and Eric jumps in.

"We can find positions for both of you with the circus. It is not a problem."

"We also have ways of bequeathing everything to a relative, and later, you appear as that relative to claim your inheritance next time we return to Earth," I assure them both.

"Okay, well, that sounds reasonable, and thank you. We had planned to try and find out about my birth family anyway, and this is a big help," Mark says solemnly.

A small smile appears on Eric's lips. "It just so happens our next stop is Celestia. We canceled the rest of the tour, and we will be leaving immediately after we can retrieve your belongings. My brother is not well, and the Celestian healers may be the only ones who can save him."

The group reacts favorably to this just as Agent Smith groans on the floor. I let my mist surround me again.

"Right, let's take care of this then." I wave a hand, wiping his last memories, and help him to his feet before straightening him out. I make him think he has a migraine coming on and that he just wants to be done with this alien crap.

"Well, what was the verdict?" he demands, looking at me.

CHAPTER FOURTEEN

Lila

"Susie and Mark are one hundred percent human," Xavier announces to Agent Smith, who smirks triumphantly at Aura.

Aura looks at Xavier like he stabbed them in the heart.

"But unfortunately, they now know the truth about aliens and can no longer be trusted to return to their previous lives. We will be taking them with us to protect the secret."

Agent Smith's smirk quickly drops. "What? No. That's not how this works," he argues, shaking his head. "They will return to their previous lives, and we will monitor them to make sure they don't reveal any secrets." I see the moment Xavier's cousin gets sick of Agent Smith. He waves a discrete finger, and Agent Smith's eyes glaze over before he continues.

"On second thought, maybe it is best you monitor them. Less work for us."

"Okay, great, now let's take a look at this last alien, the one you claim is Aaz'axian." Eric still sounds skeptical, but the smug grin returns to Smith's face. God, I hate this dude. My fangs ache to bury themselves into his neck and rip his throat out. They click down into place, and I slap a hand over my mouth.

Whoa! My eyes widen, and I look at Xavier with panic. He takes one look at me and freezes the room, much like he did when Saxon was feral, and allows his mist to fade away once more.

"What's wrong, phoeall?" he asks, pulling my hand away from my mouth. I peel back my lips to show him my fangs, and his eyes heat with lust.

"Hungry?" he asks, and I shake my head.

"No, the other H word," I tell him, and he chuckles.

"Horny?"

Again, I shake my head. "No, homicidal. I want to rip that motherfucker's throat out." It's comical how quickly the lust turns to concern, his eyes becoming as wide as mine and his mouth popping open in surprise.

"Not what I was thinking at all."

"What am I going to do?" I whine pathetically.

"Well, I'm going to go out on a limb and suggest that your bloodlust is probably triggered by the fact you're hungry. Your body is probably still adjusting to the change, and you may need to feed more frequently until it evens out some more. Remember this is all new to us too, but we will do our best to get you through it." He pulls me close to him and wraps his arms around me. I rest my head on his chest, but all that does is make my fangs throb harder. His blood rushes through his veins just below my ear, and my mouth waters.

Yup, definitely hungry.

"Can you pop me back to the ship so I can find Saxon?" I ask, feeling completely out of my depth, and his arms stiffen. I pull away from him and see he's frowning at me. "What's wrong? Did I say something to upset you?"

"Why can't you feed from me?" he asks.

"Oh... Oh! I wasn't sure if you would want me to. This is all new to me too, and I was afraid maybe you wouldn't want to see that side of me."

He loses the frown and cups my face with his hands. "Phoeall, nothing about you could scare me away. Everything about you is sexy and wonderful and kind, and this is just one more aspect of you. Please feed from me. I want to provide for you too."

Xavier's permission snaps the final thread I had been holding so tightly to. With a growl, I spin and tackle him. We fly backwards down the space between both sets of cells until I slam him into a wall. Although I'm kind of lost to instinct, I'm still cognizant enough to check that I haven't hurt him. He's fine, if the bulge in his pants is anything to go by. He's taller than I am, so I climb his body and wrap my legs around him. He spins us, supporting me between the wall and his body. My pussy rubs against his hard cock, and I moan. God, that feels good.

I strike, my fangs sinking into his neck. He shouts at the pain, but my venom quickly takes hold and morphs it into delicious pleasure. I groan as the taste of him flows over my taste buds. Just like his cum, his blood tastes like Twizzlers. Fuck, how did I get so lucky? Suddenly, we're both naked, and as I take a long draw of his blood, he thrusts his cock deep into my pussy. It's my turn to shout at the intrusion.

"Fuck." Xavier is lost to the potency of my venom and pounds into me, so all I can do is hang on tight and ride the sensations.

The tentacles at the base of his dick quickly work my clit to get me where I need to be, and I run my tongue over the stream of blood that escaped before latching back onto the puncture marks. I take a couple of large mouthfuls as Xavier drives my pleasure higher and higher, my rock-hard nipples rubbing against his chest with every thrust.

Feeling full, I seal the wound and throw my head back against the wall, and when his eyes meet mine, we combust. My orgasm detonates, sending shockwaves of rolling pleasure through my body at the same time I feel Xavier empty his seed into me.

Smug satisfaction fills me as this strong,

imposing being comes undone before me. This powerful male wants me to be the mother of his children and fills me with his seed whenever he can. I want to be dripping with his cum. His and Caspian's and Link's and Saxon's and Nikos's and.... Holy fuck, that is not me. Fucking horny bitch kraken. I'm going to be permanently pregnant if she has anything to do with it.

Xavier's grip on me softens, and he leans in and tries to kiss me, but I quickly put my hand over his mouth. He arches an eyebrow in question, and I shrug. "Blood breath!"

He chuckles, jiggling us, and I catch something moving out of the corner of my eye.

Oh my fucking god! I turn my head slowly and see a shadowed figure standing in the last cell—a figure that, by the looks of his shadowy movements, is jacking off.

"Ah, Xavier, I thought you froze everyone," I whisper into his ear. He hasn't noticed the figure yet, and he leans his forehead against mine, his dick still a happy camper deep inside my pulsing pussy. His tentacles tease my clit, trying to encourage me to go for another round.

"I did," he replies as I squirm, trying to get him to put me down. Finally, he withdraws.

I feel a gush of his seed slide down my leg as he lowers me to the ground and steps back. I look down at my now naked and even more exposed body and squeak, pulling him back against me. He giggles, sounding a bit delirious, and while I would normally be stoked at the power of my pussy and fangs, right now I need him cognizant.

"Damn it, man. There is someone in that cell, and judging by the puddle of cum that is now on the floor, I would say we just gave him a show that he hasn't seen or participated in for a while."

Xavier freezes, and I'm suddenly clean and reclothed back in my uniform, as is he. He slowly turns to look into the darkened room, then he presses a button on the wall next to the cell, and it illuminates the room. The being inside still has his cock in his hand, but he shields his eyes with his other.

"Holy fuck." The words slip from my mouth as my eyes are drawn directly to his cock. I could blame the kraken for this one, but nope, it's all me.

His cock must be covered in tiny little barbs, because his hand is covered in blood, as is his thick, long length. Although I just fed, my fangs throb in want once more.

Goddamn it. Back the fuck off, bitch. That cock is a lethal weapon that would tear my insides to shreds, I chide internally.

Big challenge, my kraken whispers, practically humming with anticipation. Oh my god, that's it, she's a fucking psycho.

"Holy shit." Xavier stares at the creature too, but he seems to be both fascinated and revolted.

I drag my eyes away from the barbed, blood-covered cock and take in the rest of the creature. Humanoid and wearing a pair of black cargo pants, which are undone and hanging around his hips, he is covered in long and short spikes. The long spikes have sheer membranes draped between them. There isn't any hair on his head, just a crest of more spikes, but his color is stunning. He looks like an opal, all greens, reds, blues, yellows, and pinks. I look at his face, and staring back at me are black eyes with the smallest elongated slit of a white pupil. His ears are pointy like Xavier's, and he has the cutest button nose with full lips and high cheekbones that have a line of ridges along them. He has little ridges on his chin as well. The skin between his ridges, bumps, and spikes is smooth and shimmery, and when the light hits it right, it is kind of mesmerizing. I realize that I should be repulsed, but he is strangely handsome in a very animalistic way that has me feeling things I shouldn't be feeling.

"Agent Smith was telling the truth. This is an Aaz'axian. Now where the hell did he find you?" Xavier sounds intrigued, and his words seem to trigger something in the alien. He tears his gaze away from me, tucks his dick back into his pants, and swipes the bloody, cum-covered hand along his pant leg before he does them up. His whole body starts to shimmer, and the alien is replaced with a human—or the glamour of a human. He's handsome as fuck, with shaggy black hair, piercing green eyes, and a golden tan over his bare torso. He sneers at the two of us before stalking into the back of the cell and throwing himself on his bed with his back to us.

"Well, that was fucking awkward," I mutter as we make our way back to the frozen group. "I never would have done that had I known he wasn't frozen."

Xavier looks down at me and scoffs. "Please, my beautiful intimate. You forgot I can feel what you're feeling, and when you realized he watched, you got a secret thrill. You are an exhibitionist."

I scowl at the warlock. "It's rude to call a girl out on it though, and it's more that horny bitch kraken of mine." I can tell by the way he looks at me that he doesn't believe me.

We move back to where we were, and Xavier unfreezes everyone. Thankfully they don't even realize it, although Xane does side-eye his cousin.

"Just this way, he's in the last cell. We leave him in the dark because he gets agitated when the lights are left on." Xavier waves his hand, and the light in the last cell winks out. Hopefully the puddle of cum is gone, otherwise that's going to be hard to explain.

Xavier and I follow along silently. I notice that Aura and their group are also silent. I guess Eric is the only one in for a rude surprise. I just hope my grandpa doesn't keel over with shock. Considering we guard the orb of power, and one of the very beings who wreaked destruction through the galaxy in pursuit of it is here, it could be a disaster to allow him aboard our ship.

Smith flicks the light switch on the wall, lighting up the room. The alien is still in his glamour form, and he still has his back to us on his bed. Smith pulls the little black remote out of his pocket before calling, "Brannock, please assume your natural form so my friends can see."

Eric's jaw clenches like he's grinding his teeth at being called Smith's friend.

The alien ignores him.

"Brannock," he snaps, and the alien continues to ignore him. A slimy, satisfied grin crosses Smith's face. "You give me no choice." He raises the little remote and pushes a button.

Although his back is to us, I can see him stiffen and start to convulse. His glamour slips away, revealing his true form. His skull and back have a line of long spines running down the middle, with two lines of shorter spikes on either side of it. There are three long spines sticking out of each shoulder, and between all of these long spines are a thin, sparkly membrane.

He groans and rolls onto the floor, landing flat on his back. The spines fold down like they are flexible. Well, that's handy, otherwise lying on his back, or anywhere really for this dude, would be nearly impossible. He has a line of short spines running down both arms, and his chest has rows of small spines as well. He turns his head and bares his teeth at us. He has razor-sharp fangs like mine, but he has two on each side. I wonder if he drinks blood. With four puncture marks, it would flow quicker. Does that mean he's more evolved than the Vilaxians?

My mind returns to what's happening in front of me as Agent Smith presses the button again. This time the alien curls into a ball, his spikes springing out like they are protecting him. Although we can't hear it, I can see that he's screaming in pain. I go to stop Agent Smith, but Xavier beats me to it.

"If you press that button again, I will flay your skin from your body." The violence in his tone sends a shiver down my spine, but it's not from terror, it's from pure fucking lust. *What a perfect mate, protecting the weak.* Oh fucking hell. Someone just shoot me now. My kraken has lost the plot. I'm going to have to let her out. Maybe Caspian can fuck her into a coma or something. She purrs at my thoughts.

Smith slowly lowers the remote.

"How did you even get that collar on him? We told you it was only for an emergency," Eric asks as we watch the poor alien roll around on the ground.

"Tranqed him and installed it. Look at him, you can't tell me that he isn't scary."

Aura scoffs. They and the rest of their group have been quiet up until now. I'm almost positive they don't want to draw his attention. I don't even think he'd really noticed they were all out of their cells with how hyper-focused he was on this guy.

"He's not even in warrior mode. That's when you need to be worried."

"Warrior mode?" Agent Smith's eyes light up. "You mean he has another form apart from that disgusting one?" He waves a hand at the sparkling opal-like man, who I think is gorgeous. Like, he's so pretty it's kind of sickening. I would never have guessed by looking at him that he was one of the most feared races in the galaxy.

He presses a button on the wall again, and we can suddenly hear the being inside. His groaning starts to change to laughter, and he rolls over, grinning at Smith. "Your prejudice only allows you to see what you want to see. You made assumptions, and I wasn't about to give you information for free." Whoa, his voice is smooth like honey and kind of soothing. I could happily listen to him talk all day.

"Show me this warrior mode, or I will light you up like an anglerfish, you freak." Smith waves the remote in his hand again, but it flies out of his hold and into Xavier's. Smith dives for it but hits an invisible wall and stumbles back. He reaches for his gun, but of course it's not in its holster because Xavier obliterated it when he pointed it at me.

"You have two seconds to return that to me before I summon the guards," Smith growls, and Xavier just snorts, but before he can say anything, Eric steps in.

"We are wasting time, and I've seen enough. We

will take him into our custody, so there is no need for you to have the remote or see his warrior form."

"Wait! Maybe I need to keep him here. He was very helpful on the raid at the Pleasure Inn, so maybe he can be of some use."

I can practically see the wheels turning inside this horrible man's head, but Eric is not having any of it.

"No. I will not let you exploit an alien. What are his charges anyway?"

"He became intoxicated and showed his alien form in public and caused a riot. You know that goes against the terms of residency, and then when we arrested him, we found he is unregistered anyway."

"Yes, I was wondering about that. We have no records of ever transporting an Aaz'axian, so he must have made his own way to Earth. We need to determine how and breach any holes there might be in the process." Eric seems a little flustered. That, combined with learning that Aura had unregistered aliens in their house as well, indicates that there are other ways onto Earth, and that is not a good thing.

"See that it doesn't happen again, and when you find out, I would like a report please." Smith grinds his teeth before spinning and heading out of the cell block. "I'll leave you to organize the prisoner. Miss Adams can accompany me, and I can have all that paperwork scanned and turned into electronic documents for you to take."

Xavier and Eric both go to argue, but I hold up my hand. "It's fine. The quicker we can get out of here, the better, and I'm not completely defenseless anymore." I flash them my fangs, and they both back down, much to my delight.

"We will see you on the platform. Fifteen minutes, Lila. If I have to wait longer than that, I will be coming to find you," Xavier says loud enough for Smith to hear. He doesn't stop, but he does stumble slightly, which makes me grin. I nod and hurry after him, so ready to be done with this.

CHAPTER FIFTEEN

Lila

Smith's shoes clicking against the floor are the only sounds as we make our way through the corridors. I slow as we reach the door that caused me to react before. Again, I feel a strange thump inside my chest and a great need to know what is on the other side. Involuntarily, my hand raises to the palm pad, but a hand slaps down on my wrist, encircling it and stopping my forward momentum.

"What do you think you are doing?" Smith demands, looking between me and the door, a hint of worry in his eyes.

Frowning, I shake off the sensation and shrug. "I'm not sure. Sorry. I guess I was turned around, I thought it was through that door," I lie my pants off, and he seems to buy it.

"Come along. I gave the paperwork to my

assistant earlier, and she should have it all ready to go now. The sooner I can get you aliens off my turf, the better." He mumbles that last bit. I guess he doesn't know or probably doesn't care about advanced hearing.

"You don't seem to like your job very much. Why do it then?" I ask him, and he turns back to glare at me.

"Because someone needs to keep the scum sucking invaders in line." He reaches a door we haven't been through yet and pushes through, not waiting for my response. I mean, I don't really have one, and his attitude makes it obvious that he hates us.

Through the door is an office with a few cubicles with people working at them. A lady stands up in one. When we get close, I can see she is basically the female version of Smith—all button-down black suit with a hard look in her eyes.

"Here are the contracts, all scanned in." She passes a thumb drive to Smith.

"Does it have *everything* on it?" he asks, emphasizing everything. Wow, because that's not subtle at all. I'll have to warn Eric to search it for viruses or spyware or whatever.

"Yes, sir. Everything you asked for is on it," she says in a clipped tone before turning her back to us and returning to her seat.

"Great, there you go. You should probably hurry. You don't want to keep your family waiting, and the Aaz'axian needs to be transferred into a cell as soon as possible. He likes to fight the control collar." Smith's smarmy grin returns. "Just head back out the door and to the right, you can't miss it." Just like that, he turns his back on me and leaves via another door.

"Well, okay then, great to see you. Can't wait to do this again. Not!" I call after him. I head back the way I came. I go to turn left, but my eyes drift back to the door that causes me to feel so strangely. Could I even get through the biosecurity lock? I doubt it, and although I gained some extras from bonding with Saxon, none of that includes powers to override something like that.

"Lila!" Grandpa Eric's voice sounds impatient, and when I turn in his direction, he's waving me forward. "Hurry up, I want to return to the ship. Susie and Mark still need to get their things before we can leave Earth, and the sooner we get to Celestia for John, the better."

I leave the mysterious door. I'm sure it's nothing anyway. I mean, it's not like they are hiding aliens, since they are all in plain sight here.

I'm the last one to make it onto the platform. The Aaz'axian appears to be immobilized by a spell of Xavier's making, so he is floating and unable to move. He also looks to be unconscious, which probably isn't a bad thing. He didn't look happy to see us, and who knows how long he's been in Agent Smith's clutches and what kind of treatment he has seen. I guess we can get to the bottom of all of that when we get home.

"Is this safe?" Susie asks, looking super terrified as she holds Mark's hand. He doesn't look much better, and Aura inserts themselves between the two of them, draping an arm over each of their shoulders.

"As safe as sitting on the sofa at home." They press a kiss to each of their cheeks as I reach through Xavier's mist and grab his hand just before we all dissolve into tiny little particles.

When we land back at the ship, Cas, Link, and Saxon are waiting for us. Crimson sees Saxon and smartly salutes him. He acknowledges her with a quick nod, and she relaxes again. Eric claps his hands.

"Right. Xavier and Saxon, you take our new guest to the cells. Until we can get his side of the story, I'm not prepared to have him roaming around, so he can keep Natalia company until we can at least begin our journey to Celestia. Lila, please show the others to the empty suite that is on our level."

"There's an extra one? I thought it was just you and me and the captains up there?" I ask my grandpa, and his eyes dim slightly.

"It was the one we had set aside for you, and it has been sitting empty for years. It has enough rooms for everyone to have their own, but you moved into your parents' suite."

"Oh!"

Xavier rubs a mist shrouded hand over my back in support, knowing my mood just dropped.

"Then we need Mark and Susie to return to their home and grab their things, and we need to do that ASAP. The circus pod should be docking with the main ship in the next hour or two, and I want to be able to tell Captain Potter to launch us into hyperspeed as soon as it does." Eric is wringing his hands in agitation, and Caspian slaps a reassuring hand on his shoulder.

"Relax, my friend. We've got this. Link and I will accompany Susie and Mark and help them with whatever they need, and Lila can show the others to their room. Find William and check on John."

Eric sags with relief and smiles gratefully at my mate. I just want to ride him like he's a bucking bronco for how sweet he's being, but that will have to wait, unfortunately. Maybe we'll go swimming, and we can let the krakens out. A wave of approval washes over me, followed by one of impatience. *Damn beast can never be happy.*

With that decision made, we all go our separate ways. Saxon and Xavier head in the direction of the detention cells, and we leave Cas and Link, who had both changed their appearance to something more human, behind with Mark and Susie—but not before they all give me a quick hug and kiss. Instantly, I feel better and steadier, prepared to face the job ahead.

My poor friends look to be a little shell-shocked, which I can completely relate to, but we don't have time to talk them through it. I'll make sure they know how to program alcohol in their replicator. Poor things are about to get a crash course in everything alien.

"If you would just follow me." I hold out my hand and gesture for Master Gasm, Xane, Crimson, Savannah, and Ricky to follow me. "I'll show you to your rooms."

"Thank you, that would be wonderful. I need to change into a more comfortable body." Aura winks at me, and I kind of just stare for a moment. Ah, right, Morpheian of course. Seriously, this still doesn't get any easier.

"Oh my goddess, this is so exciting! The actual Galaxy Circus." Savannah claps her hands with excitement, and Crimson smiles indulgently at her. "I can't believe we're here."

"Have you ever seen it? I would have thought with Xavier being Xane's cousin, you would have seen it before."

"Oh no. Whenever they were in town, Xavier would come see us so he could use the—oof." Savannah breaks off after Xane elbows her in the side. "Ow, what was that for?"

"I'm sure Lila, Xavier's intimate, doesn't need to hear about why he was visiting us," Xane says quietly out of the side of his mouth, but it's too late, and that cat's out of the bag. Savannah frowns and looks at me.

"Oops, sorry."

"Meh, it's no big deal. I've met his harem. I saw two of them pleasuring a stingray dude who had two cocks, then said stingray dude shriveled up until he was only a mummified husk. Ah, fun times. So while I'm aware he has a harem and was not particularly picky about where he put his cock in the past, I know what I mean to him. I doubt he would disrespect me by straying now that he knows what we are to one another, and once that intimate bond is locked in, if he wants to play with my other mates, well, I wouldn't be opposed."

Aura grins widely and holds up their hand. "Damn, girl, give me a high five. Now that's how you embrace the poly lifestyle. More bodies means more fun."

"And let's face it, there's only one of me, and my vagina would be quickly out of commission if I was fucking four men daily."

"Actually, Skarrian women have vaginas designed to cope with multiple lovers. Something in our feminine lubrication is self-healing." A voice from behind us has me jumping. So far, the corridors have been fairly clear. The flight deck level where the teleporter is, and also where our suites are, isn't really ever crowded with people, so to see someone is a surprise.

Whirling, I put my hands on my hips. "Fuck,

you scared the hell out of me, but that is good to know," I tell my friend Magenta, who is beaming widely. She has her bright pink hair pulled back in a ponytail and is wearing her GC uniform. She must have stayed behind instead of going back to the circus pod.

"Aura! I heard a rumor you were here." She throws her arms open and runs at the Morpheian.

How the fuck did Magenta hear that? We've been here all of two minutes. Maybe she was stalking the corridors waiting for me anyway, sneaky bitch. Also, how does she recognize Aura? From what I can tell, this is not their normal form. They embrace like lifelong lost friends, but it doesn't seem like there is any sexual tension. Magenta then goes on to hug the other three as well before stopping at Ricky.

"Oh, you're new. I've never seen you before." Her eyes scan the pretty cyborg before she holds out her hand. "I'm Magenta, and I'm Skarrian." What she is really saying is I'm Magenta, and I'm slutty, but I'm almost certain everyone knows this by now.

He blushes, his skin sparkling even more than usual, and shakes her hand quickly before stepping behind Xane without saying a word.

She sighs and looks at Aura. "Adorable."

They grin. "I know, right?"

"So how did you come to be here?" Magenta tucks her arm into Aura's, and they take the lead.

"Where are we going?" she calls back to me, not waiting for Aura to answer.

"The spare suite on our level that was supposed to be mine," I call back, and she stops, dropping Aura's arm and whirling around.

"Are you okay with that?" she asks. I see concern in her eyes, and I love this girl just a little more. I can't wait for her and Susie to meet. We are going to be like the three musketeers.

I wave my hand, gesturing for them to continue. "Yeah, it's fine, whatever. I'm using Mom and Dad's, and it's not like they are ever coming back." A lump develops in my throat for my parents, even if my actual memories are fuzzy at best.

She stares at me a little longer before turning, and we continue on our way. It's quite a walk to the last suite on the far side of the ship. I absently listen to Aura and gang explain how they came to be here, but I'm a little lost in my own thoughts, and a hand on my shoulder has me stumbling slightly.

"God, sorry, I didn't mean to startle you," Xane apologizes, helping me steady myself. It's so weird looking at this warlock. He looks so similar to Xavier, but he doesn't put off quite the same amount of power. Even when he's powered down, Xavier crackles, but Xane's power feels like a pleasant buzz.

"That's okay, I was lost in my own thoughts."

He smiles gently at me, somehow knowing I had

been thinking about my parents. I hope he wasn't using his damn warlock powers on me.

Before I can scold him, he continues. "I never met them, you know. We didn't arrive to run the Pleasure Inn until a couple years after their death, but of course I know the story. I think any alien who resides on Earth does. Not to mention the Adams' search for their missing grandchild. We were all put on alert to keep an ear and eye out for a child exhibiting strange powers. Year after year when no rumors surfaced, we figured you died as well, though your grandpas never gave up their search."

I nod my head, unable to talk now that my throat has closed off with my emotions.

"I just wanted to say welcome to the family. I couldn't be happier for my cousin, and I hope you forgive our first interaction. I'm afraid your friends had me a little off balance." He has the decency to look embarrassed, and I decide to throw him a bone, especially after he made an effort to be kind.

"I would say they have you a little more than off balance." I wink at him lasciviously, and he chuckles.

"Yes, they were an unexpected but delightful surprise. I'm not sorry in the least that they have to come with us. I'm pretty sure they were going to try to look into Mark's family, but now we have an excuse to stay with them."

Thankfully, my overwhelming emotions have disappeared with this new topic, and I can't deny feeling thrilled for my friends. This seems to be a little more than a booty call for all involved, and it means I'll have my Susie right where I want her with no lies between any of us—besides the one about the orb of power, which no one knows. I am going to have to tell Cas and Saxon about it eventually. I just kind of want to enjoy the honeymoon period before I tell them about the huge responsibility we are going to undertake. Hmm, maybe I should tell them before so they have a get out of jail free card.

Up ahead, Magenta stops in front of a door, and I stop feeling a little ill. All these reminders that my parents aren't around are throwing me off. I got so used to not thinking about it, but here, I can't help but be reminded that my parents are no longer with me.

"Lila!" Magenta is staring at me with a frown, so I guess she may have been talking to me for a while.

"Ah, yeah, sorry. I'm a little tired. My blood rose bonding with Saxon must have taken more out of me than I thought." Suddenly, Crimson is in front of me. She's taller than I am, and I have to lift my head to look up at her.

She leans in and sniffs me. "I thought I was wrong, but I'm not, am I? You are a blood rose, and you say you're General Saxon's. Wow, I'm sure that didn't go over well with his clan." Crimson looks positively gleeful at the thought.

"Radella and Estrella had a conniption. They tried to put a stop to it, but Xenos and Hale wouldn't let them."

"Xenos is here too?" Crimson's eyebrows almost jump off her face. "The queen doesn't like it when both her nephews are away from her."

"He came when Saxon had to be sedated," Magenta explains.

"Why was he sedated?" Crimson looks back at me, and I shrug.

"I'm new to all of this, and it gave me a little time." I wait for her to explode much like the girls did, but she nods calmly.

"That was smart. I see the general has landed himself an intelligent blood rose. This is good. Well, are we going to stand around all day, or are we going in?" Everyone looks at me expectantly, but I just can't. My parents' memories are going to have to wait for another day.

"You guys go. Magenta will help you with anything you need. I just can't, I'm sorry," I apologize and use my speed to escape back to my own room. I need my own alcoholic beverage now.

Please, Lord, let me still be able to get drunk.

CHAPTER SIXTEEN

Saxon

Although I manage to control my facial expression, my emotions are rolling. I can't believe what I'm seeing. How did an Aaz'axian end up on Earth? And how exactly did the Earth Alien Alliance get their hands on him? What did he do to draw their attention to them? There hasn't been a sighting in years. I'm sure most of them use a glamour to blend in, so what happened with this guy?

All of these thoughts whirl through my mind as the warlock and I make our way through the ship to the detention cells. He's bound up in a spell and unconscious, so he's really no trouble, but I am dying to ask him some questions.

"So?" Xavier breaks the silence that had been hovering between us. "I never would have thought you and I would end up bonded to the same woman." He finally brings up the subject we'd both been tiptoeing around—not that we've really seen each other to discuss it. I've been sedated, and he's been dealing with a wayward harem.

I chuckle, glad to have the subject out there now. "I know, right? I had seriously thought that you and I would be feeding off each other for the rest of the tour. I couldn't stand the thought of drinking from my clan."

"And my harem was being stingy with their emotions unless they were getting something in return. Lila is a blessing for both of us, but I won't deny that I'm going to miss feeding from you. Your anger and aggression were always so fucking tasty."

"And your power-filled blood is delicious." I think about what Link said. Even though I haven't discussed it with Lila yet, I'm going to broach the subject with Xavier since he's already comfortable feeding me. "The doc actually suggested that Lila may not be able to fully sustain me. Although her body has changed, she still may not be able to provide the amount of blood I require. He suggested that I would need to feed from others." I pause, trying to get my thoughts in order. "The thought of having to feed from others hurts. I don't want my blood rose to feel inadequate and betrayed. Link suggested that feeding from her other mates may be a solid alternative. Will you still feed me if I need it?"

I can't see it, but I can practically feel Xavier smirking at me through his mist. "Absolutely, as long as I can get a bit of quid pro quo. I also want an invite into your bedroom with Lila sometimes, even if I just watch and feed, but I'm sure the two of you together are really something."

"I will speak to Lila about this. She needs to be the one to make the final decision."

He slaps me on the back. "Believe me, our mate will agree, she's got a kinky streak a space leap wide."

The detention levels are on the last floor of the mothership just before the circus pod's docking station. That level still shows as red in the elevator, so it still hasn't arrived back from Earth. We get off, and there's an office for security personnel. Normally it's empty because we never have anyone in the cells, but today, it's manned. The guard has his feet thrown up on the console and is leaning back in his chair with headphones covering his ears and his eyes closed. I'm about to tell him off for his attitude when a god-awful screeching sound penetrates my hearing. Xavier's mist floods back into his body as we both clap our hands over our ears.

"What the fuck is that?" he demands, and I shake my head, not wanting to remove my hands— not that they are blocking out the horrible racket. I bump the guard with my hip, and he startles, dropping his feet to the ground and leaping up. He relaxes a little when he sees us.

"What is that noise?" I demand, and he frowns, pointing at his ears and shaking his head. Right, he can't hear me. "Can you do something about that?" I ask Xavier, and he quickly waves a hand, and a barrier goes up around us, blocking out the sound. I breathe a sigh of relief and drop my hands, as does the warlock. The guard reaches up, removes his headphones, and sighs with relief.

"Thank you. She has barely stopped for a breath since you brought her in here," he tells us. "I had to find headphones to block out the racket. It was driving me nuts."

"That's the lightning cat?" I ask with disbelief, and he nods.

"Yes, fuck, you would think someone was in there killing her, but I've gotten up and checked a few times, and she's just in cat form, pacing around the cell and blasting it with lightning every now and again. Thankfully it's warded and protected, so it just bounces back off. It tends to hit her, which then makes her madder. Last time I looked, she wasn't looking so hot—a bit fried around the edges to be honest." He can't hide his glee as he imparts this information.

"I'll ward her cell against noise so you and this guy don't have to suffer through it," Xavier offers, and he quickly agrees.

"That would be great. So what's this guy done?" he asks, turning to look at the new prisoner before his mouth drops open in shock. He takes a step back involuntarily before quickly recovering. "Is that what I think it is?" he asks, the brief glimpse of fear covered by fascination and not a small amount of bravado.

Most of the time, the detainees from Earth haven't really done anything wrong except for expose themselves to the wrong person, and usually that's by accident, which is what this guy apparently did too. Usually, we let them out of the cells, but we need to question him first.

"Yes it is. We'll just stick Brannock here in the farthest cell away from Natalia, but let's allow her to have a good look at him as we go past. It might frighten her into silence," Xavier suggests, and I scoff.

"Not likely. She is a stubborn woman who believes she has been wronged. They don't scare easily."

Xavier winces. "No, my friend, you are right, they certainly don't." I guess he's thinking about the harem member he just killed. She wasn't going to give up her fight, and I doubt Natalia will be any better.

Xavier releases the sound barrier, and the noise has stopped. I sigh with relief as Xavier starts moving our prisoner. He floats the still unconscious man down to the last cell. As we pass Natalia's cell, she snarls and leaps at the barrier, her claws extended as she foams at the mouth. She smashes against it and slides to the ground. Shaking her head, she picks herself up, her fur bristling and looking a little singed, and tries again. Once more, she hits the barrier and slides to the ground. This time when she picks herself up, she paces back and forth along the length, not taking her eyes off us, that yowling sound returning.

I slap my hands over my ears. "Fuck, can't you do something?" I demand of my sometimes lover, and he rolls his eyes at me. "Damn Vilaxian hearing," he grumbles but waves a hand, erecting a sound barrier around her cell.

"Like you can tell me that wasn't affecting you as well," I snap, and he shrugs, but I see his shoulders droop at the lack of noise. He can pretend he wasn't affected, but I know the truth.

Xavier lays the prisoner gently on the bed before stepping out and activating the cell forcefield. He then waves a hand, unbinding the Aaz'axian and waking him from his impromptu rest.

His eyes are slow to open, but when they do, he jumps to his feet. He groans and puts a hand to his head as he looks around, then he takes a deep breath and drops his hand to his side. Clenching his fists, he returns to his human glamour. "Where the fuck am I?" he demands when he sees the two of us on the other side of the cell.

"Relax, you're in the containment cells in the mothership of the Galaxy Circus. We have a few questions for you. If you answer them to our satisfaction, we will release you and you can decide where you want to go and what you want to do." Xavier does all the talking while I observe. The alien's heart rate is unusual. If I'm not mistaken, he has more than one, like a Vilaxian. In fact, I think he may have three. They beat irregularly, with each one pulsing after the other, making it seem like one continuous heartbeat, and then on the fourth, it pauses momentarily before the first one kicks in again. One, two, three, stop. One, two, three, stop.

I scan his body. His heart rates are certainly fast, and I can see a bead of sweat forming on his brow. He seems nervous and agitated, but I can't really blame him. I don't really have a baseline to judge him off of, so I'm not going to be all that much help.

A whisper of a touch brushes across my mind, and I know it's Xavier asking for entrance. I nod my head, and he projects his thoughts so the alien can't hear.

What do you think? he asks me, and I shrug.

I don't know. I have no baseline to judge him, so I'm afraid I won't be much help.

He has a wall around his mind that is almost impenetrable. I think I could get through it, but it would cause him excruciating pain. Xavier sounds matter-of-fact, like he doesn't care about that. *But I think he may be another case of Smith being a prejudice asshole.*

I sneer at the mention of the Earth agent. I have met him before and almost ripped his throat out. It's why Eric doesn't allow me to retrieve prisoners anymore. *The only thing we really need to know is how he came to be on Earth, so let's ask. We have no record of him using the GC as transport. If he answers without hesitation, I say we trust him. He is but one Aaz'axian, so how much trouble could he be?*

Have you ever gone up against one in warrior form? Xavier asks, still eyeing the alien who seems to understand we're having a private conversation, but he looks to be getting impatient.

No, never. As far as I was concerned, they had died out after the war.

A few survived, but most of their women died, so the few that were left went into hiding. I am too young to have seen them in action, but my grandfather would tell stories that induced both fear and awe. He did say that most of them were against the war, but their leaders were brutal and would kill off any dissenters. Maybe you should ask him to spar with you one day.

"Well, what the fuck are you looking at?"

I guess he's reached the end of his patience, and I don't blame him.

"Why don't you take a seat and get comfortable? This won't take long." Xavier waves a hand, and two chairs appear on our side. He casually takes a seat, crossing his legs as he elegantly adopts a pose of indifference. I know better. I can practically feel the concern radiating off of him, and I know it's his need to keep Lila safe, and this man in front of us could be the ultimate predator.

The being throws his hands up in frustration but

takes a seat on the bed. His back is ramrod straight, and he crosses his arms aggressively.

"Ask what you want to know," he demands, and as I take a seat on the other chair, I see the warlock arch his eyebrow in amusement before it quickly drops again.

"What is your name?"

"Brannock Zarax."

"Why were you on Earth?"

"To live a quiet, peaceful life," he replies flatly, his heart rate staying constant as far as I can tell.

"How did you come to be on Earth?" Xavier asks, voicing the question I want to know the answer to the most.

Brannock sighs and uncrosses his arms, leaning on his thighs with his elbows. "When our race was on the brink of extinction due to the mistakes and hubris of our leaders, those of us who survived the war fled to all corners of the galaxy. We knew it wouldn't be long before the Aaz'axian race was merely a bad memory for most of the galaxy. Like the Una's, we would fade into a thing of cautionary tales. A group of us, men from the unit I was in during the war, chose Earth as our sanctuary. This was before the Earth Alien Alliance. Aliens were little green men, and Roswell was far in the future. With our ability to glamour, we were able to blend in, and we lived out our lives. Some of my crew grew despondent and decided to end their lives. With no chance of a mate and not being able to have a real relationship with a human woman, since we were unable to show them our real forms or explain why we age so slowly, they fell into a deep depression."

I can see Xavier's nostrils flare as Brannock's deep sadness fills the room. He doesn't feed, though, he just tastes them on the air. Warlocks are big about consent.

"How long have you been on Earth?" I ask, and I see him think about it.

"About one hundred years, give or take a few. We perfected changing identities every twenty to thirty years, moving on, and starting new lives. It does become wearing after a while."

"And how did Smith come to find you?" Xavier asks, and his sadness disappears and the anger returns. He jumps to his feet and starts pacing back and forth.

"I don't know exactly. I think that one of my old friends may be a traitor. I very rarely drink, and once a year, we get together for a reunion of sorts. This year, it was in Vegas. We all met at a restaurant, had dinner, and then went to a bar after. I was mostly sober, and since my glamour is a little tricky to hold when I'm intoxicated, I don't often indulge. Suddenly, I felt off, my head was spinning, and I wasn't in control of my body. I dropped my glamour. Of course the whole bar freaked out. Agent Smith arrived quickly. I remember thinking that was strange. He arrested me and told everyone it was a gas leak, and they were hallucinating. Everyone in the bar was treated by medics. I think they had some solution in the drip that muddled their minds and made them think I wasn't the only weird thing they'd seen that night..." He trails off, and Xavier and I exchange a glance.

"Why would Smith want to arrest or expose you?" Xavier sounds skeptical, but he's only voicing what I was thinking.

Brannock sneers. "Because Smith hates aliens. He would do anything to see the Earth rid of them. I think he may have teamed up with someone to ensure he gets his way. Despite what it appeared like, I don't think the others and me were the only aliens in captivity. I overheard some of the soldiers talking when they took me on the bust of the Pleasure Inn, and I heard them referring to the others and how they probably won't survive many more tests and that they needed new subjects. Don't be surprised if some of the clients from the Pleasure Inn mysteriously disappear. Smith knew he couldn't do that to the master and their family because they are well known, but a few clients of the brothel probably won't be missed."

It's quiet as we mull over what we just heard. None of what he says surprises me. I don't know why it hadn't occurred to us to search the place before now. Maybe we were too trusting, and the Adams brothers have been mostly lost in their grief for their son, his wife, and their missing wife.

Do you believe him? Xavier asks.

Yes, his heart rate didn't jump except at the mention of Smith and, well, I'm sure everyone has that reaction at the mention of his name.

"Okay, thanks for being honest with us, Brannock. I'll talk to the boss men, but I don't see any reason why you can't leave the cells soon. Maybe you should think about where you want to go," Xavier tells him as we stand up. He waves a hand, and the chairs are gone as quickly as they appeared.

"Earth, I need to go back to Earth." He sounds almost desperate, and I shake my head.

"Sorry, buddy, but you are done there. Maybe one day once Smith is nothing but ashes, you can return, but for now, you're going to need a new home. Let us know what you decide. We will do our best to help you in any way we can." Xavier sounds sympathetic. It's such a surprise to see the fearsome warlock show his compassionate side. Lila has worked wonders already, and they are not even bonded.

"Aggghh. Fine." Brannock slumps back down on the bed, looking despondent. "I'll think about it." He lies down and gives us his back.

We leave him be and head back the way we came. When we pass the other occupied cell, Natalia is no longer in cat form. She starts to shout at us, but we can't hear her because of the sound barrier. Xavier drops it just in time for us to hear her yell, "I will make you pay for this. You and that bitch and that omega are all dead. My mother will —" The sound cuts off as Xavier re-erects the barrier.

"Nobody needs to listen to that shit or look at her naked body." He waves a hand and covers her with a dress similar to what I've seen her in before. She looks down, and we can see her scream. Lightning bursts around the room before bouncing off the barrier and sending her flying backward. She hits the wall and slides down, her hair, mane, and fur sticking up like she stuck her finger in a power socket. She's dazed but alive, so we keep walking.

"Come on, let's go share what we learned with the boss men." Xavier waves to the guard who nods his goodbye.

"You think we can trust him?" I ask the warlock, and for a moment, he doesn't reply.

"I have no idea, but I'm going to give him the benefit of the doubt. If he and his unit have been living on Earth for a hundred years, they could have easily taken over, but they didn't. I think that goes a long way in proving they aren't just creatures of war."

"I hope you're right. We have enough drama at the moment. We don't need to add a power hungry alien to the mix," I tell him, but a small feeling of foreboding prickles inside me. I can only pray that I am wrong.

CHAPTER SEVENTEEN

Link

W e watch as Lila leads the Pleasure Inn family away. The quick hug and kiss we exchanged was not long enough for me to surreptitiously check how she is doing. She seems to be stable, so maybe I was worried about nothing, but only time will tell. I think I may need to sit down with both her and Saxon and examine what his blood intake requirements are, then we can work out if she is going to be able to supply him enough or if he will have to substitute feed.

It's not a conversation I'm looking forward to. If I know Lila, and I think I'm getting a good handle on her, she's going to be disappointed if she can't feed him exclusively and feel guilty that she's his blood rose when he could have a Vilaxian blood rose who could give him everything he needs.

She doesn't have anything to worry about though. Just from watching him, I can see he thinks she hung the moon and the stars. While before he had been happy to mingle with the circus crew, he always had a slight cloud of woe surrounding him, like he was just going through the motions and not really enjoying life to the fullest. I had heard rumors that he had grown weary of his clan and was feeding elsewhere, though I am not sure who has been sustaining him, but two of the girls have been very vocal about it not being them. To be honest, recently, the whole clan has been taking advantage of the club and intoxicated crew members looking for fun. It's practically become a sport to feed one of the Vilaxians and see how many times you orgasm while they feed. I was beginning to worry that some of our crew members were becoming addicted to the bite, and I was going to need to give blood transfusions. Maybe with the three new Vilaxians who arrived, that will cease now.

I'm so lost in my thoughts that I don't notice Caspian vibrating next to me until Susie squeaks and steps backward. Cas has changed from his glamour to his half form, and his eyes are flashing between his normal color and the black of his beast. A low rumble is coming from deep inside his chest.

"Is he okay?" Mark whispers as the two of them try not to draw his attention.

Before I can answer, Cas does.

"Yes," he grits out from between clenched teeth. "My beast really wants to see his mate. He doesn't like that she walked away from us."

I place myself in front of the barely controlled shifter and grab his shoulders, drawing his focus to me. "Cas, the quicker we do this, the quicker you can find her and go for a swim. In fact, I bet you'll find her hiding in the pool once she's done with them. It seems to be her go-to place when her emotions overwhelm her, and I bet they are running rampant now that she's had reminders of her parents' deaths."

He struggles, a tentacle wrapping around my leg and creeping higher. His eyes flash to black and stay there.

"Seriously, get it together. Let's get this done, and she's all yours. She would want you to help her best friends. She's placing a lot of trust in you to make sure they get what they need." I shake him, trying to get him to see sense.

Those words seem to do the trick, and the tentacle's grip turns from something that was borderline painful to a gentle, apologetic caress before it slides away.

"Shit," he gasps as his eyes return to normal and he looks down at his shredded clothes on the floor. "I'm sorry. He is feeling needy after her bonding with Saxon and wants to reaffirm his place in her life."

I pat him on the back before going over to a cupboard, pulling out a spare uniform, and tossing it at him.

He changes back and slips on the clothes, not caring one little bit about Mark and Susie. I cover a smirk when neither of them avert their eyes, taking all of Caspian in.

"Lucky Lila," Susie mutters, and Mark grunts his agreement.

"Okay, let's be on our way, shall we? What is your address?" I ask the two former humans who tell me, and then I program it into the machine.

The trip to their home takes no time, and the two of them rush around, throwing things into bags and gathering items they want to take with them.

"What are we going to do to fake our deaths?" Mark asks me, and I'm confused for a moment.

"Is that how they are planning to explain your absence?" Cas asks as he helps Susie pack up their home.

"Yes. They think it will be easier, and we can come back and claim to be our relatives later."

"Do you have wills? Do you need to contact a lawyer and make arrangements in case of an accident? You could leave everything to Lila. She will be able to claim everything for you," I suggest, knowing my girlfriend's backstory is her joining the circus.

"My will already makes Lila the beneficiary," Susie says.

"I have mine going to a charitable foundation. I had no one I wanted to leave it to until Susie, and I haven't had a chance to change it to her."

"Okay, so a quick call to your lawyer is needed. Advise them of the change to the beneficiary. Then, in a week's time, we'll have one of our tech specialists put in a death report for the two of you, and then the relevant authorities will be alerted, and all of those wheels will be put into motion. Or even better, may I suggest you change from your current lawyer to the firm that handled the search for Lila? They are owned by an alien and handle all Earth residing alien affairs, from creating new identities to getting them social security numbers and passports."

Mark spends the next hour on the phone doing what he needs to do. I speak to Mr. Ryding, the lawyer at the firm who was in charge of the search for Lila, and advise him of the situation. He quickly takes over Mark's and Susie's affairs, expediting them for us.

We need to make the house look like it's still lived in and like they planned to come back, but it also needs to be future proofed. Mark and the lawyer arrange it so the apartment will be kept for "Lila," and a company will come in once a month to clean it.

"Mr. Ryding has made it so Lila will be able to transfer all our assets to our new identities, including the life insurance. Mr. Ryding has also assured me that if we choose to return to Earth, he can create new identities with our original education and qualifications so we can easily pick up jobs," Mark explains to Susie at the end of his call.

Finally, they are organized and have gathered everything they want to bring with them into one pile. I activate my watch, and the teleporter transports everything and everyone in one go.

Mark and Susie stumble slightly once we arrive back at the ship.

"Oh, that's going to take a little bit to get used to." Susie grips her stomach and swallows a couple of times.

There are a couple of the crew already waiting to help us transport their things to the room they have been assigned. They'll be on the same floor as Cas and Lila.

"Once you're both settled, why don't you come down to my clinic so I can do a workup on you both? We can see how close you are to obtaining powers, Susie, and Mark, I can show you around, and give you a rundown on how everything works. You are both welcome to come and go in the clinic as often as you want. I know that keeping busy when something is on your mind is a great distraction technique. Also, I'm sure Lila will want to give you the tour of the ship. There are quite a few places she has not explored yet either. She was basically confined to her room the week we spent here between the UK and the US."

"That would be awesome. I'd love to see what kind of tech you have and how much more advanced it is than ours." Mark sounds excited, and Susie smiles indulgently at him.

"Geek," she teases, "but why was Lila confined?"

"I'm sure she will want to tell you everything, so I won't spoil it for her. She's really happy the two of you are here."

"Ah, guys, I'm going to leave you. I can't hold my shift back any longer." Caspian waves goodbye and disappears without waiting for any of us to respond. Poor guy, he did well holding it together this long. Sometimes the Fluxxian beasts completely overrule the person in charge.

"Come on, I'll show you the way while the crew brings everything." I gesture for them to leave the teleporter room, and I can practically feel their excitement. "Your room is on this level. The control deck and a couple of suites are also up here—the Adams brothers', Lila's, and what is now yours," I explain as we walk down the corridor before stopping at the elevator. "This elevator will take you up and down and sideways depending on what button you press when you get inside. The ship is rather big, and we will get you each one of these." I hold up my hand, showing them the communicator watch. "It contains a map of the ship and GPS, which will give you directions if you ever get lost. It can also put you in contact with whomever you wish to speak to." I don't bother pressing the button for the elevator, opting to keep walking.

We get to a viewing window and stop. I step back as Mark's and Susie's mouths drop open at their first glimpse of space. I can't stop the smile from forming when the two of them press against the glass like children at a zoo, trying to take in everything at once.

"Holy fuck," Susie says, reaching subconsciously for Mark's hand.

I can see these two are in sync with one another, and I so desperately want this for myself with Lila. Not seeing her all that much over the last twenty-four hours and worrying about her during her bonding with Saxon made me realize how much I've come to care for her. Her resilience with everything that's been thrown at her is nothing short of admirable, not to mention she's sweet, funny, kind, and sexy as fuck. I hadn't realized how much I wanted to have someone to share my life with. I'd flat out been avoiding it because the people throwing themselves at me were always chosen by my mother, or people who were more impressed with me as heir to the Pleasure Bot Industries empire than me, Dr. Link. It's why the circus was the perfect escape. No one cared who I was here.

Susie and Mark murmur quietly to themselves, marveling over the sight before them. To me, it's normal, but I can imagine seeing it all for the first time must be nothing less than extraordinary.

"I think the scope of what we're doing only just hit me," Mark comments as the two of them step back from the viewing window. "Sure, the aliens and teleportation and all of that was eye-opening, but I didn't comprehend the amazing thing we're doing until that view just there. We're in space, something most humans will never experience."

"Not to mention we're on our way to meet a whole other race who may be your family." Susie squeezes his hand reassuringly, but she is unable to hide the excitement and nerves she's feeling.

"Speaking of which, if you want me to run your DNA, I can do that. It won't take long to find out if you are the missing Celestian heir. All of that information is on an official database from when they went missing. We can know within minutes if you are or not."

I think what I said has shocked them both, and they exchange a glance that seems to be full of words.

"Ah, yeah, I'd like that. Not knowing is kind of driving me crazy. Not that it will change anything, but at least I can go into meeting them prepared."

"Have they been advised of your possible existence?" I ask as we start walking again, and Mark shakes his head.

"No, not yet. Aura was going to message someone, but they didn't get a chance to before we were raided. I admit, I'm worried about how they are going to react. What if they don't care after so long?"

"I very much doubt it. By all reports, the royal family, especially the queens, has been despondent since you disappeared. The only thing holding onto the crown is King Jotan. There have been rumblings of a republic, but so far, he's managed to hold onto the monarchy despite his partners not being fully functioning."

"Do they have other children?" Susie asks, and I shake my head.

"No. Celestian reproduction is fascinating in that it involves magic, and each partner needs to want that baby. If they don't, the magic won't happen no matter how hard they try. Again, rumors say they have tried for another child, but I guess someone's heart wasn't in it. Pining for their missing child would be enough to stop the magic from happening."

"Magic?" Mark sounds curious.

"Yes, I don't know exactly what kind, but I do know that every partner in the relationship needs to be involved. Celestians are polyamorous, and if there are same sex people in the relationship, they are always sexual. I'm not sure of the mechanics, but everyone needs to have sex with each person in the group, and then the magic takes over. From what I understand, the magic takes a piece from each partner, combines it, and then implants it into whoever has been chosen to carry the child. If it is an all-male grouping, the magic allows for one of the males to temporarily carry a baby. The baby is always a genetic blend of each partner. This also works with non-Celestian partners."

We finally make it to the room they have been assigned. I knock, and it's answered by Crimson, who looks relieved to see Mark and Susie. She pulls them both into a hug. "I was worried you would change your minds and stay," she says when she pulls away.

"I don't think that was ever an option—not that we'd want to," she quickly reassures Crimson when her face falls slightly.

"I'm going to leave you to it and let you settle in for a while. The others can explain about the replicators, and someone should have delivered communication watches by now." I look at Crimson for confirmation.

She nods and holds up her wrist. "They did. I'm excited to get out and explore. Come on." She pulls them both inside and then waves to me.

"We'll see you soon. I really want to have the test done," Mark calls over his shoulder.

"Just send me a message. I won't be far away if I'm not in my clinic." The door closes behind them, and I turn, moving toward Lila's room. I want to check on her before I go back to my clinic. I need to reassure myself she's still coping with the change.

She was looking a little flushed when they arrived back from Earth, and I want to ensure that's because Xavier put it there and it wasn't some adverse reaction to the change.

When I get to her room, I knock on the door, but there is no answer, so I press my watch.

"Find Lila," I order it. It takes a moment to scan the ship.

"Lila Jenson is on the Aquilia level," the mono-syllable robot voice replies. I smile. I was almost certain it was going to tell me that.

"Find Caspian."

"Caspian is on the Aquilia level."

Good, he found her. I'll leave them, but as I make my way to my clinic, I send a message for them to find me once they have finished their swim.

Back in my clinic, I collapse into a seat and sigh. It's been a busy couple of hours, and I really could do with some food. Just as I'm about to get up and program my replicator, the incoming call alert sounds. Looking at the big screen in front of me, I grimace at the name it's displaying.

Deianira Delrose, my mother.

Fuck, what does that woman want now?

I press the button to accept the call, and her face appears on the screen. We take a moment to study each other. My mother has a mane of luxuri-ous, shiny, copper metal-colored locks with matching eyes. She has sharp cheekbones and lush lips, and she is curvy in all the right places. It's all part of being the CEO of Pleasure Bot industries. I know she didn't look like that when she was younger, but she has manipulated her nanobots so she has an appealing package despite being rotten to the core.

"Son," she finally says, looking down her nose at me.

"Mother," I reply, sounding equally as unenthusiastic. "To what do I owe this pleasure?"

She scowls at my obvious sarcasm. "I have been trying to reach Josa, but he is not answering his communications."

I scoff, unable to contain my laughter, and her scowl deepens.

"What is it, Link? Stop being obtuse."

"Well, there is a good reason why you can't reach him. He's dead."

Her scowl turns to a look of fury. "What? How? Who is responsible? I will bring my wrath down on them."

I lean back in my chair and cross my arms with a smirk, knowing this will drive my mother crazy. "Josa made an unwise political alliance which almost resulted in the Adams brothers' granddaughter's death."

"That's hardly worthy of a death sentence," she scoffs insensitively, and I tamp down my own wave of anger. I don't need her paying attention to how much I care about Lila.

"To you, maybe, but the Adamses value their

family members, not to mention she is the Crown Prince of Westalin's intimate. He was none too happy with the situation and meted out his own punishment, as is his right."

Now this gets a worthy reaction. My mother pales and shrinks back from the screen slightly, but I still catch it. The woman is off balance, and I love seeing it. As big as her political ambitions are, she won't risk catching the eye or the wrath of the warlocks. My mother is not stupid enough to take on one of the superpowers of the galaxy.

"Well, that is unfortunate." She recovers quickly, sighing like she's been inconvenienced. "I guess I will have to select you a new fiancé."

I sit up in my chair and shake my head. "I assure you that will not be necessary. I am in a relationship, and I am very happy."

Her eyebrows jump in surprise, the only outward sign of emotion on her face. "Oh? Who?" she asks, and I hover a finger over the button.

"No one of any interest to you, Mother. I'm sorry to cut this short, but I have a patient coming in soon. Give my love to Father if you see him." I cut off the call before she can start badgering me for answers, but just before the screen dissolves, her surprise gives way to fury once more, and I shudder at the look in her eye. My mother is scheming, and that is not good, but it's a problem for another time.

I have other things to worry about now, namely

finding the DNA profile of the missing Celestian heir so I can compare it to Mark's when he comes down. That will keep me distracted until Cas and Lila surface again.

CHAPTER EIGHTEEN

Caspian

It's all I can do to stop myself from shredding my clothes and shifting midway to the right level. My kraken would destroy the elevator if he exploded in here, and then I'd be in big trouble, so I hold him in as I make my way to the Aquilian pool.

The minute the doors open on that level, he pushes his way through, and I manage to get us out of the elevator and strip off my clothes before my body makes a full shift.

Mate, he bellows inside my head before letting out an ear-splitting roar that makes the calm water of the pool ripple. He throws us into the pool, allowing me to navigate and not forcing me to the back like he usually does when he takes control. The water is bright as we make our way farther into the depths of the pool. The reef, which is normally teeming with fish, is strangely deserted, but I guess that's no surprise with him being the apex predator in the pool.

A blur of color out of the corner of our eye has my kraken rolling and bracing for impact. The blur collides with us, the force sending us tumbling off course, our tentacles wrapping around the offending creature. My kraken roars, unhappy that he has once again been cockblocked from his mate. He bares his teeth and snaps at what has attacked us, but then quickly withdraws at the sharp, stabbing pain in our side. We release the offending creature and fill the water surrounding us with ink, making it impossible for anyone, including us, to see, but he barrels through it, the ink having no effect on him this time.

Ha! You will not be able to stop me so easily this time! A voice echoes through our mind. *You caught me unaware last time, but I activated my forcefield before I attacked*, he gloats, brandishing his trident at me as he appears directly in front of me. If I squint, I can make out the shimmer of magic that surrounds him. Apart from their shape shifting and singing abilities, this is one of the other things the Aquilians can do. *Bad kraken! You must not ravish without consent. My little sea squirt is weeping at the bottom of the pool in the jewel cavern. I do not think she wants your giant member penetrating her lovely soft depths right at the moment. She needs comfort, not cock.*

Nikos's ridiculous words have us both pausing

and considering what he just said. Lila is crying? I guess memories of her parents pushed her over the edge on top of everything else, not to mention she may still be recovering from her blood rose bonding with Saxon. Turning our backs on the surprisingly thoughtful merman, we continue in the direction of the jewel cave but at a slower and less sexually frenzied pace. I can feel my kraken's worry for his mate. Although human emotions don't really register with him, it's more animal instincts. He does understand the concept of sadness and hates that his mate feels this way. We dart in and out of the coral reef until we get to the special cave.

We pause just outside the entrance, my beast unsure if we should approach Lila or not, but I quickly push myself forward and do a half change, assuring him I will make sure our mate is alright. He grumbles somewhat, but her well-being is more important than anything, so he will wait his turn.

Swimming through the entrance, the strange phosphorus light that glows down here, makes all the gems incrusted in the wall sparkle and shine. I find Lila huddled on one corner of the cave and, surprisingly enough, sheltering in a giant anemone that seems to have appeared overnight. She's curled up on her side, and her eyes are closed, but her face is blotchy like she's been crying. The anemone tentacles wave back and forth, caressing her body in a soothing motion.

I should probably just swim away and leave her

be, but my heart aches at the thought that she's been crying and exhausted herself enough that she fell asleep down here in a very unfamiliar place. So, instead of leaving, I push my way through the anemone tentacles. The stings feel like electrical shocks, but my body soon adjusts, and the sensation fades away. I gather her into my arms, wrap my tentacles around my sleeping mate, and nuzzle into her neck. She groans, and as her eyes open, a sad little smile crosses her face as she hugs me back, her own tentacles tangling with mine.

Hello. Did you get Mark and Susie all settled? she asks into my mind. Of course her first thoughts are about someone else. She is so attentive to everyone else's needs.

I did, baby, but what about you? Are you okay?

She sighs and snuggles into me, grabbing another tentacle and draping it over her.

I am, but it's been a lot, you know? Being reminded that there was a suite for me and that I'm living in my parents' space was all a bit much. My memories of them are fuzzy at best, and I guess it's just a big reminder that they are not here, teaching me everything I need to know, or that I could have grown up knowing about all of this.

And how do you feel about bonding with Saxon? I ask, addressing the other question that's been bugging me. *Just like me, you didn't really know him, and I want to make sure you're doing okay.*

A slow smile spreads across her lips, and she leans in and kisses me softly. *I'm good... great, really, because just like you, he's been sweet and attentive, and the sex was out of this world. I mean, there could be worse things to endure than having to feed a sexy vampire every day.* She pulls back and studies me closely. *Are you okay? I don't want you to feel left out or ignored or anything like that, so if you start to feel that way, especially when I bond with Xavier and Link, I want you to tell me.*

A grin spreads across my face. *Link too, huh?*

She blushes slightly and shrugs. *Link's the only one I've really had a choice about. He's my choice, and I'm hoping once I ask him, he'll say yes.* She pauses for a moment, and I can see her thinking about something. *How does one ask another to fuck her and give her many orgasms until they are sealed in holy matrimony?*

I will be happy to give you as many orgasms as you want, my pretty periwinkle. I will put my sea cucumber in your clam, and you will have mind-blowing orgasms. Nikos's voice pierces my brain, and when Lila winces, I can tell it's in hers too. We both turn, and there, peeking through the anemone tentacles, is the annoying merman.

How can you hear our conversation? Lila asks, sitting up and scowling at the merman. *I wasn't actually talking about you. I don't want to have sex with you.*

His face drops, and I kind of feel bad for the poor guy. On his planet, he's in demand, so I don't think he's ever had to work for anything in his life. It's actually kind of amusing seeing Lila shut him down every time.

His smile returns, and he shakes his finger at her.

Oh, my little snappy crab, I know you are telling me lies. He turns, and on his shoulder is Lila's Skarrian attraction mark. *This is telling me you want to stroke my fins and maybe my giant manhood as well. I promise it would be so good.* He runs his hands down his chest and over his tail, smiling. *I will teach you to coax it out of my slit and how to handle it just right.* Something undulates under the skin, and a slit forms in his scales, pulsing a little. I think Lila and I were slightly mesmerized by it all, but a stinging anemone tentacle brushes against me again, and I jolt out of my daze.

Damn it, Nikos! Did you just use your voice to coerce us? Away with you. I unwrap myself from my mate and shoo him away.

He swims backward, laughing in delight. *I will wear you down, my sweet rainbow fish*, he calls back before disappearing out of the cave.

I return to where Lila is still lying inside the anemone. I settle down beside her, but she's wearing a pensive look on her face.

Why is he wearing my mark? I don't like him at all, she asks, sounding confused, and I try to smother the grin that wants to break out. I don't think I succeeded, however, because she scowls at me. *I don't! He's a misogynistic, rapey, full of himself asshole.*

Yeah, but he's hot, right? And kind of adorable with all that arrogance. He is bound and determined to win you over. I think it's awesome you're making him work for it. The guy hasn't had to work for anything in his life.

She continues to scowl as she mulls it over, and then she sighs. *He is sexy, and I can't deny that mermaid sex fascinates me. Although it would have to be above the surface, because I can't breathe underwater in my human form, and I'm not sure my half form and the merman are compatible.*

I chuckle and pull her into my arms. *The merman won't care. He seems happy to stick his dick into anything.*

She screws up her nose. *Ew, do you think I need to worry about diseases from him then?*

I chuckle and shake my head. *No. All of the circus workers take a shot that protects us against anything sexually transmitted. You would have had the same thing when you first arrived. Link would have done it when he implanted your translator. Also, I don't think Nikos has been having sex with anyone since he's been on board. He tends to stay in the pool and not venture out like the others. It's probably why he's so damn horny.*

She's quiet for a moment, and my beast starts to stroke a tentacle up and down her own tentacles, caressing them and brushing closer and closer to her sexual opening each time.

What was that slit and the thing that was moving under it? Was it what I think it was?

If you're guessing that it's his cock pouch, then you're right. The slit is sealed until they are feeling amorous, and then it opens. In mer form, the female needs to coax it out of the slit by rubbing their tails together and swimming around the male. This also creates slick for the female, which makes it easier for her to accept his member into her own sexual slit. Once she accepts him into her body, their scales lock together and they mate while swimming through the currents of water, bound together until they both orgasm and the female's body releases the male."

She shudders as my beast slides his tentacle in and out of her sexual opening, teasing her.

Oh wow... that... She pants slightly. *That feels so good. Is it weird that I'm enjoying this? I feel kind of dirty and kinky and I'm conflicted.*

Being in half form? I ask, even though I'm pretty sure that's what she means.

She nods, biting her lip as her eyes flash back to her beast's again. I take her mouth with mine, tangling my tongue with hers, and nip her lip at the same time I pluck her nipples with another tentacle, the little suckers latching on and sucking them.

It's all perfectly normal for shifters, baby, but we can stop if you feel uncomfortable, I tell her, pulling away, but she grabs me and holds me in place.

Don't you dare, she growls, her beast pushing its way to the front.

What do you say we shift fully and let our beasts play? I think you'll find they are both easier to handle if we do.

A purring sound comes out of her mouth, and she nods her head. I remove my tentacles from her body and pull away. She tries to hang onto me, but I untangle her tentacles from mine.

We need to move out of the cave, our beasts are too big to shift in here, I coax her, and she follows me out of the cave.

Our beasts push forward swiftly, and we shift from our half form to full animal form.

Let your beast take over, I tell her. *I'm not sure we need the mental scars of their mating.*

I hear her hum her agreement, but then her mind fades out, so I allow mine to do the same. A little nap is probably just what I need right now.

W hen I wake up, I've returned to my human form, and Lila and I are lying on the entrance platform near the elevator. I hear a humming sound next to us, and when I turn my head, I find Nikos sitting on the edge, comb in hand, brushing his long, golden locks like a mermaid cliché. When he sees me move, he tosses the comb back into the water quickly and leers at us, wagging his eyebrows. "Is it my turn now? Your beasts are insatiable, and their copulating was magnificent. It has me all worked up."

"What did you do? Watch them like a David Attenborough Animal Planet documentary, you perv?" Lila mutters, lurching up and cupping her breasts with her hands and crossing her legs.

Nikos frowns at her movements, disappointed

that he can no longer see her naked bits. "I do not know what that is, but yes, it was very entertaining. Unfortunately, I cannot relieve myself in this form without mermaid assistance, but I would be happy to change to my two-legged form so you could help me. Either of you."

He makes it sound like he would be doing us a favor, and I want to grin at the audacity of it all, but I'm pretty sure he would take that as encouragement. He starts to drag his tail out of the water, and Lila quickly holds her hands up to stop him. His eyes widen with delight and lock onto her breasts, and she quickly slaps them back over.

I can't help it, I snort with amusement. The two of them are ridiculous, and I think Lila is just prolonging the inevitable, but if that makes her feel more comfortable, then I'm not going to say a word. She's already struggling with the multiple mates without choices thing. At least with Nikos it would be her choice. Aquilians don't have fated mates like a lot of other species.

"Get away. If and when Lila is interested in pursuing more with you, she will let you know," I growl at the merman, who changes his teeth to shark's teeth and bares them, hissing at me.

"Fine, but stay out of my pool until you make a decision." He picks up his trident, which had been lying next to him on the deck, flips himself off the edge, and disappears into the depths without another look back.

"Fuck!" I groan, getting to my feet and holding my hand out to Lila.

"What does he mean by that?" she asks, taking my hand and allowing me to help her up. I pick up the shirt I discarded earlier and hand it to Lila. She pulls it on, covering her delicious body, as I pull on my discarded pants and pick up my shoes and all of her clothes.

"What he means is that we won't be allowed to swim in here while he has a tantrum."

"But we need it." She stares at the pool long-ingly, and I wrap an arm around her shoulders and steer her to the elevator, pressing the button.

"We will be okay. We're headed toward planets where we can actually swim in their oceans, unlike Earth, and I have a feeling now that our beasts have been allowed out together, they will be satisfied for a while."

The elevator closes behind us, and I press the button for our floor. It moves up, and I see Lila concentrate internally.

"I can't actually feel her at all. It's kind of peaceful. She always has some kind of opinion to impart." She snuggles into my side, and I press a kiss to the top of her head.

"Mine's the same, but I can tell he's content, smugly satisfied, and happy, so I guess we know what to do if either of them get too pushy in the future."

"Kinky kraken sex for the win." She holds up

her hand for a high five, and I give her one as the door opens on the right floor. We step out and walk down to our room. As we pass the grandpas' room, the door opens, and Eric sticks his head out.

"Ah, there you both are. Do you have a moment?"

Lila looks down at her naked legs. "Can you give me ten minutes to change?"

"Yep, sure, but then come back here. William and I need to talk about something with you." Eric sounds serious, unlike the playful fun guy he's been in the past.

"Okay, we'll hurry," she assures him and takes my hand, dragging me quickly to our room.

"I wonder what they want?" she murmurs as we enter, and I drop her hand.

"There's only one way to find out," I tell her, and we both hurry to our respective rooms to get dressed.

CHAPTER NINETEEN

Lila

A long, hot shower later, I'm feeling a little more stable. The last forty-eight hours have been memorable to say the least, and my emotions have been all over the place, but for the first time since I became aware of her, my beast is satisfied, and that is one less thing to worry about for the moment. I can finally concentrate on other things, like my newly cemented bond with Saxon, my only a little older mating with Caspian, and finally, my ill grandfather. I didn't believe when they first told me John had been poisoned. Who would want to poison him? Out of all three of my grandfathers, he's probably the nicest and certainly the least annoying. It's like trying to poison Santa Claus. Unthinkable.

Drying off, I dress in a pair of yoga pants and a

hoodie, wanting comfort over style, and go in search of Cas. I made him shower after me because if we had been together in the same one, I probably would have ridden his cock like a pogo stick. I can't seem to resist any of my mates. Speaking of which, I need to find time to talk to Link. I desperately want to bind him to me. There's an irrational side of me that won't be happy until I seal him to me in the Skarrian way, but I want to make sure it's what he wants. I know what it's like to have that choice taken away from me more than most, and while I love Cas and I'm sure it won't be long before I feel that way for Saxon, I still want Link to have a choice.

If he isn't interested, though, I'm not sure what that would mean for us. I guess we would have to stop having sex, and I'm not sure I can just be friends with him since what I feel is so much more than friendship.

"Cas, are you ready?" I call through his open door. He's not in the bedroom, so I'm assuming he's in the bathroom.

"Yeah, I'm just moisturizing my tentacles. They seem to be a bit dry. I'll just be a moment," he calls back, and I'm speechless for a moment. Moisturizing his tentacles? You know what? That's a problem for future Lila. I turn and head out to the kitchen, programming the replicator to pour me a big ass glass of wine. While I wait, I think about my predicament.

Fucking hell, how do Skarrians cope with these stupid biological rules? I mean, who only has sex five times before deciding they want to spend the rest of their lives together? There must be a lot of non-mutual orgasms happening in relationships. I can just see it now. *No, honey, it's my turn for an orgasm, you got the last one. Now get down on your knees and open your mouth.*

No wonder Magenta is so free with her body. The grandpas did explain that it's easier on Skarr. You grow up with people who you end up in groups with. By the time you reach sexual maturity, you basically know who you want to spend the rest of your life with. The grandpas and my grandmother had known each other since they were children, and there was no doubt in any of their minds that they would bond. Apparently, it is common to have a sort of Skarrian Rumspringa, though, when they turn eighteen. It's basically spring break spread out over a year, where they get out and explore the planet, drink, take drugs, party hard, and sow their sexual oats. It's fully acceptable—even though you may have made a decision on your family group— for every member to fuck as many different people as they can just to make sure they are truly happy with their choices. It's actually a requirement, and you can't officially get married without having done this.

Sure, there is nothing to stop you from forming the bond with your chosen ones, but the Skarrian government won't acknowledge it without an official ceremony, and you can't have the ceremony without producing your... I guess fuck passport is the best term for it. It lists all sexual relations for your eighteenth year. This assures officials you are happy with your decision. Seriously, it's so fucking weird, I'm still having a hard time wrapping my head around it.

The replicator beeps, telling me my wine is done. I reach in and pull out the glass before taking a sip. It's a bit tarter than I prefer, and I shudder slightly, but by the second mouthful, I've adjusted. I sigh, feeling some of the tension drain out of my body before taking another sip. Yup, this is what I needed. It would be even better if Susie was on the couch with her own glass, but it is now a possibility, so I'm not too upset that she's not here right at this moment.

"Everything okay?" Cas asks, coming up behind me and putting a hand on my shoulder. I sink back into him, my gorgeous, caring husband, and sigh again.

"Yeah, just a lot going on in my mind." I turn so I'm facing him, careful not to spill my wine, but stop and frown, looking him up and down. He's in human form and wearing sweats. "I thought you were moisturizing your tentacles?"

"I was, and then I changed form. They seem to absorb the lotion better if I don't run around on them for a few hours after."

I open my mouth to ask more questions but quickly slam it shut. *Future Lila problems.* "Have I told you how much I love you today?" I ask him instead, then I wrap my arms around him and lean my head against his chest, which is covered in a hoodie similar to mine. When I look up at him, there's a huge smile spread across his lips.

"No, but feel free to tell me as many times as you like, I love hearing it," he says and leans down and kisses me. It starts to turn heated, so I pull away.

"Come on, I think we've let the grandpas wait long enough. If I know them, one will be knocking on our door in no time."

I take his hand with my free one and drag him and my wine toward the door.

"You know I feel the same way," he tells me, and I turn back and grin at him.

"Yeah, I do, but you're right, it's awesome to hear it, so keep telling me."

It's not long before we're knocking on the door to my grandpas' suite. Eric must have either used his speed to get there or just been standing on the other side, because it opens before I've even dropped my hand.

His sigh is full of frustration as he gestures for us to come inside. "Finally, you're both here. Now we can start this family meeting."

My eyes slide to all the people waiting on the sofa, and a big grin crosses my lips because it's not just William waiting for us, but also Saxon, Link, and Xavier as well. I love that my grandpas have included all of them, but I still need to have that convo with Link. Maybe I should do it before the family meeting, because I have a funny feeling that I know what this is going to be about.

"Well, come on, don't just stand there." William waves us forward, but before we do, I stop Cas and lean in to whisper to him.

"I really need to talk to Link for a moment. Can you distract the others so I can have a quiet word with him?"

"Of course," he agrees, and we move over to the long sectional.

Cas takes a seat on the end, but I make my way down the line, stopping first at Xavier and giving him a kiss before moving farther down to shuffle my butt between Saxon and Link. Turning to Saxon, I smile at my newest husband, still feeling the slight awkwardness of a new relationship.

"Hi, I missed you," I tell him, and he leans in and nuzzles my neck, giving it a nip without breaking the skin before pulling away.

"I missed you too. Glad to see you're okay after your swim."

I feel my eyebrows jump in surprise. Leaning forward, I place my glass of wine on the table while I gather my thoughts. "You know about that?" I'm not sure if he's talking about the mental breakdown or our krakens doing the beast with the two backs.

"Yes. I searched for you after I finished with Susie and Mark," Link tells me.

"And the Aquilian merman messaged me to let me know." Saxon has a confused little purse to his lips that makes me grin. Huh? The can of tuna has a surprisingly thoughtful side. Extremely surprising.

"I'm okay. I really needed the swim, and Cas joined me, and we let our beasts out to frolic. I'm feeling a lot more stable, and she seems to be satisfied for now."

"Good, but I still want to do another full exam when we're done here just to make sure." My sexy doctor has the cutest little furrow between his silver eyebrows, and I just want to reach up and smooth it out, so I do. The frown drops, and his gaze turns from concerned to soft.

"I missed you too," I whisper, moving a little closer and letting the rest of the background noise fade away. I hear Caspian ask Xavier and Saxon about the Aaz'axian, but I tune all that out so I can focus on the cyborg in front of me. "Cas is distracting the others so I can ask you a question."

I take one of his hands in mine. It's the arm with the display screen built into it, and I run my finger over it, marveling at the fact that there is a seamless join between it and his skin. You would think it would be obvious, but if my eyes were closed, I wouldn't even know it was there. It is turned off at the moment and blank, so my fingers don't activate any programs as I continue to caress his skin, awkwardly considering how to approach this topic without making too much of a fool out of myself. I know we discussed it earlier, and he said he was in, but I'm trying to make this official, a proposal I guess, and I just know I'm going to fuck it up.

"Lila, look at me." Link places a finger under my chin and lifts it so I can't avoid looking into his molten silver eyes. "What do you want to talk about?"

"Well, I just wanted to double-check that you want to be here. Like Eric said, this is a family meeting, and the other three are all destined to be my mate, but you actually get a choice. I know we've been seeing where this will take us, but Skarrians don't really have a lot of options for prolonging the getting to know you part of the relationship unless we want to forgo sex, and from the way my body has been acting, we are highly sexual creatures, so I don't really understand how we ended up with the five goes and then we're bonded physiology."

I'm rambling because I'm nervous, but he just sits there, giving me his full attention.

"I guess what I'm asking is—shit, I don't know what I'm asking. My mind, which is firmly entrenched in human traditions, is telling me that it is too fucking soon to ask you to marry me, but fuck, I want to. My body, on the other hand, is riding me hard, insisting that you are ours and to ride *you* hard. I guess I kind of need to know if you're on board." A sudden lump develops in my throat. "Because I guess if you're not, I'm going to have to put an end to this relationship before my feelings develop even deeper, because I'm already in pretty deep." I break off finally, getting everything out in one great big word dump.

Link has a perfect poker face, and I have no idea how he is feeling by looking at him. Right this moment, I can see the machine part of him vividly. It's almost like he's not even breathing, and my heart starts to race even harder. Fuck, he doesn't want this.

I go to pull my hand out of his. "Gosh, I'm so sorry, I thought we might be on the same page."

Just as I remove my hand, he clamps his down hard, stopping me from going anywhere. "We are. I'm sorry, but my emotions overloaded me, and I short-circuited for a moment and needed to reboot. Yes, yes, I will marry you," he all but shouts before hauling me into his lap and kissing me hard.

I place my hand on his cheek, kissing him back just as hard, completely thrilled with his answer. Dropping my hand, I start to remove his shirt, desperate to get on with the bonding part of the evening, when a cleared throat penetrates my happiness, and I freeze. Holy fuck, I was going to seal this bond in front of my grandfathers. Seriously, someone needs to neuter me, because I'm like a horny dog humping everyone's legs. I peel back from Link, releasing my hold on his shirt, feeling my face flame with embarrassment. I turn on his lap, staying on it so Eric and William don't catch sight of the very prominent erection he is rocking.

My other mates are all smiling with amusement, but William's eyebrow is cocked, and Eric's arms are crossed, and neither of them look impressed. "Whoops, sorry," I say.

William sighs. "It's fine, we know what it's like, but this conversation needs to be had first. Strange things have been happening, and in light of the situation, we need to brief your partners on everything."

"Brief us on everything?" Xavier can't hide the curiosity in his voice, and Eric waves a hand.

"Can you secure the room against listening ears?" he asks my warlock, who quickly complies. The seven of us are surrounded by a large, domed purple barrier.

"No one should be able to penetrate that," Xavier assures us, and Eric and William exchange glances.

"Lila knows this, but the four of you need to know too. The Galaxy Circus is not just a diplomatic trade and peace keeping organization. The specific reason it was originally created was to guard the orb of power." When I look at William as he explains our mission, I realize that he looks exhausted. In fact, both he and Eric look like the weight of the world is on them at the moment.

I feel Link's entire body tense beneath me, and Saxon sits upright, completely at attention, like his military training just kicked into overdrive.

"Holy fuck," Xavier mutters, and when I look at Cas, his blue skin has paled significantly.

"The Adams family are the guardians of the orb, and it has been in our possession since the end of the Una's and Aaz'axian war. Lila will be the next guardian, and any of her mates will also be bound due to the nature of the arrangement. All of you will be in danger if this information gets out."

The room is silent as we let the guys absorb this information.

"The oath of loyalty that the circus performers take when they join is somewhat of a smokescreen in that it is a spell that pledges their loyalty to us and doesn't allow them to turn on us in the event that this knowledge becomes public. It is also why we have so many powerful families as part of the circus."

"I knew it," Link mutters. "But if you have the orb, then why don't you use that to heal John?"

I jump to my feet. "Holy shit, Link's right. We can heal him right now."

Eric and William shake their heads, their faces grave.

"Unfortunately if we use the orb to heal John, it will give off a pulse that will call every person who has ever wanted world domination directly to our doorstep. The thing can't be destroyed, and it can't be used unless we want to advertise its location. It's basically useless. Our ancestors promised the Una's that we wouldn't use it unless we had explored all other options. In the end, if we need to use it to heal John, we will, because if he dies, then the orb becomes unprotected unless we hand its protection over to you."

"It's been a long time since the war, and the orb has basically faded into memory, so most people won't even remember its existence," Xavier argues, and Eric shrugs.

"Yes, but the ones who do are the ones we need to worry about. John's illness is too suspicious not to worry us. What better motivation than to kill one of us so that the orb is no longer protected?"

"But the suspect list is short. Apart from us, Lila's parents, and now Lila, no one else knows we have the orb."

"But Lila's parents are dead, so they wouldn't have told anyone," Caspian points out, and Xavier stiffens.

"Hang on. What if that's what they told my parents during the secret conversation they had in the memory hidden in Lila's brain?"

Eric and William exchange another loaded glance before William nods. "Yes, we have considered it, but Alina and Marcus would not have told Cronus and Xylene unless they trusted them without a doubt. They entrusted their only child's well-being to them. No, we don't believe they are involved at all."

"What about your wife?" Saxon asks carefully. "She disappeared without a trace and no body has ever been recovered."

I wince at the suggestion and at the devastated looks on my grandfathers' faces, but they don't get angry.

Eric sags in his seat. "Yes, it is something we have considered as well. Liliana never reappeared, and although she could have been lost to the vastness of space, none of us have felt the bond break. It's why we have never given up looking for her or moved on with another woman, but we also have to accept that she may have been tortured or coerced into giving up the information."

The room falls into a heavy silence as we all take in the troubling information.

Before anything else can be said, the communication screen on their wall lights up. William reaches over and presses a button, and Bubby's face appears on the screen.

CHAPTER TWENTY

Lila

"Go ahead, Broderick," William orders the captain.

"Good evening, sir. Sorry to interrupt. The circus pod has docked with the ship, and we are now ready to make the leap into hyperspace. I have set a direct course for Celestia."

"Actually, we need to change that. Iceen is on this side of Celestia, and from what Xavier and Saxon tell me, it would be best if we stopped there first before going to Celestia. We can't be carting that she beast around in the brig all over the galaxy."

"Certainly, sir. I will make the changes." We see Bubby moving, and I guess he's changing what he needs to. "It will take us approximately fifty-five Earth hours before we are in Iceen's orbit. I will

263

ensure that we have the necessary clearance to dock at their space station and for you to beam down to the planet."

"Excellent, and I will advise the matriarch that we are returning her wayward daughter, as well as informing her of our endorsement of the Astrea streak as the next matriarchal family. I'm sure she will not step down easily and there will be a fight, but that may all be over with by the time we arrive. Maxsim would have informed his mother of our support by now, and hopefully she will have taken steps to ensure that insufferable female has been removed from power."

"Excellent, sir." Bubby nods. "I will sound the ten-minute alarm for the hyper leap." The screen clears, and seconds later, a siren similar to the one in the circus pod starts to play over speakers in the room. Everyone stands up, but I stay seated. I will be finishing my glass of wine before anything else happens.

"We will continue this conversation about the orb once John is back to normal, but we thought it would be best that you all knew. I trust you will keep it to yourselves, but think about what I said. You may notice other strange things that have been happening," William says as Xavier removes the sound barrier.

"Come on, Lila, you need to strap in for the jump."

Link tries to pull me to my feet, but I stubbornly

hold my place on the sofa. "Oh no. The last time this happened, I ended up mated and pregnant."

Caspian chuckles and ruefully runs a hand through his hair, having the grace to look a little embarrassed. I mean, it took two of us to tango, so the blame doesn't lie solely in his court, but when I jumped into that pod with him, I was expecting nothing, and it got wild, weird, and wonderful.

"It's not like that. You literally stay strapped in for five minutes, and there are seats all over the ship. You can even bring your wine if you want," he coaxes, but he hit the magic words, so I stand up and drain my glass before going to the replicator to order another.

"Fine, but if I find myself naked and pregnant with another mate that isn't one of the four here, then I am holding you responsible." I think about what I just said and frown at the glass I just emptied. "That's pretty strong stuff, isn't it?" I ask as I pull the fresh one out of the replicator.

Xavier wraps an arm around my shoulders and escorts me out of the suite. When we get to the corridor, I blink in surprise. Seats have popped out of the wall all along the hallway, and everyone has strapped themselves into one. My warlock leads me to one, helps me down, and assists me with the straps.

"Yes, the wine you are drinking is Husad mead. It is from Husadavia, an uninhabited planet in the Kavar system. The planets and animals on it are carnivorous and lethal, and it takes a special kind of being to harvest the fruit from the halla bush. It's quite popular and potent. Don't have any more after this one unless you don't want to remember the rest of your evening," he suggests, taking the glass out of my hand and sipping it. He then passes the glass to Link. "You better have some also and even out this playing field."

"What do you mean?" I ask, watching my precious wine disappear into Link's luscious mouth.

"Well, you're halfway to hammered, and I'm almost certain the minute we reach hyperspeed, you're going to jump Link and take care of that matter you were discussing previously."

"Did you all hear that?" I ask, looking at the men strapped in around me, feeling my cheeks heat.

"Yes, Lila, we all have enhanced hearing. There was no hiding you proposing to Link, as awkwardly adorable as that rambling mess was." Eric chuckles, and William joins in.

"Doesn't she remind you of her mother? Alina was always awkward as can be. She would turn as red as a tomato every time Broderick and Marcus would tease her about things. They would gang up on her. I'm pretty sure she finally worked up the courage to invite Bubby into their group when they had their accident." The affection he has for my mother is evident in his voice, and I feel a pang of longing again. I really need to spend some time just talking with my grandpas and learning everything I can about my parents.

Well, great, so everyone knows that I want to jump Link's bones. I mean, I'm pretty sure they already knew that, but they are going to specifically know that in a short period of time, I'm going to be rocking his mind with my mad sex skills.

"I'm not sure I needed to hear that, Lila," William tells me, looking slightly ill.

"Wait… Did I say that out loud?"

"Yes, Lila, your inside voice has become your outside voice. I told you that wine was strong." Xavier chuckles as I squirm with embarrassment.

The flashing red light turns blue, and Captain Potter's voice comes over the loudspeaker. "Prepare for jump in three… two… one… Go!"

The ship shudders slightly, and then it's like we hit Mach fifty in the space of a breath. My body is thrust back against the chair, and my internal organs feel like they are being squeezed through a meat grinder. I would groan, but all the air has left my lungs. My eyes feel like they are about to pop out of my head, and black spots appear in my vision.

Just as soon as it started, it's over once more.

The pressure on my body releases, and I can finally suck in a breath of air before it whooshes out on a moan of pain. "Holy fuck, that was horren-dous," I rasp, trying to get control of my body again. I can't seem to get my limbs to cooperate with me, but I'm glad I didn't poop my pants. "Help! My body won't work!" I call out, not even able to look at Link.

"It's okay, give it a moment, and everything will come back online," Link coos next to me, sounding completely normal.

"How are you not affected?" I demand.

"It's completely normal for all of us. Such a big ship takes an immense amount of power to get into warp speed. Trust me, after you do it a time or two, you won't notice it either."

"There are tricks to it. Taking a large breath and holding it helps. But yeah, the first few jumps are a bit much," Xavier assures me as a tingling pins and needles feeling washes over my body.

"Ugh, that's not much better," I mumble as I wiggle my toes and fingers, trying to speed the sensation along. Finally, I regain control of myself, and I can swivel my head and take in everyone else. None of them seem to be having the same kind of problems as me, so hopefully they are right, and my body will adjust. "So what now?"

"We stay strapped in until Captain Potter gives us the all clear. It's to make sure the ship has stabilized in warp. Sometimes, and I mean very rarely, it will fall out of warp, and we have to do it again," Saxon explains, reaching over, grabbing my hand, and giving it a squeeze.

"Fuck, really?"

"Yes, but it hasn't happened for ages. It's usually

when the warp core needs an upgrade, and it just had one before we docked at Earth." Eric smiles at me, and I think it's supposed to be reassuring, but one can never tell with him.

"So what happens now?' I ask.

"What do you mean?" William looks confused.

"Well, is there anything special that has to happen while we're traveling?"

His frown disappears, and he shakes his head. "Nope, you just do whatever you want. Travel is dealt with by the flight deck crew. You can shop or go to any of the entertainment outlets on board. If we were going to another show, the performers may rehearse if they want to change their act or fix something in it, but your time is yours."

"Excellent. I'd like to propose a family dinner, but I feel like we need to wait until John is able to attend as well."

"As soon as we're done with Iceen, we'll head straight to Celestia, and they will be able to help us with John. He will be thrilled to have a family dinner." Eric smiles softly, and I know I've said the right thing.

"Before we do anything else, I want you on my table again for a full examination." Link puts his foot down, and he sounds forceful and sexy. I feel my nipples pebble with desire, remembering what happened the last time I was on his table. "I want to check on your changes to make sure your body is adjusting, and I want to scan the babies just to double-check that everything is alright with them."

I press my hand against my little paunch. My little beasties. They have been secure and snug, and I think they are mostly okay. The fuck me vibes have certainly settled slightly. I'm wondering if my kraken being satisfied has anything to do with that.

"Okay, I'm down for that."

"While you examine Lila…" Xavier winks suggestively, and I roll my eyes, but he's not wrong. I totally want to play doctor and nurse with my cyborg. "I will look in on Aura and your friends to make sure they have everything they need and advise them of the quick stop on Iceen."

"That would be great, thank you. I bet they are feeling the effect of the hyper jump too." I look down the corridor in the direction of their suite, but because of the curve, I can't see or hear anything.

"Mark is also probably still digesting the fact that he is the heir of the Celestian throne," Link says conversationally, and I feel my head whip around to look at him.

"Really?" I gasp.

"Oh yes. I ran some tests on him and Susie while you were swimming. I confirmed his identity, but we decided we wouldn't say anything until we got to Celestia. Susie is very close to activating that ball of power inside of her, so I advised her to continue drinking the water and let us know if anything strange happens. Eric, William, and

Magenta have all volunteered to assist her if anything does occur."

"That is smart. If we told the Celestian royal family that information, I'm not sure they wouldn't come to us. They are also probably used to imposters claiming to be their lost child. I'm sure they have their own way of telling. It's better to wait and let them find out for themselves." William is all business now. "We also need to continue that conversation from before, but not here and not now. For now, we will continue with business as usual, but be on the lookout for anything suspicious."

"Lila, I need to deal with my clan and dissolve my ties to them," Saxon announces seriously. He gives Eric and William a guilty look. "We also need to discuss the continuation of the act and whether or not they want to continue working with the circus."

William waves a hand at Saxon. "Eric and I will leave you to make whatever decisions you deem reasonable."

Saxon's eyebrows jump in surprise, and Eric chuckles. "Saxon, my dear boy, you just married the heir to the circus, so that makes you co-owner when we hand all of this over to her. These decisions will all be yours eventually, so why not start early? That's one less thing Will and I have to worry about."

I smother my giggle as Saxon's mouth drops open in surprise. He stutters a couple of times before he gets himself together. "Ah, yes, okay.

Thank you for your trust. I will not let you down." He bows his head respectfully.

"And I will advise Echo and Maxsim that our next stop will be Iceen. As far as everyone knows, we were heading directly for Celestia. They may need to make preparations."

"Thank you, Caspian. Please ask them if they intend to stay or return to Iceen. In light of the leadership change, Maxsim may want to stay and support his family. If they do decide to stay on their home planet, we will need to scour the universe for a new act." William sounds aggravated at the idea, but that's a problem to worry about in the future.

"Woo-hoo. Look at us all gelling and shit." I throw my hands into the air and wave spirit fingers. "Team Adams and mates are amazing."

Everyone looks at me with disbelieving expressions, and I raise an eyebrow.

"What? Too much?"

"Maybe just a little." Eric holds up his hands, showing me a little, while the others all nod.

"Party poopers," I grumble, dropping my hands just as the red lights switch off and the siren ceases.

"Warp is stable. You may all be unseated," Captain Broderick announces, and I sigh with relief, clicking the button on my harness release and jumping up out of my seat. The minute I step away from it, it folds up and slides seamlessly back into the wall.

"Wow, that is super cool," I say, running my

hand over the wall. "You can't even feel a seam or anything."

I feel someone crowd in behind me and lean down. "That's nanotechnology. If you come with me to my clinic, I'll show you what else nanotechnology can do." Link's words are barely a whisper in my ear. I know he did that deliberately to rile me up and so my grandpas didn't overhear him. I shudder as I think of my last demonstration of his amazing nanobots.

Whirling, I grab his hand. "I'll see you all back here later, right?" I ask, looking to my other three mates, stopping on Xavier. "You might as well move all your crap from your room into mine too. I mean, it's only a matter of time before we get to Westalin. Not to mention I don't like it when you're too far away from me."

Xavier's expression almost makes me laugh out loud. I think I completely blindsided him, if the open mouth and wide eyes tell me anything. One point to Lila. I like to keep my tricky warlock on his feet. He thinks he's cleverer than the rest of us, so an occasional surprise will keep him humble.

"Did you get your things moved in?" I ask Saxon, and he nods.

"Yes. In between everything else, I found time to return to my room. I do not have much of sentimental value, so it didn't take long. Lila, I was thinking maybe tomorrow we could go down into the circus pod and use the arena to test out your new abilities," he offers, and I squeal and throw my arms around him. Of course I misjudge my strength, and the two of us fly into the wall, Saxon cushioning the impact with his body. He grunts and slides down onto the floor, taking me with him.

"Oh fuck. I thought I'd gotten a handle on that," I cry out, checking him over for damage.

He shakes his head and grabs my hands, holding them in place. "Extreme emotions will probably trigger you for a little longer, at least until you have had some time to get used to them."

I scramble to my feet and hold out a hand, carefully hauling him up. "I'm so sorry," I apologize, brushing him off, though he doesn't really need it. I don't like seeing him wrinkled and feel the need to do something.

Again, he grabs my hands and leans in. "Do not worry, my beautiful blood rose, you can kiss all my boo-boos better after you have seen to your cyborg's needs." He inhales deeply when his nose presses against my neck.

"Are you hungry? It's been a while," I ask, and when he pulls back, his magenta eyes are glowing, and I can see his fangs have dropped.

"Yes, I can smell the abundance of blood in your system and know that you are ready to feed me, but I can wait until you are done."

"You can tell that?" I ask, cocking my head to the side before stepping in and getting on my tiptoes to shove my nose into his neck. I inhale deeply, and sure enough, the smell of marshmallows and choco-late flood my senses as well as the unmistakable scent of copper. My gums throb, and my stomach rumbles, which is weird since I just drank from Xavier not that long ago. "Oh yes, well, I guess you and I have a date for dinner then," I tell him, and the smug smile that crosses his lush mouth is panty wetting. It takes all my strength to turn away from him.

I look around, and I'm surprised to find William and Eric are missing. "When did that happen?" I ask the other three, and Cas grins.

"The minute Saxon started sniffing your neck, they bailed. They went to check on John in the clinic."

My stomach sinks. Fuck, John is in the clinic. There is no way I want to play doctor and nurse with Link in there now. They must see the dismay on my face, and Xavier brushes across my mind before chuckling out loud. I should reprimand him, but he has been very good at staying out of my head, and do I really want to admit about me being selfish and wanting sex when my grandpa has an unknown toxin ravaging his body?

"She is upset because she was hoping for a little role play-down in the clinic and has just remem-bered that John is down there too," Xavier shares, and my other guys all look at me with heat in their eyes and no judgment whatsoever. God, I love them. They are fucking amazing.

"It's okay, baby. I have a private treatment room that is soundproof. We can still check you all over," Link assures me.

"Well, what the fuck are we waiting for?" I grab my lovely cyborg by his hand and drag him in the direction of the closest elevator. "I'll see you all later, right?" I call back, and they all respond in the affirmative.

"Okay then. Good luck with your clan, Saxon, and Xavier, tell Susie I'll speak to her soon," I say, but once we reach the elevator, I turn my attention completely to the man in front of me. As the doors open, I push him back against the wall, ready to ravish him, but he stops me.

"Wait!"

CHAPTER TWENTY-ONE

Lila

My stomach sinks, and I step back. Does he not want this? Is he having second thoughts? Fuck, it hasn't even been half an hour since I asked him to bond with me. Was I so crazy that he's backing out?

"No, Lila, it's not what you're thinking. I definitely want to bond with you. Nothing would make me happier," Link assures me, and I look up, scowling at him.

"Do you have mind reading capabilities that I don't know about?"

He smiles and pulls me back into his arms as the elevator starts to move after he presses a button. "No, I haven't suddenly developed mind reading abilities, but I am getting to know you. As much as I want to bond with you here and now, I need to be certain that your body is coping with the current new bonds and that if we go ahead with our own bonding, that no extra strain or pressure is going to be put on you and the babies. I also need to ensure that your own ball of Skarrian power is still stable and not being suppressed by your changes, and that your body is adjusting to the DNA changes that have happened."

"What do you mean?"

"Well, your body has basically rewritten your DNA twice in a short period of time. You now have the ability to shift into both half and full kraken form, not to mention the new and interesting addition to the internal walls of your vagina." I smirk at the thought of the guys' reactions when they feel my pulsing sucker powered pussy. Now that upgrade was definitely awesome. "As well as the addition of the babies in your womb, you now have a larger heart and denser bone marrow for extra blood production. The fact that you are still standing, let alone functioning, is kind of mind-blowing. I really want a Celestian healer to look you over before we add any more extras to your repertoire."

The elevator comes to a stop at the right floor, and we step out before making our way to the hospital wing.

"But bonding with you will be different, won't it? I won't get anything from you."

"No, but it's still tradition for me to give you some of my nanobots, which I really want to do, and I don't want your body to reject them." My confusion fades, and I beam at him. He still wants to go ahead with this, and he's just thinking of me and the babies. "Okay, I can be patient as long as you promise to move all your stuff into our quarters. I don't want to be apart from any of you more than I have to."

"That sounds like a fair deal." His voice hitches slightly, and when I look at him again, his eyes are shining with emotions.

The clinic is quiet when we enter, but I hear a low conversation, which draws my attention. Not waiting for Link to guide me, I head over to where I can see my grandpas. I push through Eric and William and look down at Grandpa J. His normal golden skin looks sallow and pale, and while I know he's sedated and being given painkillers, there's a grimace on his face like he's still in pain. I take his hand in mine, and his skin is clammy and cool.

"Oh, he doesn't look good at all." I look at Link, and I can see the helplessness on his face.

He sighs, running a hand through his hair before tapping one of the monitors surrounding John. "I've done everything I can. He's stable for now, but it's not stopping the poison from moving through his body. Thankfully it hasn't latched onto anything else vital, and it seems to be happy swimming in his bloodstream. There is, however, a small amount of damage to his heart." He points at what must be a scan of John's heart. "This black section here shows damage, but I don't think it's life threatening. The antiviral mix that I injected him with, in the hope it might help, seems to be keeping it from progressing further, but it hasn't eradicated it. I'm at a loss, I've never seen anything like it. To be honest, the toxin acts similar to nanobot technology. When a cyborg wants to change something on themselves, nanobots rearrange to form the desired result. Cyborgs' entire bodies are made of nanobots, as well as living tissue, so for them it's no big deal, but nanobots trying to rearrange cells that don't contain the same tech just does damage. If it was straight nanobots, however, it would have destroyed the heart completely. It is like the poison has been mutated with nanotech that is programmed to mimic other illnesses. Does that make sense? John looked like he was having a heart attack, but his heart is one hundred percent healthy except for that small section that had the toxin on it. There is a small dark patch in his brain too, but it's so minute that it might not have been obvious that there was something wrong."

"Holy shit. He has been super emotional. We thought it was because we found Lila and the reminder that we lost Alina, Marcus, and Liliana." Eric looks at Will who confirms what he said.

"It was very unlike him. He is the most even-keeled of us, and he is usually just quiet when he's sad, but there were some outbursts that were very out of character for him."

"Even the first day I arrived. Remember when he bungled telling me about aliens?" I remind them. "You thought it was just because he was so nervous and excited."

"You're right. So John could have been carrying this poison for a while." William rubs a hand across his chin. "Eric, do you remember the day before Lila arrived? John was complaining about having a sore hip at dinner. He grumbled about the miserable weather in England and how he never believed it before when people said it affected the way they felt. I didn't think anything of it because we aren't spring chickens anymore, but what if that was when he was injected?"

Eric thinks for a moment before he slowly nods. "We had dinner with the crew, and we announced that we found Lila and she would be joining us and that everyone had to be on their best behavior. The three of us wandered around the dining room to get a feel for their reactions. It was only after that when we were on our way back to our quarters that he said something about the pain. I suggested he come see you, Link, but I guess once Lila arrived, that all slid to the background."

"The pain probably went away too. If that's the case, I'm almost a hundred percent sure that there is some kind of cyborg tech in the toxin. If that was any other injection site, the puncture wound would have faded, but nanotech injection sites always stay because if they have to be removed, then they have to be drawn out the same place they were injected."

"Can you draw this out of him now?" I ask, feeling excited at the prospect, but my stomach sinks when Link shakes his head.

"If I try without knowing the exact combination, I could mess it all up. Only the person who created this can withdraw it, and unfortunately, it also means that there could be no cure. They could have programmed it to resist any tampering."

The silence in the clinic is heavy as we all contemplate the fact that John might not recover from this at all.

"Lila, honey, this makes that other thing we discussed earlier all the more important. Maybe it would be best if we performed the ceremony sooner rather than later." William sounds grave as he looks down at his brother, his hands clenched in the bedsheet.

"No. Not yet. Let the Celestians look at him, and if they can't help him, we can revisit that discussion." I don't want to discuss the possibility that I may lose one of my grandfathers after only just finding them again.

Will sighs and nods his head as Link blanks the screen before turning back toward us.

"For now, no more damage is being done to him, and the Celestians' medical knowledge is extensive. They will have archives, and I'm sure there will be something in there that will help us cure him. I've never heard of them failing at anything. It's rather remarkable really." His admiration for the Celestians is clear, and it eases my worries slightly. "But for now, it's time for me to run all the tests I need to on you." He grabs my hand and leads me toward a closed door.

"I'll catch up with you two later. Why don't you try to get some rest? I have a funny feeling we are going to need it," I call back to my grandpas who quickly agree.

"We'll take turns. I don't want to leave John on his own," Will replies.

"Xavier already came and warded the room earlier. No one but the four of us can get in here, I promise, and all my monitors are set to alert me if anything happens. Just go. He will be fine," Link assures my other grandads who reluctantly give in. We watch as the two of them leave the clinic, the door closing automatically behind them, and I breathe a sigh of relief.

"I'm so worried about them," I tell my cyborg as he puts his hand against a screen and opens the door in front of us. When we enter, I can see it's another exam room similar to the large one outside, just more private.

"They will be okay, and so will John. Everything will work out." It's a promise I'm not sure he can keep, but I appreciate the sentiment.

He helps me up onto the bed.

"This room is for anything contagious. It has its

own self-contained life support system, but we've never had to use it."

"I appreciate the privacy, even if we're not going to play doctor and nurse today."

He chuckles as he grabs a portable device out of a nearby cabinet. "I promise there will be plenty of doctor and nurse role-playing once we get the all clear from the Celestians. Now, how are you feeling? Are you hungry?" he asks as my stomach decides to let itself be known. "You ate a lot just before you went down to collect the detainees."

"Way to food shame your girlfriend," I grumble at him, and he chuckles.

"No, not at all, I just want to gauge if your new powers are increasing your food intake. Are you hungry for blood?" He helps me lie down and then starts slowly running the machine over the length of my body.

"I am hungry, and I did have blood from Xavier when we were on Earth, but I don't think that was hunger so much as Agent Smith triggering my bloodlust. To stop me from killing him, Xavier fucked me and satisfied my bloodlust that way."

"Okay, good. We are learning what triggers you. Bloodlust is triggered a lot easier in young Vilaxians than older ones. It's why they don't start their military service until they get it under control. They go through two kinds of changes in their early lives. They are born with the need for blood, but that's like any baby, a hunger triggered by the innate need to survive and thrive. It's not until they go through puberty around the age of twenty when they begin having other bloodlust urges. Violence, sexual attraction, and extreme emotions can all trigger the need to feed," Link explains as he stops the machine at my lower stomach and pushes a few buttons.

"You seem to have all the knowledge," I tease him, and he smiles.

"I did my research once you made your decision to bond with Saxon so I could help you through it. Basically, you are the equivalent of a Vilaxian teenager and are going to find your bloodlust is triggered easily. Hopefully with the four of us, we will be able to keep it under control so you don't feel the need to attack anyone."

I grimace at the thought of causing an incident because someone pissed me off. "I better not go anywhere on my own for a while." I know my limits, and I don't have patience for idiots, but they don't deserve to have their throats ripped out either. Well, Smith might have, but we can save that for another day. Hopefully by the next time I see him, it will be a moot point.

Link is frowning, still hovering over my stomach and pushing a few buttons on the machine, and I begin to worry. "Is everything okay?" I ask, but he doesn't answer, and I feel my heart rate rise. "Link?"

"Just give me a moment. The conclusions have come back inconclusive, so I'm rerunning the tests."

Now I'm really starting to panic.

"The babies?" If I hurt them from bonding with Saxon, I will never forgive myself, and I doubt Cas and his kraken will either.

The silence in the room is strained, and I feel my fangs drop from my gums and my bloodlust rise with my panic. I grip the sheets in an effort not to lunge at Link in my heightened state of mind.

This seems to draw his attention from the screen, and he looks up at me. His eyes widen in shock when he sees me. "Oh fuck, Lila, I'm sorry. Here I was, just telling you we need to keep your emotions under control, and I made you panic. The babies are fine. Their DNA makeup has changed slightly from the previous test. I think maybe they took on some Vilaxian traits as well. We won't know until they are born, but at this stage, it hasn't done them any harm."

I feel my heart rate drop significantly, Link's words reassuring me, but I still can't help but feel guilty—and angry. Angry at the people who interfered with my and Saxon's bonding and forced the issue. Except two of them involved are already dead, and the other two are insignificant nonissues now that Xavier has stripped them of their powers. There's nowhere for me to direct my anger, so I will hang onto it for now.

Link moves on from my stomach, moving farther up my body to my chest. He purses his lips, and I feel my panic rise. That, combined with the anger that's still riding me hard, is not a good combination.

"Damn it, Link," I growl between gritted teeth. "You are not doing my bloodlust any favors."

He glances at me again and lowers the machine, putting it to the side before he slowly reaches for my hands, not making any sudden movements. "Sorry, my sweet. Sometimes I get caught up in what I'm doing and forget about everything around me. Nothing is wrong, I'm just trying to make sure that your heart and lungs and everything are coping with the new changes. I find the changes to your body fascinating. It's not every day I get to witness these amazing things."

"Fine, but can you do it with a blank face so I don't worry when I see your expressions change? Or you can even smile creepily all the way through it. I think I'd prefer that to the rest of your expressions."

He chuckles and kisses me, and I inhale his scent. He smells like the air before a thunderstorm, all fresh with an electric tinge to it. It's intoxicating, and my fangs throb with want.

"Link," I grind out. "I am hanging onto my sanity by a very fine thread. You need to back away very slowly and put some distance between us."

"Why, Lila? I won't mind if you drink from me if it will help you." Link's words snap that thread, and I pounce, moving so fast that I have him on his back beneath me on the bed before he has even realized what's happened.

CHAPTER TWENTY-TWO

Lila

Link blinks up at me adorably from where I have him pinned to the hospital bed, but I'm lost to the bloodlust. A quiet, continuous growl rumbles from my chest as I run my nose along the length of his neck. His hands grip my hips as I grind against him, my bloodlust making the other kind rise as well. I watch as his pupils dilate, swallowing the silver irises until they are no longer visible. I stroke my hands down his body as I settle myself comfortably on top of him, pleased that he's pinned and unable to move.

I use my tongue to probe the thick vein in his neck, plumping it before striking hard. He stiffens and grunts at the sharp bite of pain, but soon enough, my venom kicks in and he becomes loose and compliant beneath me as his blood flows into my mouth. Holy crap, it's like drinking an energy drink—sharp, tangy, and delicious. I feel his fingers tighten on my hips as I grind down harder onto his erection, dry humping him as I drink, and he thrusts up, doing the same. It's not long before our teenage style movements have me on the crest of an orgasm.

One of his hands slides into my yoga pants and under my soaked panties. I groan as he thrusts two fingers deep into my pulsing channel, but then they start to grow, shifting and moving until they completely fill the space. I release the suction on his neck and throw my head back, moaning loudly as he pounds them in and out. It doesn't take long before I'm flying over the edge, my orgasm ripping its way through my body. I'm not sure how long I ride the wave of pleasure, but when I finally come down, I'm panting hard, and I drop down against Link's body. He removes his fingers, which have now returned to normal, and sticks them into his mouth, sucking them clean.

"You taste so fucking good," he rumbles in a low voice before wrapping his arms around me and leaning in to kiss me. Before he can, I hold my hand up and place it across his mouth, stopping him. He raises an eyebrow, unable to question me with my hand on his lips.

"Blood breath," I explain, flushing slightly, and he pushes my hand away.

"I don't care," he tells me, but instead of letting

him kiss me, I push up and shuffle down the bed, reaching for his pants.

"But I do," I mumble, unable to look him in the eyes. Tugging at his zipper, I try to undo his pants to return the favor, but he places his hand over mine and stops me.

"Lila, I'm fine. Your venom combined with your sweet little body grinding on me and your own orgasm proved to be my undoing. I'm going to need a change of pants." He grins, not embarrassed in the least, and it's contagious. I feel my own smile spread across my lips.

"Does that count as mutual orgasms?" I ask, climbing off of him and helping him sit up. I took quite a bit of blood, and I don't want him to feel light-headed.

He shakes his head. "No exchange of body fluids, so we're good," he says, reaching up and feeling around his neck. There's no wound because I remembered to swipe my tongue across it when I let go. "Vilaxian venom is really quite amazing," he says when he pulls his hand away and sees that there's no blood.

"Are you okay? I didn't take too much. It's weird, but there's like this thing inside of me that tells me when you've had enough. It was the same with Xavier too. Saxon, not so much. We were kind of in a sexual bloodlust frenzy, so I wasn't paying attention, but he seemed fine after. I think."

"He was, and so am I," Link assures me. "How are you feeling? More emotionally stable now?"

I smile goofily at him, patting my stomach. "I feel great. I'm as full as a leech and feeling pretty fucking amazing after that orgasm. I think after some real food, I could probably sleep for a day. It seems like so much has happened in the last forty-eight hours."

Link slides off the bed and pulls me into a hug. I rest my head against his chest and sigh with contentment. "So much has happened! I think a meal and chilling in our quarters sounds like a good plan. I know you probably want to see Susie and explore the ship since you haven't had a chance to yet, but that can all wait until tomorrow, or the next day. We have plenty of time to do all of that, and I want to make sure all of my readings are correct."

A yawn creeps up on me, and I slap a hand over my mouth. I was going to argue with him, but now I can't, so I nod. "Okay. How about we go past your quarters so you can get changed and grab a few things to move into mine? The guys can help you with the rest tomorrow. In fact, I bet Xavier would just teleport it all there and save us the work."

He chuckles and pulls away, grabbing my hand. "You may be right. Okay, let's do this, my pants are starting to feel uncomfortable."

We leave the private room, and I give John a kiss on the forehead on the way past. Link checks all his vitals before we leave, satisfied with the readouts. He locks up the clinic, and we move in the direction of the elevator.

"I will probably return here after dinner. I don't want to leave him alone for long periods of time."

I feel my bottom lip drop in a brief pout, but I mentally slap myself.

Get over yourself, Lila, he's looking out for your grandpa. Stop being so selfish.

"I understand. I appreciate all the professional care you're giving both me and Grandpa J," I tell him as he stops in front of a door halfway between the clinic and the elevator.

"Lila, I would do just about anything for you," he says, kissing my cheek before putting his hand up on the entrance panel.

The door slides back, and we step into a living area. It's decorated in a minimalist style. He has the typical picture window, like all the other rooms I've been in, but the rest of the room is different than any others. There is no dining table or kitchen, just a replicator in the corner. The rest of the room is filled with a huge sofa, and the surrounding walls are covered by book-filled shelves.

"Oh my god," I whisper as I turn in a semicircle, taking in all the books. You would think with the advanced technology that he would just use a tablet or something, but no, these are all leather-bound, paper-filled books. The room smells amazing. I stop at one shelf that is built around a fire-place. "Does that work?" I ask him, gesturing to it, and he smiles. He walks over to it and flicks a button on the wall, and it leaps to life.

I throw my hands up in the air. "That's it, you can't move into my place. How could you abandon all of this? That's not right. I'll have to move here." His face had fallen, but he's chuckling again by the time I finish.

"I'm sure we can figure out a way to move it all to your quarters. If you told your grandpas, they'd arrange to have your room extended and redesigned next time we are back on Skarr." He turns his back to me and heads in the direction of his bedroom, while I run my finger over the length of a spine.

"What are all of these about?" I call to him.

"There's a little bit of everything—romance, history, and planetary and alien species information, not to mention medical textbooks," he replies, but something in the corner of the room has me squealing.

"Oh my god, there's a ladder!" I look down, and I hadn't noticed before, but there's a track running the length of the shelves in an arc, as well as one along the top of them. I hurry over to it and pull it away from the wall. I slide it back and forth a few times to make sure it slides easily before pushing off and jumping. My foot lands on one of the rungs as I wrap an arm around one higher up. I throw my head back and toss my other arm out, and then I shout with joy as I ride the ladder along its path. When I get to the end, and I have to hang on tightly so I don't fly off, I find Link leaning against his bedroom door, his eyes filled with laughter.

"Did you enjoy that?" he asks. He's changed out of his uniform and is in sweats like Cas was wearing earlier.

"I am calling you Beast from now on." I point my finger at him before pointing to our surroundings. "The only thing missing is a rose under a glass dome." I'm almost certain when I look back at him, he's going to be confused, but he crosses his arms and smiles indulgently.

"Does that make you my beauty?"

"You know *Beauty and the Beast*?" I ask as he crosses the room and holds out a hand to help me down. I take it, his hand slightly cooler than mine. He places a kiss on the back of it before dropping it and moving the ladder farther back against the wall.

"Of course. Earth has so many wonderful stories. I think their imaginations are so vivid because of the lack of magic, but a good portion of my fiction novels come from there. Come on, let's go. Your other mates will be getting impatient, and I don't want to be on the receiving end of their annoyance."

He flicks the switch on the fireplace again, and I allow myself one final glance before I follow him out. Outside the door, he stops and grabs my hand, holding it up to the entrance pad. He pushes a few buttons, and it beeps green.

"There, now you can come and go as you please until we can figure out how to get you your very own library," he tells me.

"Best mate ever." I sigh, leaning forward to kiss him but stopping again when I remember the blood breath.

He shakes his head and rolls his eyes. "Come on, let's get you some food and drink, and then maybe you'll let me kiss you again."

When we get back to my room, Xavier has moved all of his things into one of the spare rooms and is lounging indulgently on the sofa. Neither Cas nor Saxon have returned yet.

"What is this?" he asks as Link and I step into the room. "Some kind of kinky sexual device, and if so, how does it work?" Xavier is holding up the knitting loom that I bought when Link and I went shopping in Vegas.

I snort with amusement as I go over to the fridge and pull out a bottle of Skarrian water, popping the top and taking a long pull of the delicious liquid. "Making yourself at home I see, Snoopy." I wipe my mouth with the back of my hand.

I see Link smile out of the corner of my eye. He

knows what it is now, but he also thought it was for something else when he first saw it. His mind went to torture, but of course Xavier's didn't.

"Well, I don't like to think I've been missing out on something exciting." Xavier smirks at me, holding the loom over his crotch and winding the handle.

Link chuckles as I roll my eyes.

"No, it's for making garments. I was going to make you one, but now that I know you've been snooping without asking, maybe I won't." He pouts but throws the loom onto the couch and starts looking at the games I put on a shelf under the coffee table.

I wave Link over to the empty bedrooms. There are three left after Saxon, Cas, and Xavier claimed theirs. "You can have any one of these, and if what you say is true, then we can furnish it to your liking when we return to Skarr. The bathroom is communal, and you have a door that leads to it, as do all of us. There is a locking mechanism that will lock out everyone else if you want it to, but I've noticed most aliens aren't too picky about being naked. There are a couple of separate toilets as well." I wave to another door. "Down there is another living area with a big screen TV and some gaming systems that I haven't checked out yet, and I guess that's kind of it," I say apologetically. I thought the suite was huge, but now that I'm filling it with men, it seems kind of small, and I feel bad because Link has to leave behind his library, and Xavier doesn't have anywhere for the sunken lounge he had in his rooms.

"Lila, don't be upset. All the living areas are designed to cater to each species or individual wants and needs. We will be able to change it to how you want it." Link drags me over to the couch where Xavier is, and he reaches out and pulls me down next to him, wrapping an arm around my shoulders and tugging me closer.

"Not to mention all the other ship facilities. Most of the crew are very social and use everything. There are gyms, theaters, bowling alleys, and the recreational holodeck, which allows you to program anything you like. Plus, apart from the Aquilia pool, there is one available to everyone else as well. Then there are all the retail and dining outlets. This ship is our home and our way of life."

"Yes, don't you worry about us. I know I wouldn't want to be anywhere but here. Now, what do you feel like eating for dinner, Lila?" Link went back to the kitchen replicator after depositing me in Xavier's capable arms.

"He's right, you know," Xavier whispers in my ear as he runs a caressing finger up and down my arm. "All four of us are thrilled to be here. Now tell your future husband what you want for dinner." His touch brings goosebumps to the surface of the arm he's caressing, and he chuckles when I shiver.

"As much as I want to say surprise me, I kind of

need some normality. How about a double bacon cheeseburger, fries, and a chocolate shake?"

Xavier groans beside me. "That sounds delicious. Make it two, Link, but can I have a vanilla shake?"

"Let's make it a clean sweep, and I'll have the same, and a banana shake." Link presses a few buttons, and the machine starts whirring before it produces the meals one after the other.

"That is still nothing short of phenomenal," I remark, thinking about whether something like that would work on Earth, but I guess it really wouldn't. I asked someone to explain it to me, but when William began speaking about synthesizing on a molecular level, my mind sort of turned to when I can get my next pedicure, and I tuned out the whole thing. I'm just happy it works, because I am a terrible cook.

Xavier and I get up from the couch and go over and grab our plates. The three of us sit at the table when I feel a touch of guilt. "Should we wait for Cas and Sax?"

Link and Xavier smile at the nicknames, but Link shakes his head. "No, Lila, you need food, and the two of them will understand."

Xavier stands up and goes over to the wall communication systems.

"I'll reach out to them and find out how long they are going to be, but start eating. Hopefully they can make it here for dessert." He wiggles his eyebrows suggestively, but I ignore him and, using both hands, grab my enormous burger. I'm not sure that I can eat the whole thing, but I'm going to give it a try.

CHAPTER TWENTY-THREE

Echo

Lying in my nest in cat form, I watch my alpha mate stalk back and forth across our den, his tail twitching in agitation. He hasn't been able to get a hold of his mother or her mates via the comm link, and I can tell how worried he is. The sound of our doorbell ringing has him growling and stalking off down the corridor to answer it.

I consider chasing him down, but I'm super comfy where I am, and maybe by the time he gets back, he will be in a better mood. I roll onto my back and think about the compulsory meeting we attended. The pretty human girl was there, and she smelled even better than before. She was with the Vilaxian, and I could tell by the way he was looking at her that they mated like the rumors were saying. It was all the other Vilaxians could talk about while we were waiting for the meeting to start, and two of them were not being quiet about their displeasure, but Saxon's brother quickly shut them down. I wonder if he is going to stay with the circus. I wonder if any of them are.

I'm also uncertain of our own fate. I will go wherever Maxsim does, and if he chooses to stay on Iceen to support his mother, well, then that's where I will be too. It would be nice to be surrounded by family again. Yet there is something about Lila that calls to me. It is very strange. I am an omega, so I should only be attracted to alphas, and only lightning cat alphas at that. We do not mix with other species. It is taboo. That's not to say it doesn't happen, but it wouldn't be a permanent thing, and it is usually beta cats who indulge.

Alphas and omegas have needs that are not met by other races, and we would never invite another species into our streak. So then why does her scent make me want to roll around in it and present for her? She is not an alpha, so she would not be able to knot me, but I feel my heat coming on quicker and quicker every time I get near her. I think I might shift and go see if I can find her. Maybe she would like to go see a movie with me. It would be nice to go out in public and not worry about getting killed if I want to hold a pretty girl's hand and make out in the back of a dark theater. It would be even better if Maxsim was there too. We could both make her feel really good in the dark.

A sound in the tunnel has me sitting up. Maxsim is returning, and if my nose isn't mistaken, he has Lila with him. I run a paw over my mane to make sure it's not sticking up at all angles, but when he appears, the breath I was holding escapes in disappointment. It's her kraken mate, and they must have had sex recently, because I can smell her all over him. I want to drag him into my nest, roll all over him, and lick the scent of her from his skin. A growl of jealousy rolls out of my mouth before I can stop it, and I feel my lightning power up, wanting to strike the intruder down so I can claim his mate for myself. Fucking hell, this just became a problem. I try to tamp it down, but my instincts are winning out over rationality.

Both of them look at me. Caspian seems wary, but it's the complete shock and hurt on Maxsim's face that finally has me controlling my emotions. My overwhelming guilt puts my lightning out in a flash.

"I am very sorry to intrude once more." Caspian bows his head at me in respect, mistaking my reaction to his presence in our den. "I just came to let you know we are rerouting directly to Iceen. Natalia is causing problems in the brig, and the Adams brothers wish to avoid creating an international incident by returning her to her mother in a bad way. I thought I would come personally and let you know. The Adams brothers are also interested in knowing if you have made a decision about your continued position with the circus. If you all decide to leave, we will need to find a new act, and the sooner we can put out feelers, the better."

I leap out of my nest and pad over to my mate, taking a deep inhale of the kraken on the way past. My cock throbs in its sheath, but thankfully, it stays retracted. I butt my head against my alpha's leg in comfort, and he absently reaches down and strokes between my ears. It feels good, and I don't clamp down on the purr that rumbles from my mouth. I know he would be happier if he could reach his mother and discuss everything with her, but he will need to make a decision soon.

"I haven't been able to reach my mother and discuss the situation with her. To be honest, this has me worried. It also has me leaning toward saying we will be leaving the circus. I can't speak for Trace, Sim, and Fuse, and they must make their own decisions as alphas in their own streak," Maxsim tells Caspian, though I can feel that he does so hesitantly. He does not like to admit any weakness to anyone.

"Do you think something has happened to her?" Caspian asks, crossing his arms and spreading his legs slightly. Unlike the last time he was in here, he is in his humanoid form and wearing appropriate clothing for the temperature of our den.

"Unlikely. My mother is much stronger than the reigning matriarch, but she wasn't interested in politics while everything was fairly run. Our current matriarch is fine, but it's the fact that she has proposed Natalia as the next matriarch that is worrying. She's not a ruler my mother would willingly support. If she has to step up and challenge to win, then she will. What worries me is that Echo will become more of a target if we choose to stay on Iceen. My mother will probably change the laws regarding male omegas so they are protected, since she has never agreed with turning a blind eye to killing them, but it will take time for the mindset to change. Female omegas can be incredibly possessive, jealous, and territorial."

I chortle at his words and weave my way around his body. All female lightning cats, no matter their designation, are possessive, jealous, and territorial, though they do get slightly better once they have formed a streak and are secure within it.

Caspian frowns. "I apologize for my ignorance, but why would female alphas kill off male omegas? Can they even breed with female omegas?"

"No, they can't. Female alphas are rare, there hasn't been one in a hundred years. They would need a male omega to breed with."

"Can a male alpha and a female alpha breed?" Caspian seems fascinated with our way of life. I guess it's interesting from an outsider's perspective.

"Yes, they can, but there would be a dominance fight beforehand, and again, they often end in bloodshed or death."

The kraken runs a hand through his hair and blows out a breath. I break away from my alpha and creep toward him, unable to resist his scent anymore. I slink along the ground, and he's so caught up in the information he just learned, he doesn't notice. "Being a lightning cat is complicated. I kind of understand why you volunteered to join the circus. It will be a shame to see you go, but I completely understand the family first motto. Now that I have Lila and she is pregnant, all of my priorities have changed. Everything has become about keeping her safe and happy, so anything else is just background crap. Though I do have it a little easier because I'm sharing her with three others."

I stop my forward momentum at those words. Three others? Thankfully Maxsim asks what I want to know, so I keep shuffling forward and listen for the answer.

"Three others? I thought she was only mated to you and the Vilaxian."

"She is also Xavier's intimate and will be bonding Dr. Link in the Skarrian way."

I get to the kraken's feet. Sitting up, I stick my nose into his crotch, inhaling deeply, and he yelps in surprise.

"Holy fuck!" He jumps back, and I feel smug that I was able to creep up on him.

He tries to push my head away, but he smells intoxicating, and I push back before standing up, rubbing my body against his, then nudging him. He stumbles back, and I keep nudging him, herding him in the direction of my nest. He keeps trying to push me away, but although I may not be as big and strong as Maxsim, I'm still a big cat, and unless the kraken shifts into half form, I can easily maneuver him.

"Echo!" Maxsim growls at me, but he doesn't put any alpha command behind it, so I ignore him. Only a couple more steps, and the kraken will fall into my nest. I push harder, determined to get him there before Maxsim loses his patience and orders me to stop. The kraken, caught by surprise, doesn't even notice, and suddenly finds himself hovering over empty air. He shouts as he drops down into my nest. I see him brace for pain, but his eyes widen with surprise when he finds a soft landing.

Not giving him a chance to get his bearings, I leap into the nest, landing on top of him, and rub my body all over his, purring as I try to get as much of Lila's scent into my bedding as I can.

"Echo, enough."

My body seizes up with the alpha command, and I feel my body become pliant as I relax into the kraken. His hands are in my fur from him trying to wrestle me off of him, but now that I've stopped, he relaxes underneath me and absently strokes my fur.

"What's going on?" he demands, looking up at Maxsim who is staring down at us with a frown pinching his brow.

"I am not sure. Echo is acting weird. It's getting

close to his heat, and his actions are that of an unmated omega." My alpha does not sound happy, and I know I will probably be punished for my behavior, but I can't help myself. Something is driving me to cover myself in the Earth woman's scent. I'm not sure what that means.

"Well, that's clearly not the case since you are his mate, so what else could it be?" Caspian continues to stroke his hands over my fur almost like he's reluctant to remove them. I preen, knowing how soft and silky my pelt is.

"Shift, Echo."

I can hear the confusion and anger in my mate's voice as he orders me to shift. He must be really mad to do that, because an ordered shift is painful. I yowl and roll off Caspian, my body contorting and bones cracking as they reshape into my bipedal form. I'm panting with exhaustion by the time it finishes, and I stumble slightly as I get to my feet. Caspian kindly puts out a hand to steady me. I stare up at my alpha, feeling mixed emotions—anger that he commanded me to shift in a painful way instead of just asking, and guilt because now I have to explain my predicament.

If we were back home on Iceen, it wouldn't be unheard of for us to take a few more into our streak if we found someone appealing, but it never would have been another omega. We wouldn't be able to share with one another. It would cause continuous infighting until one took out the other, so it would have only been betas or another alpha, and only then if Maxsim okayed it.

"What are you doing?" he asks, crossing his arms and still looking down at us.

I feel the kraken get to his feet behind me, and with one quick movement, he leaps back up next to my alpha. I stubbornly shake my head, refusing to answer. Maxsim growls, but Caspian just holds out a hand, offering to help me up.

"It's okay, Echo. I'm not upset, you just surprised me." I take the proffered hand, even though I don't need it, and allow him to pull me up and out. To my disappointment, I wasn't very successful in transferring her scent from him to my nest. It mostly smells like an ocean breeze, which is what the kraken smells like.

Unashamed of my nakedness in front of our guest, I turn my back and walk away from Maxsim, still hurt that he ordered me to shift. "Can I get you something to drink?" I ask the kraken, heading over to our replicator. I press a button and order my favorite Iceen freezie. This conversation is definitely going to require some alcohol.

When I turn back, Caspian is glancing awkwardly between Maxsim and me, and he shakes his head.

"No, but thank you. Maybe another time. Look, I'm going to leave the two of you alone. Just let one of the Adams brothers or Lila know what you decide to do."

Caspian leaves without an explanation for my weird behavior, but Maxsim hasn't stopped staring at me with his lip peeled back in a snarl.

"What was that?" he demands again, and this time he puts the alpha command behind his words.

"Fuck you, Maxsim," I manage to snarl back before my omega compulsion kicks in and I have to answer him. "He smelled like the Earth girl. I want that smell in my nest."

He snarls and leaps toward me, grabbing my mane.

"Why would you want that? She is a pathetic human. She cannot be anything to you."

Wow! I'm not sure he even realizes how much he sounds like Natalia now.

"Why not?" I'm stubborn, and I refuse to give in to his jealousy.

"Because she is not a lightning cat, and she is not an alpha. She can't give you what you need. How empty would you feel without a knot stuffing you full?" His voice has dropped to a low rumble, and he mutters all of this into my ear, knowing it will trigger something inside me.

Sure enough, my cock, which has been semi-hard since I shifted, hardens even further. He pulls my head back and bites into my neck over his claiming mark. He is not gentle, his jealousy insisting he reassert his dominance over me, and I shiver with excitement as all thoughts of the Earth girl float away.

I whimper, and I feel his lips turn up into a smirk against my neck as his own cock hardens against my back.

"I think we need to finish what was interrupted before. I think you need to be reminded of who your alpha is." He tightens his grip on my mane and drags me over to my nest before shoving me into it. I allow him to manhandle me and fall into it, excited and breathing heavily in anticipation. Suddenly, Lila's scent hits my nose, overpowering the previous scent of the kraken, and I almost come in my nest. Maxsim jumps down into it and wrinkles his nose at the smell, growling angrily.

"I'm going to fuck you and fill you with so much cum that you will never smell her in our nest again. I will paint your body with it if I have to and remind you whom you belong to. Now present for me."

The last words are laced with alpha command, and I roll over, giving him my ass. He leans in and bites down on my neck again, wrapping one of his big hands around my weeping cock. He drags a claw along it, and I grunt in pain as he uses his other hand to probe my entrance.

"Look at this, you are dripping with slick, ready to take my cock like a good little omega." Maxsim's voice is still growly and gruff, but it causes my fur to stand on end. He shoves two fingers in roughly, and I grunt with the intrusion, the sharp bite of pain quickly turning to pleasure as I adjust to them. I rock back, pushing myself onto them, needing more, and he removes his fingers before slapping my ass hard.

"No, I am in charge. You will take what I give you when I give it to you." He smacks my ass again. "You have been a bad omega, lusting over a girl who can't give you what you need." He smacks my ass again, and I jolt forward, my cock sliding through his hand, bringing me a combination of pleasure and pain, and I yowl out loud.

He caresses where he smacked, and his voice gentles. "If you need another alpha for your heat, we can start looking for one when we get home, or even a pretty beta to suck your cock while I fuck you hard with my knot. That would be fun, wouldn't it?" He tries to appease me, but I say nothing. Thankfully he didn't use his alpha voice, because I don't have to admit that only Lila will do. As an omega, I should be in charge of who we let into the streak, but Maxsim is so very alpha he has trouble wrapping his head around that. His mother's mates always get an equal say in everything.

I don't say anything, but I don't think he was looking for an answer. All I want right at this moment is his knot. With my heat getting closer and closer, I need it rough and hard and fast. "Now, Maxsim, please," I beg, and he chuckles smugly, all thoughts of Lila gone from his mind.

"Yes, my omega." I feel him line himself up and slowly push into the ring of my asshole. I'm slick, though, and he prepped me well, so I don't want slow. I'm still super annoyed at him despite being desperate to fuck, so I slam myself back on his cock, shouting at the intrusion before purring when that pain blooms to pleasure. He leans over me, and I brace my hands, ready for what's to come.

"I'm going to fuck you so hard you'll forget your own name, let alone that little Earth girl's." He pounds into me, his body curled over mine, still gripping my cock firmly in his grasp. It's weeping so much now that it provides enough lubrication so it's a smooth glide.

"You're my omega, and no pretty little Earth girl with big tits and a round ass is going to take you away from me." The words come out all garbled with emotion—jealousy, lust, and a small amount of admiration. My alpha is not so indifferent to Lila's outward appeal after all. "I'm going to stuff you with my knot and fill you with my cum." He pulls my head back and bites me again. This time his teeth are sharp and puncture my skin like it's tissue paper. He pulls back and laps at the mark, licking up the blood he's drawn as he continues to work his cock in and out of me. I feel his knot punch against my ring with every thrust, but he hasn't been forceful enough yet. He's waiting for me to beg, punishing me for my interest in Lila.

Having him in my ass and feeling his grip on my cock quickly gets me to my peak, but it's not enough to push me over the edge. I'm going to have to give him what he wants.

"Please, Alpha. Please knot me," I implore, and I feel more slick ooze out with his next thrust, coating the base of his dick and knot.

He tightens his grip on both my mane and my dick and slams home. His knot pushes past the final line of resistance, and he growls as it starts to swell inside me. I moan and shake as it gets bigger, locking him deep within me, and then in the next breath, my orgasm detonates. My ass ripples around him, bringing on his own release, and I feel his seed shoot deep within me.

Locked inside of me, he can no longer move, but his hand continues to stroke my cock, milking me of my cum. He reaches around and catches it with his other hand, completely surrounding me with him, then he brings what he caught back up to his mouth before using his tongue to lick his hand clean, growling as his knot continues to pulse deep inside of me, drawing out my own pleasure. I pant and whine as he runs his hand over my cock again, spreading the remainder of my cum all over it and up my body.

I collapse into my cushions, muffling my cries with the pillow and breathing in Caspian's and Lila's combined scents. I spasm around Maxsim's cock again, but he's not paying any attention to what might have caused it, thankfully.

Finally, he curls himself around me, his cock still

lodged deep as we remain locked together for the next little while. He strokes a hand over my back, running his fingers through my fur and cooing words of praise. "Such a good omega taking his alpha's knot. We'll find you some more streak mates, ones who are compatible with us and won't bring shame to my mother's family." He's muttering all sorts of nonsense now, sounding more and more like Natalia.

I feel a pang of longing for the Earth girl, and I'm not sure if it will ever go away.

CHAPTER TWENTY-FOUR

Lila

When Saxon returned from visiting his clan, he was in a foul mood. While Hale and Velorina were happy for the dissolution, Estrella and Radella are fighting it with everything they have. I distracted him momentarily by feeding him and rocking his world with my mad sex skills, but as we lie in bed together later, I can tell it's still bothering him.

He's distracted, and while I find his fingers running through my hair comforting, I can tell when he thinks of something that makes him angry, because his fist tightens and he pulls hard. I don't even think he's noticed he's doing it.

"You know, I was so lost in the moment during our bonding that I didn't notice your cock is literally like a rabbit vibrator," I comment conversationally, trying to distract him from his turmoil. "All those ridges and bumps were fucking amazing, but then it started to vibrate too, and, well, I scored the husband jackpot." I'm desperately trying to lighten the mood, but I don't think he's even hearing me. A wave of anger rushes over me. Those petty fucking bitches better not run into me in the hallways, because I will tell them what I really think of them. Sighing heavily, I swing my legs over the bed and stand up, making my way to the bathroom. He doesn't even say a word, he's so caught up in his own thoughts.

I wasn't kidding about his cock. He fucking made me see stars, and I'm a bit wobbly on my feet. He drank deeply too, so I'm feeling a little light-headed. When I feel something slide down the inside of my leg, I look down and scream.

Thick, red fluid coats my legs. Oh my god, I'm having a miscarriage. My babies. I feel a breeze, and Saxon appears in front of me, grabbing me.

"What's wrong, my blood rose?" He looks around the bathroom, on high alert.

I throw myself into his arms and sob. "I'm losing my babies. Call Link or take me to the clinic quickly."

"What? No! We didn't do anything that should cause a miscarriage," he argues, and I point at the mess between my legs.

"Yes, there's no denying it."

He gently pushes me backwards and looks down, and then he starts to chuckle.

"What are you laughing at, you insensitive asshole?" I scream at him, smacking his solid chest.

"Oh, my sweet blood rose. That is the color of my cum. That's what's making the mess on your legs." I stop smacking him and look down again. "You didn't notice during our bonding because we were so caught up in it and everything was covered in blood, so it didn't stand out."

"Really?" I gasp, and my heart rate settles as I drag in a shuddering breath. "I'm not losing the babies?"

"No, my darling, you're not. Well, I mean, unless you count all the potential ones," he jokes and presses a kiss to the top of my head. "I'm sorry you were so scared."

"I really was. I didn't realize how much I wanted them until there was a possibility they would be gone." We stand there with his arms wrapped around me as I get myself together again.

"Why don't you wash off? You will feel better after that," he suggests, pulling away and leading me to the pool.

He holds my hand and helps me down the steps. I hiss when the steaming hot water hits my body, but soon enough, it's easing all the aches, and I sigh with contentment. Saxon doesn't follow me in, he just blows me a kiss and returns to our bedroom. I spend ten minutes floating, letting my own thoughts drift as my body does the same thing in the pool, before I quickly wash myself. Getting out, I grab a big, soft, fluffy towel off the heating shelf and use it to dry my body. When I'm done, I wrap it around myself and head back out to my room and my large wardrobe. Saxon is nowhere to be seen, and I feel a little put out about that. He could have at least told me he was leaving. I guess his drama with his clan is worse than I thought. He doesn't seem like he would usually be so thoughtless about my feelings.

Although it's nighttime, I'm restless, so I decide that maybe getting out of my room and taking a walk around the ship wouldn't be a bad thing. I've seen a few places, like the restaurant Link took me to for dinner and the cafe where I had drinks and coffee with Magenta, as well as a couple of other things, but there is so much more to explore. I also still haven't seen Caspian this evening. He hadn't returned when I took Saxon back to my room.

I don't feel comfortable going to sleep for the night without seeing my mate, so I grab a pair of skinny jeans, a cute top that displays the girls to perfection, and a pair of ankle boots. Dressing quickly, I do my hair and makeup and head out to the living area. I stop and look around the empty room. No one is in sight. Huh, where could everyone have gone?

Suddenly, my watch beeps, and I look down at it and smile. My thoughtful cyborg has sent me a message telling me he returned to the clinic to watch over John for the evening. Well, at least that is one wayward future husband accounted for, but what about the other three?

I poke my head into Saxon's bedroom, but it's empty. Next, I check Xavier's bedroom, and I find my warlock curled up on his bed, fast asleep. He's lying spread eagle on his front, and the covers are at the bottom of his bed. I want to sink my teeth into his naked ass. He asked before I dragged Saxon off to my bedroom if he could feed from our emotions, which we were both more than willing to allow him to do. I'm almost certain we fed him as full as a tick and this is him sleeping it off. I'm tempted to wake him, but I have a feeling he doesn't often feel this full or sleep this soundly, so I make the decision to leave him be. I'll leave him a note in the kitchen telling him where I have gotten off to.

I creep in and pull the covers up over his naked body. He must have kicked them off in his sleep. He doesn't move a muscle, which shows me how truly exhausted he must have been. Since I've known him, he has constantly been on full alert. I'm just glad he feels comfortable enough here in our rooms to really relax.

I push his hair back from his cheek and press a kiss to it before leaving him be. I turn off the light and pull the door shut on the way out.

One more future husband accounted for. Now I just need to track down my two actual husbands.

Grabbing my access card and slipping it into my

back pocket, I leave our rooms. I make sure I set the locks to keep Xavier safe before I leave and send a message to Link, telling him what I'm doing.

"Okay, be careful and have fun," he replies.

As I walk toward the elevator, I use my watch to locate Saxon. He's in the Vilaxian clan's quarters. I guess he went back to try and negotiate the dissolution further. He didn't tell me much, but he said if a clan cannot agree on terms of a dissolution, then it needs to go before a committee headed by the queen. I think what frustrates him the most is that a member of a clan finding a blood rose is usually accepted as an automatic dissolution of that sanguinista's membership to the clan, but the two girls refuse to acknowledge that I am Saxon's blood rose. They believe that being a non-Vilaxian is cause for me to be denied bonding. Too late, because it's already happened. I said that to him, and he grimaced, then he told me they have ways of breaking blood rose bondings. Usually it's only used when one is a criminal sentenced to death to save the innocent partner.

I'm not feeling really reassured about that. I understand that it's preoccupying his mind, but it would have been nice if he'd at least given me a kiss goodbye.

Okay, three down, one to go. "Find Caspian," I instruct my watch. The little Galaxy Circus emblem flashes while it searches for him before a map pops up on the screen. It shows Caspian at Orion's Belt.

Huh, I wonder what that is. I press a couple of buttons and bring up a glossary. Oh, it's a bar. Why would Caspian be at a bar? I thought he was going to speak to the lightning cats and check in on his friend, Silac, and the other new shifter, Tirrian.

Well, I guess I was looking for something to do, and I haven't been to that one yet, so I press the right level on the elevator and wait while it starts moving.

It's on the level below the one with the restaurant and club I went to with Link. It doesn't give much information, just says it's a good place to grab some food and drinks with friends and maybe catch a show, so maybe it's a cabaret lounge. Okay, I like a good performance.

When I arrive on that level and step out into the walkway, I can hear the noise of a crowd of people. Smiling in anticipation, I walk in the direction of the sound, looking forward to grabbing a drink and some food with my mate. I hear a pulsing beat, and I start to sway my hips in time with the rhythm as I walk. Sweet, maybe we can get our dance on too. Link was such a great dancer, and I bet Caspian is as well.

When I arrive at the entry to the establishment, there is a couple standing outside, making out like crazy. Neither of them is wearing many clothes. Looking around, I wonder if I should suggest they take what they are obviously moving toward somewhere private, but cheering, whistling, and clapping from inside draws my attention. Leaving them to it, I enter Orion's Belt, but the act must have left the stage, because it's empty. Pouting at missing out on what must have been a good show, I look around the room, trying to find Caspian amongst the crowd.

The interior is set up with a stage at the back with a catwalk that juts out into the room. Surrounding this catwalk are tables and booths. Probably about fifty percent of them have patrons in them. Down in front. directly before the catwalk, is a large booth, and that's where I find Caspian with Silac and the new dragon. When I get closer, I can see they all have beverages in front of them, but Cas's is still full, and he looks slightly uncomfortable.

His eyes widen when he sees me approach, and he jumps to his feet. "This isn't what it looks like," he blurts out.

I giggle and give him a kiss before sliding into the booth and pulling him down next to me. I'm sandwiched between him and Silac.

"It looks like you're having a good time with your friends, and I'm okay with that."

"Woo-hoo, hell yeah, Lila. Cas, your woman is amazing!" Silac holds up a hand to high-five me, and I return the gesture. He's in humanoid form today, and I really want to get a good look at him, but short of bending down and peering under the table, I'm shit out of luck. Cas still has a worried little frown on his face, but I just pat his leg.

"Hi, Tirrian, how are you?" I ask the dragon who has been nothing but hostile to me. He stares at me, his dragon eyes unblinking as he crosses his arms over his broad chest. He's not wearing a shirt, and the lights of the club make the holographic effect of his scales and skin shimmer and shine. He's fucking stunning, with the oil slick black skin and shimmery, holographic pink scales on his wings which are tucked in tight against his back, but all that attractiveness doesn't make the ugly attitude any better.

"I was good until you got here," is his gruff response, and I want to say that I ignore the vitriol, but that shit hurts.

"Tirrian," Silac scolds, but I wave him off.

"It's okay, Silac. I get it. He's Dylan's cousin, and he would feel resentful of the way he got removed from the circus."

"Because you're a mate stealing whore and then influenced your grandpas to get rid of the competition," he snarls and leans forward aggressively.

My mouth drops open in surprise, and Caspian stiffens next to me.

"Is that what you were told?" I ask, a little surprised that the dragon alpha would spread lies.

"I didn't have to be told. My cousin was kicked out of the circus, and when I got here, the love of his life was shacked up with frellscum.

"Hey now, that's enough." Caspian slams his hands on the table and stands up. "You know nothing. I never even considered mating with Dylan. My kraken would not allow it, and I never gave him any impression that I would."

"Not to mention Dylan was a man-whore of epic proportions. Was Cas supposed to stand around and wait while Dylan fucked anything that walked, or didn't, on the ship?" I point out dryly.

"And he was kicked off because he attacked Lila, not because he was competition. He wouldn't accept that my kraken made the choice. He pushed forward, mated, and bred her and took it all out of our hands. I'm just lucky that Lila was gracious enough to forgive and accept us." Cas sits back down and grabs my hand, squeezing it. The love in his eyes is obvious when he looks at me. "When he heard this, he lost it and tried to shift and attack Lila. At no stage did Dylan ever ask me to be his mate. We hadn't even had sex for a long time because he was happy sticking his cock into everything else. Dylan didn't want to be tied down, and I made it perfectly clear to him that my kraken would not mate with him. My kraken is fussy, he wanted a female to bear his young, and a surrogate was not going to be a suitable replacement."

Cas looks at Silac when he says this, and I have a feeling that maybe there was something between the two of them in the past. Silac nods with understanding in his eyes, and I make a note to ask Cas about it later when we are alone.

"Well, I'm happy for you, my friend—for both of you. We need another round of drinks to cele-brate." Silac waves a hand, looking over my shoulder for a waitress.

Tirrian is still silent and judgmental, and I guess it's going to take more than an explanation to win him over. I shouldn't care whether the dragon likes me or not, but I should be wary. His cousin turned out to be a duplicitous asshole, so I'm sure the trait runs in the family.

I feel more than see someone arrive to take my order. When I turn my head to ask for a rilaxious, the words stutter to a stop. Standing in front of me is a tall, stacked, half naked voluptuous three-breasted, four-armed woman. She has mottled green skin, except for her nipples which are bright orange, and a pretty face with tusks and backward facing horns on her head. She's wearing sparkly black hot pants and nothing else, and holding a tray with one set of arms and a tablet with one of the others. She puts the last on her hip and poses, smiling brightly.

"What can I get you boys?" she asks, ignoring me completely as she bats her eyelashes at Silac.

I groan silently. Great, another passive aggres-sive female. I'm so sick of all this shit.

"Oh, I didn't see you there. Hi, lovely, what would you like?" She moves all her attention from the naga to me and smiles brightly. "Sorry, we don't get a lot of women in here. I'm Tully."

Phew, crisis averted. She seems nice enough, but I have a feeling there's a reason they don't get a lot of women in here, and that explains why Cas looked so nervous before.

"Lila." I smile and wave. "I'll have a rilaxious," I tell her, and she makes a note on her tablet.

"And we'll have another round of the same, thanks, beautiful." Tirrian's attitude has done a full one eighty, and he's smiling at Tully. Holy fuck, he's hot when he smiles. Oh, who am I kidding, he's even hotter when he's aggressive. He makes my kraken's tentacles curl. She likes his whole grumbly, growly façade. Me, not so much.

She nods and makes another note. "I won't be long." She turns and walks off just as the lights dim and unfamiliar music blasts through the sound system. The track is sultry, seductive, and slightly Middle Eastern sounding, which makes me think of hot nights in Marrakesh. Sure enough, when a spotlight appears in the middle of the catwalk, my suspicions are confirmed. This is a strip club. Standing there is a tall, voluptuous female—or I'm guessing it's female considering most of the bar is made up of male patrons. Now that I think about it, that should have been my first clue. I'm really going to need that drink now. I hope Tully returns quickly.

CHAPTER TWENTY-FIVE

Lila

She has blue skin and smooth, tentacle-like appendages coming from her head that are undulating in time to the music, but that's all I can make out because she's wearing an outfit that seems to be made up of layers and layers of fabric draped over her like a harem girl's veils. The only parts of her face that are showing are her eyes and forehead. I'm not close enough to see the color of her eyes, but there seems to be some kind of glow in them, and the pupils are elongated like a snake's.

She starts to sway to the music, and the crowd who had been cheering and clapping falls strangely silent. Her arms start to undulate in a way that's similar to Bollywood dancing, and her hips sway. She takes a step and removes one of the veils covering her body, swinging to the music. It's fascinating, but I'm not turned on. I watch as this behavior continues, and she dances back and forth, removing more layers. She passes close to us at one stage, and I blanch in shock when I realize the tentacles on her head are actually writhing snake-like creatures. Holy shit, a real-life Medusa. I look at Cas, dying to ask questions, but he's staring at the performer, completely slack-jawed and mesmerized. I glance to the other two shifters and find they are both the same way. Glancing around the room, I realize every single creature in here seems to be in the same state. A wave of worry rushes over me.

I try to stand up, but I'm still sandwiched between two mesmerized shifters, and even with my new strength, I'm not sure if I could move them. They seem to be paralyzed, and the only thing that indicates they are still alive is the rise and fall of their chests.

I stay put, knowing that this performance has to be finished soon. She's finally down to two layers. One still covers her face, and another layer of cloth is wrapped around her body like a towel. She shim-mies and spins, giving us her back, then she reaches up and grabs the bits of fabric with both hands. She opens it wide and slides it down her body, exposing her back. A pair of small, blue, bat-like wings stretch out on either side as she drops that layer, exposing a naked butt. She turns, and it's like the whole crowd takes a breath at the same time. Her breasts are large, and her body is hairless. There is a crosscut incision in her stomach that doesn't look like a wound, but an actual part of her body. She moves sensuously across the stage and takes a seat in the chair, reclining back and spreading her legs.

Well, this just got awkward. Unlike Susie, my tastes don't run to both sexes, yet I still can't look away. Movement at the side of the stage has me looking to see what is going on. The female gestures to a man in the crowd, beckoning him toward her. He stands up and does as she bids. His movements are wooden and awkward, like he's not in control of his own body. He's big and brawny, and I think I recognize him as one of the performers from Caspian's first act—one of the jugglers. He has the same slack-jawed look that the rest of the crowd has. He mounts the stage and stops just in front of the naked female. She gestures to him, and he strips off his clothing and changes form.

He looks like a demon from Earth mythology. He has red, leathery skin, big horns, and his own set of large, bat-like wings, and jutting out in front of him is a humongous cock. My vagina yelps and clenches tight, but not from want, from horror. Even my kraken is silent at seeing the size of that thing. It would tear us apart, and I'm not down for that. The naked female reaches out and runs a finger over the erect penis in front of her. We still can't see her face, so I have no idea what she thinks of it, but she grabs hold of it and starts to lean back, pulling the man toward her by his cock.

I watch on in horror and train wreck fascination as she slides the massive appendage into the opening in her stomach. I can't hear her above the music, but she throws her head back and thrusts her body up, taking more and more of it into her. The man grabs hold of her and starts to rut in and out of the slit in her stomach. Clear fluid leaks out with every forward thrust, and I can't tear my eyes away from what's happening. The female is splayed out on the chair while the demon creature rails into her. His tail is sticking out straight behind him like it's an erection too. All of a sudden, there's another appendage, this one probing between his butt cheeks.

Oh my god, that looks like a snake as well. I follow the path of its body to see where it came from, and I stare in horror when I find its origins— it's coming from her pussy like something out of *Aliens*. I watch as it forces its way between his butt cheeks until it's fucking him at the same time he's fucking her. The music dies down, and all I can hear are animalistic growls and grunts and hisses as the two copulate in front of us.

I squirm uncomfortably on my seat. I can't decide if I'm turned on or horrified by the sexual display going on in front of us, but I know two things for sure. One, this is not what I thought I would be doing tonight or that this was where I would find my husband, and two, I can't believe my grandpas let this happen.

Just as the grunts and groans reach a crescendo, she tears the final veil off her face, and I slam backward in my seat. Her face is a mouthful of teeth, like a snake, and her nose is just two slits, much like Lord Voldemort from the children's story. She snatches the demon creature's arm, brings it to her mouth, and bites down hard into the crook of his elbow. He shouts and thrusts hard and must find his release. She releases his arm from her teeth and squeals high and loud. The female's stomach slit starts to ooze thick, yellow, pus-like fluid that makes me want to gag, and when she pulls her pussy snake from his ass, a trail of thick black liquid flows out to puddle at his feet.

I wrinkle up my nose. Yeah, I've made up my mind, I'm not turned on, and that was all kinds of fucked up. Suddenly, Tully appears on the stage. She's holding a weapon, and it's pointed at the female. The female grins and holds up her hands as Tully steps forward and pistol whips the guy. He shouts and shakes his head, and then he releases an ear-piercing scream when he realizes where he is. He stumbles backward, removing his cock from her stomach. Another bare breasted server of the same race as Tully comes onto the stage and wraps a towel around the now shuddering man, who turns and vomits off the stage. She then helps him off to the side.

"Turn it off," I hear Tully demand, and the woman chuckles evilly.

"No. Why should I? I have them all in my thrall."

Tully snorts, and without turning away from her, she calls out, "Lila, slap Caspian hard for me. Pain will knock him out of the trance."

I don't hesitate to do as she asks. Something is not right here. I think Tully needs all the backup she can get, and I'm just not at that level yet. I slap Caspian hard across the face, putting a little of my Vilaxian strength in it to guarantee it works. He grunts and slumps forward, grabbing his head. I don't have time for this shit. "Ah, Caspian, we could do with a little help here please."

He lifts his head and blinks owlishly at me, then turns to look at where I'm pointing. His eyes widen in shock, and he jumps to his feet.

"Fuck me. Silac, you fucking idiot." He reaches around me and punches Silac in the jaw. This has the same effect on him as my slap did on Caspian. He drops his hands and groans, shuddering. "You never said a Madova was the main performance. I could fucking kill you right now." Cas is so angry, his eyes are slits as he glares at Silac.

Silac shakes his head, reaches over, and pinches the still tranced Tirrian hard on the nipple. This has the desired effect, and he becomes quiet and angry once more. "I didn't know, neither of us did." Silac looks to Tirrian for confirmation, and he gives him a brief nod. "I'm not sure anyone did. I can't imagine the Adams brothers being okay with that.

We're just lucky she didn't shift mid-session and eat him. That's what usually happens."

"Someone needs to explain what the fuck I just witnessed and what the fuck was wrong with all of you." I'm feeling off balance and kind of grossed out.

Cas is practically shaking with anger. "The female creature is a Madova. They come from a planet with the same name. They are parasitic in nature and only shift into a humanoid form for breeding. Their animal form is reptilian, kind of like a Chinese dragon with long, slender bodies and wings. The species is completely female. They are able to mesmerize males of other races into copulating with them. The males cum into the hole in their stomach, which fertilizes the eggs. She then deposits the eggs inside the male. That was what that thing in his ass was doing. They keep them alive and can control them like a puppet while their eggs incubate, but when it gets close to hatching time, they shift and kill the male, usually by biting off their head. The flesh then rots and helps incubate the eggs. When the babies are born, their animal form will eat what is left of the host."

"What I want to know is how did one come to be on this ship?" Tirrian sounds angry. I imagine he is not a creature who doesn't like to be in control of his own body. "Who runs this bar?" he demands of Tully, who shakes her head.

"My sister and I do. We never hired this thing,"

she spits out the words, and the Madova laughs again, looking quite comfortable reclined back on the chair. "We hired what we thought was a Filani. She had all the right documents and references, but was always covered in the traditional Filani garb, so we didn't know any different."

"Filanis can be just as dangerous," Silac points out, and Tully shakes her head.

"There are good and bad people in all races. Most Filanis only take the smallest amount of life force during sex, nothing that damages the partner, but it's also why they never settle down. They need to constantly have sex to feed, but there are some who will kill their partners. This is nothing new in the galaxy," Tully argues. "Unlike these parasites. Gilani needs to see the doctor now. We need to find a way to extract the eggs."

I can't believe what I am hearing.

"So you are saying that this one took the place of the real woman you hired? But why?" Cas asks, stepping out of the booth, and I follow him. I can feel Silac and Tirrian at my back, so I turn and whisper to them.

"Can the two of you wake the rest of the men from the trance and get them out of here? I don't think it's safe."

Thankfully Tirrian doesn't argue or sneer, he just quickly agrees, and then they work their way around the room as I tune back into the conversation.

"Tell us why you're here," Tully demands, her gun still pointing at the Madova.

The Madova chuckles and shrugs. "Maybe it was just my breeding time and I was looking for a suitable partner."

Cas shifts into half form, shredding his clothes, and the two of us mount the steps to back up Tully.

"I somehow doubt that. No man is willing to breed with a Madova, it's why you need to put us all into a trance," Cas snaps.

She hisses, and a long, forked tongue flickers in and out of her mouth. I shiver in disgust. Now, on Silac, that shit is sexy, but seeing this female do it just creeps me out.

"Why are you really here?"

She starts to laugh again, and this time more yellow pus starts to ooze out of the gaping hole in her stomach. That thing still hasn't retracted, and it's no wonder, considering the size of the cock that had been in it. I feel nauseous just looking at it.

"I just can't do this with all of that." I gag a little. "Can we cover her up?" I ask.

One of Caspian's tentacles grabs the last cloth she removed and quickly drapes it over her. She doesn't move.

"Why isn't she moving?" I'm curious as to why she is just sitting there, unconcerned.

"She can't. She's paralyzed for a short time. They both would have been if Tully hadn't stepped in."

"Shall I call Xavier and get him down here? Maybe he can rifle through her brain and find out why she's really here," I suggest, and he looks at the female once more.

"Last chance to admit why you're here, or I will call the warlock down and he can force it out of you."

She hisses, and I see her pussy snake start to retract as all of the ones on her head stand up and flare their hoods.

"Ah, I think the paralysis is wearing off." I point out the movement in case Cas missed it.

"Just let me kill her. No good can come of this." Tully waves her gun, but Cas holds up his hand as Tirrian and Silac join us on stage. The female's eyes widen, and she licks her lips as she gazes at them, and when I turn to see why, I find Silac has shifted into his half form as well.

"A naga. You would have been a suitable carrier for my eggs. What a shame I did not pick you out of the crowd," she hisses and pouts.

Silac flares his hood and slithers closer, looking down on her. Her eyes start to glaze slightly, but she shakes it off and hisses at him, as do the snakes on her head. He flares his hood wider and starts to weave back and forth in front of her. This time her eyes glaze over fully.

"Why are you here?" he demands once more.

"The orb of power is rumored to be on this ship. I was sent to find it." I feel my stomach lurch and my skin prickle with panic. I stay very still, not glancing at Caspian in the hope that I do not give myself away.

"By whom?" Silac demands.

"The Syndicate," she replies in a monotone voice.

"Who are the Syndicate?" Silac is asking all the right questions, but this time, she shakes her head.

"I don't know, nobody does, and if anyone finds out, they are quickly dealt with."

Silac folds his hood back and lowers his body before turning to us.

"Thank you." Caspian slaps his friend on his shoulder. "I know you don't like doing that."

Silac shudders. "No, it makes me no better than her," he spits out, but I disagree.

"Lila, what do you want to do?" my mate asks me, and when I turn away from the female, the three of them are looking at me, waiting for an answer.

Swallowing some bile, I turn to Tully. "Kill her," I order, and in a flash, she pulls the trigger. The gun shoots light and puts a small, smoking hole in the middle of the female's forehead, followed by one in the middle of the chest and two in the stomach. Her eyes glaze over, and she slumps, the life extinguished from her body.

"Thank you, Tully," I say to the woman who lowers her gun and turns pleading eyes on me.

"I am so sorry, Lila. Please don't fire us."

"It's fine, Tully. I'm not blaming you. There must be a better way of checking if people are who they say they are."

"There is, except we've never needed it before, but things are changing." Cas looks at me, and in his eyes, I see that he understands that this just became an even bigger problem.

"Why would they think the orb of power is here? It's been missing since the end of the war." Silac has a little frown on his face that makes him look all confused, and it's cute as fuck, but Tirrian is studying me with eyes that I wouldn't hesitate to guess miss very little. I wonder if he heard my heart rate jump. Fucking hell, I hope he's not going to become a problem.

"No idea. I'm sure it's just one of those silly rumors that pop up occasionally, kind of like myths and legends on Earth." I brush it off, and it seems to satisfy Silac, but Tirrian doesn't look as convinced.

"Well, that's about as much excitement as I can take for one night. Can I leave you to clean up this mess and see that Gilani is taken to Link? I know he's down in the clinic now," I ask the girl, and she quickly agrees.

"Yes, of course. Sully and I will take care of it, and again, we're sorry." She bows her head and hurries away, I assume to check on the demonic male and her sister.

I look at the dead female once more and shudder before turning my back. "Well, I wish I could say this has been fun and a beautiful bonding experience, but it really hasn't. Maybe next time you could avoid taking my husband to the death dealing strippers." I raise an eyebrow at the other two, and they exchange a glance.

"Sorry, Lila," Silac mumbles, but Tirrian just scowls at me.

"Right, good chat. See you later, I guess." I grab my husband's hand and drag him out of the strip club.

"Lila," he starts as we make our way to the elevator.

I hold up my hand. "Not until we get home and I can get Xavier to put up a barrier," I plead, and he stops.

"No, I just wanted to apologize for going to the strip club. It wasn't planned, it's just where they were when I went looking for them." I wave him off and press the button to call the elevator car.

"I don't care about the strip club. I trust you. Hang out with your friends wherever. I'm just shaken by the whole Madova thing. I guess all of the races I've met so far have been mostly peaceful. Seeing her and hearing about their race reminds me that I have so much more to learn, and things aren't always black and white or safe. I'm going to ask Saxon to work on my new powers tomorrow."

"That's smart. I forget that you are so new to all of this. Iceen is still a good day and a half away. We will probably arrive late tomorrow night and stay in orbit until the morning. Iceen is too inhospitable during the night to risk being caught outside. They don't allow people to transport directly into the dwellings. There is a landing pad, and we will use a shuttle to get down there, but that is also weather dependent."

"Okay, good then. We need to tell my grandpas what happened too, but I really don't want to worry them even further," I say as we step in, and it takes us to our floor.

"Let's not for now. Link can check over Gilani, and in the morning after your training with Saxon, we can tell them. Let them have a good night's sleep. God knows they are worried enough about John without adding to it."

He wraps a tentacle around my waist and drapes an arm over my shoulder as we walk to our room. I rest my head on his shoulder and sigh. "There's never going to be a dull moment here, is there?"

He shakes his head and presses a kiss to my temple. "Not since you arrived, and I wouldn't have it any other way."

CHAPTER TWENTY-SIX

Lila

T he next day, Saxon brings me down into the circus pod soon after breakfast so we can work on my new Vilaxian strength.

When we arrive, Xenos is there, as are Hale, Velorina, and two unfamiliar Vilaxians. The nasty bitches are nowhere to be seen.

"Lila, I'd like you to meet my brother, Xenos." Saxon drags me over, and I blink, staring at the man in front of me. I didn't get a good look the night Saxon and I bonded. Instead, I played possum, not wanting to draw more attention to myself, but it's like looking at my husband with longer hair. I glance between the two of them, and they both grin at me.

"Twins?" I ask, and Saxon nods.

"Welcome to the family, Lila." Xenos pulls me into a hug, kissing my cheeks. "We're so very happy that Saxon has found his blood rose."

"Thank you." I smile gratefully at him. I was truly worried that he was only putting on a happy face for his brother, but he seems genuinely pleased.

"Let me introduce you to my clan." He waves the two strangers over, and both of them approach with happy, welcoming grins, and I feel a relieved breath escape me. "This is Dante and Kavita." He points to the male and female respectively. Both of them are tall and intimidating, like all the sanguin-istas. Dante has luscious brown curls that flop over his lavender-colored eyes, and Kavita has long, pin straight, red hair that falls to her ass, dark eyes with red flecks in them, and ruby red lips. They are both fucking stunning. Out of the corner of my eye, I see Hale and Velorina eyeing them like they are a tasty snack that they'd like to eat up.

"Welcome, little one," Dante says, repeating the same actions as Xenos and kissing my cheeks.

"We are so happy to meet you. Well, I am happy to have another female in the family." Kavita grabs both of my hands and squeezes them.

"Hey, what am I?" Velorina sounds annoyed and puts her hands on her hips.

"But you won't be family much longer, will you?" Kavita doesn't turn back to look at her, so she misses the hurt on Velorina's face.

Wow, so things just got fucking awkward.

Hale growls and steps forward aggressively. "Fuck you, Kavita," he spits out, and in a flash, Xenos is in his face, chest to chest.

"Watch how you speak to my clan member."

"How about she thinks before she opens her fucking mouth?" Hale doesn't back down, and Saxon pushes between them.

"Enough. Now is not the time or place." He looks at me guiltily. I guess he hasn't been completely honest with me.

Hale steps back and runs a frustrated hand through his ice blond hair, making it stick out awkwardly. "It's nothing against you, Lila. We both know Saxon wanted out for a while. Both of us have had similar feelings, but the other two are making things difficult. We don't want it, but it looks like they are going to force a mediation on us."

"Mediation?" I ask, looking at each of them, hoping someone will answer.

Saxon sighs. "We need to go before a committee and explain the reason for our clan dissolution. It's messy and prolongs the process, and it also makes it harder to find a new clan because the other members get the reputation of troublemakers." His eyes are full of sympathy as he looks at Hale and Velorina. Hale has stepped back and wrapped an arm around the other woman, comforting her.

"I'm sorry. My words may have been insensitive.

I apologize." Kavita has the grace to blush prettily. "I didn't mean to attack you, I am just so angry at the other two. There is no reason this should be happening. They are only causing problems for everyone. A blood rose bonding is an automatic dissolution." Kavita walks over and wraps her own arms around Velorina in comfort, and I see her melt into them.

"Are you two going to behave?" Saxon looks between his brother and Hale, and now that I'm paying attention, I realize the air is filled with sexual tension.

Saxon told me these two clans used to be combined, but when they got assigned to the circus, Xenos and the other two decided to stay on Vilax. Being in the circus was beneath him. I wonder what changed their minds, or if they were ordered to. Maybe that's why there is so much tension between him and Hale—or they used to fuck. I'm going to go with that.

"Because if you're not, you can all leave."

They quickly agree, and before long, I'm being put through my paces. They test my speed, strength, reflexes, and reactions. I'm put through the wringer, but I'm almost on par with Velorina who, by her own admission, is the weakest in the clan.

"This is freaking awesome. I was so disappointed when I didn't get any Skarrian powers, so it's nice to have these to rely on until we can see Xavier's parents and get mine unlocked." I'm breathing heavily, and Saxon passes me a bottle of Skarrian water. I twist off the top and down it all in one go.

"Okay, last test, my sweet blood rose," Saxon says, taking the empty bottle out of my hand and putting it to the side.

"Flying?" I can't control the excitement in my voice, and the others all chuckle.

Saxon nods. "Yes, it's the main reason I asked the others to join us. When you're learning, it can be unpredictable, and you should always have experienced flyers around to help you."

I squeal quietly and do a little dance on the spot then clap my hands. "Let's do this!" I shout, and they all look at me strangely, so I wave my hand. "Never mind. Show me what to do."

"Well, if you have the ability, and you may not," Saxon warns gently, "you just push off into the air and think about where you want to go and how fast."

"So like Superman?" I say, and a little furrow of confusion appears between his eyebrows. It's so freaking cute.

"Who?"

"Never mind. Can one of you show me?" I ask, looking at the others, and almost like they are in sync, they all bend their knees and launch themselves into the air. Just like that, the five of them are flying around the dome. I watch carefully, and I can see that they shift their bodies to direct themselves.

Streamlining makes them go faster, and making their bodies bigger slows them down. They twirl, tumble, somersault, and glide, looking majestic.

"Are you ready?" Saxon draws my attention back down and holds a hand out for me.

"Yeah, okay. But promise not to let me fall?" I ask, putting a protective hand over my tiny baby bump.

"Of course, my sweet blood rose. I will never let anything happen to you," he tells me, pressing a sweet kiss to my lips.

"Come on, Lila. Get your ass up here," Hale calls, and I take a deep breath, bend my knees, and jump.

I lift maybe an inch off the ground and drop back down. I feel my face fall in disappointment.

"No, don't be sad. It's okay, sometimes it takes a couple of tries," Saxon quickly assures me.

"Yeah, and sometimes it takes pushing you off a cliff." Hale snickers, and Velorina slaps him on the back of the head.

"Shut up. You'll scare her, you idiot."

The five of them are upright and hovering on the spot, waiting for Saxon and me to join them. Hale and Velorina are on one side, and Dante, Kavita, and Xenos are on the other.

"Try again," Saxon encourages, and so once more, I take a deep breath and bend my knees before pushing off as hard as I can.

This time I do manage to leave the ground, but

it's slow and awkward, kind of like doing bunny hops in a car, and my arms and legs are flailing. I scream, but Saxon is right next to me, hovering gracefully in the air.

"Good, Lila. Now you need to look in the direction you want to go and kind of kick off," Saxon tells me.

"Kick off what?" I yell, still flailing wildly. I can hear the others above me quietly laughing, so I look up at them and give them my middle finger. My body shoots upwards in the direction I was looking. Hale was the one who was in my line of sight, and I hurtle toward him, unable to slow myself. His grin drops and his mouth opens as he realizes I'm not going to pull up in time. He braces for impact when hands grab my legs and yank me to a halt.

He sighs with relief, and I'm so close, I feel his breath ruffle my hair. I look down and find Saxon and Xenos have a hold of my ankles.

"Whoa, that was close," I exclaim, my body hovering in place now that my movements are being controlled by someone else.

"Wow, Lila, I've seen Vilaxian children with more coordination than you." Velorina's eyes are wide with shock, and I can't really be upset with her —I am a disaster.

"How about two of us help her move around until she gets the hang of it? I remember my mother and father doing that with me and my siblings when we were learning to fly." Dante smiles at me encouragingly.

"Holy crap, that was the worst flying I have ever seen." A voice from below has us all looking toward the ground. There, my magenta-haired friend stands with a hand shielding her eyes as she looks up at us. Suddenly, she starts to rise into the air. My mouth drops open in shock. I'd forgotten Magenta could fly. It's one of her Skarrian abilities. Soon enough, she's eye level with me, smirking with her arms crossed. "Dude, you are going to need some serious lessons, but there's no time for that now. Xavier sent me to find you. You need to be outfitted for Iceen." Her gaze drifts away from me, and she waves a couple of fingers at Velorina. "Hi.

Velorina smiles and propels herself closer. "Hello, pretty girl." She picks up Magenta's hand and presses a kiss to the back of it. Hale moves to their side.

"We missed you at the club last night," he tells her, and I watch in surprise as my Skarrian friend blushes prettily.

Now hold up. Mags is a whore, but these two just made her coy. What the fuck am I missing?

"Hale, why don't you introduce us to your pretty friend?" Xenos releases my leg and moves to join the group, with Dante and Kavita going to.

"Great, now I'm chopped liver," I grumble to myself, and Saxon pulls me through the air until we're facing each other.

"The most delicious liver I've ever tasted." He nudges my nose with his, and I giggle but then push him out of the way. I want to see how this all plays out.

Hale's face sours, but he waves a hand. "Magenta, meet Saxon's brother, Xenos, and his clan members, Kavita and Dante."

"Hi, I saw you in the act the other night. Thanks for coming and helping out." Magenta is polite and shakes the three newcomers' hands. "Anyway, I'm going to steal Lila away. We'll be close to Iceen soon, and she needs to be briefed on protocol. I might see you at the club tonight," she tells Hale and Velorina.

"We'll get Nixie to join us, it will be fun," Hale replies, and the two girls blush again. Fucking hell, I need to grill my friend about what's going on.

Magenta turns to me. "Okay, let's go."

"Ah…" I look at my husband, who just chuckles. He wraps his arms around me, and we start to lower.

"Don't worry, sweetheart, we will work on it later. At least we know you do have that ability." His words make my chest puff up with pride. He's right, I can fly—not well, but I can do it. Practice only make me better.

"Lots of practice," Magenta mutters next to us as she keeps pace with us on the way down. This time, I flip her off, and she and Saxon both laugh.

"Wow, with you two as friends, who needs enemies?"

"Seems like you've got plenty of those too," Magenta muses, and this time I bare my fangs at her, feeling my bloodlust rise.

"Whoops, sorry." Magenta holds her hands up in apology as our feet finally touch the ground and my body regains the feeling of weight. Huh, I hadn't noticed before that I had been feeling weightless.

"Just give Lila half an hour to feed, and then she will meet you at the shopping precinct," Saxon suggests, and Magenta salutes us.

"Sure thing, General. I'll drop the information on your watch. Drink heaps so that you don't feel like gnawing on my neck," she says before walking away.

"Oh, I didn't think you minded being gnawed on," I retort sassily, and it's her turn to flip me off. I laugh. Yeah, payback's a bitch named Lila.

"Come on, my blood rose, let's get you topped off so you don't kill your friend."

I'm happy, well fed, and well fucked when I finally find myself in the shopping district an hour later. Magenta is sitting in the same cafe I'd met her at not all that long ago. She's sipping something that smokes furiously and has an empty plate next to her.

"About fucking time," she grumbles when she sees me and stands up. She tosses back the rest of her drink in one go, her eyes watering slightly. Placing the glass back on the table, she grabs my hand and starts towing me toward one of the clothing stores.

"Sorry it took a little longer than I thought. I needed to eat after expending all that energy this morning." I don't elaborate and tell her what I needed was blood, but she's not stupid.

She narrows her eyes and squints at me. "Yeah, sure, eat. Now spill the tea. I want to know everything about your blood rose bonding and what it's like to drink blood, not to mention what sex with a Vilaxian is like."

"But I thought you had a thing going with Velorina? Surely you know what sex with a Vilaxian is all about."

"I do, but we haven't gotten to the sex part yet. Not really," she mutters as the door to the store slides open and we enter. I look around in amazement at all the different styles of clothing. Sure, there's everyday wear that you would see in any clothing store in cities on Earth, but there are other things that you would only find in specialty or costume stores.

"Hello. How may I help you today?" a polite

voice calls out, and from behind a mannequin wrapped in a shimmery cloth, a being appears. I say being because I'm not sure if they are male or female, and I have no clue what race they are. I really need to do better with my alien research.

I can't see their legs because they are wearing a long skirt-like garment, but they seem to be gliding over the ground. Their skin is a mauve color, and they have long, spindly arms. Their head is round like a human's, but they have a snout with two, black beady eyes, kind of like an insect. They have no hair, but they do have ridges and bumps all over the back of their skull, all in the same mauve color as the rest of their skin. I can't see a nose, and the snout ends in two pouty lips that seem to be covered in red lipstick.

"Hi, Tynka. How are you today?" Magenta asks, bowing slightly at the creature.

Their pouty lips turn up in a smile. "Ah, Magenta." She bows back. "I am very well indeed. What can I do for you and your friend?"

"This is Lila Adams. Lila, this is Tynka, the preeminent clothing designer on the ship." As Magenta does the introductions, the creature's eyes widen in surprise before she's smiling even wider.

"Lila, it is a pleasure to finally meet you." She bows, so I return it and smile back.

"You too, Tynka." I look around the store. "It looks like you have an amazing selection here."

"Well, the circus keeps me on my toes

depending on where they are performing. I need to outfit everyone in suitable garments, but I do love my job, and I am forever grateful to your grandpas for giving me a chance."

"No matter where we go, our clothes are always a hit, and Tynka ends up with orders from throughout the galaxy. She even has a factory on her home planet of Sotda XV where they make everything."

Tynka's mauve cheeks tinge red, and she lowers her head. "It is nothing special," she says modestly.

"It certainly sounds like it is," I praise her, and she lifts her head again.

"You are too kind. Now, what can I do for you today?"

"We are heading to Iceen to drop off that hell beast," Magenta tells Tynka who shudders visibly.

"Thank goodness she will no longer be with us. Although they don't venture out often, she was in here just before our Earth stop and wanted a new dress. She made me change it five times before she was happy, her lightning crackling threateningly the whole time."

"Lila will be joining the away party to the surface, so she needs something suitable for the cold climate of Iceen. We don't need our little circus heir turning into a Lilasicle." Magenta and Tynka giggle, and I start to worry.

"Is it really that cold down there?" I ask, and Magenta shrugs.

"Colder probably. Iceen is fairly inhospitable. Only the lightning cats and the yalani, as well as some low-level life-forms, live on it. I think their lightning helps regulate their temperature, but they are so damn secretive."

"Come, I have the perfect outfit for you. It will keep you warm, and you will look fabulous at the same time." Tynka moves smoothly away from us, and Magenta whispers out of the corner of her mouth.

"Our conversation is not done, just postponed," she threatens me, and I raise an eyebrow.

"Same. Don't think I forgot that you didn't answer my own question either."

She sighs and rolls her eyes. "Fine. After Iceen, we'll have a girls' night. Your mates have been hogging you, and Nixie is dying to see you again. We can invite Susie too, if you want."

A night with my best friend and my two new ones sounds like heaven to me. "Deal. I'm in, and I promise I'll tell you what sex with a male Vilaxian is like, because don't think I didn't notice the tension between you and Hale too, and the interest the other three had as well."

"They are only interested in me as a blood source. Vilaxians like Xenos wouldn't lower themselves to having a fling with another race. Not all of them are as open-minded as Hale and Velorina. Look at how Estrella and Radella reacted to you being Saxon's blood rose," she mutters as Tynka stops in front of us, and the conversation ceases.

As Tynka starts to pull clothes out and pass them to me, I think about what I saw high in the rafters. The sexual tension was off the charts, and I think my friend doth protest too much.

But clothes now, sex talk later.

CHAPTER TWENTY-SEVEN

Maxsim

I haven't slept a wink since we arrived at my home planet. I still haven't been able to get in contact with my mother. Echo called his mother and requested if she could find out where mine is, but we haven't heard back from her either. I suspect something is amiss and something has happened to them both. It will be up to me to find them.

The ship has been orbiting Iceen for the last eight hours, waiting for the faraway sun to reach the side the landing platform is on. The temperatures are way too frigid for anyone other than lightning cats to venture out before it is up. Long ago, our ancestors made it so that people couldn't transport directly into a building. There's a special electrical charge that runs through the cave walls and our home structures that disrupts a teleport beam. This way they have to use the arrival platform and brave the weather on the short walk to the nearest dwelling. We were hoping this would deter most invaders or people with not so honest intentions. Not to mention anyone visiting is a little frosty, so it makes negotiations on our side more favorable because all they want to do is warm up.

Echo and I arrive at the teleporting room ten minutes before we are scheduled to beam down. I know that others will be accompanying us, but I'm surprised by how many when we get there. I thought it would just be William and Eric, but Caspian and Dr. Link are both here, as well as the Earth girl.

She and Link have a quiet, whispered conversation off to the side before he pulls her into his arms and presses a kiss to the top of her head. I wrinkle my nose at the smell that starts to drift over from her. Next to me, Echo whines softly, and I feel a scowl cross my face. That girl is going to be a problem.

"Ah, Maxsim, great. Seems like you have the same idea as us. We just want to get this over and done with," William addresses us, and Eric and Caspian both wave.

I look around the room. "Where is Natalia?"

"Saxon and Xavier went down to the brig earlier. They were going to release the Aaz'axian Brannock and show him to a spare room. He hasn't decided where he wants to go yet, so we've offered him refuge here for now. It can't be easy having your life completely upended just because one man in the Earth Alien Alliance is an asshole. I'm sure we can find something for him to do. Anyway, they are going to grab her once they have taken care of him. They should be back any minute," Eric explains, pushing a couple of buttons on the controller. Officer Kirk is nearby, but I know Eric likes to be hands-on.

The door opens behind Echo and me, and we step away from the doorway, but it's just Trace, Sim, and Fuse. The other three cats move into the room, and William raises an eyebrow at us.

"Well, have you all decided what you are going to do? Are you going to continue with the circus or stay on Iceen when we leave?" he asks, and I exchange a glance with my fellow cats.

"Trace, Sim, and I would like to stay on with the circus if that is okay with you. We were hoping that maybe Minx would be able to come in place of Natalia," Fuse answers, speaking up for the three of them.

William huffs. "Not if she's going to be a problem like Natalia was."

"She's nothing like Natalia. She's sweet, kind, and gentle," Trace says quickly, and Sim nods.

"Yes, we want to mate with her, so if she doesn't want to come, we will be leaving."

Eric and William exchange a glance, and I have a sinking feeling they are going to say no.

"Oh, let her come," a husky voice interjects. We all turn to look at Lila. "You've been dealing with Natalia this long, and from what I understand, she hasn't made any friends on board. How much worse can Minx be? We need an act, and the cats are a big draw, plus she may be just what the boys say she is." She gestures to my streak mates, who are all looking at her like the sun shines out of her ass. A small growl slips out from between my lips, and she must hear it, because her eyebrows rise, and she turns to look at me with surprise in her eyes.

"And you two?" William asks.

Echo nudges me, and I sigh.

"It all depends on what we find when we get to Iceen. My mother has not responded to any of my calls, and now neither is Echo's. I am worried Mazlan, Natalia's mother, may have done some-thing to both streaks in an attempt to hold onto her matriarch role, which is against our laws. If she is challenged, she must fight to hold her position. Challenges are taken very seriously on Iceen."

"Why doesn't a male challenge for the posi-tion?" Caspian asks. "It's quite obvious that the males are bigger than the females. You five are way bigger than Natalia, even Echo as an omega, and would easily defeat her in a fight. I'm assuming the rest of the males on the planet are the same." Caspian seems confused by our matriarchal society.

"Mostly because we are taught to respect our traditions from a very young age. This is how it has always been and always will be. We have no problems with that, but there are laws against males and females fighting against one another. If a male does challenge a female, then he must appoint a female proxy, and vice versa," I explain.

By then, the sound of Natalia arriving becomes apparent to all of us. She is screeching so loudly she can be heard through the closed door. I cannot wait to be done with her. The immense relief I feel that she won't be able to attack Echo anymore is breath stealing.

"Holy fuck, that's loud," Eric complains, putting his hands over his ears.

"I would like to meet this Minx, and we will decide from there as well as see what the situation is down there. I would like to spend as little time as possible on Iceen, because I want to get to Celestia for John," William tells us firmly as the door opens, and Xavier and Saxon drag a struggling and worse for wear Natalia into the room.

"You will all pay for this. My mother will rip your intestines out when she hears of my treatment," she screams at us.

Lila and Link have moved closer to us in a bid to get out of the way, and I see Echo's nostrils flare as he scents Lila. Jealousy starts to niggle at my mind. Why her? Why not another lightning cat? Or really, why anyone at all? We are all each other needs.

At that moment, Natalia catches sight of him,

and she lunges toward him with her claws out, surprising Saxon and Xavier who struggle to contain her. Before I can even react, Lila is in front of Echo, protecting him, her own fangs bared. Her eyes glow just like a Vilaxian's during bloodlust.

"Step back, Natalia. I haven't fed this morning, and your neck is looking mighty tasty despite the risk of a fur ball," Lila snarls at her, and I watch in amazement as Natalia actually stops and listens to her. It's almost like she's in a trance as she steps back and allows Saxon and Xavier to get a better grip on her. The minute they tighten their hold, she starts to struggle again, hissing and spitting insults.

"Wow, she really is a nasty bitch, isn't she?" Lila stares in amazement as the threats and foul language continue to spew forth.

I frown when I see Echo is huddled close to her, and she has put her glove-covered hand on his back and is rubbing him reassuringly. I don't even think she realizes she's doing it. My own jealous rage erupts, and I feel my claws extend and the teeth in my mouth change to fangs. I can't help the growl that escapes my mouth.

She turns to look at me in surprise, and that's when she recognizes what she's doing. She removes her hand slowly and holds it up. "Oh relax, Maxsim, I was just protecting your mate," she says, and with shock, I do exactly as she says.

My jealousy recedes, as do my claws and fangs. Not because I wanted them to, however, but because she said it. I feel a rush of horror replace my fear. What is she? Is that Vilaxian compulsion?

"Why don't you shut up?" Lila shouts at Natalia, who hasn't even stopped to take a breath during her rant. The room instantly falls silent. Now everyone looks at Lila, who appears as surprised as everyone else.

"Hmm, I guess maybe you got compulsion too," Saxon muses.

"Enough, let's get this done. Xavier, restrain her, and for fuck's sake, gag her. I cannot listen to that shit anymore," William demands and strides up onto the platform.

Everyone but Dr. Link is wearing Iceen approved clothing. As everyone else follows William, I see Echo admiring Lila's outfit. She's wearing all white, which must appeal to him because it's the color of his fur. They look very pretty standing side by side. The pants are skintight and hug her curves, as does the top which dips low in front. The material isn't very thick, so I'm guessing it's specially treated to withstand cold temperatures. In fact, everyone is wearing outfits that are easy to move in, so maybe they are anticipating trouble and have dressed accordingly.

She's paired it with a long, fur-lined white coat and thick, knee-high boots. I watch as she brings the hood up over her head, covering her hair. She places herself between Echo and Natalia on the small platform despite the warlock having immobilized and silenced her.

I'm not even sure she realizes she's done it. She's distracted as she talks to her kraken mate, who is in his human form and covered in the same kind of outfit as everyone else. I quickly insert myself between my mate and Lila while she is preoccupied. My skin itches at the thought of having her too close to him.

"Okay, Link, hopefully we won't be long," Eric says, the last to step onto the platform.

"Good luck, and I'll let you know if anything changes with John." The cyborg doctor waves goodbye as Officer Kirk hits the transport button.

Our bodies dissolve into molecules, and we are transported down onto the planet's surface. When we reform, I take a deep breath, smiling at the smell of home.

"Holy cold as a witch's tit," Lila mutters behind me. The wind is howling so loudly it's hard to hear her, and the icy particles in the air sting the face as everyone puts their head down to protect against it.

Suddenly, a yellow barrier surrounds us, blocking out the weather completely, and the noise falls away.

"Fuck, I could kiss you," Lila says, and Xavier turns and smirks at her.

"I'll claim it later."

"I know you all told me it was bad, but that was way worse than I expected," she replies as I take the lead, moving toward the large capital building which isn't far away. The snow is knee high, and it takes the others a little longer to move through it than us cats, but eventually, we make it to the double doors.

"Maybe it would be best if you took the lead. I would like to search for my mother," I tell William, who quickly agrees.

"Would you like me to search for her like I searched for the cyborg? It is no problem and would be done a lot quicker than if you have to go room to room," the warlock offers, and my mouth drops open in surprise before I can stop it. He chuckles, his mist-covered body jiggling slightly with the action.

"I really have been antisocial, haven't I?" he says conversationally to Caspian and Saxon.

"Yes, you're a real asshole," Saxon responds dryly.

"I've never heard you complain before," the warlock mutters under his breath, and I don't think most people hear it, but my hearing is better than the other cats'. I quickly recover from the revelation that the warlock and the general have been lovers in the past. That was a well-kept circus secret. There had never even been a rumble of that gossip.

"I would appreciate it," I say, bowing my head in thanks before pushing through the door. We all enter the great building, and I let the door close behind us as Xavier drops the barrier. It's only slightly warmer in here than outside. The current matriarch doesn't believe in coddling her people. If you want to be warm, you should stick to your own dwellings.

Xavier creates a ball of light in his hand, and it quickly divides into a number of individual balls which zip off to explore the building while I lead them to the receiving room. A set of guards stand on the outside. I recognize them as two of the matriarch's sons—sons from the same litter as Natalia—and although we were once friends, I brace for an attack, but they both just nod their heads at me and open the doors.

"Go get her," one whispers as I walk past, and a memory of him appearing on my family's doorstep with whip marks across his back pops into my mind —whip marks his mother had given him while she had been teaching Natalia to be a leader.

William takes the lead with Eric by his side, and Saxon and Xavier follow behind with the quiet, frozen Natalia between them.

I can see Mazlan sitting on her throne at the end of the room. Next to her and back a bit is Minx and their younger sister Soshi. She's only ten, but it looks like Mazlan has been instructing her. Mazlan smirks until she catches sight of Natalia, bound and silent, and then she stands up, lightning crackling around her as her sky blue fur stands on end.

"What is the meaning of this? Why is my

daughter tied up like a criminal?" Mazlan demands, pointing a claw at William. "Explain yourself."

"Your daughter has been found guilty of conspiracy and aiding and abetting a wanted criminal. Out of respect for you, I have allowed her to live and returned her, unlike her co-conspirator, who was sentenced to death."

"What did this criminal do? Surely it can't be so bad as to warrant death. My daughter wouldn't help a murderer."

"He conspired to kill my intimate, which is an automatic death sentence." Xavier steps forward, shrouded in mist, and I watch as Mazlan flinches before steeling her spine.

"Only on your planet. Warlock laws have nothing to do with Iceen. Let her go."

"Warlock laws are recognized worldwide, including on the Galaxy Circus starship where this crime took place, but as she was not directly involved, she has been spared. Be mindful, however, that she will not be spared a second time." Xavier waves a hand and releases Natalia from her confines.

It takes her a moment to recover, but once she does and she realizes where she is, she smirks and struts up to stand next to her mother. I see her lean in and whisper in her ear before she stands back up.

"I challenge Echo to the right of being Maxsim's mate."

Anger infuses me, and I feel my lightning flare

up, crackling around my body. I stare at her with disbelief, amazed at her cunning. She waited until we returned to challenge him because then it could be witnessed by everyone. Echo's fear drifts into my nostrils, and it's all I can do not to strike out with a bolt of electricity. I reach for his hand, giving it a squeeze of reassurance, and purr quietly under my breath.

"Summon the citizens of Iceen. Challenges must be witnessed, and Echo must ask for a stand-in, as is our rules," Mazlan announces, sounding bored, but I hear a door open behind me. Mazlan looks up, and her jaw drops open in shock.

"Well then, I challenge you, Mazlan, for the position of matriarch, and I don't need anyone to stand in for me." Hearing my mother's voice brings me so much relief, and I feel Echo, who has been standing next to me, sag with relief too.

Turning, I find my mother and her three mates, as well as Echo's mother, Jalin, and three of her four mates. Echo's omega father is missing though, and he grabs my hand, squeezing it tight with worry.

"Astrea, I thought you were in my dungeon."

"On what charges?" I demand, and Mazlan chuckles.

"I don't need charges. I'm the ruler."

"Oh, I believe you do. I shall alert the Galactic Council to the matriarch challenge. I'm sure they will be very interested to hear about your wrongful imprisonment." Eric pulls a tablet out of his jacket and starts typing a message to the galaxy authorities, and Mazlan hisses at him.

"When I win this challenge, I will stop any citizens from Iceen from ever performing in your circus again."

"That's fine by me. It's no skin off my nose." Eric doesn't even look up at her, deeming her threat a nonissue because my mother will win this challenge. It's just Echo's challenge I need to worry about.

Who are we going to find to stand in for him?

CHAPTER TWENTY-EIGHT

Lila

"Holy fuck, it's cold on this planet," I mutter to my mates, who are all huddled around me, trying to keep me warm while we wait for the citizens of Iceen to arrive for the challenges. We've moved to a big outdoor stadium, and no one else seems to be bothered by the frigid temperatures. They come in droves in both bipedal and cat form, all here to bear witness to the challenges about to take place. The lightning cats from the circus are standing off to the side. Maxsim's and Echo's families are surrounding them, and they are whispering quietly amongst themselves.

Trace, Fuse, and Sim had an amusing and awkward reunion with Minx, Natalia's sister. The four of us watched in fascination as they introduced her to my grandpas who then proceeded to grill her.

She doesn't cower, but I can tell she's not comfortable, so I make my way over to the group, leaving the warmth and comfort of my guys.

"You're really going to continue to interrogate the poor girl?" I demand, interrupting Eric's next question. "Even I can see with my small amount of alien experience that this girl is nothing like her sister. "

"Lila," William scolds, and I raise an eyebrow at him.

"Hey, you're the one who said I needed to take charge and that the lightning cats were going to be my next task once we got John sorted, so I'm making an executive decision. If Minx wants to join us, I'm all for it. At least that way we'll still have four lightning cats. We still don't know what Echo and Maxsim are going to do." I wave my hand in the direction of their group, and when we turn to look at them, Maxsim and his mother are staring at us, their eyes predatory and scary. I shudder and turn back to my group.

Again, the male cats are looking at me like I just did them the biggest favor, and that may go a long way toward me being able to control them in their cat forms.

"Fine, this is on your head." William stabs a finger in my direction and stalks toward Maxsim and his mother. Eric smirks at me and pats me on the back before turning to Minx.

"Welcome to the circus," he says to her before hurrying after his brother.

Minx grabs my hands. "Thank you. I don't know how to repay you, but I will," she gushes, and I feel my brow wrinkle in confusion.

"It's no big deal," I protest, and Minx shakes her head.

"It really is. When my mother loses that challenge, we will be relegated back to the general population, and Natalia will be on the warpath. She will kill anyone who is in her path to making a good match. Why do you think she challenged Echo? She knows Mother is going to lose, so she is trying to make the most of the situation for her own selfish needs."

"But surely someone here is stronger than her. There has to be an alpha female who will beat her, one who will be happy to stand in for Echo and Maxsim. They may even ask her to mate with them as a thank you," I argue.

"No, there are no alpha females, or none who are unmated. Only omegas and betas have been born for years, and none of us will dare step up and take that challenge. We all know how vicious and aggressive Natalia is, and in the event she loses, she will make the winner's life a living hell. The circus is the safest place for me."

My heart sinks. "So does that mean no one will stand up for Echo?"

"No, they won't, so it looks like she will win the

challenge by default." Trace wraps an arm around Minx's shoulders, giving her comfort as Sim and Fuse crowd in behind them.

My eyes drift over to where the male omega is surrounded by his family. His mother has tears streaming down her face as Mazlan steps up to a dais and silences the now crowded arena.

"The first challenge of the evening is issued by my daughter, Natalia, against the abomination omega, Echo. Who here will stand in his place as his proxy?" The crowded arena falls silent, and only the sound of Echo's mother's sadness can be heard. Not a single person steps forward, and Mazlan's grin becomes smug, as does Natalia's, who has stepped up next to her.

"Well then, this challenge has a clear winner, my daughter, as no one will step in as proxy, so Echo automatically loses," Mazlan declares as Maxsim's mother shouts out her protests.

I feel myself step forward. "I'll take that challenge," I call out, my voice echoing around the arena.

"Lila, no!" Caspian shouts. I turn back to look at him. Saxon and Xavier are holding him back, so I hurry over to the three of them and grab his hand.

"I can't let that bitch win. It's akin to rape. The other females are terrified of Natalia, and although Maxsim hasn't been all warm and fuzzy, I refuse to let Echo lose him."

"The babies," Cas hisses at me, and my stomach sinks. "I'm not sure if you or they will survive a lightning strike."

Fuck me. How did I forget about that gem of an ability? I bite my lip, turning back to the crowd.

"She has Vilaxian abilities now, so she will be fine," Saxon assures Caspian, putting a hand on his shoulder. "She can move fast enough to avoid it."

Xavier puts his hand against my stomach, and I feel a warmth sink into my skin. When he pulls back, he's smiling softly. "The babies are happy and safe and fully protected now, and they said to tell you to kick that bitch's ass."

"Right, that's a dollar into the swear jar for all of you, damn it," I tell my children, half horrified and half proud at the message they just sent me. We are in so much trouble.

I look at Cas, and he lets out a sigh of relief and nods. "Go get 'em, tiger." He leans in and kisses me, and they both back away, allowing Saxon to escort me over to the middle of the arena.

"Challenge accepted. When I win and kill you, and your mates die too, I will be feared throughout the lands." Natalia roars loudly before unleashing her claws, jumping down off the dais, and stalking toward the center of the arena.

"She's cocky, and she angers quickly. You have your speed and strength, so knocking her out is probably your best bet. I know you have your martial arts experience from Earth, so combine those two skills, and you should have no problems. All you have to do is avoid her lightning."

"What constitutes a win?" I ask, and Natalia hears it.

"Your death." She curls her lip back and hisses.

"If my granddaughter dies, Mazlan, I will see that you pay." It's Eric who threatened the matriarch, and I turn to see him floating above the crowd with a gun pointed at the matriarch, the red laser beam illuminating the middle of her forehead.

She nods her assent before announcing, "The first to tap out or be rendered unconscious will be the loser. The fight will not stop until this happens, no matter how much you are bleeding. If you die because you are too stubborn to admit defeat, then that is neither my nor my daughter's fault," she warns me, and I nod, acknowledging her words.

Eric accepts this and lowers himself, tucking his gun back into his clothing.

"Begin." She smashes a mallet into a gong sitting next to her, and it rings throughout the stadium. People start to yell, scream, and cheer.

Natalia immediately fires up her lightning, aiming it at me. I use my speed and quickly step to the side, and it hits the ground where I had been standing, sending up sparks.

"You've got to be quicker than that," I taunt the hell beast, knowing the angrier I make her, the worse her accuracy will be. I wonder if the lightning is unlimited or if her ability to use it will wane as she tires.

"I will eat your intestines when I gut you, and then I will gut that pathetic abomination of an omega, but not before I fuck his mate in front of him and have him knot me," Natalia spews at me, and I feel my fangs drop and my bloodlust rise at the thought of her hurting the pretty, soft omega. There's just something about him that makes me want to protect him.

"Hahaha. How are you even going to do that? You don't have the right parts. A beta can't take an alpha's knot," I goad, and she smirks as the two of us circle each other, trying to make the other flinch with sudden movements. We must look ridiculous.

"When your mother controls the illegal trade of omega hormones, you can. Where do you think all the male omegas go? Killing them would be a waste when we can milk them for their slick and synthesize a drug for betas. There's a reason my family have been matriarchs for so long. We are smart," she gloats quietly, and it's so loud with the crowd screaming encouragement, I don't think anyone else hears it.

"Maybe instead of killing him, we'll add Echo to our milking stock. His mother's omega mate has been an absolute asset to our program, and I'm almost certain he's Echo's biological father. It would be quite the turn-on for Maxsim if I smelled like his mate."

I was angry before, but now I see fucking red. "Why don't you shut your fucking mouth?" I growl at her, and it's like I flipped a switch.

She stops talking instantly, and her eyes widen in shock. I'm not sure what just happened. Did I just compel her to be quiet? When I had tried compulsion yesterday with Saxon's and Xenos's clans, I wasn't able to successfully compel any of them. They thought I hadn't received that ability.

She lunges at me with her claws out in front of her, and I dodge, but I'm not quick enough, and she rakes them over my arm. I scream in pain. It's not deep, but it hurts like a bitch.

I hear my family and mates shout in distress, but I don't let it distract me. If I turn my head, I'm as good as dead. I quickly move farther out of reach and bring my arm up to my mouth, swiping my tongue along the wound, and the venom in my saliva quickly heals the lesions.

Again, her eyes widen, and she screams in frustration.

"Now, now, no need to be sad. Why don't you smile?" I tease her, and she is suddenly wearing a joker worthy grin.

Holy fuck, I really can compel her.

I take the opportunity her surprise gives me and dart forward, throwing a huge punch at her. She flies backward, landing on her ass and groaning in pain.

"Lila!" a voice calls, and I turn to see Maxsim's

mother standing on the edge of the arena. She beckons me over, and when I see Natalia is still down, I speed over to the female.

"What?" I ask the woman, and she grabs my arm.

"Listen, don't talk. You are a whisperer. Natalia is going to have to obey anything you say. I have no idea how. It is a Skarrian ability that was hunted into extinction many, many years ago by lightning cats who didn't want anyone to control them. Use it and end this."

I've been keeping an eye on Natalia, and she is finally back on her feet. Astrea steps back, nodding her encouragement, so I use my speed to get back into the fight. Natalia tries to strike with her lightning again, but she's too slow, and I roundhouse kick her in the head at the same time I say, "Sleep!"

She twirls around from the force of my kick before landing flat on her face. She doesn't move a muscle, since the whisperer ability put her out like a light. I've done it, I've won. A small amount of guilt fills me, but when I turn to see Maxsim and Echo embracing, I feel a sense of satisfaction and a small amount of jealousy—damn horny kraken— but when the two of them turn to look at me, Echo is staring at me the same way he looks at his mate. I feel a pang of longing, but Maxsim is still scowling despite what I just did for the two of them.

He's off-limits. He has a mate, and we need to leave

them be, I tell my inner kraken, but I freeze, paralyzed with shock, when another voice answers.

They are yours, they just don't know it yet.

Holy fuck, just what I need, another damn voice in my head. Is this a whisperer thing? I need to find Astrea and demand she tell me everything.

The arena continues to chant my name, and it echoes around the huge space. I'm slightly dazed at the new revelation, but I hold up my hand to wave to everyone. I hear Minx scream my name from the dais, and I turn to look just as a bolt of blue lightning hits me directly in the chest.

I seize up, and the pain that jolts through my body is so bad I can't even scream. My limbs convulse furiously, and then there's blackness.

CHAPTER TWENTY-NINE

Lila

My first conscious thought when the pain in my body registers with my still foggy brain is *holy fuck, knock me back out again*. I feel like Bubby hit me with the starship and then reversed over me.

I groan and try to turn my head away from the annoying light that shines brightly through my eyelids.

"Ah, there she is," a voice so beautiful I want to weep at the sound of it says from somewhere above me. "Come on, Lila, open those pretty eyes so that your mates can see for themselves that you are okay."

My eyelids flutter, but I keep trying. All I want to do is please that beautiful voice. The light is bright when I finally get them to cooperate, and I groan again, slamming them shut.

"Oh sorry, dear, try again," the voice coaxes, and when I do, the light has dimmed considerably. That's when I notice that the light is coming from the stunning woman with huge-ass white angel wings who is standing above me.

"Oh my god, I fucking died. That bitch killed me. Oh, I hope Maxsim's mom eviscerates her. So how long until I get my own wings? I want to go back and see that match so I can cheer on Astrea."

The being erupts into laughter, which sounds like an angel's laugh, all perfectly in tune, unlike my own goose honk. Oh right, it is an angel's laughter.

"No, Lila, you did not die. Your mates and family brought you to us as quickly as they could, and we were able to stabilize your body," the gorgeous, blonde-haired beauty assures me.

"Stabilize me? The babies?" I ask, finally able to move my limbs as I wrap my hand around my tiny baby bump, ecstatic to feel that it is still there.

"Yes, the lightning strike activated the rest of your Skarrian abilities, as well as overloaded your body, causing you to blackout. For now, your babies are fine, but your body has been under a huge amount of stress, so I have recommended to your family that you initiate the birth as soon as you possibly can."

Give birth soon? Holy fuck, I'm not ready for that. I can barely keep them safe inside me, so how am I going to manage once they leave my body?

"Hang on, how do you know the lightning strike activated my Skarrian powers?" I ask the beautiful woman who I now realize must be Celestian.

She steps aside, and my bed is surrounded by all of my mates as well as Eric and William. I guess they haven't fixed John yet. I feel a pang of disappointment and guilt. They have been too busy seeing to me to get to him yet. Caspian reaches for my hand, and Saxon takes the other. Xavier brushes a hair out of my face as Link squeezes my foot. I beam at them.

"Lila, the reason we know about your abilities is because your body started to change. First, you took on the features of a lightning cat with pretty stormy blue fur, a tail, and fluffy ears, but then you became shrouded in mist just like Xavier when he reached you. When we got back to the ship, we decided to test you, and we detoured past Tynka, and you became a Vengi. We then brought Tully into the clinic, you became Tutva. Lila, you are a mimic. It's a rare Skarrian ability that hasn't been seen in a very long time. It allows you to take on the characteristics of any race or being you come across, and once you do it the first time, you can always access it. It's incredible," Eric gushes, but William is pale and has his normal frown on his face.

"But it will take a while to get a hold of this ability, and your body cannot handle the extra stress with the babies. It will become dangerous for them, so we will return to Skarr, and you will have the babies so that all of you are safe," he tells me, his tone leaving no room for argument.

"Thank you, Corethea. I don't know how we can ever repay you," Cas says to the beautiful angel woman, but she shakes her head, smiling brightly.

"There is no need for repayment, for you have returned my boy to me. We will never be able to repay your family for bringing him to us. We have been despondent and without hope for so long, but now our family is reunited. Poor Jotan finally has some support, and we will find out who took Marcus and make them wish they had never been born. We are forever in your debt." Whoa, I just caught a glimpse of Corethea's wrath, and if I were the person who stole their baby, I would be on the other side of the galaxy by now.

I bet they are cocky, though, and they will trip up eventually.

"What about Grandpa J?" I ask, trying to sit up. Saxon puts a hand behind my back and helps me up. His eyes are glowing, and his fangs are out, so I can tell my being unconscious has triggered his bloodlust. I wonder if I can feed him.

I struggle to get up, and it's only when I put my hands down to push off the bed when I realize why.

"Agghh! I have wings!" I scream, accidentally plucking a feather out as I pull my hands away. I scream again at the burst of pain.

"Slowly… Yes, your mimic abilities took on Corethea's capabilities the minute she entered the room." Xavier sounds amused, but when my eyes drift to him, I suddenly realize he's not covered in mist, and the worry in his eyes is evident.

"I can see you." I point at him, momentarily forgetting about my extra appendages.

"Yes. We owe these people everything. Although my spell protected the babies, it didn't occur to me that the lightning cats would be dishonorable. I wasn't prepared for an attack while you weren't alert." I hear the guilt in his voice, and I shake my head.

"I didn't either, but I guess we should have. What happened once I was hit?"

"Astrea didn't wait, she ripped out Mazlan's throat. Matriarch challenges are to the death," Eric says quietly. "But if she hadn't, I don't doubt one of these guys would have."

"And Natalia?" I ask, my heart racing, worried that they killed her before we could discover the location of all the male omegas.

"Alive but in the dungeon for now," Saxon growls, and I know he needs to be fed, but I just can't do it. I grab hold of Xavier's shirt and pull him closer to whisper in his ear.

"Take Saxon and feed him please." I register how pale he is too. "And yourself," I encourage him, pushing my acceptance and love toward him.

"You would be okay with that?" he asks carefully.

I kiss him on the cheek. "Of course, but next time, I want to be the meat in the sandwich, okay?"

"It's a deal." He kisses me swiftly and peels Saxon's hand out of mine.

"Go," I tell him. "Neither of you are any good to me if you're undernourished, and I can't provide for you at the moment." I feel slightly guilty but just as horny as well. My body and mind are a mess.

They leave, and I look at William. "What happened to Echo, Maxsim, and the others? Did they come back on the ship?"

He shakes his head, and my stomach sinks. "No, but they will join us again once the show restarts."

I heave out a frustrated sigh. "There's something I need to tell you." I explain what Natalia told me. The colorful words that fill the room would make me laugh in surprise if the situation wasn't so serious.

"I will go call Astrea and let her know. They will search for them." Eric moves toward the door.

"If they have issues, ask Xavier to help them. He was the one who freed Maxsim's and Echo's parents, so I'm sure his little balls of light will be able to find them," I tell him before he can leave.

Once he does, I look at my angel savior. "So how do I turn off the feathers?"

She giggles musically. "All you have to do is

picture yourself as you normally look in your mind, and they should shift away."

"So I need to know what I look like in each form to be able to take it again?" I ask as I concentrate on doing what she said. Sure enough, I feel the wings disappear. I have no idea where they go, but suddenly, they aren't there.

"Yes, that is correct, but please don't practice this until after you have your babies. Only Xavier's protection prevented you from losing them during so many changes."

I swallow the lump in my throat and quickly nod my head. "Okay, so no shifting. Got it."

"She will have to shift into half form as part of the birthing process. Will that be okay?" Cas sounds worried, but I can't get past his comment. Fuck me, there is so much I don't know about this process. I really need to talk about it with him again. The last conversation was post orgasm and I felt too good to really take any of it in.

"That will be fine," Corethea says. "I will take my leave now. I want to join my family."

"Of course, and thank you again." William presses his hands together and bows reverently to her. She smiles and takes her leave, and I watch in awe as those big, beautiful, white fluffy wings go through the door.

I remember the question I asked before I discovered my wings. "Grandpa J?" I ask again, and

William sighs, taking a seat as Link moves around to take the hand Saxon is no longer holding.

Link sighs. "Queen Tabbris looked at him while Corethea worked on you. She confirmed what Link told us. The toxin is nothing like anything she has seen before, and her magic was not able to remove it."

My heart sinks, and I feel tears well up in my eyes. "So what now?"

"Well, it's not all bad news. She was able to tell us about a plant that is found at the bottom of the deepest mine on Rilu. It only blooms once a year on the spring equinox. That flower has the capability to heal any wound or illness. It is also rumored to be able to resurrect the dead if they have been dead less than twelve hours."

"Holy fuck, why has nobody ever heard of it before?"

"Because there are only a handful of plants, and if everyone was to know, it would soon become extinct. The Celestians are guardians of this knowledge, but because they have the ability to fix most ailments, they don't have need of the plant," Link explains, and William sits forward, propping his hands on his knees.

"Because of you, Lila, and the fact that we were able to reunite them with their long-lost son, they were willing to tell us."

"Well, what are we waiting for? Let's go!" I throw back the sheets and try to swing my legs off the bed, but my body screams in protest, and I can't stop the groan from slipping out.

"Lila, stop," Cas demands, pulling the blankets back up. "You can't get up yet, and we don't want you coming across another Celestian and changing again."

I pout. "Is that going to happen every time I come across someone new? Because that could get old really quick."

Link shakes his head. "No, once the babies are born, everything should stabilize, and you should only change if you will it by picturing it in your mind like Corethea said."

"Fine, but you should all go without me. Don't wait."

William stands up and grabs hold of the foot that Link had been grasping. He smiles and gives it a squeeze.

"No, my beautiful granddaughter. The Celestians have him in a stable stasis, and the spring equinox on Rilu is not for another two months, so we are all going to return to Skarr, and you will have your babies, and then and only then will we go to Rilu and find the cure for John."

I look between the three remaining men, seeing the seriousness on their faces, and I know I'm outvoted.

Nerves rise up, and my stomach rolls as I nod. "Okay, well, I guess that sounds like a solid plan."

The three men chuckle, and I roll my eyes at

them. I'm not sure what they want me to say. Once again, the decision has been taken out of my hands, and while I can't wait to meet my children, I feel like fate has fucked me up the ass with a cactus. But hey, I guess what doesn't kill you makes you stronger.

It's with mixed feelings that I start to get out of bed once more, but again, they stop me. "No, Lila, we will stay here tonight. The Celestian royal family wishes to honor us with a dinner."

"Cool," I say, but Link shakes his head.

"Unfortunately, you will need to stay here. We can't risk you changing."

Okay, that's it. My already bummed mood just hit rock bottom, and I feel my lip drop in a pout.

"But Caspian and I will stay here and keep you company," he finishes, and I perk up a bit.

"Yes, we can talk about what needs to happen now to bring the babies out of stasis." My head swings to my kraken mate, and when I see the heat in his eyes, I know that is going to be a discussion I don't want to miss. I seem to remember sex will trigger it or something.

"Okay, well, enjoy your dinner then, Will. Oh, and say bye to Susie and Mark for me. Tell her I'll call her as soon as we get to Skarr. I want to hear all about their reunion."

"And she wants to hear about the fight. She was beside herself when she found out you had been attacked. She sat by your bed the whole time. We figured it was safe enough because she hasn't exhibited any of her own abilities yet. Actually, she was a huge comfort to us all because we couldn't be with you. We will forever be in her debt," Cas explains, and I grin. Of course my bestie was there for me. We are ride or die, and I would have liked to have seen them try to keep her away.

William stands up and chuckles before coming around and nudging Caspian none too gently out of the way. He leans in and presses a kiss to my head.

"Tonight, you need to rest. When we get home, you can start the process." He growls the last part to Cas, who quickly nods his agreement, and once again, my lip drops into a pout, but then I think of something.

"But where are we going to live?" I don't really want to have sex in my grandpas' house. The ship is different because there's decent distance between us, not to mention soundproofing and Xavier's handy barriers, but being in a small house changes everything.

"We have a big estate. One of the wings is yours, and we began renovations when we found you," he tells me with a wry look on his face. I'm pretty sure he knows why I'm asking, and from the look on his face, he feels the same way. "Your wing has an amazing view of the ocean. I'm sure your krakens will be very happy."

With that, he gives us a wave and disappears,

leaving me alone with my husband and fiancé. I snuggle down and then pat either side of me. The bed I'm in is big enough for the two of them to slide in next to me. They do, and both press a kiss to my head, but I sit up, suddenly remembering something.

"Do either of you know what Astrea said to me during the fight?"

Caspian presses me back on the bed, and he and Link exchange a loaded glance. Great, now what?

"Apparently one of your Skarrian powers is that you're a whisperer," Link says quietly, and Caspian bites his lip.

"Well, what the fuck is that?"

"A whisperer is someone who is able to control lightning cats. It's so very rare because the bloodlines were hunted to extinction. You can imagine lightning cats didn't take kindly to having someone from another race be able to control their actions. It's kind of like compulsion in a Vilaxian."

I think about how Natalia did exactly what I told her. "Yeah, okay."

"That's not it." Cas sighs. "A whisperer is sexually compatible with all designations of lightning cats. You can take an alpha's knot or knot an omega."

I scrunch up my face. "How does a female knot an omega male or female?" Not that I have any interest in it, but I'm fascinated.

"I'm not sure. When I checked my database, the information was vague. Something about a lock. I'm sure if we ask Astrea, she could tell you more."

"Why would they hunt the bloodlines to extinction? Wouldn't that help inject new blood into the race?"

"It was a racial purity thing. They didn't want other species infecting their bloodlines. Betas have the capability to breed with other races, but it is frowned on, and any lightning cat with a different race in their streak is often shunned."

"Well, that's a load of bullshit. Does that mean I have a whole race of lightning cats gunning for me now?"

Cas chuckles.

"Not now that Astrea is in charge. She and Jalin think you can do no wrong after you stepped in and took Echo's place. Words like gallant, brave, and fierce were thrown around. I think it's safe to say whisperers are about to have a revival in a more positive frame."

"Well, if I'm the only one around, that's not going to do much good," I grumble, a wave of exhaustion rolling over me. A yawn escapes before I can stop it.

"Yes, but it might be something Skarrians have hidden in fear of being killed. Hopefully more will come out of the woodwork. Astrea said it might be what is needed so that female alphas start being born again," Link explains.

"Rest now, Lila. There is plenty of time to talk about that and the pregnancy process. Tomorrow, we will be on our way to your home. I can't wait to see it, and I can't wait to meet our babies. It won't be long now." Cas leans forward and presses a kiss to my belly as my eyes drift closed, feeling safe and secure snuggled in with my loves.

GALAXY CIRCUS GLOSSARY

PLANET ICEEN

Lightning Cats

They are a shifter race that has two forms—a bipedal human form and their cat form. Their bipedal form is humanoid in shape, but they are covered in a soft downy fur except for the front of their torso and genital area. They have sharp teeth, big ears, and long tails in this form. Their animal form is similar to a saber-toothed tiger from Earth. They can shoot lightning from their tails, and it can be used for defense and attack.

They are a matriarchal society and live in family groups called streaks. They have alpha, beta, and omega distinctions, but there is always a female alpha who acts as head of the family.

Alphas have a rut, and omegas have a heat. Only alphas and omegas can breed with one another, and betas can only breed with their own designation. There are male and female omegas.

Both have breeding capabilities, but male omegas are rare. Most are killed once their designation is discovered to prevent competition with females for coveted positions within the streak.

The planet Iceen is a frozen tundra of caves and outcroppings, and the streaks usually have two dwellings—a cave for their animal form, and a dome-like, insulated glass building which they live in with their streaks.

Maxsim (Alpha Lightning Cat)

The leader of the streak of lightning cats that performs in the circus, despite it being a matriarchal society. Maxsim is a dark aqua blue that ombres out to snowy white in the legs, with black, tribal style markings across shoulders, chest, and arms. He has high cheekbones, cat ears, feline eyes, a tail, and fangs, which are bigger when in animal form, as well as a broad chest and well-defined arms. Fur covers his body when in humanoid form, except for a patch across his chest and groin.

Maxsim keeps the rest of the streak safe from an aggressive Natalia.

Natalia (Beta Lightning Cat)

Only female in the group that performs in the circus. She is heir to her matriarchal streak, but is a beta designation. Natalia has pale blue fur all over, with long black hair, high cheekbones, cat ears, feline eyes, a tail, and fangs. She has small breasts, a slender, toned body, and a lean backside and legs. She has a naked patch across her breasts and down to her groin.

She wants to form a streak with Maxsim, Trace, Fuse, and Sim, but they are alphas and cannot breed with her. She took her omega sister's place, who was supposed to be the one performing with the circus.

Echo (Omega Lightning Cat)

He is a pure white lightning cat, with a smaller frame than Maxsim's, and built much more delicately. His designation is omega, and he has survived because he comes from a rare streak with a male omega. The streak, with help from the warlocks, protected him while growing up. They hid it, and he presents himself to the world as beta. He wants to form a streak with Maxsim, but not Natalia. She discovered he is an omega and keeps trying to kill him.

Other cats in the group
Trace (**Alpha Lightning Cat**)
Fuse (**Alpha Lightning Cat**)
Sim (**Alpha Lightning Cat**)

Mazlan, Natalia's mother and matriarch of the lightning cats (Omega)
Sky blue fur.
Minx, Natalia's sister (Omega)

Shoshi, Natalia's younger sister (omega)
Ten years old.

Jalin, Echo's mother (Alpha)
Astrea, Maxsim's mother (Omega)

Yalani

An abominable snowman type creature with shaggy white and gray fur. They are good at blending into their surroundings. It is a hunter-gatherer species that lives in caves on Iceen. Eight to nine feet tall, they are an aggressive species that will attack if they feel threatened. They live solitary lives unless mated and raising a family.

PLANET SKARR

This planet is the birthplace of the human race. The original humans were exploring Skarrians who crashed on Earth, and because they no longer had access to the magical waters, lost all their supernatural abilities.

Skarrians are mostly polyamorous and have attraction marks that show up on both parties' bodies. If attraction wanes on either side, the marks disappear. Skarrians find themselves bonded to others after five rounds of sex, which requires them to orgasm simultaneously. Skarr is basically a sister planet to Earth in that it is made up of ten different land masses surrounded by pink oceans, but it has different species of plants and animals.

When reproducing, all bonded members of the family must participate to produce a child.

Lila Jenson (Liliana Adams)

Orphaned at a young age, she moved from foster family to foster family, never really fitting in anywhere, though nothing terrible happened to her. One family put her into gymnastic lessons and self-defense courses to keep her out of trouble. She has no real goal in life but has always thought that there must be something more than working in a bar and having the occasional one-night stand.

She is average height with a curvy figure, long chestnut hair with turquoise streaks, golden skin, and green eyes.

Lila discovered she has grandparents who are still alive, and they invited her to learn their family business.

Currently, she has shown no signs of having Skarrian powers despite an impressive first showing.

John Adams, William Adams, and Eric Adams

Triplet brothers who appear to be in their late forties, they possess chestnut hair, tall, slender builds, and emerald green eyes.

They have been searching for Liliana, also known as Lila, for years, and are thrilled to have finally found her. They are also the CEOs of the Galaxy Circus and guardians of the power orb.

William has a buzz cut and is gruff.

Eric has long hair, which he wears in a man bun, and is the joker and tease in the family.

John has short, tousled hair and is the kind and

loving brother, but he is subject to spirals of depression.

Alina and Marcus Adams (Dec.)

Lila's parents moved to Earth in order to raise her in relative safety, but they were killed in a car accident. Alina had blonde hair and green eyes, and Marcus had brown eyes and the same chestnut hair as the grandpas and Lila.

Magenta

She is a performer in the circus. When on Earth, she uses the circus silks, but on other planets, she uses her levitation powers. Magenta has bright pink hair and pale skin. She is mid height with a slim build and light blue, almost gray eyes. She has been a lifeline for Lila when it comes to all things alien.

Broderick Potter (Bubby)

Captain of the mothership and Marcus Adams's best friend. He has red hair and a red beard with crystal blue eyes. He's rugged and well-built and thrilled to meet Lila.

Phillip and Fiona

They are Lila's twin cousins, but not on the Adams side of the family.

Fiona has long, curly red hair, brown eyes, and freckles with a tall, slim build.

Phillip's red hair is cropped short, and he has brown eyes and freckles with a tall, slim build.

They oversee the dinosaur act. The dinosaurs were hand raised in the zoo on Skarr.

Captain Lester

Captain Lester is an alternate captain for the mothership and circus pod. He has an abrasive personality and a voice like he smokes two packs of cigarettes a day.

Terrans

Security officer for the circus pod and brother to Ferrans.

Ferrans

Security officer for the main ship and brother to Terrans.

Susie (A Night Most Wicked)

She is Lila's best friend, with dark, mahogany skin, chocolate-colored eyes, and black corkscrew curls. She's a nurse and previously lived with Lila. Recently, she drank the waters from Skarr, activating a dormant spark of power.

PLANET FLUXX

Fluxx is a sister planet to Skarr, and its waters have magical properties too, but it gives its inhabitants the ability to shift into another creature. Fluxxians are animal shifters with three forms—humanoid while retaining coloration and some features of their animal, half form, and beast form. Fluxxians can use glamour to blend in and must do this when on Earth and in public. Fluxxians have fated mates, and their animal will dictate how they reproduce.

Caspian (Kraken Shifter, Lila's First Mate)
Caspian performs in the first act in the circus, shifting into half form and juggling multiple items with his tentacles.

He has mottled blue and purple skin, piercing stormy blue eyes, nipple rings, and vivid purple hair shaved on either side with a long section on top the drapes over one eye. His tentacles are purple and blue when in half form. Caspian's beast form is large. Male krakens implant their partners with their eggs via an ovipositor, and the womb then fertilizes the eggs, basically doing the opposite of a human. Fertilized eggs can lie dormant inside the female for a long time until she is ready to give birth. Drinking a large amount of the male kraken's cum tells the eggs that you are ready for babies. Four weeks later, they are born in kraken form. Two weeks after that, they are able to shift into their human form for the first time. Krakens can have anywhere between one and six babies at a time. Non-kraken mates will have their biology changed when given the mating bite. This allows them to carry a kraken's eggs for their partner.

Dylan (Dragon Shifter)

Dylan is in the first act of the show, which is a fire breathing act where he actually breathes fire.

He has ebony skin, a metallic black shimmer to his scales and wings, yellow and green reptilian eyes, and fangs. He also has sharp cheekbones, and his nose flattens slightly in half form.

Dylan is the man whore of the circus. He befriends Lila early on, only to betray her later and get kicked out of the circus for his act of aggression.

Silac (Naga Shifter)

Silac is one of the shifters who replaced Dylan in the first act. A naga shifter, he has tousled, emerald green hair in his humanoid form, with long, lean muscles and nipple rings. His eyes are orange and black. When he is in half form, he has a snake body from the waist down, with emerald green scales covered in horizontal orange stripes and black diamonds. Naga males have a hemipenis that hooks in to hold their partner close during copulation, and their mates give birth to live young.

Tirrian (Dragon Shifter)

Tirrian is the dragon shifter who replaced Dylan in the first act. Where Dylan was pitch black, he is more like an oil slick black. He has a shimmer to his skin that flickers from green and gold to pink and blue. He appears holographic depending on what angle you look at him from. In half form, his wings are the same color, and his scales are holographic pink. He is tall, broad, and muscular. His hair is black with pink streaks in it, and his eyes are black with lines of pink in them. He's an asshole.

Dragons can only have young with female dragons or their mates. Once again, a mating bite will change a non-dragon shifter mate to allow them to lay eggs. Eggs are incubated by the couple for two months before being born. They must be kept at a certain temperature to ensure a live birth. Homosexual dragons can hire surrogates to help them with reproduction if they wish, and it is common practice for young dragons to offer this service as a way to start their own hoard before they wish to begin their own family. There is a website that can help facilitate this.

PLANET CYBERTRONIA

A technologically advanced planet inhabited by life-forms that are half organic, half nanobot technology, allowing them to change their features at will. Reproduction occurs through intercourse, but parents program their respective organic matter with the traits and features they wish their babies to have. Once the baby is born, their source code is imprinted on a microchip, which is then deposited into a secret storage facility for safe keeping.

Pleasure Bot Industries is one of the main sources of employment for Cybertronia. They produce lifelike robots for sexual pleasure and are one of the galaxy's most popular purchases. Pleasure Bots are not like cyborgs, in that they are incapable of thoughts, feelings, or responses that have not been programmed into them.

Link (Cyborg)

Link is the ship doctor for the Galaxy Circus and is one of Lila's boyfriends. His skin tone is peach with a shimmer. He has silver hair and eyes. He is built like a swimmer, with long, lean lines, a tapered waist, and broad shoulders, and he is able to change his body parts at will. Cyborgs can't lie.

Josa Spears (Cyborg Nurse)

Josa is the nurse to Link's doctor, but he was hired by Link's mom to spy on him and the circus. He was promised Link's hand in marriage and a share of the Pleasure Bot Industries fortune if he complied. He has the same shimmery skin tone as Link, with metallic green hair and eyes. He has a slender, feminine frame and a dirty attitude.

Deianira (Cyborg A Night Most Wicked)

CEO to Pleasure Bot Industries and Link's mother. She doesn't like to be told no.

Ricky (Cyborg A Night Most Wicked)

Sent to Aura as a gift from Deianira. Blond hair, tan skin, and gorgeous body.

PLANET VILAX

Vilax is home to a race of blood drinkers, the sanguinistas. Much like Earth's legend of vampires, this race is strong, fast, and has heightened senses. They can fly and are very hard to kill. Their bodies will regenerate as long as their body parts are close to one another. To kill them, you need to burn both of their hearts. They are a warrior race and one of the fiercest in the galaxy. Military service is mandatory for all Vilaxians.

Vilax only gets five hours of sunlight a day, so while they are not allergic to the sun, they do prefer the dark. Sanguinistas drink blood because their bodies cannot process their own red blood cells. They have a fated mate called a blood rose, but not everyone finds them. They live in family clans, and blood sharing can be a sexual thing, but with children, it isn't.

Saxon (Sanguinista)

Saxon is part of the aerial troupe in the circus. He has magenta-colored eyes and thick, short black hair that's long enough to run your fingers through. His body is muscular and broad, and he has pale skin and fangs.

Hale (Sanguinista)

He is in the same troupe as Saxon and is Saxon's best friend. He has blond hair, teal eyes, and fangs.

Radella (Sanguinista)

Estrella (Sanguinista)

Velorina (Sanguinista)

Xenos (Sanguinista)

Saxon's twin brother, his hair is longer and worn tied back.

Dante (Sanguinista)

Chocolate brown hair that falls in floppy curls over his forehead and lavender-colored eyes. Tall and athletic.

Kavita (Sanguinista)

Pin straight long red hair that falls to her ass, dark eyes with a red flecks in them, and ruby red lips. Tall and athletic.

Crimson (Sanguinista) A Night Most Wicked

Long red curly hair, tall, toned, and lean. Crimson is antisocial and could never fit in with a sanguinista clan, so once she finished her compulsory public service for Vilax, she got a job working at the Pleasure Inn so she would have a variety of options for feeding. Clients like being bitten during sexual relations. She was in relationship with Savannah prior to Xane and Aura taking over the brothel. Aura bestowed a mating bite on her, permanently joining her in their group, and she stopped seeing clients.

PLANET WESTALIN

This is the warlocks' home planet. Warlock powers include, but are not limited to, mind manipulation and control, teleporting, and manifestation. Powerful warlocks have harems to feed from because they are psychic feeders who feed from strong emotions. Weaker warlocks and other creatures make up these harems. Weaker warlocks benefit from it, as they are able to feed off the stronger warlock at the same time and get a temporary boost in power. Members of the harem receive a wage and a comfortable position within the warlock's household. Powerful warlocks are able to absorb powers and life force, but it is frowned upon and is only used as a punishment. Warlocks have soulmates they call intimates. When a warlock finds their intimate, they no longer need a harem to feed from.

Xavier Colest (Crown Prince)

Xavier is one of the most powerful beings in the galaxy, only second to his parents. He is mostly with the circus because he gets bored easily. He helps with glamour to confuse the humans. He has purple/blue eyes and long indigo hair. His body is lean and muscular, and he has piercings in his ears, nose, and eyebrow. His ears are pointed, and he has lavender-colored skin with silver markings.

Xylene Colest

Queen of the Westalins and Xavier's mother. She was best friends with Alina and Marcus Adams, Lila's parents.

Cronus Colest

King of the Westalins and Xavier's father. He was best friends with Alina and Marcus Adams.

Xane Colest (A night Most Wicked)

Nephew of the king and queen and former strike team commander. Mate to Aura Gasm, master of the Pleasure Inn, and powerful warlock. He has long indigo hair shaved at the sides, exposing more silver tribal like tattoos on his skull, and is tied back, and there's a top hat covering it. Silver rings line both ears, as well as in his eyebrow and his bottom lip. Sharp cheekbones with eyes that look to be purple and pouty lips. Rescued Aura when they were enslaved on an illegal brothel ship.

Elyan (Warlock, Head Harem Girl in Xavier's Harem)

Nambra (Warlock, Harem Member)

She has red hair and a voluptuous figure.

Lexus (Warlock, Harem Member)

She has short dark hair and a petite frame.

Ara (Warlock, Harem Member)

Ara has pale pink hair, eyes, and skin.

Jastia (Warlock, Harem Member)

Jastia possesses buttercup yellow hair, eyes, and skin.

Sinath (Rasque, Harem Member)

The Rasque is a humanoid race that looks like an Earth grasshopper. They have segmented arms and legs with plated body structure. Their penis is covered by plated sections, which retract when manipulated. Once the penis extends, claspers lock the copulating couple together.

Mithus (Milobar, Harem Member)

He has a stingray-shaped head and body, with arms, legs, and a barbed tail. Mithus has two penises, which both have barbs that activate during intercourse, locking them within their partner.

Zanorn (Morpheian, Harem Member)

A race of metamorphs, they are able to take any shape they desire. In natural form, they are like a blank slate with limited features and gray skin.

Topirey (Dionall, Harem Member)

Dionalls are plant creatures with two forms— one is an upright humanoid sentient form, and the other is a stationary plant form which is similar to the Earth's Venus flytrap, only a lot larger and it feeds on flesh. They have leafy foliage on their head and sharp teeth and are able to grow their body parts at will.

PLANET AQUILIA

Aquilia is seventy-five percent water, and the Aquilians are an aquatic species with three forms—humanoid, mer, and beast form. In beast form, they resemble an Earth dolphin, but are scaled and have sharp teeth. They come in a variety of pastel colors. In half form and on two legs, they retain the pastel colors and cannot glamour. They require a glamour spell if they want to tour Earth. Family groups are called pods. Aquilians rarely leave their home planet, and if they do, they will return once they form a pod so that their young are born in their home waters.

Nikos (Aquilian Prince)

Nikos is one of the performers in the dolphin show in the circus. He is a member of the Aquilian royal family, but not in line to inherit. He is arrogant and horny. He has pastel green skin, and his scales are pastel green and gold. His hair and eyes are metallic gold.

Nixie (Aquilian princess)

Nixie is Nikos's sister and also a performer in the circus. She's friendly and fun and is interested in exploring the galaxy. She does not want to get trapped by being mated on Aquilia. Nixie is also open to trying relationships with other species. Her colors are pastel blue and gold, with metallic gold hair and eyes.

Galaxy Circus Pod Members
Joaquin
Nolani
Marin
Dorado

PLANET RILU

Rilu is a desert-like planet with small green oases dotted across its land surfaces. There are no above ground oceans or seas, but there are large underground ones which provide fresh water for the inhabitants of the planet. At each of the oases, which usually center around a small lake, are wells which provide fresh drinking water for travelers. Some of the larger lakes have permanent villages established for trade. The people of Rilu are nomadic tribes. They raise larnuks and are miners. Under the surface of Rilu are extensive gem mines, and the people of Rilu mine the gems for trade and to feed their larnuks.

Larnuks

These are creatures much like Earth's Pegasus, possessing both wings and a horn. They come in the same colors as the gems that are mined on their planet—emerald, ruby, sapphire, gold, and amethyst. They eat gems and spout fire, and they have sharp, vicious teeth. They are bred and raised by a larnuk mistress or master who will bond with their herd. The larnuk will bite them, and a lock of their hair will turn the same color as the larnuk's. The more streaks a master or mistress has, the more larnuks they control.

Rilax

Rilax are berries that grow in the mines alongside the gems. The berries are used to make rilaxious, a pink alcoholic beverage popular across the galaxy. It is slightly bubbly with a thick, creamy consistency.

Zala (Larnuk Mistress)

Zala is the larnuk mistress for the circus and is in charge of that portion of the show. She has exotic, Middle Eastern looks with darker skin and wavy, pitch-black hair with streaks of color in it from her horses. Her eyes are a pale blue, almost white, rimmed in kohl, and framed with long black lashes. She is tall and slim, and her body is covered in silvery scars from bonding with her horses. Five appear in the show, but she has more.

PLANET MORLASH

Home of Morpheian race. They are shape shifter who can merge into any form, metamorphs. They are hermaphrodites and all members of the race have breeding capabilities. They usual assume a preferred form which is either male or female, Aura prefers to be both.

Morpheians are polyamorous and bestow a mating bite in their natural form to seal their mate to them. It is quite a painful process ensuring that the mate is genuine.

Aura Gasm Proprietor Pleasure Inn (A Night Most Wicked)

Aura was kidnapped by alien sex traffickers as a teenager and forced into an illegal brothel where they were regularly abused to keep them in line. Developed Stockholm syndrome and tried to defend their captors when the ship was raided by a warlock strike force led by Xane. Xane, besotted by Aura, nursed them back to health and have been together ever since.

PLANET CELESTIA

Celestians are what humans would call angels. All Celestians have wings and powers. Powers tend to be emotive in nature, healing is one of the powers, as is being able to manipulate emotions. Celestians glow with heightened emotions, the color they're glowing tells what emotion they are feeling. Lavender is horny.

Celestians are also polyamorous, and reproduction involves a magical process that combines everyone's DNA ensuring the child is a part of all mates before depositing the embryo into the chosen carrier.

Savannah (A Night Most Wicked)
Tall and voluptuous with a long mane of blonde curls, and silver eyes. Savannah is a product of rape and forced breeding which should be impossible with the way Celestians breed. She was cast out by

her mother as a baby, never fitting in anywhere, teased, and ridiculed. She made the Pleasure Inn her home as a way to make herself feel good. Crimson taught her she didn't need to have sex with someone to be loved.

Mark (Marcus Aurelias) (A Night Most Wicked)

Stolen from his parents by unknown assailants. Needs to go through activation ceremony. Mark is Susie's boyfriend. He has black hair and gray eyes, and worked as an emergency room doctor. Mark is also bi.

King Jotan Angelis

One of Mark's fathers and a fierce king who has hung onto the monarchy while his mates have been mourning.

Queen Corethea Angelis

One of Mark's mothers, blonde with large white wings, and a talented healer.

Queen Tabbris Angelis

One of Mark's mothers and also a talented healer.

PLANET RECCEDEA

A lush, foliage-covered, tropical planet with frozen poles on either end. It is the birthplace of the dinosaurs found in the circus. Many species of dinosaurs that once roamed the Earth continue to survive and thrive on this planet.

Vigolash

Viggy is a red and black tyrannosaurus rex. He was trained from a baby, and acts just like a giant, overgrown golden retriever.

Htaed

Htaed is a yellow and orange velociraptor, who was also trained from a baby, but is unruly and kind of crazy.

PLANET AAZ'AX

The leadership of this race was cruel and vicious and wanted to use the orb to conquer other lands. They possessed it momentarily and laid waste to a number of planets, but the Una's were able to take it back. By then, the Aaz'axians weren't doing well. A mysterious illness had taken most of their women, and women of other races wanted nothing to do with the men. Their species has been on the brink of extinction and were finally able to dispose of their tyrannical leadership. Remaining survivors scattered to planets far and wide. The Aaz'axians are distant ancestors of the Vilaxians. Although they do not require blood, they can consume it, but it acts much like alcohol and drugs to a human. They have the ability to glamour, and they have two natural forms, their warrior form which is humanoid, but their shoulders and backs are covered in ridges and their body looks like they are covered in thorns. With their green skin and blood-red hair, they resemble a rose. And their everyday form which is again humanoid but he is covered in spikes, long and short. Comparable to an Earth's lionfish. The long spikes have sheer membrane draped between them. They don't have hair just a crest of spikes, but it's their color that is stunning. They look like an opal, all greens, reds, blues, yellows, and pinks. Originally people thought they were two separate races because of how different they look.

Brannock

Hiding on Earth. Escaped there with his unit over a hundred years ago when the Una's and Aaz'axian war finished. Moves every thirty years and changes identities. Uses a glamour to blend in. Can't hold his glamour when intoxicated.

OTHER ALIEN RACES

Una's

A race of highly intelligent, peaceful, powerful beings who created the power orb that the Galaxy Circus protects. The now extinct race had powers that were fueled through sexual energy. They didn't have mates or partners, it was just a free-for-all orgy.

Their war with the Aaz'axians dwindled their numbers until there were only a handful left. Their energy was absorbed into the orb when they turned it over to the Adams brothers. They used the Adams' ancestor's blood to link it to them, and if it leaves their line, anyone remaining will be absorbed too.

The power orb was supposed to be a clean, free source of energy capable of powering planets across the galaxy. It can be used as a weapon of mass destruction, but cannot be destroyed because the galaxy would implode.

Darklarkian (Planet Elos)

Elf-like race identifiable by their pointy ears and black skin, and green, snake-like eyes.

Snarkle (Planet Cereabosto)

Humanoid bodies with two heads. Each head has a mouthful of sharp teeth

Pistadon (Planet Laxo)

Bird-like creature similar to a pterodactyl. Sharp beaks and beady eyes, they have no feathers, look like a freshly plucked chicken. The only feathers on their body surround their cloaca. Red and yellow spike like feathers circle this opening protecting it from unauthorized penetration.

Seiomann (Planet So)

Magic race with subjugating powers. They can make it so a being cannot access their powers. They also have the ability to freeze a person in stasis. They appear floating draped in a dark cloak with only discernible feature are three red eyes.

Telazions (Planet Telaz)

They sold the tech for the iPhone to Steve Jobs.

Nengh

They perform as clowns in the circus. They have detachable limbs and are able to adjust their body's size and mass. They are humanoid in shape, but they are orange with feathery tufts instead of hair. They use a glamour provided by Xavier to appear human when on Earth.

Jelliads

A race of purple gelatinous amorphic creatures. They are sentient and communicate via telepathy. The feed from the atmosphere of their home planet but they can also feed on orgasmic energy. They can change their shape and the breed asexually.

Bacalacian

From the planet Bacalac they are humanoid form in that they walk upright and have two legs but they have a red armor plated outer shell, bright red when on high alert, orange at rest. They have two pincers in place of arms, that are razor sharp and dangerous. Their torso is triangular with two eyes on stalks sticking out of the top and a mouth opening with a single pair of teeth on top and bottom which grind food between them.

Dodarran

A demon counterpart to the Celestians.

Gilani: member of the circus. In the first act with Caspian, one of the jugglers. He has red, leathery looking skin and big horns and his own set of large, bat-like wings.

Filani

A race of beings that can be likened to succubus and incubus. So beautiful they can seduce with their looks and can absorb someone's life force during sex to feed.

Madova

This race has only females, and they have two forms. Humanoid with hypnotizing gaze, snake-like appendages for hair, fangs, nose slits, and wings. A snake like appendage that comes out of the vagina and penetrates the male to lay eggs. They have sex through an X-like opening in their stomachs.

Animal form, shifts into a serpent dragon with wings, spits venoms, and bites the head off the male they have sex with once the babies are ready to be born. Babies then consume the remaining body.

Tutva

Four-armed humanoid race. The women have three breasts and two vaginas, and the men have double cocks and only one nipple in the middle of their chest. Tall and built with tusks and horns. Kind of like orcs. The come in various shades of green, gray, and brown

Tully and **Sully** are sisters who run Orion's Belt

Vengii (Planet Sotda VX)

Tinka - No legs, mushroom style base and long spindly arms with mauve skin. Round back skull like a human, but the front half tapers down into a snout. Black beady eyes no hair, ridges, and bumps all over the back of their head. Snout ends in pouty lips. Seamstress and fashion designer for the Galaxy Circus.

DICTIONARY

Phoeall (fo-all): Warlock for…

Vigolash: Obedient one in Aaz'axian

Sandar worm: native to the planet Westalin, they are large creatures that turn soil over in their paddocks between crops. They eat all organic matter left from past crops, leaving it free for farmers to plant the next crop.

Silax worm: Native to Rilu, it lives in the mines and is a pest. Their secretion kills the rilax berry plant. They are trapped, and their secretions are used to make achom.

Achom: A drink that is like a blend of coffee and chocolate with a chili vodka kick.

GIN: Galaxy Information Network.

Karta monster: A large, kaiju style creature the size of an elephant.

Cirillion: Little bundles of fluff with big eyes.

Lastovian hog:

Saturn's Rings: A restaurant on the mothership.

Edalaxion Space Station: A space station with dodgy bars and meeting spaces for the dregs of the galaxy.

Celesian Brothel: A popular brothel if you want to have sex with living beings as opposed to sex bots.

Jaxa bird: A bird native to Westalin, it looks like a cross between a peacock and a phoenix. Its tail is a fanned bloom of fire.

Kala mouse: A marsupial found on Westalin.

Coolmy shell: This is a crustacean found in Aquilian waters.

Farlucks: A creature from Westalin similar to an Earth fox with three tails and pink fur. They are an aquatic mammal.

Husad Mead: From Husadavia, an uninhabited planet in the Kavar system. The planets and animals on it are carnivorous and lethal and it takes a special kind of being to harvest the fruit from the halla bush. It's quite popular and quite potent.

Mitavin: Rodent found on space junk and in space stations. Skeletal beings with a tail like a beaver and body like a racoon.

Treason: Board game like monopoly but you invade planets.

THANK YOU FOR READING!

I hope you enjoyed the book. It would be super awesome if you could leave a review wherever you bought it, because I love to hear what you thought of the story.

Want to see what happen next for Lila and friends? I'll be putting up a preorder soon for the next one so keep an eye out for it.

Also do you want to know what happened to Susie and Mark on their trip back from Vegas? Get the Galaxy Circus Halloween Novella
A Night Most Wicked.
A Rocky Horror Picture Show retelling.

In the mean time why don't you check out one of my other series. You can find everything on my website at www.lexiewinston.com

ACKNOWLEDGMENTS

To my cover designer Jessica, of Raven Ink Covers. Thank you for making the covers exactly what I envisioned, you nailed it and all of them.

Thank you to both Jess at Elemental Editing and Val at SCW Editing. My book is pretty and readable thanks to you guys.

Galaxy Circus is a real passion project for me. I love writing it and I hope to keep working on it for a little while longer. There will be at least 2 more books. A novella in between Whisperer and book four; which will be titled Performer.

And lastly to you guys the readers. I love what I do, and probably would do it regardless if anyone read them or not, but you guys make it that much sweeter so thank you.

Until next time, happy reading

Lexie